With Promises To Keep

Ellie Dean lives in a tiny hamlet set deep in the heart of the South Downs in Sussex, which has been her home for many years and where she raised her three children. She is the author of the Cliffehaven Series.

Also available by Ellie Dean

There'll be Blue Skies
Far From Home
Keep Smiling Through
Where the Heart Lies
Always in My Heart
All My Tomorrows
Some Lucky Day
While We're Apart
Sealed With a Loving Kiss
Sweet Memories of You
Shelter from the Storm
Until You Come Home
The Waiting Hours
With a Kiss and a Prayer
As the Sun Breaks Through
On a Turning Tide
With Hope and Love
Homecoming
A Place Called Home
Love Will Find a Way

Ellie DEAN
With Promises To Keep

PENGUIN BOOKS

PENGUIN BOOKS

UK | USA | Canada | Ireland | Australia
India | New Zealand | South Africa

Penguin Books is part of the Penguin Random House group of companies
whose addresses can be found at global.penguinrandomhouse.com

Penguin Random House UK,
One Embassy Gardens, 8 Viaduct Gardens, London SW11 7BW

penguin.co.uk

Penguin
Random House
UK

First published 2025
001

Copyright © Ellie Dean, 2025

The moral right of the author has been asserted

Penguin Random House values and supports copyright. Copyright fuels creativity, encourages diverse voices, promotes freedom of expression and supports a vibrant culture. Thank you for purchasing an authorised edition of this book and for respecting intellectual property laws by not reproducing, scanning or distributing any part of it by any means without permission. You are supporting authors and enabling Penguin Random House to continue to publish books for everyone. No part of this book may be used or reproduced in any manner for the purpose of training artificial intelligence technologies or systems. In accordance with Article 4(3) of the DSM Directive 2019/790, Penguin Random House expressly reserves this work from the text and data mining exception.

Typeset in 11/12.5pt Palatino LT Std by Jouve (UK), Milton Keynes
Printed and bound in Great Britain by Clays Ltd, Elcograf S.p.A.

The authorised representative in the EEA is Penguin Random House Ireland,
Morrison Chambers, 32 Nassau Street, Dublin D02 YH68

A CIP catalogue record for this book is available from the British Library

ISBN: 978–1–804–94774–6

Penguin Random House is committed to a sustainable future for our business, our readers and our planet. This book is made from Forest Stewardship Council® certified paper.

To all those who take on the role of mother.
It is the hardest, but most fulfilling dedication
any of us will ever experience.

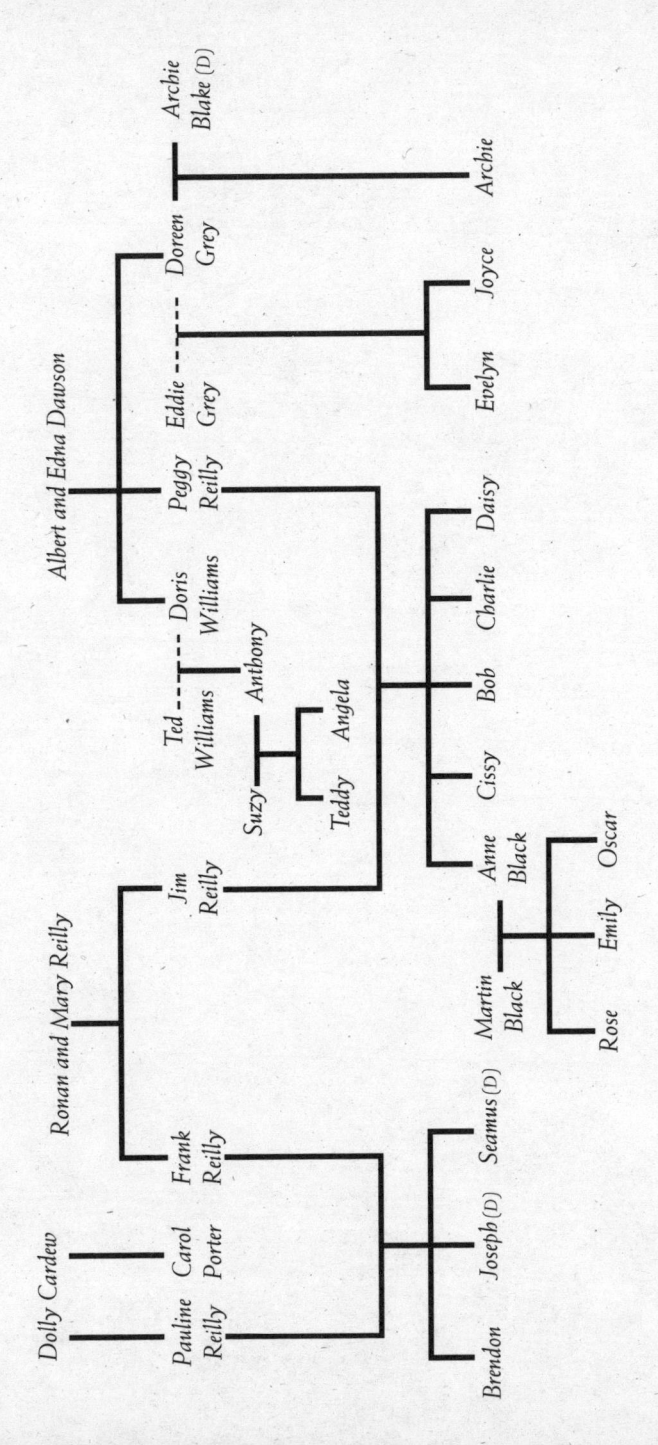

The Cliffehaven Family Tree

Dear Reader,

Here we are again, another year over and a new one beginning. What will this new year of 2025 bring us I wonder? The world seems to be in turmoil, but there is always the sanctuary of diving into the world of a good book, and being lost in the magic that the turning of the pages reveals.

With Promises to Keep was a difficult book to write, as there was a great deal of emotion involved. I have come to know and love my characters so well, it is always hard to see them struggle to attain their dreams. But with fortitude and determination, they make their way towards those goals, and I'm forever cheering them on.

I do hope you enjoy Danuta and Stan's story. Until next year – adieu – and may you be blessed with good health and happiness.

Ellie Dean x

Acknowledgements

As always, I'm hugely grateful to the fabulous team at Cornerstone for their unstinting efforts in getting my stories as perfect as possible before they go out into the world. I would like to give special thanks to my editor, Emily Griffin, who kept working on this book right up to the point where she was about to give birth to her sweet baby boy. Congratulations, Emily, he's perfect!

My thanks also go to Teresa Chris, who has journeyed alongside me right from the very beginning of my career as an author. I do appreciate all you have done, and know how hard you've worked on my behalf.

1

December 1946

It was only four-thirty in the afternoon, but the late December day was already closing in as district nurse, Danuta Kowalcyzk, lit the night-light and gently drew the blankets over Bobby Smith's narrow shoulders. She resisted disturbing him with a soft kiss on his tear-stained cheek, but gazed down at him, her heart aching with love for the orphaned child.

He was not quite six years old and couldn't possibly understand what had happened during the last traumatic few days – let alone the implications of how it would affect his life. And yet the death of Gracie, his mother, and the consequent upheaval it would cause must be tended with great care – for his future, and that of his newborn brother, Noel, was uncertain and plagued with difficulties.

Danuta took a tremulous breath. This was the precious calm before the inevitable, stormy intrusion of the authorities with their meddling enquiries and obstructive red tape that must surely come, but at least he was in familiar surroundings and safe for now with the very capable Florence Hillier.

Tiptoeing from the bedroom, she closed the door on the sleeping child and stood for a moment in the hallway of the flat to gather her strength. She hadn't slept for two days, and so much had happened in the past week, she'd barely been able to think straight, let alone deal with the conflicting emotions inside her. The elation of having the chance to be a mother to Gracie's Bobby and baby Noel was tempered with grief for the tragic loss of their young mother.

Any hope she felt that this could be the start of the family she'd always yearned for was quashed by the stark reality that although she and Stanislav had been granted British citizenship, there were still some who were biased against their Polish roots. And no authority would grant them care of two vulnerable children while they lived in a fisherman's shack in Tamarisk Bay.

Then there was the dread she felt of being forced to break her promise to Gracie that she would adopt her children and love them as her own – a heartfelt and sincere promise made in the heat of a dramatic moment as Gracie lay dying – and one she was determined to keep despite all the odds that would be set against her.

Knowing these negative thoughts were far from useful, Danuta shook them off and went to join Florence in the warm, cluttered kitchen of the ground-floor flat. Florence had lived alone until she'd taken in Gracie and her little boy after they'd been made homeless. She usually ran a tight ship, but Danuta noted that the kitchen table still held the detritus of hurried meals, and the sink was filled with dirty pans and dishes – but then the circumstances she'd found herself in were far from normal. Florence clearly had little heart for housework and was now deep in thought as she huddled close to the range fire, the twinkling lights of the small Christmas tree in the corner cruelly illuminating a drawn face, prematurely aged by recent experience and deep regret.

Danuta knew the older woman blamed herself for not seeing how ill Gracie had been, and no amount of reasoning could convince her otherwise. And yet, Gracie had hidden her pregnancy, and deliberately avoided seeking the urgent medical aid she'd needed after giving birth to Noel secretly and alone in an old caravan up in the hills and then abandoning him at the church, for fear of being found out. But she'd left it too late to ask for help, and tragically paid the ultimate price, leaving little Bobby in a bewildered Florence's care, and her newborn baby at the mercy of the authorities. It was only by great good fortune that Solly and Rachel Goldman had stepped in to take care of baby Noel until things were resolved.

Danuta sat beside Florence and took her hand. 'Bobby's sleeping, Florence, so I'll just clear up the kitchen and come back in the morning,' she murmured. 'Go to bed. You look worn out.'

Florence slowly emerged from whatever thoughts tormented her, her brown eyes shadowed with grief. She squeezed Danuta's hand. 'The kitchen can wait. You should go back to that husband of yours and get some rest. You look dead on your feet, and he must be frantic by now wondering where you've got to.'

'I telephoned Stanislav from the hospital last night when it was clear Gracie was close to the end.' Danuta looked at the watch pinned to the bib of her rather crumpled nursing apron. 'But, yes, I must go home. There is a lot to tell him.'

'So, he doesn't know Gracie's last wish was for you to adopt Bobby and the baby?'

Danuta shook her head. 'It is not a conversation to be had on the telephone. But I did call into Beach View to tell Peggy Reilly and her family, and I suspect she's already contacted Rachel and Solly Goldman with regards to Noel's parentage.'

Florence's gaze sharpened. 'And how did Peggy take the news that it was Gracie who'd secretly given birth in that caravan and then abandoned her baby in the church?'

Danuta had a fleeting image of the Reilly family gathered amongst the glitter and baubles of Christmas, their faces etched with heartache on learning that their beloved daughter, Cissy, had suffered not only a vicious rape, but a subsequent miscarriage and loss of everything she'd worked for over the past year – and that she'd kept it secret until a very worried Peggy had called for a family council of war that morning. Peggy was no doubt regretting her actions, for the revelations that had come out of it had been shocking – but at least the secret was out now and the healing could begin. *There have been too many secrets of late*, Danuta thought sadly, *and the consequences will be felt long after today.*

She kept these thoughts to herself, knowing she must never reveal what had happened to Cissy. 'They were shocked to hear about Gracie, and although pleased for me, they were concerned that our circumstances could prove a huge stumbling block to our adopting the children,' she replied quietly.

'You could have trouble from Rachel Goldman,' said Florence. 'She's taken to Noel and could make a good case to the authorities for keeping him.'

A dart of alarm hit Danuta, but she quelled it instantly. 'I cannot think of these things now, Florence,' she said, standing to draw the other woman to her feet and pull her into a brief hug. 'Go to bed, and I will see you tomorrow. For now I must go home and speak with Stanislav.'

Florence nodded and walked with her to the door. A blast of icy air hit them as they parted on the doorstep. 'Drive carefully, Danuta. The country roads will be lethal in this frost.'

Danuta nodded, and glanced up at the black sky which was now sprinkled with cold, bright stars.

With a shiver, she climbed into her car and turned the key in the ignition. Frost was already thick on the ground and tracing the silhouettes of the leafless trees, and not for the first time, she wished their home wasn't so isolated.

Beyond the chalk cliffs that protected Cliffehaven, and tucked neatly on the shores of Tamarisk Bay, sat the dilapidated fishermen's cottages where Danuta and Stanislav had made their home. Wing Commander Baron Stanislav Kowalcyzk tugged at his flowing moustache as he glanced again at the kitchen clock and realised that only a minute had passed since the last time he'd looked. He leaned heavily against the sink to ease the throbbing in the stump of his right leg – it had been playing up for the last two days, and the one on his left leg was starting to complain too.

He knew he'd been overdoing things at the airfield, but that wasn't his main worry as he stared out at the frost glittering on the bank of tamarisk in the reflective glow from the kitchen light. Danuta had not been home for two nights, and during the past week she'd merely dashed in for something to eat and a quick change of uniform before hurrying out again. He understood and loved her compassion for her patients, but their first Christmas as man and wife had been spoilt, and now he was worried for her safety. The long, hilly drive from Cliffehaven to Tamarisk Bay was difficult enough in good weather, but with the sharp frost on the ground it could be dangerous, and with little sleep, she could so easily lose concentration.

'You'll be no help to her if you've worked yourself up into a gibbering wreck,' he muttered in Polish. 'Trust her to take her usual care and do something practical.' He drew the curtains against the black night and turned from the sink to the temperamental stove which was their only source of heat. There was a pot of vegetable soup waiting to be warmed through, but the fire beneath it smouldered and smoked, the wood too damp to ignite properly.

Cursing under his breath, he pulled on his overcoat and scarf in an attempt to ward off the icy draughts that whistled beneath doors and through rotting window frames, and then grabbed the poker. But no amount of prodding seemed to make any difference, and he was forced to accept he'd have to clear out the stove and start again.

The stump on his right leg throbbed more persistently as he emptied everything into the big bucket set at the side of the hearth, riddled the grating in the bottom to get rid of old clinkers and ash, and then began to carefully place kindling, paper and a few lumps of anthracite into the mouth of this beast he'd come to hate now winter had set in – and which seemed determined to frustrate him. He struck a match, watched it catch the paper beneath the kindling and then held a sheet of newspaper in front of it to encourage it to draw up the chimney pipe.

He heard the flames roar, saw the scorching on the paper, and with a sigh of cautious relief, knew the fire had caught, so he carefully added a couple of small dry logs and a few more nuggets of fuel before shutting the metal door. He washed his hands, then sank onto a kitchen chair to massage his stump and watch the blaze through the stove's murky window, praying it would stay alight long enough to heat the house and the soup before Danuta came home.

He glanced up at the clock and realised only half an hour had passed – it had felt longer – but then every minute that his Danuta was out and about in all weathers felt like a lifetime. Where on earth was she? And why hadn't she rung since last night?

Surely she must realise by now that he'd be worried sick about her?

Beset by visions of her stranded in a ditch somewhere, he shoved himself out of the chair, meaning to go out in search of her, but was brought to a sudden, agonising halt by red-hot stabs of pain in his right stump. He collapsed back into the chair, gasping for breath, his fingers urgently fumbling to unbuckle the straps that held the prosthesis so firmly to the pulsating wreck of his thigh. He'd known he'd overdone things, but had stubbornly ignored the warning signs and carried on flying the cargo planes, as well as helping to load and unload them. After all, he'd reasoned, he had a commitment to Roger and Martin who'd given him the chance to fly again after losing most of both lower limbs during a wartime dogfight over Holland, and he needed to earn enough money to get out of this place and provide a proper home for Danuta and any child they might be permitted to adopt in the future.

The leather straps fell to the wooden floor with a clatter and, hissing with pain, he gingerly eased the padded prosthesis away from the inflamed stump. It was as he'd suspected, swollen and angrily red – but on closer inspection there seemed to be darker patches embedded in the tender flesh – and that was truly worrying. He'd been warned by the doctors that if he didn't lose weight and take proper care of his stumps, infection could set in and that could mean a further operation to cut away more of what was left of his legs.

Refusing to contemplate the possibility that his carelessness could bring him serious trouble, he reached over to the cupboard beneath the sink for the methylated spirits and the soothing creams he'd need to ease the pain and hopefully stop any infection in its tracks. But he'd have to keep this from Danuta; she had enough on her plate without adding to it, so he'd dress the stump and leave the prosthesis off for now. Once the Christmas holidays were over, he'd find a moment to go and see the doctor if it hadn't improved.

Stanislav had always been a believer in doing things for himself, and although losing both his lower legs had been a terrible frustration, he was determined to live life as normally as possible and not make a song and dance about it. Why worry Danuta unnecessarily when it was probably just a matter of clean dressings, rest, lots of padding, and a few pills and a swig of alcohol to kill the pain?

His expression was grim as he cleansed and dried the throbbing stump and, after a thick dusting of antiseptic powder, he bandaged it up again and set about taking off the prosthesis from the other leg. That stump didn't look half as bad, but he treated it carefully, and once that was done, he relaxed back into the chair, opened his last bottle of vodka to assist downing the pills, and waited for Danuta to come home.

Peggy Reilly felt wrung out from all that had happened that day but, as a mother and wife, she knew she had little option but to keep going. She'd do no one any good by falling apart at the seams. If nothing else, she silently reasoned, carrying on with her normal routine would stop her from thinking. She gave the large pot of ham and vegetable soup a good stir and then turned her attention to the bubble and squeak which was slowly frying in a pan. They would have that with cold meat and pickles, she decided.

'Are you all right, Peg?' murmured Jim, coming to stand behind her and snake his arms about her waist.

'About as all right as any of us is,' she replied, leaning her head back against her husband's shoulder as she continued to stir the soup. 'But I brought this on myself, didn't I? It's all my fault everyone's so upset.'

'Leave that,' he said firmly, taking the wooden spoon and turning her to face him. 'After all the gossip and speculation over the identity of the mother of that abandoned baby, it's hardly surprising you were at your wits' end and suspecting all sorts. But without you forcing the issue, Cissy would not have been able to tell us what happened to her. You gave her the opening and thank God she took it.' He softly kissed her brow. 'She can start to heal now, Peg – and that has to be a good thing, doesn't it?'

'I suppose so. But to think of what she went through, Jim. I can hardly bear it.'

His expression darkened. 'I'm not happy about it either, and if I meet the bastard who did that to her, I'll have his guts for garters.'

Peggy softly placed her fingers against his lips, noting the anger in his blue eyes and understanding the frustration behind it. 'That won't solve anything or make Cissy better, Jim. You have to put the thought of revenge right out of your mind if any of us are to move on from this.'

'Easy to say, Peg. Not so easily done.' He released her and slumped down into one of the kitchen chairs to light a cigarette. 'Da will not forget or forgive that swine – and neither will I. He should be punished for what he did to our girl – and that sister of his is no better, covering up for him like she did.'

'We don't know for certain it was Clarissa's brother, Jim. Cissy was careful not to name him.'

'Aye, that might be the case, but I can put two and two together, Peg.'

Peggy gave an inward sigh. Jim wouldn't let it go and she couldn't say she blamed him, but seeking revenge wasn't the answer – not when there was only suspicion, and Cissy certainly wasn't inclined to name her rapist, who by her own account was a dangerous and very powerful adversary. 'If you want to help our girl, then you'll have to swallow all that anger and concentrate on what she needs to get over it. Love and care and some kind of work to give her a reason to get up in the morning – that's my prescription.'

'I just want to know why the hell she didn't come straight home and tell us what happened,' hissed Jim, aware of footsteps approaching from across the hall.

'Because she was frightened of how we'd react,' she hissed back. 'But she's told us now, and as a family we're going to surround her with love and support, so stop going on about it. Now, help me get this heavy pot of soup off the heat.'

Jim's grim expression told Peggy he wasn't convinced by her argument, but he got a tea towel and lifted the pot away from the ring just as the elderly Cordelia and Bertie Double-Barrelled came into the kitchen, closely followed by Cissy.

'It's cold cuts, soup and bubble and squeak,' said Peggy with all the cheer she could dredge up. 'I hope you're all hungry.'

'Actually, Peggy, I don't think I could eat anything,' said Cordelia, sinking into the fireside chair. 'What with everything that's happened today, I feel very out of sorts.'

'But you must have something, Cordy,' said Peggy, her tone sharp with anxiety. 'It's a bitter night and you need food inside you to help keep you warm.' She looked to Bertie for support.

'Yes, my dear,' he murmured. 'You need to keep your strength up, and you know how difficult you find it when the cold inflames your arthritis.'

'I can't eat, Bertie,' she replied crossly. 'And it's not the arthritis that's bothering me.' She eyed Peggy and

Jim sharply over her half-moon spectacles. 'It's being left out of things that really pains me.'

'We didn't want you upset, Cordy,' Peggy protested. 'We were going to tell you, honestly.'

'I might be old, Peggy, but I'm not stupid. I knew something was afoot long before this morning when Gloria and her lot turned up shortly before Rachel and Solly arrived with that baby. But you seemed determined to keep it to yourself, and left me here in the kitchen worrying myself sick over what was going on in the dining room – and imagining all sorts. And then Danuta came with the news about poor little Gracie. It's all quite knocked me for six.'

'To be fair, Cordelia, we didn't know anything for sure until this afternoon,' said Jim. 'We only had our suspicions, which proved to be wrong in the end – but the reality turned out to be far more complex.' He placed a gentle hand on her shoulder. 'We're sorry you felt left out. It really wasn't our intention.'

Cordelia regarded him coolly, clearly not mollified. 'I don't suppose it was, Jim, but that's how it felt.' She took off her glasses and rubbed her eyes. 'I'm sorry to be so sharp,' she said on a sigh. 'It's been a long, worrying day, and I'm worn out.'

Cissy, looking pale and drained, squatted down at Cordelia's side. 'We all love you very much, Grandma Cordy, and Mum and Dad were only trying to protect you. Please don't be angry with us.'

Cordelia softly touched Cissy's cheek. 'I'm not angry, my darling, just sad that none of you could trust me with your troubles.'

Cissy acknowledged this statement with a regretful smile. 'It's done now, Grandma Cordy, so will you just eat a little something – for me?'

Cordelia's eyes glistened with tears. 'Sweet girl, so caring even when I know how badly you've been hurt.'

She glanced at the concerned faces around her and then reluctantly nodded. 'I'll eat if that's what you want, Cissy, but only if you sit with me and have something yourself. You're far too thin.'

Cissy's smile was wry – a glimpse of her old self in her twinkling eyes. 'You're not exactly robust, Grandma Cordy,' she teased. 'A puff of wind would probably blow us both off our feet.' Cissy helped her struggle out of the chair and guided her to the table.

Despite the delicious food, the atmosphere was heavy with unspoken thoughts, and Peggy soon realised that none of them were really hungry, and, like her, probably just wanted to crawl into bed, pull up the blankets and shut out the world. But there would be little rest for her and Jim tonight as their sons, Bob and Charlie, would be home soon, and Cissy was determined they should know what had happened to her – or at least, the bare bones of it – so there'd be no family secrets.

Sighing, she pushed her half-eaten meal away and sipped her tea. Cordelia's outburst had dismayed her, but there wasn't much she could do about it except reassure her that she was indeed a part of this family and would never again be left out of things. At least her youngest, Daisy, would be staying with Rosie and her grandfather tonight, which was a blessing. Daisy was only five and far too young to understand any of it, although she must have noticed the tense atmosphere in the house since Cissy's return home, and was bright enough to start asking questions. But, please God, that was for another day.

'I think I should start to wend my way home,' said Bertie, rising from his chair to reach for his hat and coat. 'My church warden duties mean an early start tomorrow, and I fear I've encroached on your hospitality long enough.'

Ignoring Peggy's soft protest, he went round the table and gently took Cordelia's hand. 'Try and get a good night's sleep, my dear.'

'I will,' she said. 'And you be careful on the roads.' She kept hold of his hand and looked up at him, her blue eyes worried behind the half-moon spectacles. 'Will you still honour your vow to sponsor Noel now he's to be adopted by Danuta and Stanislav?'

'My word is my bond, Cordelia. I have no intention of breaking it,' he replied firmly. 'Goodnight, everyone.'

Peggy wished him goodnight and watched him leave by the back door, wondering if she'd imagined the fleeting look of doubt in his eyes at the mention of his promise. But it seemed Cordelia had seen it too.

'I think dear Bertie has made a promise he may not be able to keep,' she said tremulously. 'He has such a good heart and I know he means well, but he's only got a few savings and relies heavily on his army pension. I really don't see how on earth he can afford to sponsor Noel too.'

'Noel's in the lap of luxury now he's being fostered by Rachel and Solly Goldman,' soothed Jim. 'It could be a long time before the authorities allow Danuta and Stan to take him and his brother on, so I shouldn't worry about it too much. Besides, I think he was planning to leave Noel well set up in his will – not actually pay for his keep now.'

'I suppose so,' she replied, her expression doubtful. 'But I still worry that it's preying on his mind.'

As exhausted as she was, Danuta drew her little car to a halt on the brow of the hill which overlooked Cliffehaven and climbed out. The cold wind stung her face and made her eyes water, but it was exhilarating to be out in the open after the long hours in that stifling hospital room waiting for poor little Gracie to breathe her last.

She dug her gloved hands into her coat pocket and nestled her chin into her scarf as she surveyed the sprawl of the town beneath her. It followed the curve of the crescent bay that lay between chalk cliffs and rolling hills, and spread out to the north and east. The waters in the English Channel undulated like dark, flowing silk beneath a cloudless, star-studded sky, the bright moon gilding the white ripples breaking on the pebbled shore, and in the clarity of this still night, she could see the glow from the distant shores of France.

Her gaze followed the ribbons of coloured lights that edged the High Street to the bright shimmer of the large Christmas tree that stood outside the Town Hall. From this bird's-eye view, she could make out the pale gleams from behind curtained windows, the tall spire of the church where she and Stanislav had first met, and the progress of an ambulance making its hurried way to the beacon lights of Cliffehaven General in Camden Road. Cliffehaven had grown since she'd first arrived at the beginning of the war, for where there had once been fields were now new houses, a large factory estate and a forest of prefabs going up behind the railway station.

She followed the curve of the bay to the nearby valley and the ancient church of St Cuthbert's where she and Stanislav had taken their marriage vows, and the remnants of her family were buried in the cemetery overlooking the sea. Those first months in England had been filled with anguish as she'd had to come to terms with learning of her beloved brother's death during the Battle of Britain, and then losing the baby she'd so desperately wanted. But Peggy Reilly had given her a loving home at Beach View and become like a second mother, easing her pain and helping her to find her feet again as an outsider in a strange new land. Cliffehaven was her home now – hers and Stanislav's, but neither of them would ever forget Poland, and the families they'd lost during Hitler's rampage through Europe.

Danuta realised she was becoming maudlin. She climbed back into the car, glad of the warmth from the heater, and set off for Tamarisk Bay, slowing only as she approached the large house owned by the local factory owners, the Goldmans. There were lights in every window and it looked warm and inviting – not least because she knew baby Noel was there, snug and safe in Rachel's care. But she resisted the temptation of going to see him tonight, for he would no doubt be asleep, and Rachel and Solly would need time to come to terms with the news of Gracie's death and her last wishes.

The streetlights had come to an end now she was out on the narrow country road, and under the bright moon, the shadows lay deeply beneath the overhanging trees that bordered the Cliffe estate. Frost glittered in puddles and on the grassy verges, lacing the hedgerows with delicate tracings of ice. A fox slunk out of the shadows and darted in front of her, and with a racing pulse, she just managed to avoid him without skidding on a patch of black ice.

Turning off the lane where the estate's border of trees came to an end, she drove up the steep slope, glad for once of the rough chalk track which meant the tyres could get good traction, and not send her slithering and sliding as it did after heavy rain. Breaching the hill, she paused for a moment to prepare for what was to come. Stanislav would, no doubt, be cross with her for not keeping in touch more regularly, but there were so many important things to discuss tonight, and she needed a moment to gather her thoughts and bring some clarity to the extraordinary turn of events caused by Gracie's passing.

She eyed the line of flat, tar-papered roofs peeking above the steep bank of tamarisk. Spirals of smoke rose from the three chimney pipes into the thin air, and a warm glow from the windows seemed to welcome her home. She took a deep breath and slowly drove down the hill towards the thicket of gorse where Stanislav's especially adapted car was parked.

The three fishermen's cottages had been built almost a century before on a flat shelf of land that jutted out between the chalk bank and the steeply sloping shingle beach, and although they now had electricity and a telephone line, very little else had changed.

They were owned by Frank Reilly, Peggy's brother-in-law, who lived in the end one and moored his fishing boat above the high-tide line. He'd done repairs to the roofs and weathered wooden walls, and slapped on a lick of paint and preservative where it was needed. Consisting of three main rooms and a bathroom the size of a cupboard, they were draughty, and the ancient stoves used for heating and cooking were far from efficient – but they offered shelter, and as there was a dearth of places to rent in the aftermath of the war, Danuta and Stanislav counted themselves lucky to have it.

Parking the car, she grabbed her medical bag and made her way carefully down the slope, past Frank's to her own front door, surprised that Stanislav wasn't there waiting for her. The door opened straight into the kitchen, and she found him snoring away in front of a roaring fire, the pot of soup in danger of boiling dry on the stove.

Once she'd removed the pot, she scrutinised her husband anxiously as she took off her coat, hat and gloves. He looked flushed and had, unusually, removed both prosthetics long before bedtime. She noted the empty vodka bottle and the fresh bandages on his stumps, and knew instantly that he'd overdone it again. 'Stan, my love. I'm home. Wake up,' she said softly in Polish.

'Mmmm?' His heavy-lidded eyes were bleary and bloodshot. 'Danuta,' he mumbled, still fighting to emerge from his deep sleep. 'I've made soup.'

She kissed his warm cheek and gently tweaked his luxuriant moustache. 'I see that,' she replied. 'It's a good thing I came home when I did or there would be nothing left but a burnt pot.'

He roused himself to sit straighter in the chair. 'I'm sorry. I didn't mean to fall asleep, but I haven't been able to rest with you away for so long.'

She eyed the clutter of bandages, powders and creams that sat on the kitchen table alongside the depleted vodka bottle. 'You've been overdoing things again, haven't you?' she scolded gently. 'Honestly, Stan, you know what the doctors said. You must learn to take things slowly.'

His reply was to pull her to him and smother her face in kisses. 'I know, and I will now the December rush is over.' He silenced her protest with a long, passionate kiss. 'My God, it's good to have you home again,' he sighed.

Easing herself away, Danuta noted the wince of pain he tried to hide as she brushed against his right stump and decided not to comment on it. There was little point in lecturing him, no matter how gently, for he wouldn't take any notice and would just carry on in his own sweet way until he was forced by the doctors to rest.

She ladled out the soup, cut slices of the rather stale bread and quickly toasted them on the hotplate. 'I'm ready for this,' she said, sitting at the table. 'I can't remember the last time I ate.'

'Was it very bad at the hospital?'

'I stayed with Gracie after Florence took Bobby home last night. I don't know if she realised they'd been there, and of course Bobby's too young to really understand what was going on. But Gracie was heavily sedated and not in pain, so the end was very peaceful,' she replied, those last few moments etched in her memory.

'I don't know Florence. Is she a good woman? Will she look after Bobby?'

Danuta drank some more soup before replying, for she needed to choose her words carefully. 'Florence is Peggy's right-hand woman at Solly's factory,' she began. 'She took over the management while Peggy nursed Daisy through the measles. She's in her forties, I would guess, and a bit of a stickler for getting things done properly, but then she was something high up in one of the civilian services during the war. She's never married, and doesn't seem inclined to do so, but she has a good heart and will be kind to Bobby until other arrangements can be made for him and baby Noel.'

Stan slurped his soup and then followed it up by chewing on a hunk of toast. 'I expect Rachel and Solly will take them both on. Rachel's already besotted with little Noel, so it stands to reason they'll want to keep the brothers together.'

'They are good people, and for now, things should be left as they are.' She paused. 'But Gracie's last wish for them was not to be with Rachel and Solly.'

He tensed and held her gaze across the table as if he had an inkling of what she was about to say. 'And what was her final wish?'

Danuta couldn't hide her joy any longer. 'She wants you and me to adopt them, Stan,' she babbled in Polish. Reaching across the table, she grasped his hand and grinned at his astonishment. 'Just think of it, Stan. Our own children to love and cherish – a proper little family. Something we thought we'd never have after what those Nazi brutes did to me. What greater gift can anyone give?'

His expression was unreadable as he took in her radiant face and shining hazel eyes. 'It is indeed wondrous, Danuta,' he said finally.

Danuta felt a stab of fear quench her excitement. 'You don't seem so delighted by the idea.'

'It is not going to be possible, my darling.'

Her spirits plummeted, and she eyed him in confusion. 'Why are you being so negative? It's not impossible, Stanislav – of course it isn't. Not once we find a better place to live – and Rachel promised to help us with that, remember?'

Stanislav regarded her solemnly. 'But will she still help us if it means she will lose Noel? She has already spoken of her hopes to adopt him.'

'I know that, Stan,' she retorted. 'But even Rachel must realise that she and Solly are far too old to adopt two such young children. The authorities would never allow it. Besides,' she added heatedly, 'it would be going against what Gracie wanted, and Rachel wouldn't do that.'

'Rachel is a good woman, I agree, but things have changed with Gracie dying, and we really don't know how she will react to this news.' He tightened his grip on her fingers, his expression sad. 'Money and influence count for a great deal, Danuta,' he said softly. 'You must take the stars from your eyes, my darling, and see things as they really are.'

Danuta was blinded by tears.

He released her fingers and reached to cup her cheek in his large hand. 'I know how desperately you want us to have a child, my darling, but we have so little to offer. And two children are a huge responsibility.'

Danuta could feel the tears coursing hotly down her cheeks. 'We have love enough for two,' she whispered. 'We can cope with anything as long as we have that.'

'Sometimes,' he replied sadly, 'love is not enough.'

Ronan Reilly had come to the conclusion that, now he was in his late sixties, he was far too old for all the drama the day had brought. He was also wise enough to realise he had to swallow the anger and thirst for revenge against Cissy's attacker, for it would serve no purpose, and ultimately eat away at him.

He'd walked back to the home he shared with his much younger wife, Rosie, shortly before five that afternoon to find she had yet to return from the pantomime matinee with his granddaughter, Daisy, for which he was thankful. He didn't feel ready to tell Rosie about the revelations that had come out of the afternoon's family meeting, for despite his good intentions, he was still eaten up with impotent fury over what had happened to Cissy. The dogs, Harvey and Monty, were pleased to see him, however, and it was a relief to all of them to go out for a walk after being cooped up indoors all day.

He'd returned from his tramp across the nearby playing fields an hour later in a better mood, and although he could see that Rosie was aching to know what had happened earlier, it had been impossible to say anything until little Daisy was safely tucked in bed. Once this had been achieved with the aid of a story from her favourite book, they'd sat closely together on the couch with the dogs at their feet, and Ron had told her everything.

'You were right to think Peg's idea of a council of war would be opening a can of worms,' sighed Rosie, her head resting on his broad shoulder. 'But at least the mystery of the abandoned baby's mother has been solved. Although I'm sure the gossips will have a field day over that juicy titbit,' she added sourly. She looked up at him. 'I can't believe you and Peggy thought Cissy was the mother.'

Ron shifted his arm from round her shoulders and, to mask his shame at ever thinking such a thing of his granddaughter, began to fill his pipe. 'All the evidence seemed to point that way,' he mumbled. 'To Gloria's niece, Sandra, too, for that matter – but of course it turned out Sandra was struggling to come to terms with the fact her husband was a liar and master manipulator, and she was secretly preparing to divorce him.'

Rosie reached for the onyx cigarette box on the coffee table. 'Poor girl. What a piece of work he turned out to be. She'll be well shot of him if you ask me. But it's Cissy that really concerns me. How is she ever going to get over it all?'

'She's a Reilly. She'll find a way as long as we stick by her.'

Rosie tapped the end of the cigarette on the back of her hand. 'It's all such a mess, isn't it? Poor Peggy must be at her wits' end. And I have serious doubts about Danuta and Stanislav being allowed to adopt those children.'

'Me too, especially if they continue to live in Tamarisk Bay. I know Frank's done work on the cottages so he could rent them out, but it would have been better to knock the whole lot down and start again.'

Rosie looked at him in surprise. 'You've changed your tune, Ron. I seem to remember you saying they were a memorial to your parents and the uncle they'd inherited them from.'

Ron took his pipe from his mouth and studied the burning tobacco. 'Aye, they were – and believe me, we were glad of them when we arrived here from Ireland with little more than the clothes on our backs. But times change, Rosie, and we need to move with them. Those shacks were falling down when I was a boy, and they're not much better now. I told Frank he needed to rebuild, but he was in too much of a hurry to earn rent – now it's too late.'

'It's a great shame you have tenants in the beach-front cottages by the town's fishing station. They'd have been much better off there.'

'They're good, long-term tenants and, as fond as I am of Danuta, I'm not about to throw them out for her or anyone else,' he replied.

Rosie lit the cigarette and snapped the gold lighter shut. 'Well, I feel sorry for Danuta. She's longed to have a baby, and now she's finally got the chance, everything seems to be set against her. We have to do something, Ron. We can't just let the authorities steamroller through all her hopes and dreams.'

'To be sure, I don't know what we could do to help in any practical way, Rosie. Being on the local council, you know better than most that we're going through a housing crisis, and there simply isn't anywhere for them to go. Danuta reckons Rachel has promised to help her find somewhere in town – or at least she did before she fostered Noel and became possessive. I just hope she keeps her word and doesn't make it even tougher for Danuta than it needs to be. But I fear it's all in the lap of the gods from now on.'

'Hmm. Rachel has influence and money. She could certainly put up a strong case for keeping the children.' Gloria gave a deep sigh and rested her head against Ron's shoulder once more. 'It's all so unfair, isn't it?' she murmured.

He stroked her platinum hair. 'That's life, Rosie, me darling. But if Danuta is meant to have those wains, then it will happen.'

A thoughtful silence fell between them and the only sounds in the room were the crackle and hiss of the fire in the hearth and the occasional whine and yip of the sleeping dogs.

Ron puffed on his pipe, his thoughts returning to the time when Danuta had first come to Cliffehaven. It seemed so long ago, but in reality it had only been six years, and there had been many a time since that he'd wished he could turn back the clock and change that fateful day he'd asked her to put her life on the line. A great deal had happened to all of them in those war years, but especially to that heroic young woman, whose exploits with the SOE could never be revealed or fully rewarded.

Danuta had managed to escape from Poland early in 1940 and, with the help of the underground network of partisans, had somehow crossed a war-torn Europe to get to England in search of her brother, Aleksy, who'd been billeted with Peggy at Beach View. The girl had shown great courage to get as far as England, and even the news that Aleksy had been shot down during the Battle of Britain had been met with the stoic acceptance of someone who'd already lost her parents and her lover in the turmoil of war.

However, it had been harder to overcome the heartache of losing her lover's baby, and he knew it had taken all of Peggy's motherly love and understanding to help her rise again. And then she'd been met with prejudice over her Polish roots at the hospital, forced to work as a menial in the laundry instead of using her nursing qualifications on the wards. For a short time she'd driven an ambulance – much to the terror of any pedestrian who happened to cross her path – but had proved to be brave and efficient during air raids. It seemed she was determined not to be beaten by anything.

Ron had been living at Beach View at the time and, intrigued by this slip of a girl who seemed to fear nothing, he'd quietly followed her progress through every barrier she'd breached. The girl clearly had many admirable qualities but, to his mind, they were being wasted. He'd decided to do something about that, for he knew someone who could put them to better use if Danuta was prepared to risk everything.

After discussing his idea with Dolly Cardew who was working for the SOE, he'd approached Danuta, and she'd snatched at the opportunity to do her bit in the war against Hitler. When she'd left for Bletchley Park and the weeks of intense training she would have to go through, it was in secret, and even Peggy thought she'd been offered a nursing job in London.

His pipe had gone out, but he didn't want to disturb Rosie who was leaning so comfortably against him, so he set it aside, rested his head against a cushion and closed his eyes. He had little idea of what Danuta had gone through during her time with the SOE, because it was all top secret and even his long-standing friendship with Dolly wasn't enough to break the strict code of silence. But he'd learnt since that she'd finally been captured and put in the hands of the SS. Quite by chance, it was an allied air raid which had rescued her, and having made her escape with the help of the French underground partisans, she'd been put on a hospital ship and brought straight back to England.

His heart ached with remorse, for he could only guess what those SS brutes had done to her, and it was only through Peggy that he'd discovered she could never again have children and her body would forever bear the scars of their torture.

It had been Dolly who'd made sure she got the very best of care, and used her not inconsiderable influence to get her granted British citizenship as well as the nursing documents needed to confirm her status as the fully qualified theatre sister she'd been in Poland. Ron smiled. The indomitable Dolly had been a force to be reckoned with – but then he'd learnt that as a callow youth who'd adored her. A small part of his heart would always belong to Dolly.

Feeling rather guilty at these thoughts, Ron kissed the top of Rosie's head. He was at peace with the knowledge that Rosie now ruled his heart and Dolly would always be his dearest friend, even if she was now happily married to Felix and living in America. However, it was Danuta preying on his mind, for she was once again to be faced with a formidable challenge – and this time, she might not have the weapons to win.

2

Danuta had barely slept, and when she did doze off, she'd been tormented by images of Noel and Bobby being torn from her arms by a succession of cruel-faced persecutors bearing a close resemblance to the SS sadists who'd tortured her. She'd risen as dawn had broken over the sea, and without disturbing a snoring Stanislav, had dressed, made a flask of tea and left a note for him before going out into the bitter morning to her car.

She let the engine idle in the hope the heater would warm the little car she affectionately called 'Betsy' for her rounded curves and comforting reliability. As she waited for the frost to melt on the windows, she watched the rising sun sparkle on the water in the small bay. Frank's boat was no longer moored on the beach, so she assumed he'd been out all night and was probably coming in with his small fleet to the fishing station beneath the Cliffehaven cliffs now the tide was turning.

With the car comfortably warm, she released the handbrake and let it roll silently down the hill to the valley before touching the accelerator. She didn't want Stanislav waking up and stopping her. They'd talked late into the night, and with his warnings still ringing in her head, she needed to find out for herself what Rachel intended to do.

The large house sat almost on the brow of a hill several miles from Cliffehaven, and was sheltered from the main road by a neat hedge of rhododendrons. Danuta parked the car and surveyed the drawn curtains over the many windows. There was a stillness about the house which told her that the occupants had yet to rise from their beds. She looked at her watch and realised it was far too early to disturb them, but she was on edge, and didn't have the patience to wait until a more civilised hour. There was a five-day-old baby in the house. It stood to reason someone had to be up.

Climbing out of the car, she pushed through the ornate wrought-iron gate and headed along the brick pathway to the imposing oak front door shadowed by a wisteria-covered porch. She tugged on the iron bell-pull and, hearing the clang echo through the house, she almost lost her nerve. But it was too late now – and this was too important.

The door eventually opened to reveal a sleepy-eyed Rachel, dark hair tousled and tumbling over her shoulders. Her eyes widened at the sight of Danuta standing on her doorstep. 'I wondered when you would come,' she said, opening the door wide. 'But it is the most ghastly hour, my dear, and that damned bell has woken Noel.'

Danuta stepped over the threshold to hear Noel's wails drifting down into the grand entrance hall. 'I'm sorry, Rachel. I didn't mean to wake him, but I needed to see you.'

Rachel closed the door and tightened the sash on her silk dressing gown. 'You'd better come up while I see to Noel,' she said, heading for the stairs.

Danuta hadn't missed the coolness in the older woman's eyes, and her misgivings multiplied as she followed her up the elegant sweep of plush carpeting to the first-floor landing where Noel's cries rang out. She felt guilty at having woken him, but at least this would give her a chance to hold him and, if Rachel allowed, to change and feed him.

Rachel swept into one of the rooms off the landing and headed straight for the lace-draped cot. She reached down to pick up the squalling baby and held him against her shoulder. 'His bottle and everything are in there,' she said above the noise. 'If you could sort that out while I change him, it would be helpful.'

Danuta went into the small room that she guessed had once been a dressing room – but which was now home to piles of pristine nappies, tubs of formula, bottles of sterilising liquid, and enough baby clothes to kit out an entire shop. Refusing to dwell on the realisation she could never provide such luxury, she filled the kettle from the tap over the tiny basin, spooned formula into a jug and took a clean feeding bottle from one of the overhead cupboards. As she waited for the kettle to boil, she peeked through the doorway to enviously watch Rachel change the baby's nappy.

Noel was grizzling now, his plump little arms and legs waving about as he wriggled and squirmed to combat Rachel's efforts. But Rachel was clearly no novice when it came to changing nappies, for within moments, the terry towelling was firmly pinned in place, the waterproof pants pulled on, swiftly followed by a clean pair of knitted leggings. The tiny vest was fought against momentarily, but it too was soon in place and the matinee jacket neatly buttoned over it. Rachel swept the hair out of her eyes with elegant fingers that glittered with diamonds, and then scooped Noel up to kiss and nuzzle his sweet neck.

Danuta heard the kettle whistle and turned back to make up the formula. She didn't like the jealousy that was raging through her, and certainly didn't want Rachel to see it in her expression. And yet her hands were shaking as she tested the heat of the formula on her wrist.

'You can feed him if you'd like.'

Danuta turned at the sound of the soft voice and saw Rachel standing in the doorway with only compassion in her brown eyes. 'I would like it very much,' she managed through a throat tight with grateful tears. 'Thank you.'

'There's no need to thank me, Danuta,' said Rachel, indicating a low upholstered chair beneath the window. 'Sit down and I will hand him to you.'

The feel of him was a balm despite the racket he was making, and once she'd again tested the heat of the formula, she plugged that demanding little mouth with the rubber teat, whereupon he began to hungrily feed.

'Blessed silence,' sighed Rachel, sinking onto a chaise longue. 'If nothing else, Danuta, that small baby has a powerful set of lungs.'

Danuta smiled down at him as he greedily drank the formula. His eyes were closed in concentration and his tiny fists were curled beneath his chin. He was so perfect, she couldn't find the words to express the depth of her feelings.

'I know why you've come, Danuta.'

She tore her gaze from Noel to look at Rachel. 'Peggy rang you, didn't she?'

Rachel nodded. 'Solly and I were shocked and saddened to hear about little Gracie. She came to work for Solly after her husband was killed early on in the war. She was a good girl, hard-working and almost painfully honest. It's such a tragedy she felt she had to hide away from everyone like that.' Rachel sighed and ran her manicured hands over the silk of her dressing gown. 'I do hope that what she did won't taint the lives of her children. People can be so cruel with their gossip.'

Danuta looked down at Noel, who'd finished feeding and was now sated and drowsy. She set the bottle aside and held him over her shoulder to wind him. Noel gave an enormous burp which made both women smile, and she rested him back in her arms to watch him sleep.

'How do you feel about Stanislav and me adopting Noel and his brother?' she asked tentatively.

Rachel was silent for so long that Danuta eyed her in alarm. 'Rachel?'

'I have to be honest with you, Danuta,' she said, her gaze drifting to her tightly clasped hands. 'I do have reservations.'

'Reservations?' Danuta's pulse was racing. 'Does that mean you and Solly will not support me and Stanislav in this?'

Rachel looked back at her, eyes wide with surprise. 'Whatever made you think that?'

'You have all this,' Danuta replied, gesturing distractedly at their surroundings. 'You clearly adore Noel, and can give him and Bobby so very much more than we ever could.' She took a breath. 'And you have a lot of influence in this town,' she added quietly. 'The authorities are bound to be on your side.'

Rachel bit her lip. 'Oh, my dear girl,' she breathed. 'I didn't realise . . .' She got to her feet and gently took Noel from Danuta's arms and placed him in the cot beneath a warm blue blanket. Drawing Danuta to her feet, she took her hand. 'He'll sleep for a couple of hours now. Let's go downstairs where we can talk.'

Cissy had slept well, and without troubling dreams, for the first time in what felt like an age. She'd woken in the small room she'd slept in as a child, stretched luxuriously and slowly padded out to the bathroom to get ready for the day. It wouldn't be an easy one, but her Aunt Doris and her sister Anne had to be faced. Once that was done, all the family would be in the know, and she could only hope that that would be the end of it, for the repeated retelling was taking its toll mentally as well as physically. Her Aunt Doris could prove tricky, though, for there was no guarantee as to how she would react to the news.

She stared at her reflection in the bathroom mirror, added a swipe of red to her lips and fluffed out her fair hair in defiance of Doris and anything she might have to say. Feeling lighter in spirit now everything was out in the open, and ready to face the others, she headed downstairs to the kitchen where she found only her mother busy at the table.

'You're up early, Mum,' she said, giving Peggy a hug.

'Bob and Pippa are leaving today and I wanted to sort out some food for them to take with them. It's a long drive back to Somerset.' Peggy stepped back from the embrace and studied her daughter thoughtfully. 'You look much better this morning, darling. I'm guessing you slept well?'

Cissy nodded. 'Better than I expected.' She poured a cup of tea from the pot on the table, then went to put some bread into the toaster. 'Where's everyone else?'

'Your dad's having a lie-in; Cordelia's still asleep, and I suspect the others are too after their late night.' Peggy took her hand. 'You did well last night with Bob and Charlie,' she murmured, 'but I'm sure they'd have understood if you'd told them what that man did to you.'

'They didn't need to know it all, Mum. The loss of my baby was enough.'

Peggy nodded, her eyes sad.

Cissy lightened her tone. 'Anyway, it's a new day, and there are things I need to do. Could I borrow your car, Mum? Only I want to see Anne and check on Sandra before I have to face Aunt Doris.'

'Of course you can, dear. But do you really want to see Doris on your own? Wouldn't it be better if I came with you?'

Cissy shook her head and grinned. 'I'm a big girl now, Mum. I've come up against far worse than Aunt Doris, believe you me.'

Peggy didn't look convinced, and there was the light of battle in her eyes. 'Well, if you say so. But if my snooty sister utters one word out of turn and upsets you, I'll punch her nose.'

Cissy chuckled. Rescuing the toast before it burnt, she carried it to the table.

Peggy plonked down into the chair beside her and continued to butter bread for sandwiches with rather more verve than was needed. 'If you're going to borrow my car, you must remember these country roads are far more challenging than the ones in London, especially now the temperature has dropped to almost zero.'

Cissy swallowed a mouthful of toast and home-made blackberry jam. 'I'm sure they are, Mum. But I need to talk to Anne. I've missed her, you know.'

She saw Peggy raise an eyebrow and grinned. 'I know we're chalk and cheese and that when I was at home we constantly fell out over almost everything, but she is my sister – just as Doris is yours.'

Peggy blinked in astonishment before putting down the butter knife. 'Doris is a cross I have to bear, Cissy, but of course I'm glad you're going to confide in Anne. She's always been very sensible, and a good listener.'

'Whereas I never have been, of course,' Cissy countered without rancour. She held up her hand to silence her mother's denial. 'You know I'm right, Mum. Anne's always been the steady, practical one. I should have listened to her long ago, and kept my feet on the ground and my head out of the clouds.' There was a wry twist to her mouth. 'After all, Mum, look where that led me.'

Having no reply to that, Peggy squeezed her fingers and carried on making the sandwiches.

Ron had left the house in Havelock Road just after dawn had broken. It was bitterly cold, and he noticed that Harvey was moving his hindquarters quite stiffly as they headed up the silent and deserted High Street. The old boy had been reluctant to come out at all and was finding these cold mornings a bit of a trial; perhaps he should have left him snoozing by the fire.

He patted the lurcher's head and received a lick on the hand in return. 'We won't go far, wee man,' Ron murmured, ruffling his brindled fur. 'And tonight we'll just go for a slow stroll around Havelock Gardens.'

Harvey's eyes were knowing as he gazed back at him. But before Ron could change his mind and take him back home, the old dog shook himself and gamely hobbled after his pup, Monty, who was galloping up the hill some distance ahead of them.

Ron gave a deep sigh and plodded after him. Harvey had been with him for almost sixteen years, and it was clear he was now feeling his age. There would be no more long walks over the hills – no more outings with the ferrets, or into the woods hunting pigeons or pheasants. It was time for him to retire, to stay at home and dream of his glory days in warmth and comfort.

He blinked away sentimental tears and dug into the deep pocket of his poacher's coat for his handkerchief. Blowing his nose and wiping his eyes, he exchanged the handkerchief for his pipe. If this was to be Harvey's last long walk, then he would make sure he enjoyed it. They would take it easy up the hill to the rolling countryside that lay beyond the town and visit some of their favourite haunts – perhaps sit a while by the ruins of the old farmhouse – and if Harvey was too tired to make the journey back, he would carry him home.

Ron got his pipe lit to his satisfaction and kept an eye on Monty who was darting about sniffing every lamp post and doorway. With Harvey at his side, he plodded past the building site where a new, fancy Odeon cinema was going up in place of the old one where Jim had worked as a projectionist before the war. Everyone in Cliffehaven was delighted, for it would mean an end to cramming into the ramshackle scout hut to watch outdated films on an unreliable projector, or having to catch the bus into the next town.

There was to be a new Woolworths, as well as a bingo hall and several other smaller shops catering for the tourists who flocked to Cliffehaven in the holiday season. All in all, the town was being reborn, and it was all through forward-thinking people like his Rosie who'd fought the rail company to keep the trains coming, and who worked so diligently on the council for the residents of Cliffehaven.

Ron approached the turn-off for the church and saw a familiar figure, well wrapped up against the cold and clearly deep in thought. As he got nearer, he realised Bertie Double-Barrelled was muttering to himself, which made Ron smile.

'Would you be after having a conversation with yourself, Bertie?'

The long-retired army officer turned and nodded bashfully. 'Guilty as charged, Ron.'

'Ach, well, it's often the only way to have an intelligent debate.'

Bertie dug his chin into his scarf and his gloved hands into his coat pockets. 'I find it's a good way to sort out problems. Clears the mind, don't you know – helps me make decisions.'

Ron grinned. 'Aye, me too, but it's usually Rosie who makes the decisions, regardless of what I want. I just go along with them for the quiet life.' He cocked his head and eyed the older man with some concern. 'Is something troubling you, Bertie? Want to share it?'

Bertie shook his head. 'It's nothing, Ron. I just haven't slept very well, that's all.'

'Me neither,' he admitted, his gaze following the two dogs as they watered a nearby drainpipe. 'And I suspect there wasn't much of it at Beach View, either. 'Tis a troubled world we live in, Bertie, but we have no choice but to carry on.'

Bertie nodded mournfully, and then looked at his watch. 'I'd better not stop and chat, Ron. The vicar has early matins and I need to get the church ready.'

Ron waved him on his way, whistled to the dogs and headed towards the steep path that ran behind the memorial gardens and up into the hills. Despite Bertie's denial, something was worrying the old fellow, and he suspected it had to do with his promise to sponsor Noel. Deciding he'd approach him another time, he turned his attention back to the lurchers. Monty had dashed off, but Harvey seemed content to plod along at his own pace, stopping now and then to sniff at something and cock his leg.

They had almost reached the top of the slope when he caught sight of Monty's backside and tail waving about as he buried his nose beneath a pile of discarded building waste and yapped excitedly.

Ron's first thought was he'd found a nest of rats or mice, and so he hurried to drag him out before he got bitten. But as he yanked on his collar, Harvey came lumbering up to put his nose into the hole his pup had made.

'Will the pair of you get out of there,' Ron growled, making a grab for their collars.

Monty was too quick and he twisted away – out of reach at a sprint.

Harvey whined and began to paw at the rough planks and bits of broken brick, heedless of the rusty nails and bits of wire enmeshed in it all.

Ron grabbed his collar and managed to haul him away, but the old dog was clearly agitated, and tried his best to get back to whatever was lurking beneath the rubbish. 'You don't want to be messing with rats, you silly old fool,' Ron hissed.

Harvey barked, tore himself from Ron's grip and began to dig frantically.

'What the divil's got into you, ye heathen beast?' muttered Ron crossly. 'Go on – out of me way and let me have a look before you do yourself damage.'

He pushed the dog to one side, got down on his knees and warily peered into the dark hole the dogs had dug. It didn't smell of vermin or rabbit, but that was no guarantee there wasn't a big fat rat hiding in there waiting to attack him. And there was nothing he hated more than rats.

'There's nothing there, ye daft beggar,' he said, preparing to get off his knees and continue with his walk. But then he heard a sound, faint but unmistakable. 'Well, I'll be damned,' he breathed as he began to carefully clear away the rubble to the plaintive cries coming from its depths.

Harvey came to help and was swiftly joined by Monty.

'Get out of it,' snapped Ron. 'You'll terrify the poor wee thing. Go. Sit. Behave.'

Both dogs lay down, noses on paws, eyes pinned to the hole, ears twitching as the faint cries came again.

As light flooded the hiding place, Ron found he was being watched by two pairs of green eyes. 'Well, well, well,' he murmured. 'What have we got here?'

He reached in and carefully lifted both the kittens out. Their fur was damp, matted and filthy on their frail little bodies, but they seemed alert enough, and both purred like small engines as he held them to his chest.

Harvey crept forward on his belly to inspect the find. He liked cats. Monty wasn't sure what to make of them and kept his distance.

Ron could feel the little creatures trembling in the cold, so he quickly tucked them into an inside pocket of his coat so they could garner some warmth from his body. 'I'd better see if there are any more,' he murmured, getting back onto his knees to peer into the hole. His heart sank, for there were indeed two more, but they were dead.

'Poor wee mites,' he breathed. 'You didn't stand a chance out here without a mother to keep you warm and safe. I bet some bastard threw you out like so much garbage.' His anger was so great he could scarcely contain it as he got to his feet.

Harvey and Monty shot up and eyed Ron expectantly, tongues lolling, tails wagging.

'No more walking today,' Ron said crossly. 'I need to get these little ones home.'

They looked at him in confusion as he headed back down the hill, and then reluctantly followed him.

Danuta had followed the older woman down the stairs and through the large hall to an expansive kitchen which was flooded in the early sunshine streaming through French doors which led onto a paved terrace overlooking a manicured lawn. Watching from a chair at the scrubbed pine table as Rachel made tea, she was once again forcibly reminded of how poor her own little home was.

There were cupboards above and below polished oak working surfaces; an enormous refrigerator had pride of place at one end; the modern gas stove, with its eye-level grill and large oven, was neatly slotted into the run of cupboards. Pretty yellow and white gingham curtains matched the padded cushions on the kitchen chairs, and the light coming through the windows heightened the yellow paint on the walls, making the room feel as if they were sitting in the very heart of the sun. Rachel's kettle was electric and there were shelves piled high with expensive china, copper pots and all manner of cookware that Danuta had never seen before.

Rachel put the teapot on the table and set out the cups and saucers. 'Have you had breakfast, Danuta?'

She shook her head, her stomach in knots with anxiety. 'I'm not hungry.'

Rachel arched one finely plucked eyebrow and slotted slices of bread into the shining toaster. She fetched butter and honey, and slid knives and side plates onto the table. 'Well, I am,' she said. 'And I find things are much easier to talk about with something in your stomach.'

Danuta realised she was stalling for time, and her spirits reached a new low ebb. The last thing she wanted was food, but it seemed Rachel was determined to stay silent on the subject of Noel until she was ready.

Rachel slathered real butter on the hot toast and spread on thick, yellow honey before pushing the plate towards Danuta. 'Eat. Then we'll talk.'

Despite everything, the sight and smell of such richness made her mouth water and before she knew it, she'd eaten both slices and did, in fact, feel much better for it. 'You said you had reservations,' she said once Rachel's plate was empty.

'Solly and I both do,' she replied, holding up her hand to silence Danuta's protest. 'We know you'll love those children as if they were your own, and that Stanislav will be a superb father to them.' She paused as if choosing her words carefully. 'But it's where you live, Danuta – and the fact that Stanislav sometimes struggles with his health which means he can't work. And you'll have to give up your nursing if you take them on.' She gave a sigh. 'Neither of us can see how you could ever cope.'

'It is my concern too,' Danuta admitted. 'But we have talked of these things, and if you can help us to find somewhere better to live, many of the problems will disappear.'

'I know I promised to help, and I will do my best. But Jacob Kaplin is an old man, still trying to get over the loss of his wife. I can't force him to sell up and move out, Danuta.'

'I realise that. I also know there are very few places available to buy or rent.' She regarded Rachel through a blur of tears. 'It all feels so hopeless, Rachel.'

Rachel reached for Danuta's hand and gave it an encouraging squeeze. 'Not hopeless, my dear, merely problematic. I am simply being realistic about the resistance you might encounter, but that doesn't mean that we will not support you in every way we can. Of course everything has come to a halt because of the Christmas holidays. But once we're into the new year, I shall do my best to find Jacob somewhere that he'll find more suitable.'

Danuta nodded, knowing Rachel would keep her word, but also knowing they might not be able to afford Jacob's house. It was, after all, in Elms Avenue, and the cost of buying it would surely be way out of their reach. 'If we can't afford to buy it and you buy it instead, would you rent it to us?'

'We'll cross that bridge when we come to it, Danuta,' Rachel replied firmly. 'You'll just have to trust me.'

Danuta realised she'd get no further on the subject so she left it for now. It would probably be many weeks before anything was resolved, and a lot could happen before then. 'I'll still have the authorities to convince,' she murmured. 'But when they see where I live compared to all this – they're bound to want Noel to stay with you.'

'Now, Danuta, enough of that. Being a mother is nothing to do with "all this", as you put it. It's about being there in times of trouble, about having a shoulder to cry on and arms to cuddle and soothe. These material things mean nothing when a child just needs to be loved.'

'But will the adoption people feel the same way? Will they see beyond the shack we live in and Stanislav's injuries to the love we can give? Or will they decide the children would be much better off with you and Solly who've already proved to be wonderful to Noel?'

Rachel gave a deep sigh and moved her chair closer. 'Danuta, you are troubling trouble before it troubles you,' she said, putting an arm round her shoulders. 'Now, I want you to stop looking on the dark side of things and listen to me.' At Danuta's nod, she took a breath and turned her so they were face-to-face.

'Solly and I talked after Peggy told us about Gracie and what she wanted for her children. And I admit that I hoped for a while to adopt Noel, because I do adore him. But Solly's wise judgement persuaded me that I was being very foolish. You see, Danuta, neither of us has ever met Bobby, and it wouldn't be fair to take one boy and not the other.'

She gave a wan smile. 'To be frank, Danuta, we're both in our sixties and far too old and set in our ways to take on a five-year-old as well as a baby, and Solly, bless his soul, is quite enough of a handful on his own, believe me.'

Danuta looked into her eyes. 'So you won't object to us taking them on?'

'Of course we won't, and we'll do all we can to help, I promise.'

Danuta grasped Rachel's hands. 'Thank you, Rachel. That means the world to me.'

Rachel's eyes were sad despite her smile. 'Don't thank me yet, darling. There's a very long road ahead of us – and who knows what we'll have to face. Just be assured we'll be with you every step of the way.'

Ron closed the front gate and shooed the dogs indoors. 'Rosie!' he called. 'Rosie, where are you?'

She emerged from the kitchen in her dressing gown, looking cross. 'Shush!' she hissed. 'You'll wake Daisy. And why are you back so soon?'

'Never mind all that,' he said, breathless from his hasty walk. He reached into his coat pocket and drew out the tiny kittens. 'I need help with these.'

'Oh,' she gasped, wide-eyed. 'Oh, Ron, how darling – and so tiny. Where on earth . . . ?'

'This isn't the time for cooing, Rosie. They're probably starving as well as half-frozen and filthy. Have we got any milk?'

'Of course. Give them to me. The fire's lit in the sitting room and I'll soon have them dry and snug.' She took the kittens and hurried out of the kitchen. Grabbing the blanket off the couch, she made a nest for them in front of the blazing fire, ensuring they were protected by the fireguard, and gently rubbed them dry with a corner of the blanket, crooning softly as they started to purr.

Ron came in with a saucer of milk, and another saucer loaded with chopped left-over duck. 'It might be a bit rich for them,' he said. 'I doubt they were even weaned before some ratbag threw them out.'

'People like that should be shot,' muttered Rosie. 'I suppose there was no sign of the mother?'

Ron shook his head and tried to encourage the kittens to drink the milk. As he suspected, neither of them knew how to lap. 'We need something to feed them with, like a pen-filler.'

'I've got a new one in my briefcase.' Rosie shot to her feet, almost tripping over Harvey who'd come to survey their latest house guests and steal the chopped duck in two gulps.

Ignoring him, Ron dipped his little finger in the milk and offered it to both kittens. The noisy one sucked it off immediately, so he repeated the exercise for the other one which soon got the idea.

Rosie came back in a rush. 'I've washed the pen-filler out just in case, but I've also found the eye dropper I used when I had that conjunctivitis. Both should do.' She dropped to her knees and filled the droppers with milk, before scooping up the smaller and quieter of the two to cradle it against her generous bosom and feed it.

Ron fed the other one, noting how hungry they both were — but at least they'd stopped shivering, and as they filled their little bellies, they grew sleepy.

With both kittens snuggled together in the nest of blankets, Harvey kept close watch, his greying muzzle on his paws, his ears twitching every time one of them stirred. Monty had settled on the couch, not sure what was happening but clearly very put out that Harvey had snaffled the plate of duck.

Rosie sat on the floor at Ron's feet. 'Poor little things,' she sighed. 'I hope they both survive.'

'They have a good chance now, which is more than can be said for the two that died out there under all that rubble. If I find out who abandoned them, I'm going to report them to the RSPCA.'

'Good.' Rosie gave a sigh. 'I don't know, Ron, what with abandoned babies and discarded kittens, the world has become very cruel.' She smiled at Harvey and lovingly patted his head. 'But all's well that ends well, and it seems these two have a very attentive nursemaid.'

'Aye, he's a good dog, Rosie. But sadly the time has come for him to take things easy.' He noted the alarm flash in her eyes and hastened to allay it. 'He's feeling the cold in old joints, and the long walks are getting too much. I'll just be taking him for a turn round the communal gardens from now on.'

Rosie reached for his hand, her eyes full of sympathy and understanding. 'You're a good man, Ronan Reilly, with a big heart, and I love you very much.'

He felt colour flood his face in embarrassment. 'Ach, I'm no better than the next man,' he rumbled. 'You're just biased because I bring you kittens to fuss over.'

She giggled and got to her feet to kiss his hot cheek. 'And lovely they are too. But they'll need feeding every hour over the next few days and nights if we're to save them. And then there will be the problem of what we'll do with them.'

'I thought we might keep them,' he said hopefully.

She eyed him steadily. 'We already have two dogs and two ferrets. Two more of anything would be rather overdoing it, don't you think?'

'Aye, maybe,' he murmured, noting how lovingly she was gazing at the two tiny scraps by the fire. 'We'll see how things go, eh?'

3

Having waved goodbye to her brother Bob and his sweet girlfriend, Pippa, Cissy returned to the house to fetch her coat and bag. Her younger brother, Charlie, was in the hall, preparing to leave for his holiday job at Jack Smith's garage, and although he'd seemed to have quite calmly accepted she'd got pregnant and then lost the baby, she couldn't help but notice how he'd avoided looking at her since finding out. She didn't comment on this, realising that at his age anything to do with sex was hugely embarrassing – especially when it involved his sister.

'Don't mind, Charlie,' said Peggy as the seventeen-year-old fled the house. 'He's at a funny age.' She grinned. 'You should have seen him after your father gave him the facts of life talk. He couldn't look at anyone for three days!'

Cissy could remember squirming with Anne after their mother had had the same talk with them. *Oh, to be that young and innocent again*, she thought wistfully. 'He'll get over it,' she said lightly.

'Now,' said Peggy, becoming businesslike. 'You do remember how to get to Anne's, don't you?'

'I've only been there the once, but I think so,' she replied.

'I've drawn a map. It's not difficult to find as long as you don't miss the turning into her lane.'

Taking the scrap of paper, Cissy kissed her mother and left the house to climb into Peggy's car. It was a grey, chilly day, and despite having to face Doris later, Cissy felt her spirits lighten as she drove away from Beach View, heading for the Crown which stood proudly – if rather shabbily – in the High Street. She loved her family and her home, and now everything was out in the open, she could at last feel the tension of the past months lift from her shoulders.

Despite having been stored away on bricks for the duration of the war, Peggy's car had been expertly serviced by Jack Smith and it now ran as smooth as silk. She drew to a halt outside the pub and because it was still far too early for Gloria to be open for business, made her way down the alley to the rear entrance.

The sound of bolts being drawn and keys turned in locks preceded the vision that was fifty-five-year-old Gloria first thing in the morning. Her dyed hair was encased in curlers and a scarf, her face was naked of the usual heavy make-up, and her plump feet were stuffed into high-heeled fluffy sandals that made her totter. Between the gaping folds of the rather ugly dressing gown floated the flimsiest of nightdresses which left very little to the imagination.

'Hello, love,' she said, seemingly unfazed by her early visitor. 'Get yerself indoors. It's as cold as a witch's tit out 'ere.'

'I'm sorry I'm so early, but I wanted to make sure Sandra's all right,' Cissy replied, stepping into the dingy hallway.

'She's as right as rain,' Gloria replied cheerfully over her shoulder as she led the way up the stairs to the kitchen. 'But I'll let 'er tell you all about it herself. I've got the kettle on.'

Cissy entered the warm kitchen which held the aromas of many meals past and quickly embraced Sandra who'd been in the middle of making a pot of tea. 'You're looking ever so much better,' she said, regarding her friend carefully, and noting there was colour in her face and her eyes were bright and clear. 'I was worried Graham would cause trouble when you got back here yesterday.'

'He wouldn't bloody dare,' retorted Gloria, dumping the teapot on the table.

Seeing Gloria's expression, Cissy had no doubt of it. 'So, what happened?'

'He'd legged it by the time we got back,' said Sandra calmly. 'Packed up his things – along with my fur coat and pearls – and presumably caught the next train back to London.'

'And good riddance,' muttered Gloria, plumping down into a kitchen chair. 'Let's hope that's the last we see of 'im, and all.'

'He took your coat and pearls?' Cissy was shocked he could be so petty.

Sandra shrugged. 'He bought them, so they were his by rights, I suppose. And anyway, I can live without them reminding me of what a fool I've been for so many years.' She reached for Cissy's hand. 'But how are you, Cissy? It can't have been easy to tell the rest of your family what happened.'

'It wasn't, but it's done now, and hopefully we can all get on without having it overshadow everything. I'm going to see my sister Anne this morning, but the hardest bit will be facing Aunt Doris. You know what a stickler she is for not letting the side down and keeping up with the snobs. She's never really approved of me and is bound to see it all as confirmation of her suspicions that I'm a flibbertigibbet leading a rackety life.'

'Too snooty by 'alf,' muttered Gloria around the cigarette she was lighting. 'And she ain't no saint. You 'ave me word on that.'

Cissy giggled with surprise. 'Really? Is there

something I should know, Aunt Gloria, or are you just making it up so I can see her in a different light?'

Gloria lifted her chin, her gaze drifting far beyond the kitchen walls. 'I knows what I knows,' she murmured mysteriously. 'Let's leave it at that.'

Cissy was intrigued, but as it was clear she'd get no more out of Gloria, she drank her tea and let the idea simmer quietly at the back of her mind. 'What will you do when you go back to London, Sandra? You clearly won't be able to go back home.'

'Mum said I could move in with her until I find somewhere suitable. I'm well paid at the Inns of Court, so it shouldn't be too hard to find something. But it'll be good to stay with her a while and get my breath back before I have to face Graham in the divorce court.' She glanced up at Cissy over the rim of her teacup. 'I'm rather hoping Graham will initiate things, because I have no stomach for airing our dirty laundry in public.'

'I doubt he'll want it either,' said Cissy, thinking of the years Graham had denied Sandra longed-for children by telling her he was impotent, only to be exposed as a liar and manipulator. 'Let's hope he'll cite abandonment because you left him and refuse to go back.'

'We'll see,' replied Sandra. 'There's nothing either of us can do until the new year, anyway.' She finished her tea and placed the cup on the table. 'As I said yesterday, I want to focus on Gracie's funeral for now. What will happen to her children, do you know?'

'Not really. The baby is being fostered by Rachel and Solly Goldman, and the little boy is still living with Florence. But according to Danuta, Gracie managed to dictate a will before she died, and she's made it clear she wanted them both to be adopted by Danuta and her husband.'

As Sandra clearly didn't know who she was talking about, Cissy explained who the Polish couple were and their circumstances. 'Mum's fretting over it all, of course, and actually it doesn't look too hopeful.'

'That's so sad,' the other girl sighed.

'I'd offer them a place 'ere,' said Gloria, 'but I doubt them in charge would take kindly to the thought of kids living above the pub.' She grimaced. 'To my mind, as long as kids are loved and cared for proper, it don't matter where they live. At least it's a roof over their little heads, and it done my boy no 'arm when he was a nipper.'

'I agree,' said Cissy, suppressing her thoughts that the rowdiest pub in Cliffehaven was hardly the most suitable place for a young boy and a newborn. She got to her feet and glanced out of the window at the gathering clouds that were darkening the sky. 'I'd better get going. The weather looks as if it's closing in, and I don't fancy getting caught out in the middle of nowhere.'

She hugged Sandra and made arrangements to meet the next day, and after thanking Gloria for the tea, made her escape from the fug of cigarette smoke and boiled cabbage.

Cissy drove up the hill past the Goldmans' elegant house and down into the valley towards the Memorial Hospital for wounded service personnel where Danuta and Stanislav had once been patients. Taking the turn-off for Anne's hamlet, she passed acres of ploughed fields, the newly sown crops lying dormant beneath the rich dark soil that glittered with frost in the weak sunlight. She could see the airfield ahead, the refurbished Nissen huts looking small against the two huge C-47 cargo planes that sat on the runway next to the control tower.

The sight brought back the memories of her war, for Cliffe aerodrome had been her home during those years of service with the WAAFs – a place of excitement, drama and the most heart-breaking losses. Too many young men had died in the defence of this country, and she was often haunted by the memories of their frightened but stoic young faces; of being bombed; of seeing planes coming in on a wing and a prayer; of names being erased from the blackboard after yet another sortie into war-torn Europe – and raucous parties where only copious amounts of alcohol could blot out the horrors.

Cissy shook off those memories, determined to remain positive. The airfield had fallen into disuse after the war, but Anne's husband Martin Black and his co-pilot, Roger Makepeace, after surviving the death march from their POW camp in Silesia and returning home, had persuaded the MOD to lease it to them. Now, in partnership with Roger's wife Kitty and a fellow pilot's widow, Charlotte, it was home to a fully-fledged air transport business, and the updated Nissen huts were providing welcome accommodation for the ground crew and their families.

Lost in thought, she almost missed the sharp turn Peggy had warned her about, and with a screech of tyres, just made it into the lane without ending up in the deep ditch half-hidden by an overgrown hedge. The lane was narrow and the trees either side formed a dark tunnel which seemed to go on for ever, and she began to wonder if she'd turned off too soon. On the point of turning back, she finally saw Anne and Martin's neat detached house standing back from the lane in a leaf-strewn garden, and breathed a sigh of relief.

She drove through the open gateway and drew to a halt on the gravel drive. But almost before she could climb out, she was bombarded by two small girls vying for attention.

'Oh, my goodness,' she exclaimed. 'Give me a minute, girls. I can't understand a word you're saying if you both talk at once.' She hugged Rose Margaret and Emily, who both seemed determined to ply her with questions, and looked over their heads to their mother who was standing in the doorway with baby Oscar in her arms and a broad smile on her face. 'I'll tell you all about London later,' she said, firmly disentangling herself to go and greet Anne.

'It's so lovely to see you again,' she said, giving her a hug. 'I'm sorry if I was a bit off with you at the tree ceremony before Christmas, but things were going on that I couldn't explain then.'

Anne hugged her back. 'Let's get indoors before we all freeze to death.'

Cissy had only been to the house once before and hadn't been that impressed. But she knew that after it had been rented out during the war, Anne and Martin had fully refurbished it, so she was keen to see how it looked now. She stepped into the square hall that was set in the middle of the house between the dining and sitting rooms and was amazed by the transformation. The tatty old carpets and dark panelling were gone, fresh paint and paper had been applied to the walls and a new runner of deep blue carpeted the stairs and upstairs landing.

Anne flung open the doors for her to admire the elegant decorations and furnishings in the reception rooms, and then led her along the hall to what Cissy remembered as a very dark, dank and basic kitchen with a crumbling lean-to for a washhouse and outside lav. She gasped in delight, for the lean-to had been demolished, and now the kitchen extended the whole width of the house to provide modern fixtures and fittings and plenty of space for the American fridge, and a large table at the centre. A pram stood by French doors which led into a large, neat garden, radiators pumped out welcome heat – and even on this dull day, the light through the many windows made the space feel bright and welcoming.

'It's lovely, Anne. My goodness. You must have both worked terribly hard to get it all done so beautifully.'

Anne blushed with pleasure and tucked her dark curls behind her ears. 'Dad, Grandad and Charlie did a great deal of it. Martin helped, of course, but he was busy setting up Phoenix Air Transport with Roger and the others.' She shot Cissy a wry smile. 'Mum was an absolute brick through all the chaos, but I think she was quite glad when the work was done and we finally moved out of Beach View.'

Cissy grinned. 'I bet she was in her element, having you and the girls home to spoil.'

Anne laughed. 'I'm not too sure about that. My two are a handful at the best of times.'

As if this was a cue to make themselves part of the conversation, the girls once again started plying Cissy with questions, and demanding she let them show her their bedrooms.

'That's enough, both of you,' said Anne in her sternest school teacher tone. 'Upstairs, please. I'll call you down when Cissy is ready to talk to you.'

With glaring eyes and stubborn chins, both girls huffed and puffed before stomping out of the kitchen and thudding upstairs. The bang of the bedroom door swiftly followed.

'Sorry about that,' said Anne with a sigh. 'The measles has kept them indoors for too long and neither is in the best of humour. I don't know how Mum coped with the four of us.'

Cissy laughed. 'She probably went into a darkened room and screamed into her pillow,' she replied. 'I know I would if I had to put up with me as a kid.'

Anne giggled. 'You weren't that bad, Cissy, just lively and full of mischief like any other child with a vivid imagination.' She hitched the sleeping baby a little more comfortably over her shoulder. 'It's easier when Martin's at home, but he's always at the airfield dealing with some endless problem. He should be back for lunch today, though, so I hope you'll stay and help us eat the mound of food we've got left over from Christmas. I seem to have overdone things on the catering front.'

Cissy felt awful at having to let her down. 'I wish I could help you out, but Aunt Doris is expecting me later this morning, and I daren't be late.'

Anne regarded her thoughtfully. 'That's brave of you.' She plonked a sleeping Oscar into Cissy's arms and turned towards the kettle. 'Well, if I can't give you lunch at least have a cup of tea and some of this lovely shortbread. I'll say one thing for Aunt Doris, she doesn't skimp when it comes to ordering things from Fortnum and Mason's.'

Cissy looked down at the sleeping baby. He was dark-haired like both his parents, and rather chubby, and smelled deliciously of baby powder. The weight of him in her arms was a reminder of what she'd lost, but she knew she had to put the past behind her and accept there would always be other people's babies. But it was still very hard to be that brave and it took a great deal of effort not to let her emotions get the better of her.

Anne filled the teapot and placed it on the scrubbed pine table next to the plate of shortbread. Sitting down, she regarded her younger sister with concern. 'I get the feeling this isn't entirely a social visit,' she said quietly.

'You always could read me, couldn't you?'

Anne nodded, took Oscar from her arms and settled him into the pram. She closed the door into the hall so the girls wouldn't overhear, and returned to the table to pour the tea and push the plate of shortbread towards Cissy. 'What's troubling you, Cissy?'

Cissy took a sip of tea, and after a deep breath, told her everything.

Danuta drove away from the Goldman house feeling more assured than she had when she'd arrived. There were still mountains to climb, but she couldn't help but feel that with Rachel and Solly on her side, things might not be as difficult as she feared.

Parking her little car outside the back-street Victorian villa where Florence had the ground-floor flat, she walked up the path and knocked on the door. One look at the older woman's weary face told her she hadn't slept well. 'Bad night?' she asked, stepping inside.

'Bobby woke up calling for his mother and wouldn't be soothed. I took him into my bed for a cuddle in the hope he'd go back to sleep, but he was too restless and full of questions about where Gracie was.' She pushed back the hair falling into her eyes and tucked it roughly back into the untidy bun at her nape. 'I ended up making him cocoa at three this morning,' she added on a sigh.

'Where is he now?' Danuta slipped off her coat and followed Florence into the cramped and untidy kitchen.

'Asleep on the couch in the lounge. He finally dropped off an hour ago. Exhausted by it all, poor little mite.'

Danuta resisted going to see him and reached for the kettle instead. 'Sit down while I make tea and toast. You'll feel better with something inside you.'

Florence sat down and didn't protest. She watched dully as Danuta quickly made a pot of tea and started on clearing the sink of the pile of dirty pots while the bread toasted. 'I wish there was more I could do to help Bobby,' she sighed. 'Poor little boy. He's so confused and frightened.'

'You're doing all that's needed, Florence,' replied Danuta, placing a consoling hand on her shoulder. 'It's vital we keep things as normal as possible and not try anything new too quickly. He's at home here, and trusts you. Once he's back at school, he'll have other things to distract him. Children that age are amazingly resilient, you know.'

'No, I don't know,' replied Florence flatly. 'I've never married – never wanted to – and as for children . . . I've never felt the urge to have them, and frankly, find them quite incomprehensible.' She saw Danuta's shocked expression and shook her head. 'Don't look at me like that, Danuta. Not all women want to be mothers.' She gave a deep sigh. 'But despite everything I just said, I feel for Bobby and his welfare and will do my utmost for him.'

'I know you will,' she replied. 'Just remember he's a small human with the same feelings and fears as us even though he's only five and can't really express them. And those fears and feelings are confusing, and he's trying to make sense of it all at the moment. He needs time, Florence, and lots of love and support.'

The door crashed open. 'Mummy?' Bobby stood there in his pyjamas, face bright with a hope that slowly faded when he realised Gracie wasn't in the kitchen. 'Where's my mum?' he demanded.

Danuta let Florence go to him, knowing that Bobby would still regard her as a stranger.

Florence put her arms about him and lifted him up. 'Mummy's gone away, Bobby. Remember I told you?'

'I want my mum,' he retorted, squirming in her arms, his legs kicking at her thighs. 'Where's my mum?'

Florence looked helplessly at Danuta, who stepped forward and took Bobby onto her lap to soothe him. 'Mummy's in heaven with your daddy and all the angels,' she said quietly once she had the child's attention.

'Can I go and see her?' he asked, tears trembling on his lashes.

'One day,' she replied softly. 'When you're a much, much bigger boy. But for now she wants you to be good, and do what Auntie Flo tells you.'

'Why can't I see her now?' His bottom lip trembled.

She held him close, her heart heavy at his sorrow. 'She's fast asleep, Bobby. She's very tired because it's a long, long way to heaven and she needs to rest. But she loves you, Bobby, and wants Auntie Flo and me to look after you.'

'Where's heaven?' His big brown eyes were tear-filled, his voice tremulous.

Danuta carried him to the window and pointed up to the lowering sky. 'It's up there, Bobby. Way above the clouds.'

Bobby thought about that for a moment and then went limp in her arms to rest his head against her shoulder with a deep sigh. 'I'm tired too,' he said, his eyelids drooping as his thumb sought his mouth.

Danuta and Florence exchanged glances before Danuta carried him to the bedroom he'd shared with his mother. She snuggled him beneath the bedclothes, found one of Gracie's sweaters which still held her scent, and tucked it in with him. 'There we are, darling,' she soothed. 'You go to sleep now.'

'Will I go to heaven too?' he asked drowsily.

'Not yet, sweetheart,' she whispered, stroking his brown curls. 'Not for a very long time. But your mummy will be waiting for you when you do.'

She sat by the bed, her whole being aching for him as she watched him drift into sleep. Coming to terms with losing his mother was only the first challenge he'd have to meet. He'd yet to be told he had a brother and that, God and the authorities willing, he was to start a new life with her and Stanislav. What he would make of Stanislav, she had no idea, but knowing her husband, he'd soon have the child laughing.

Leaving the bedroom that was cluttered with reminders of Gracie, she left the door ajar and returned to the kitchen to find Florence busy at the sink. 'He's asleep, but it will probably mean you'll have another rough night.'

'I'll cope once I've had a bit of a snooze on the couch,' she replied, balancing the last of the clean pots on the pile sitting on the drainer. 'Then I'll take him out for a walk. We both need some fresh air.'

Danuta checked the time. 'I have to get to the surgery, but I was wondering if I could bring Stanislav for a visit this evening? Bobby needs to get to know us both, and meeting Stanislav might cheer him up.'

'Whatever you think is for the best, Danuta. But I'm worried it could be too much too soon and all for nothing if the authorities don't give you permission to adopt them both.'

'I spoke to Rachel earlier. She's promised to help as much as she can – and I can't think of anyone more influential than the Goldmans, can you?'

Florence shook her head and then smothered a yawn. 'I'll see you later, then.'

Peggy had stripped the beds and optimistically hung the washing out as there was a sharp wind coming off the sea and the rain was holding off. The house was quiet for once as Cordelia had decided to stay in bed and read for a while since she was still feeling the effects of yesterday; Jim had gone over to Parkwood House to see his army mate Ernie; Charlie was at the garage; Cissy was not expected home until lunchtime, and Daisy had yet to be brought home from Ron's.

It was bliss to have the house to herself after the chaos and upsets of this particular Christmas, so she set to with a will, cleaning the kitchen and sweeping away the needles from under the tree in the dining room. Having dusted and polished in the dining room, she mopped the hall floor tiles and returned to the kitchen to empty the bucket of dirty water, make a pot of tea and have a well-earned fag while she read the local newspaper.

With the fancy Bakelite wireless burbling quietly in the background, Peggy glanced at the front page and her spirits sank. Someone had leaked the story of Gracie's death, and the fact that she'd been the young woman who'd abandoned her baby. The article left very little out, and to Peggy's mind it was a salacious piece of gossip which would do no one any good – least of all, Gracie's reputation and that of her little ones. 'Poor girl,' she sighed, folding the paper and pushing it to one side. 'Now the gossips will have a real field day. It's a faint hope that none of it will touch those children.'

The back door suddenly swung open, and Daisy came flying in with Rosie in tow. 'Mummy, Mummy, Grandpa's got kittens!' She flung herself against Peggy and, jumping up and down in her excitement, looked up at her beseechingly. 'Can we have one? Please, please, please.'

Peggy looked at Rosie over the child's head. 'Kittens?'

'He found them abandoned early this morning,' she replied, taking off her gloves and sinking into a nearby chair to light a cigarette. 'The poor little things were half-dead, but with milk and warmth, they seem to be hanging on.'

'Can we have one, Mum?' pleaded Daisy, all big brown eyes and cheeks rosy from the cold. 'Moppet's all right, but I prefer Tom Kitten. He's really noisy, just like in the storybook, and keeps meowing at me.'

Peggy raised an eyebrow at Rosie. 'Moppet and Tom Kitten?'

'Ron's been reading to her from his collection of Beatrix Potter books. Tom Kitten is ginger with white stripes. Moppet is his sister and more tortoiseshell. We had to bathe and dry them to discover what sort they were.' Rosie looked glum. 'She's the weaker of the two, but I'm hoping she'll perk up now they're both safe.'

'So, can we have Tom, Mum?' persisted a breathless Daisy.

'Did Grandad say you could?' she hedged, not really sure about taking on another pet and hoping Ron hadn't made any foolish promises.

Daisy ducked her chin. 'He said Moppet needed Tom for now, and they had to stay with him until they were growed a bit more.'

'Grown, not growed,' Peggy corrected automatically. 'But he's quite right. Being so young they need to stay together.' She looked meaningfully across the table at her friend. 'Isn't that right, Rosie?'

Rosie got the message. 'Absolutely. Harvey has taken on nanny duty, so I'm sure they're best with us for a while yet.'

Daisy slumped into a chair and folded her arms. 'It's not fair,' she moaned. 'Grandad's already got the dogs and ferrets – now he's got kittens too.' She scowled at her mother and Rosie before giving a great sigh to emphasise how hard done by she felt.

'Keep that up and there will definitely be no more pets in this house,' said Peggy sternly. 'Why don't you tell me all about the lovely pantomime Auntie Rosie took you to?'

As Daisy perked up and enthusiastically went through the pantomime scene by scene, Peggy caught Rosie's eye and shared a moment of silent communication. Rosie knew what everyone at Beach View had gone through the previous day, and as a close friend of long standing, Peggy was very grateful for her support. But the thought of taking on a kitten and all that would entail was something she didn't feel ready for, and she just hoped Daisy's enthusiasm would wane as time went on and she returned to school.

Once Daisy had run out of things to say about her trip to the pantomime, she ran off to fetch her toys from her bedroom. Peggy poured another cup of tea for Rosie and pushed the newspaper towards her. 'Whoever it was didn't wait long to sell the story,' she said crossly.

Rosie quickly scanned the headlines. 'Someone at the hospital, do you think?'

Peggy shrugged. 'Probably. But it's her funeral I'm worried about. With publicity like that, it could turn into a free-for-all. And who's going to pay for it? We can't expect Florence to fork out, and I don't see why Solly should pay – he's doing enough for that baby already.'

Rosie finished reading the article and shoved the paper away. 'Perhaps we should ask the *Gazette* to stump up seeing as they're making money out of that scurrilous bit of gossip – or at least start a fundraiser to pay for the service. Funerals don't come cheap, and Gracie deserves more than a pauper's funeral.'

'Would people pay into it, though?'

'We'll soon find out,' said Rosie purposefully. 'May I use your telephone?'

Cissy finally left Anne's and headed back into Cliffehaven. The last three hours hadn't proved as difficult as she'd expected, for Anne was indeed a good listener, and a quiet, sensible counsellor. Cissy had expected her to say 'I told you so', but those words of condemnation had never been spoken, and all she'd seen in her sister's eyes was compassion and understanding. Now, as she headed for Mafeking Terrace and Aunt Doris, she had the feeling this next visit would be very different.

Drawing the car to a standstill some way down the street from Doris's, she nervously lit a cigarette and tried to find some calm before she had to face her aunt. Like the rest of the family, she had always found Doris daunting with her bossy ways and grandiose ideas, and even as a child, Cissy had sensed that her aunt didn't like her. In all fairness, she reasoned, she had been a naughty child, and her time in the dancing troupe had hardly endeared her to her aunt who'd thought the whole thing disreputable.

She gave a sigh. Grandad Ron was the only one Doris couldn't bully, although her mother had sometimes found the courage to stand up to her. Having said that, she mused, Auntie Doreen was no pushover either. The two sisters were always falling out, and Doreen wasn't at all afraid of telling her exactly what she thought of her when she was on her high horse. It was a great pity the third and youngest sister was living so far away – she could have done with Doreen by her side today.

As time ticked away and she started to feel the cold, she finished the cigarette and drove along the terrace of identical semi-detached bungalows which lined the hill overlooking the town and the distant sea. She drew to a halt outside Doris's gate and wasn't at all surprised to find that her aunt's home was very different to all the others in the road – but then Doris had always had grand ideas.

Cissy had so far managed to avoid visiting Doris, and usually made herself scarce on the rare occasions her least favourite aunt deigned to grace Beach View with her presence, but of course her mother had kept her up with Doris's movements. Doris and Colonel John White had once been neighbours in their semi-detached two-bed bungalows, but on their marriage, they'd knocked them into one and converted the attic into a bedroom suite with bathroom, dressing room and magnificent views through the dormer windows. It did look very smart, but Cissy wondered what her neighbours thought of the transformation.

She reluctantly climbed out of the car and was almost knocked off her feet by the wind tearing up from the sea. Clinging to her hat, she was all but blown up the short path to the front door.

'Cecily!' Doris was resplendent in twinset, pearls and pleated skirt, her carefully coloured and permed hair rigid with hairspray. She didn't offer a hug. 'Do come in quickly. This wind is murder on one's hairdo.'

That hair wouldn't shift in a force ten gale, thought Cissy as she stepped into the hall. 'I hope I'm not intruding on anything,' she said politely as she unbuttoned her coat.

'Not at all,' said Doris. 'Suzy, Anthony and the children left for home early this morning, and John has taken himself off for a round of golf.' She smiled indulgently at the mention of her husband. 'We all ate far too much over Christmas, and he felt the need for some exercise. He likes to keep trim.'

She took Cissy's coat and hat and fussily placed them in the cupboard under the stairs. 'I must say, Cecily, your telephone call was quite a surprise,' she said, eyeing her with something approaching greedy curiosity. 'Nothing wrong at home, I hope?'

'Everyone's fine,' she fibbed, unwilling to sate her

aunt's thirst for gossip. To distract her aunt and give herself time to get used to being called Cecily again, she turned to admire the elegant hall. 'This all looks very smart. I'd love to see the rest of the house.'

Doris happily babbled on as she took Cissy from one elegantly appointed room to another and then led her up the stairs to the luxurious loft conversion. 'We're both delighted with the work, and in the mornings, we can sit in bed with our tea and look out of that window right to the sea.'

She finally seemed to notice that Cissy was less animated than usual. 'You seem rather subdued, Cecily.' She clutched at her throat. 'You're not sickening for something, are you?'

'I'm perfectly well, thanks, but there is something I have to tell you, Aunt Doris,' she said nervously.

Doris nodded briskly. 'I had a feeling there might be. We'd better go down, and I'll make a pot of tea.'

Cissy followed her downstairs into the warm kitchen where the delicious aroma of baking greeted them. She sat at the small table in the corner and waited for her aunt to take the scones out of the oven and make the tea. Once Doris had sat down and filled the bone china cups, Cissy almost lost her nerve. Her aunt was watching her with cool expectancy, and Cissy didn't have the first clue as to how to start telling her why she'd come. Playing for time, she lit a cigarette and nervously tapped it on the edge of the glass ashtray.

'Do stop fidgeting, Cecily. It's most annoying.'

Cissy obeyed but squirmed inside just as she had as a small child when under the cold scrutiny of this daunting aunt.

The long silence was finally broken by Doris tutting. 'As you seem incapable of speech, I can only surmise that London didn't come up to your high expectations and you've come here to explain why.' She arched a delicate brow. 'Though what business it is of mine, I really can't imagine.'

Stung by her tone, Cissy found the courage to reply. 'London did prove difficult. It's why I came home.'

Doris sniffed and patted the double string of pearls round her neck. 'I've always thought it was over-rated. The people there are a very different breed to what one is used to – unless, of course one moves in the upper echelons of society.'

Cissy glanced at her in surprise. 'I didn't realise you knew London.'

The pale blue eyes held little warmth. 'I lived there for a while. It didn't agree with me. But I'm surprised at you, Cecily. I'd have thought that sort of rackety life was right up your street.'

Cissy wasn't immune to the cattiness but chose to ignore it. 'It was for a while,' she admitted, stubbing out her cigarette. 'I loved the energy in the city, the shops, parties, theatres. But something happened – something bad – and I was made to realise that what I thought was real, was just a sham.'

Doris regarded her steadily. 'I'm guessing this bad thing had something to do with a man?'

Her tone made it clear she'd expected nothing less, but now she'd started, Cissy was determined to get to the end of what she had to say, regardless of her aunt's disapproval. 'Doesn't it always?' she said flippantly to counter Doris's frostiness. 'But it wasn't just a man that sent me scuttling back home. I realised I was living in a fantasy world, and it fell apart like a pack of cards.'

Doris remained silent, her expression unreadable. And then she gave a sigh. 'You might not think it, looking at me now, but I was young and starry-eyed once, so I do have some understanding of what it's like to be alone in a city where one is vulnerable to all sorts,' she said briskly.

Cissy remembered Gloria's words and wondered if there had, perhaps, been some truth behind them, and Doris had got into trouble all those years ago. However, the idea was so ludicrous, she dismissed it immediately, deciding to keep as calm and cool as her aunt, and remain dignified. 'Then I hope you won't be too shocked by what I'm about to tell you,' she said flatly.

Doris met her defiant gaze with little emotion. 'You clearly have something to say, so perhaps it would be best to get it off your chest, instead of going round in circles. John could be back at any minute, and I doubt you'll want him hearing about your scandalous exploits.'

'Why do you always have to assume the worst of me?' snapped Cissy.

Doris's chin went up. 'Well, you're hardly here to tell me you've achieved great things, are you? You said yourself you got embroiled with some man, and nothing any good ever came out of that.'

She suddenly seemed to realise she was being too harsh, and her tone softened. 'I'm sorry if you think I'm being judgemental, but you've always been flighty, Cecily, so one has come to expect rather less of you.'

Cissy could barely contain her fury. 'I might have known your prejudice would overshadow any sense of compassion or real understanding. I don't know why I'm surprised. You've never liked me.'

The carefully made-up face hardened into a mask of distaste. 'Don't take that tone with me, Cecily. Say your piece and have done with it.'

So Cissy did. She left out nothing and told the awful story in the harshest of tones so there would be no misunderstanding. When she'd finished, she noted the shock in her aunt's eyes and the loss of colour in her face, but refused to feel an iota of remorse. Without another word, she pushed away from the table and went to collect her hat and coat.

She was almost at the front door when Doris caught up with her and stilled her with a hand on her shoulder. 'I'm sorry, Cissy,' she spluttered. 'I didn't realise ... I had no way of knowing ...'

'Of course you didn't,' Cissy said coldly. 'But I'd appreciate it if what I told you went no further than these four walls. There's enough gossip in Cliffehaven without you adding to it.' With that, she tore open the door and ran down the path to the car.

Climbing in, she slammed the door, turned the key and raced to the end of the cul-de-sac where she did a rapid three-point turn and shot past Doris who was still standing on her doorstep. 'Bitch,' she spat, hitting the steering wheel with her hand. 'Bitch, bitch, bitch.'

By the time she'd parked outside Beach View her temper had blown itself out as swiftly as a summer storm, and she was left not only with a sore hand but a feeling of emptiness. Utterly spent, she sat for a moment to replay the unpleasant scene, and then put it firmly behind her. No one – least of all her mother – would ever know what had happened in Doris's kitchen this morning.

Doris was in such shock from her niece's revelation that she stood on her doorstep for several minutes, unable to move as the girl drove away at speed. She stayed there until she became aware of the cold wind biting through her clothes and stinging her face, and it was only then that she was able to shut the door and slowly return to the kitchen, her thoughts in turmoil.

Sinking into a chair, she stared out of the window to the garden where John had planted winter vegetables – but her unfocused gaze saw little as she battled to cope with her conflicting emotions. Cecily had been correct in thinking she'd never really approved of her, for even as a small child, the girl had been wilful and inclined to show off. As she'd grown, Cecily had joined a dancing troupe of all things, and Doris was fairly certain the girl's time up at that airfield during the war had not been spent quietly. She was too fond of music, dancing and men – so it was hardly surprising things had turned out badly in London. But what she'd gone through was utterly ghastly, and Doris couldn't help but feel very sorry for her.

However, she was cut to the quick that Peggy had not included her in the family meeting the previous day, and Doris regarded that as the ultimate betrayal – proof positive of how little her sister must think of her when the odious Gloria had been invited. But despite the anger this had engendered, it was Cissy's story that had really shaken her, for it had mirrored her own experiences in London all those years ago, and brought the past all too brutally to the fore.

Her hands shook as she lit a cigarette and let her thoughts turn back to her youth. She too had been starry-eyed and ambitious, holding down a good secretarial job and inveigling her way into the sort of social circles she'd always aspired to. There had been a man, of course, and she'd been naive to believe his promises – utterly stupid to think she belonged to that entitled and fast set of men and women who thought nothing of sneering behind her back and laying wagers on which of the men would be first to get into her bed.

She shuddered at the memory of that last night when she'd fled from the country mansion after his assault, her reputation, dreams and pride in tatters. Like Cissy, she'd been living a fantasy, and she'd had no choice but to return home to Cliffehaven. But unlike Cissy, her pride wouldn't allow her to speak to anyone of her shame, and she'd let it fester for years – hiding behind a façade of cool propriety – always mindful of her manners, but still yearning to be accepted by the upper echelons of what passed as Cliffehaven society.

Doris was suddenly overwhelmed with guilt for how cold she'd been to Cissy, when all she'd really needed was a shoulder to cry on and some understanding. What on earth had possessed her to be so cruel – so cold and unfeeling – when it had clearly taken a great deal of courage for the girl to tell her what had happened?

She recognised the self-pity and remorse as ugly bedfellows when they took hold and she became helpless to stop the hot tears that rolled down her cheeks. Scrabbling for a handkerchief to dab them away, she tried to get her emotions under control, but it was as if a long-held dam had burst, and nothing could stop the flow.

'Doris? Doris, my dear, whatever is the matter?'

Startled, she looked up at John through her tears. 'I'm fine, really I am,' she replied, hastily swallowing her tears and mopping at her face.

John pulled up another chair to sit beside her and take her hands. 'I know when my girl is hurting inside,' he murmured, his blue eyes full of concern. 'Please tell me what's wrong.'

Doris looked into his beloved face and knew she would have to tell him everything. Her secret had been held for too long, and this darling man deserved honesty. She took a quavering breath and began with Cissy's reasons for coming home.

'Good heavens,' he breathed when she finally fell silent. 'That poor, poor girl. What a dreadful thing to happen – and how brave she was to reveal it all to her family.'

'I wish I'd been as brave all those years ago,' she stuttered through a fresh wave of tears.

John's gaze sharpened. 'What do you mean?'

Doris gripped his hands. 'I went through something similar in London – although thank God it didn't lead to anything more serious than hurt pride,' she began purposefully. 'After I'd been assaulted, I came running back here, determined to keep the whole sorry episode to myself. It was clear that my family was worried about me, but I simply couldn't admit to being such a naive fool, and refused to talk about it.' She took a shallow breath. 'Then I compounded my stupidity by rushing into marriage with Ted, who turned out to be a serial philanderer and inveterate gambler.'

John silently pulled her to her feet and into his arms. He held her close until her tears of shame and regret finally ran their course, then he softly kissed her damp face. 'I'm so sorry you had to go through all that, my love,' he murmured. 'But now it's out in the open, let's put it behind us, and count our blessings. We have each other, and God willing, Cissy will soon find peace and be able to live her life without always looking back.'

'I'm so glad we found each other, John.' She kissed his lips and held him close for a moment, wishing fervently that she hadn't been so unkind to Cissy – but promising silently to do her best to make amends.

4

Stanislav said goodbye to his co-pilot, Charlotte, grabbed the two walking sticks he hated but couldn't do without, and left the hangar. He could feel his right stump pulsating and every step he took was agony, so he was eager to get home before Danuta so he could tend to it without her knowing how damaged it had become.

The temperature had plummeted, the sky was leaden and the easterly wind was whipping across the airfield, where the gulls and crows swirled and cawed as they battled against it to land in the ploughed field beyond the surrounding hedges. Stanislav tucked his chin into the collar of his greatcoat and headed towards the office hut at the far end of the field where Martin Black would be waiting for him. The distance seemed impossible, although it was merely a matter of a couple of hundred yards, but every inch was a trial, and he was quite out of breath by the time he reached it.

'Legs not so good today, Stan?' Martin looked up from the logbook with a frown.

'I'm just stiff after that long flight,' he said with all the nonchalance he could muster. He sank into the sagging leather chair beside the untidy desk with a stifled grunt of relief, and carefully stretched out his legs in the hope they'd stop hurting. 'All delivered safely. Berlin was glad to receive those medicines in the light of this latest typhoid outbreak.'

'Are you sure you can do the flight with Charlotte to

Scotland tomorrow? Only Roger's off to Holland with Kitty as co-pilot, and I'll be tied up at home with the accountants for half the day while I'm babysitting all their kids. I really don't want you overstretching yourself, Stan.'

'I'll be fine,' he said airily. 'A hot bath, a tot of whisky and a good night's sleep is all I need.'

'Well, if you're sure,' Martin murmured. He stroked the neat moustache he'd grown to hide the scarring on his face and continued to frown as he regarded the other man. Then he turned back to the logbooks and weather charts and became businesslike.

'We need to get as much as possible out to our clients before the weather closes in. I've had long-range weather reports from the Met Office, and there's some filthy stuff coming in from the north before the end of January. We can't afford to get stuck here with half our cargo sitting in grounded planes.' He threw his pen onto the desk. 'I've warned the ground crews they might have to find better accommodation for their families than those Nissen huts, but where on earth they can go, I have no idea.'

'It will be very bad?' Stanislav tugged at the ends of his luxurious moustache and did his best to ignore the persistent throb in his stump.

Martin nodded. 'Heavy snow, high winds and plunging temperatures. If the reports turn out to be right, we could be grounded for some time.' He looked up from the paper-strewn desk. 'You and Danuta should probably ask Peggy if you can move in with her and Jim for the duration. Frank and the other tenants should be warned, too. None of you can possibly survive such weather in those shacks.'

Martin's news made his spirits plunge further, for if they didn't fly and the airfield was closed, they didn't get paid. 'I will speak to Danuta, and the others,' he replied, absent-mindedly massaging the stump of his right leg. 'We will have to find a better place anyway. She has told me we have a chance to adopt Gracie's children.'

Martin's brown eyes widened. 'Good Lord. Really? Peggy told me and Anne about Gracie dying and the baby she'd abandoned, but this is news to me. When did it come about?'

'Danuta told me yesterday. Gracie put in her will her wishes for the children.'

Martin leaned back in the chair, his expression concerned. 'That must have come as a bit of a shock. How do you feel about taking on such a responsibility, Stan?'

Stan wasn't too sure what he felt but he maintained an easy-going air, unwilling to express the doubts and fears he'd had ever since Danuta had told him. 'It is a big thing to take on, Martin. I do not know these little ones, but my Danuta she longs for children, and if it makes her happy then I too am happy.'

Martin eyed him for a long moment and then nodded. 'It's up to you, of course, but I'd advise some very careful thought before you plunge into anything. And, as you say, you'll have to find a more permanent home if you stand any chance of the authorities allowing you to take them in.'

He gave a deep sigh, pushed back from the desk and grabbed his hat and coat. 'It's been a long day, and time we both went home. I'll see you at six tomorrow morning.'

Stanislav struggled out of the deep chair and as his stumps thrummed in complaint, fought for balance on the walking sticks. He was a big, heavy man, and if he fell he'd be like a beached whale, and the last thing he wanted was to show any weakness in front of Martin. He needed this job, needed the money to support

Danuta and provide for Gracie's children – and his pride simply wouldn't allow him to fail.

He stifled a groan of pain as he put his weight on his troubled stump, and slowly made his way out of the office to let Martin switch off the lights and lock up. It was now only a short walk to his car, but by the time he'd reached it, he was trembling from the effort.

'Goodnight,' he called to Martin, who was now clambering into his own car.

Martin waved back and drove at some speed towards the entrance gate.

As silence fell over the airfield and dusk began to settle into darkness, Stanislav leaned on his car bonnet to keep the weight off his tortured stump, and then slid into the specially adapted car with a grateful sigh. He was exhausted after the long, cramped flight, and the constant pain was wearing him down. As he switched on the engine and steered the car out of the airfield, he decided he would make time after tomorrow's flight to go and see the doctor who'd treated him up at the hospital for injured servicemen. This couldn't go on, and if they had any chance of adopting those children, then he had to get himself as fit as possible.

Peggy had the feeling Cissy's visit to Doris hadn't gone too well, but as her daughter seemed determined to make light of it, she had to let it go. There were already too many things to worry about, not least of which was the weather forecast. It wasn't as if it was unusual to have bad weather at this time of year, but with Gracie's funeral yet to be organised, she could only hope it wouldn't hamper things. Funerals were bad enough, but if it was cold, wet or snowing, it would merely add to the misery.

'You're looking down in the dumps, Peg,' said Jim

as he entered the kitchen and dumped his hat, coat and briefcase on a chair. 'Bad day?'

She grinned back at him as he took her into his arms. 'Not really, just thinking about Gracie's funeral, which has made me feel rather sad. The results of the autopsy still aren't through and we can't organise anything until they are.'

She returned his kiss, and then smiled. 'But on the lighter side, your father has found kittens, Daisy is pestering me to take one, and Rosie has worked her magic on the local newspaper editor.'

'Goodness me, that sounds ominous,' he chuckled before giving her another kiss. 'What's for tea? I'm starving.'

'Aren't you always?' she teased. 'It's the last of the turkey and ham minced up with veg under a potato topping.' She gently poked him in the chest. 'Don't look at me like that, Jim Reilly. I know you've had enough turkey to last a lifetime, but this really will be the end of it.'

'And glad I am to hear it. We'll all have grown feathers with much more of it.'

She waved away his moans with some impatience. 'Don't you want to hear what Rosie's been up to?'

'Mischief would be my first guess. She's as bad as Da when it comes to stirring up hornets' nests.' He sat down and helped himself to the dregs from the pot of tea as he scanned the front page of the paper. 'Go on then, you're obviously dying to tell me.'

'Well,' she said breathlessly. 'She telephoned the editor of the *Gazette*, told him who she was and really played on the fact she held a good deal of influence as an elected member of the local council.' Peggy jabbed a finger at the front page. 'Then she pointed out how that scurrilous article about Gracie was bound to cause trouble, and suggested he might make amends by starting up a fundraiser for her funeral with a generous donation.'

Jim looked up from the newspaper and grinned. 'And of course he agreed.'

Peggy chuckled. 'He didn't have much choice. You know how good Rosie is at getting her own way once she's got a plan in her head. He'll put the notice in the Saturday paper and has promised to start it off with a donation of twenty pounds.'

Jim gave a low whistle. 'That was generous.'

'He can afford it,' retorted Peggy. 'That story must have sold a good many papers, and no doubt he'll make a meal out of headlining the fact the *Gazette* is spearheading the fundraiser with that donation.'

'Well, it will certainly solve the problem of who pays for the funeral if they can raise enough. But all that publicity could backfire, Peggy,' he warned. 'The funeral could turn into a proper bun-fight if half the town *and* the press turn up to rubber-neck.'

'That occurred to me, too, but there won't be much we can do about it.' Peggy sat down at the table to finish her cup of tea and change the subject.

'Cissy went to see Anne, Sandra and Doris today. Sandra seems to be getting on all right after the to-do with Graham and making firm plans for when she returns to London. Anne was lovely with her as we'd expect, but I don't think things went well with my sister.'

Jim raised a dark brow. 'I'm surprised you're surprised,' he muttered. 'Your Doris is hardly the most understanding or sympathetic of women.'

Peggy lit a cigarette and blew smoke before fiddling with the tablecloth. 'I know, but it's probably best to let sleeping dogs lie, as it were. As long as she keeps Cissy's story to herself, then no more harm can be done. But I fear Doris likes to gossip, and what with the scandal over Gracie, she might find it impossible to keep her mouth shut.'

Jim placed his large, warm hand over her restless fingers. 'She's too aware of her own reputation to give away family secrets,' he soothed. 'I think you'll find she'll keep it to herself.'

'Let's hope so.' Peggy glanced up at the clock. 'It's almost teatime. Where on earth has Charlie got to?'

'I saw him and Jack going into the Anchor as I drove up Camden Road,' said Jim casually. 'I wouldn't worry about him, Peg. He's never missed a meal yet.'

Peggy wasn't at all placated. Charlie was only just seventeen and too young to be drinking in pubs, but this wasn't the first time she'd heard about him and Jack going to the Anchor after work. She could only hope that Ruby continued to run a tight ship and refused to serve him anything but lemonade.

Despite the lack of sleep and the long, busy day, Danuta's spirits were high as she parked the car and made her way down the slope to her front door. She was looking forward to tonight when she could introduce Stan to Bobby, and had already been to the shop to exchange her sweet ration token for a small bag of toffees. There was no harm in using sweets to encourage the child to see Stan in a favourable light.

'I'm home!' she called cheerfully.

Shedding her hat and coat, she frowned. The only reply had been the sound of snoring. Surely Stanislav wasn't already in bed?

She dumped her nursing bag on the kitchen table, noted the fire needed another log if it wasn't to die, and that nothing had been prepared for supper. Feeling rather anxious, she hurried into the bedroom to find Stanislav sprawled like a beached C-47 on the large double bed, fully clothed apart from his prosthetic legs.

These had been propped up against the bedside chair on which stood the ointments, bandages and powders he used to tend his stumps – along with a half-full bottle of whisky.

Danuta stood for a long moment just watching him sleep. His colour was quite high, and there were beads of sweat on his brow. The snoring was so loud she suspected the neighbours on either side could hear it through the thin wooden walls. But that didn't worry her as much as the sight of that whisky, and her darling husband all but comatose at six in the evening. He must have been exhausted after that long return flight to Germany, but was it just tiredness that had sent him to his bed so early?

As her suspicions rose, she tentatively eased back the trouser legs until she could see what remained of his legs. The stumps had been freshly bandaged, but she had a nasty feeling he'd been doing too much and that under those strips of gauze and padding, the flesh was red and swollen.

Deciding to leave him to sleep, she went back to the kitchen, fed the stove a couple of the dry logs Stan had stacked beside it, and turned her attention to heating up the last of the soup. It would warm them before they had to go out again into the chill night, and when they returned, she would cook the sausages she'd managed to buy from Alf the butcher. Quickly peeling a few potatoes, she chopped them up and placed them in some salted water, ready to be boiled and mashed later.

As she worked methodically at the sink, her mind was on Stanislav. He worried her immensely, because he was so careless with his health and refused point blank to take any advice, no matter how well meaning. He was a big man, well over six feet tall, with broad shoulders and a barrel chest. Unfortunately, he also had a big belly because he liked his food, and his consumption of alcohol could be quite alarming at times. And yet his lust for life was as large as he was, which was why she hadn't been able to resist him when they'd first met at Peter and Rita's wedding.

She smiled at the memory. His courtship had been relentless and unstoppable, and she'd yielded willingly, but now they were married, she could see the frustration behind the booming laughter; the determination to live every moment beneath the gung-ho carelessness of his actions. He wasn't a stupid man, but one who saw his disability as an insult to his manhood, and therefore something to ignore until it was absolutely impossible to do so. It was the reason why he'd fought so hard to get his pilot's licence back; why he volunteered for the longest flights and extra hours loading the cargo planes, refusing to allow a little thing like double amputation hinder his life.

Giving a sigh of exasperation, Danuta dumped the saucepan of potatoes on the draining board and dried her hands. If they were to get to Florence's flat before Bobby went to bed, she needed to get a move on. About to go back to the bedroom to wake Stanislav, she heard the bedsprings creak and the sound of Stanislav swearing softly in Polish as his prosthetics clattered to the floor. She decided to leave him to it as he wouldn't appreciate her trying to help.

Stanislav appeared in the kitchen doorway some minutes later. 'I didn't hear you come in,' he said, swamping her in a hug.

'I'm not surprised,' she teased. 'You were making enough racket to drown out any noise I might have made.'

He smiled bashfully and ran his hand through his tousled mop of hair. 'I woke myself up,' he admitted. 'Sorry I haven't done anything about our tea. I was very tired after the Berlin run, and the bed was too tempting.'

She thought of the allure of the bottle of whisky, but made no mention of it as she turned her back on him and busied herself by stirring the soup. 'Are you sure it's only tiredness, Stan?' she asked tentatively. 'Your legs aren't bothering you?'

'My legs are fine,' he replied firmly. 'Can't a man take a siesta without his wife worrying about him?'

'Of course he can, if that's the real reason,' she replied mildly. She tapped the wooden spoon on the rim of the large pan. 'But if your legs are causing you problems, perhaps it would be a good idea for you to see the doctor,' she suggested.

'I will see doctor when I need to,' he replied with his usual stubbornness. 'He is busy man. I cannot go to him every five minutes.'

'You last saw him for your annual check-up back in August,' she reminded him. She placed the bowls of soup on the table and began to slice the fresh loaf she'd bought this afternoon. 'Perhaps it's time to go again, just to make sure everything is as it should be.'

He grinned back at her and twirled the waxed ends of his moustache. 'If it will stop you with the nag, nag, nag, then I will go. But we are very busy at Phoenix Air Transport, and the weather forecast is not good for January. We must get the cargo out, and it is as the English say, all hands to the pumps.'

'Just promise me you'll go the minute you have time, Stan,' she urged.

'I will, I will,' he said, impatiently waving his spoon about. 'But first let me eat.'

Danuta dropped the subject and silence fell as they tucked into the soup. Once the bowls were empty, she dumped them in the sink, whisked off her apron and reached for her coat. 'We'd better hurry, or we'll be late.'

'Where are we going?'

'We talked about it last night, remember? Florence has agreed to us going to visit Bobby this evening. I persuaded her because I think it's time the child got to meet you.' She dug into her coat pocket and pulled out the bag of toffees. 'I even bought some sweets for you to give him.'

'You will bribe the child to like me?' Stanislav frowned.

'Not a bribe – not really – but it might help to break the ice.'

He shook his great head, his expression showing his doubts. 'I do not know if this is a good thing. It is too soon. Nothing is decided.'

'I realise that, Stan, but we have to start sometime. Besides,' she added softly, 'Bobby needs to know there are people who will love and take care of him, no matter how things work out.'

Stanislav heaved a great sigh. 'All right. I can see how much it matters to you, my love, but I am afraid of what it will do to you if this all comes to nothing.'

Danuta didn't want to think about that very real possibility and refused to let Stan's doubts lower her spirits. 'We have to stay positive, Stanislav,' she said firmly. 'Now, get your coat on.'

'But what about dinner?' he moaned.

'There's sausage and mash when we get back. Now do hurry up. It's getting late and it will soon be Bobby's bedtime.'

He grabbed his heavy overcoat from the peg by the door and wrapped a thick scarf round his neck before retrieving the hated walking sticks from the hall. 'I will drive,' he declared. 'That car of yours is impossible.'

Danuta hid a smile behind her scarf, and together they carefully made their way up the slope, Danuta matching his slow pace, ready to catch him should he lose his balance.

'What's all this about the weather?' she asked as he steered his car away from Tamarisk Bay and headed for Cliffehaven.

'Martin got the long-range reports from the Meteorological Office. They forecast the worst winter ever with heavy snow and blizzard conditions which will make flying impossible. It is why it is so important to do as many of the flight deliveries as possible while we have the chance. I have warned Frank and our other neighbours to make arrangements to move out. Martin thinks we should ask Peggy if we may stay with her.'

She stared at his profile as he concentrated on the road ahead. 'That sounds a bit drastic,' she said. 'Surely a bit of snow won't warrant moving house.'

Stanislav shrugged. 'I do not know. In Poland, we are prepared for such things, but in England . . . It is not for me to say. I go only by what Martin tells me.'

Danuta's thoughts were in turmoil. If the weather closed in and they really did have to move to Peggy's, then how would that affect their application to adopt Bobby and Noel? Would the whole country grind to a halt, and if it did, how would she cope on her district nurse rounds? It was all very worrying.

Peggy finished preparing the family meal, and then reached for her overcoat, hat and gloves. 'I'm off to see Florence and will eat when I get back. You're in charge of dishing up, Cissy' – she lowered her voice – 'and please make sure Grandma Cordy eats something. She's still looking tired and frail despite having spent most of the day in bed, and I'm worried about her.'

'I don't see why you can't telephone her instead of dashing out on such a cold night,' grumbled Jim.

'It's too impersonal,' she replied, ramming her feet

into her fur-lined boots. 'Florence has been an absolute brick throughout all this, and it's only right I should tell her face-to-face about the fundraiser, and to check that she has everything she needs.' She grinned at his dour expression. 'Besides,' she added, 'I need some fresh air and exercise after being stuck indoors all day.'

Jim rolled his eyes. 'All right, but you be careful. The pavements are like ice now the temperature's dropped.'

Peggy hugged him, kissed her daughter's cheek and waved goodbye to Cordelia who was sitting in the fireside chair hugging a hot-water bottle. There was still no sign of Charlie.

She hurried out of the kitchen and down the steps to the basement. Opening the back door, the blast of cold air almost took her breath away, and she began to have second thoughts. Perhaps it would be better to telephone rather than risk life and limb – but no, Florence deserved a call in person after all she'd done for Gracie.

She pulled Charlie's old bobble-hat over her ears, wound the thick woollen scarf round her neck so it covered her nose and mouth, and gingerly stepped outside. The garden path was like an ice-rink, but once she'd gained the alleyway which ran between the backs of the terraces, the ground was firmer underfoot. The council had clearly been prepared for this cold snap and the roads had been liberally sprayed with grit, but the pavements were treacherous, so she avoided them and kept to the edge of the road.

Luckily, there was very little traffic as the shops were now shut and most people had retired to the warmth and shelter of their homes. She slowly made her way down Camden Road until she got to the Anchor. Pushing open the door and whipping off the bobble-hat, she was met by the warm fug of huddled bodies, a roaring fire and pipe and tobacco smoke competing with the steam rising from damp clothes.

She elbowed her way through the crush surrounding the inglenook fireplace and found Jack and her son leaning on the bar. 'Time you went home, Charlie,' she said below the hubbub of conversation. 'And I hope that isn't beer in your glass.'

Charlie went as red as a tomato. 'It's just shandy, Mum.' He quickly downed the remains of his drink in case Peggy took it into her head to snatch it away.

'I'm surprised at you, Jack Smith,' she fumed, rounding on her friend. 'You know he's not old enough to be drinking beer.'

Jack grinned at her, totally unfazed by her verbal assault. 'There's precious little beer in that lemonade, Peg, and he's a big lad who's earned a drop after a hard day. No need to make a fuss.'

'He's only just seventeen,' she hissed, turning to her son, who stood head and shoulders above her looking sheepish. 'Your tea's on the table, Charles Reilly, and don't let me catch you in here again.'

'Yes, Mum,' he muttered, his cheeks blazing with embarrassment before he pushed his way through the crowd and made a hurried exit.

'You was a bit 'ard on him, Auntie Peg,' said Ruby from behind the bar. 'It were only a lemonade with a drop of Jack's beer added to give it colour.'

'I know,' admitted Peggy. 'I just don't want him getting into the habit of coming in here every night.'

Ruby smiled and handed her a small glass of sherry. 'To keep out the cold,' she murmured.

'I shouldn't really,' she protested weakly.

Ruby turned away to serve another customer, and as Peggy took a sip of the sherry, she caught sight of Dr Darwin sitting on his usual stool at the end of the bar. She didn't miss the looks that passed between him and

Ruby, and was happy to see that his courtship was progressing. Ruby had been her evacuee before she'd married Mike and sailed for a new life in his Canadian wilderness home. The tragic loss of Mike and the baby she'd been expecting had brought her back to Cliffehaven to start again as landlady of the Anchor – and now it seemed love was blossoming once more, and it warmed Peggy's heart.

'Hello, Peg. Jim not with you?'

She quickly turned rather guiltily to face the mountain of a man that was her Jim's older brother, Frank. Standing at well over six feet, he had the weathered complexion of a man who spent most of his life out at sea, and a large, sturdy body honed like granite from years of hard labour. 'I only popped in to make sure Charlie got home in time for his tea,' she blustered.

His handsome face was wreathed in a grin, his blue eyes teasing as he glanced at the glass of sherry in her hand. 'If you say so. Want another?'

'No thanks,' she said hastily. 'I'm not staying.'

Frank was still grinning as he greeted Jack, and then leaned on the bar to catch Brenda's eye and order a pint.

Peggy smiled inwardly as she sipped the sherry, for romance was truly blossoming beneath the roof of this ancient old pub. There was Ruby and Alistair Darwin exchanging cow-eyes, and Frank was mooning over the barmaid Brenda who seemed very happy to reciprocate. Peggy's romantic heart fluttered in the hope that 1947 might bring a couple of weddings, and by way of celebration, she permitted Frank to order her another sherry.

Stanislav drew the car to a halt outside the Victorian terraced house, and with some difficulty, managed to extricate himself without putting all his weight on his bad leg. Using the walking sticks to aid his balance on the slippery path leading to the door, he tamped down on the growing doubts that this wasn't a good idea, and arranged his face into a welcoming smile as Florence opened the door.

Danuta made the introductions and after shaking Florence's hand, he followed the two women into the narrow hall. Florence wasn't what he'd expected, although he hadn't really formed much idea of the woman who'd taken in Gracie and her son as lodgers. He'd just imagined her to be plump and matronly. But Florence was far from matronly with her slender figure and rather daunting air. In fact, he found her rather plain; clearly a spinster and – he suspected – used to having things done her way. He'd met English women like her before and respected them for being the salt of the earth as well as part of the almost invisible force of indomitable women who had kept this country moving during the war years.

'Bobby's in the sitting room,' said Florence, who seemed to share Stanislav's doubts as to the wisdom of this visit. 'He's slept on and off all day, but I did manage to take him to the swings for an hour. He's had his tea and bath, and it's really past his bedtime.' She caught the disappointment on Danuta's face and relented. 'But I suppose it won't matter just this once.'

'It's very good of you to let us come,' said Danuta. 'Have you told him we would visit?'

Florence nodded and darted an anxious glance towards the closed door before reaching for the knob. 'He's still confused by everything, so don't take it personally if he's a bit offhand with you. It's all rather too much for him to take in, really.'

Danuta patted her arm. 'We won't stay long.'

Florence reluctantly opened the door and fixed on a

smile. 'Bobby, it's Auntie Danuta and Uncle Stan to see you.'

Stanislav saw a room stuffed with too much dowdy furniture, the drawn curtains and weak lamplight making it gloomy but for the blazing fire in the hearth. The small boy was kneeling on the rug before it, in his pyjamas and dressing gown, playing with a red toy truck.

Bobby looked up hopefully, but when he saw it wasn't his mother, he ignored his visitors and continued pushing the truck back and forth on the rug.

'I'll make tea,' said Florence.

Danuta glanced back at Stanislav who was still standing in the doorway. 'I'll come and help,' she said.

Stanislav remained in the doorway, feeling stranded and not at all sure how to cope with the situation. He watched the boy, noting the dark shadows beneath his eyes and the way the firelight caught strands of copper and gold in his thick brown hair. But he also saw the clenching of that small jaw and the whitening of his knuckles as he gripped the toy and refused to acknowledge Stan's presence. The child was clearly battling to hold in emotions which must be eating him up.

Realising nothing would be gained by standing on the threshold, Stanislav entered the room and slowly eased himself down onto the sagging couch that had been positioned to one side of the hearth. The old springs complained under his weight as he sank rather too deeply into the faded cushions. Placing his sticks on the floor, he stretched out his legs, letting his trousers ride up just enough for the boy to see the leather prosthetics emerging from his size thirteen shoes.

Bobby turned his head just enough to take a peek at

those shoes, his fingers still gripping the toy truck. He frowned, and then his clear brown gaze moved up the trouser legs to Stan's flourishing moustache.

Stan grinned and twirled the waxed ends. 'Hello, Bobby,' he said quietly. 'I'm your Uncle Stanislav.'

'That's a funny name.' Bobby turned to sit cross-legged at Stanislav's very large feet, his expression curious as the firelight picked out the golden flecks in those brown eyes.

'It is a Polish name,' he replied. 'You may call me Stan if you'd prefer.'

The child thought about this solemnly and then nodded. 'Why do you and Auntie Ditta have funny names? And what's Polish?'

Stanislav rested his forearms on his thighs and leaned towards the boy. 'Polish means we are from Poland,' he explained. 'Do you know where Poland is?'

Bobby shook his head, his wide-eyed gaze never leaving Stanislav's face.

'It is a long way away from here, but one day I will show it to you on a map.'

'Is it as far as heaven?'

Stanislav's heart twisted. 'No, Bobby. Heaven is much further away, and not on any map,' he said sadly.

Bobby gave a tremulous sigh. 'That's what Auntie Ditta said.' He dropped his chin and concentrated on the sizeable shoes which stuck out on the rug before him. 'What's that?' he asked, his finger not quite daring to touch the leather prosthesis.

'That, my boy, is my magic leg.' He hoisted up the hems of his trousers. 'And look, I have two. Aren't I a lucky chap?'

'Can I touch them?' Bobby breathed. 'Will it hurt them?'

Stanislav chuckled and used a walking stick to

sharply rap them both. 'See, nothing will hurt them. Hard as rock.'

'Oh,' Bobby murmured, his eyes wide with wonder as he put a tentative finger on the heavy leather sheath. 'Are they really magic?'

'Indeed they are. You see, they help me to walk and to dance, and to fly my planes.'

Bobby's eyes widened further and a flush of excitement coloured his little face. 'You fly planes?' he said breathlessly.

Stanislav grinned as he nodded. 'You would like to see pictures of my plane?'

At Bobby's nod, he dug into the inside pocket of his coat and drew out the photographs he'd had developed the day before and forgotten to give to Danuta. Glad he'd brought them, he handed them over and watched the boy gaze at each in turn, his expression showing his delight and wonder.

'Those photographs were taken the day I got my pilot's licence back,' he explained. 'The planes are C-47 Dakotas. They were used in the war to carry troops, heavy military equipment and paratroopers, and also used for towing gliders and parachuting down things like tanks and trucks. The Americans call them Gooney Birds because when they are on the ground they look just like the giant albatross birds they'd seen in the Pacific.'

Bobby's little face was solemn. 'My dad was in the war,' he said sadly. 'He's in heaven with Mummy now.'

There wasn't much Stanislav could say to this, so they shared a silent moment to think of all those they'd both lost. And then Stanislav remembered the bag of sweets. He dug again into the pocket of the heavy coat which was beginning to make him sweat in the enclosed heat of the room. 'Would you like a sweet?' he said, offering the bag.

'Auntie Flo said I mustn't eat sweets after I've brushed my teeth for bed,' he said, clearly wanting to break this rule but not quite brave enough to do so.

'I won't tell if you don't,' Stanislav whispered, giving him a wink.

They grinned at one another and took a sweet each to happily munch in shared guilty pleasure. And then Bobby abandoned the truck, snatched up a book from a nearby shelf and clambered onto the couch next to Stanislav. 'Will you read me a story, Uncle Stan?'

He took the brightly coloured book, remembering with sadness all the times his own mother used to read to him when he was a boy. 'Five on Treasure Island,' he read out loud. 'This sounds exciting.' He opened the book and didn't remark on the fact that Bobby was now snuggling against his side, but gently put his arm around him and drew him closer as he began to tell the story.

Neither of them noticed that Danuta and Florence were silently watching them from the doorway, or saw the tears glistening on Danuta's happy face as she tiptoed back to the kitchen.

Peggy had stayed in the Anchor far longer than she'd planned, and after two sherries was glad of the cold night air to clear her head. She hurried through the narrow alleyways that led to Florence's door and was surprised to find Danuta sitting comfortably in the kitchen munching on a mince pie.

'Mama Peggy, how lovely to see you,' she said in delight, rising to give her a hug. 'The tea is fresh, and Florence has made these delicious little treats. Come, sit and get warm.'

Peggy took off her coat, hat and gloves and stretched out her hands to the welcome heat from the stove.

'What brings you here at this hour, Danuta? There's nothing wrong with Bobby, is there?'

Danuta smiled happily through welling tears. 'Far from it,' she replied. 'My Stanislav is reading him a story and together they are cuddled on the couch by the fire like old friends.'

'This I must see for myself,' said Peggy.

She tiptoed out into the hall and peeked around the partially open door. Tears sprang unbidden as she stood there watching the large man and the little boy, so attuned to each other and to the story Stanislav was reading that the outside world was lost to them.

She returned to the kitchen and hastily dabbed her eyes. 'How lovely to see them so content with each other,' she sighed.

'It's certainly a sight to soothe a troubled soul,' said Florence, who seemed determined not to show how much the little scene had affected her. 'But it is past the child's bedtime, and after the to-do over the past two days, I really can't take another disturbed night.'

'Leave them for a while longer,' begged Danuta.

'Yes, do leave them, Flo,' urged Peggy. 'Bobby will probably fall asleep mid-story, and then Stan can put him to bed.'

Florence gave a sigh and poured tea into a fresh cup. 'Just remember, Peggy, it won't be you that will have to get up in the night if he wakes crying for his mother.'

'I know, and I really appreciate everything you're doing for Bobby. Which is why I've come, really.' She settled into the kitchen chair, the hot cup of tea cradled in her cold hands as she told them both about the fundraising.

'Do you really think people will stump up?' asked Florence. 'There's very little money about, and now everyone knows it was Gracie who abandoned Noel, they might not feel like donating.'

'You could be right, Flo, but I have faith in the good people of this town. I'm sure they'll see what she did as an act of desperation, and I firmly believe there are enough charitable souls who will want to see her buried decently for her children's sake, if nothing else.'

'That's all very well,' countered Florence, 'but the gossip surrounding the baby has been vicious, and there will be many more who'll be scandalised by what she did, and regard a pauper's burial her just desserts.'

'I do hope you're wrong, Flo,' sighed Peggy.

'Well, I think Rosie's idea is marvellous,' said Danuta. 'Stan and I will be donating, and I'm sure the Goldmans will too. People must surely realise that by punishing Gracie, they will be punishing the children, and no child deserves to have their mother cast aside as if she was worthless.'

Peggy heard the passion in Danuta's voice and understood she was being reminded of how she'd had to bury her parents in an unmarked and unsanctified grave during the siege of Warsaw. She grasped her hand. 'That will never happen, Danuta. I will make sure of it.'

'But how? None of us has very much money, and if people are unwilling . . .'

'Leave it with me,' said Peggy, getting to her feet. 'Now I must be off. Jim will be wondering where on earth I've got to.'

Stanislav felt the weight of the child slump against his side and looked down. Bobby's thumb was in his mouth, his chin sunk into his chest as his eyelids fluttered with sleep. He closed the book, gently eased the little boy onto the cushions and reached for his walking sticks.

It took an enormous effort to extract himself from the grip of those sagging cushions, and it was out of sheer, bloody-minded will that he managed to get to his feet, the sturdy walking sticks almost bowing under his weight as he fought to gain his balance. His stump burnt fiercely in protest, and for a moment he had to just stand there and get his breath back, his weight on his other leg.

Looking down at the sleeping child, he silently cursed his stump; cursed his carelessness at getting shot down, and cursed the doctors who'd cut off both his mangled legs and left him like this. How simple it should have been to scoop the boy into his arms and carry him to his bed. But here he was, gasping and sweating with pain, unable to do anything.

As the pain finally began to ebb, he kept his weight firmly on his better leg, discarded one of the sticks and very carefully managed to lift the boy from the couch and hoist him over his shoulder. Steadying himself on the single stick, his breath hissed through his teeth as he hobbled towards the sound of the women talking in the kitchen. 'Where is Bobby's bed?' he managed.

Florence and Danuta rushed towards him, clearly intending to take the child from his precarious grasp.

'Leave him. I can manage,' he rasped. 'Where is his room?'

Tight-lipped, Florence indicated the next door down, and Danuta hurried to open it and switch on the light.

Stanislav carried his precious cargo into the untidy room, noting the clutter of Gracie's things strewn across the larger of the two beds, and the dressing table. The pain in his leg was now excruciating as he impatiently waited for Danuta to draw back the bedclothes on the small bed. If she didn't hurry up, he was fearful that he might drop Bobby, and that had to be avoided at all costs.

Danuta finally stopped fussing with the bedclothes, and he gratefully let her help him slide the boy from his shoulder and between the covers. He watched as Danuta softly kissed his cheek, and concentrated on fighting the waves of agony that were roaring up from his tortured stumps.

Bobby opened sleepy eyes. 'Night, Uncle Stan, Auntie Ditta,' he managed before sleep captured him.

Stanislav headed out of the room, the tears in his eyes only partially caused by the pain that beset him. He fetched his other stick from the sitting room, said a brusque goodbye to Florence, and was halfway down the path before Danuta could catch up with him.

'Why are you in such a hurry?' she asked.

'I am hungry,' he growled, struggling to get behind the steering wheel and rest his legs.

'You're in pain,' she said flatly as she got in beside him and slammed the door.

'I'm sad for that little boy with no mother and father,' he replied. 'And hungry for sausage and potato. My legs are fine.'

'Have it your own way,' she sighed. 'But if you don't go to the doctor's soon, you'll be in real trouble.'

He knew that, but he was damned if he was going to let Danuta win the argument. He would see the doctor, but not because of her nagging – not even because he'd realised things had reached a stage when something had to be done – but because he wanted to be fit enough to carry Bobby to bed without the risk of dropping him.

5

It was the last day of 1946 and, with the new year only a matter of hours away, Cissy decided it was the perfect time to deal with her past and unpack the large suitcase she'd dumped out of sight in the wardrobe. She'd deliberately avoided it until now, for it was visible proof that her old life in London was over, and her future here in Cliffehaven had still to be determined. However, a new year held the promise of new beginnings, and she now felt prepared for the challenge.

Cissy opened the wardrobe doors, and then plumped down on the narrow single bed which she'd slept in as a child to regard the smart Louis Vuitton leather case she'd bought in a sale at Harrods. She knew it contained dresses, shoes and bags which would remind her of the parties, dances and shows she'd attended, and of the people she'd once thought of as friends and partners in the luxury limousine private hire business. She bit her lip as she remembered how Clarissa and her catty cronies had shown their true colours when, through no fault of her own, she'd lost them two important clients. They'd dismissed her instantly by bringing in their well-heeled friend to invest in the company, and had all but thrown her out of the Mayfair flat.

She gave a sigh. At least they'd paid her what she was owed, and that provided her with a healthy nest egg she could use to try another venture down here. What that could be, she had no idea – but at least her parents were giving her the time and space to recover from the ordeal of the rape and the subsequent motor accident which had robbed her of her unborn baby. Not wanting to think of the traumatic days which had followed this loss, she got to her feet and hauled the suitcase out of the cupboard to heave it up onto the bed.

The beautiful clothes were crammed into the case, and she remembered all too well how she'd wept with frustration and fury as she'd packed on that awful night. The unfairness still stung, but it was the way her so-called friends had coldly closed ranks that left a bitter taste in her mouth. Cissy regarded the dainty shoes, the evening bags and gloves, the lacy froth on the hem of a silk nightgown. Each treasured piece had been chosen carefully as she'd scoured the small, discreet boutiques which sold the cast-offs of the rich. With a judicious eye for a bargain, she'd employed a widowed seamstress to make repairs and alterations, and no one had ever guessed that she'd been wearing second-hand clothes and shoes.

Cissy unpacked the dresses one by one and shook out the creases before putting them on hangers which she hooked over the wardrobe door. Gathering up the shoes, she placed them in pairs on the bottom shelf with the bejewelled and embroidered evening bags, and then turned her attention to the blouses, skirts, slacks and sweaters. She held the soft cashmere to her cheek and breathed in the lingering reminder of her favourite perfume, Ma Griffe, and with a rueful glance at the delicate bottle on the dressing table, she realised it was almost empty.

The perfume had been a gift from a charming American diplomat who'd been sent to Paris shortly after peace in Europe had been declared. He'd returned to London to regale her with the almost unbelievable story that these tiny bottles in their green and white packaging had been parachuted down as a way of advertising Carven's latest offering to the young women of France. It was an advertising coup, for the perfume now sold all over the world. She smiled at the memory of that delightful man who'd had to return to America too soon after their meeting, and turned her attention back to the contents of her case.

The beautiful lingerie was carefully folded into a drawer with the packets of stockings; the velvet pouches holding her jewellery tucked in beneath her underwear. The black velvet cocktail dress joined the midnight-blue one on a hanger, and she folded the evening shawls and long gloves away into another drawer. The case was now almost empty but for two sprigged cotton tea dresses with their matching belts. She found two more hangers and hooked them over the wardrobe handle, before closing the case and stowing it away on top of the cupboard.

Sinking onto the bed, she regarded everything with a critical eye, and then lit a cigarette. When she would ever wear half of this again, she had no idea. The hectic social life of London was far behind her, and Cliffehaven rarely held the sort of events that called for such finery. But they were her treasures – her investment – just as the few pieces of good jewellery were, for the labels inside were from famous fashion houses, and perhaps, one day, they would be worth a great deal more than she paid for them.

There was a tentative knock on the door. 'Cissy, are you all right in there?'

Cissy snapped from her thoughts, and quickly went to open the door to her mother. 'I'm just unpacking,' she explained.

'I've brought you a cup of tea,' said Peggy, her gaze flying to the clothes hanging all over the wardrobe doors. 'Goodness,' she exclaimed, depositing the cup and saucer carefully on the dressing table. 'It's like walking into a very posh department store.'

Cissy grinned and stubbed out the half-smoked cigarette. 'It is, rather,' she admitted. 'But I couldn't leave them all behind.'

Peggy's fingers softly brushed over the velvet and silk of the cocktail dresses before she turned her gaze to the line of shoes and bags. 'Lawks, Cissy, you've got more shoes than I've ever had.' She bent to pick up a pair of delicate silver sandals with impossibly high heels. 'However do you walk in these?'

Cissy chuckled. 'Very carefully,' she replied. 'Why don't you try them on, Mum? We've got the same size feet.'

'Oh, I couldn't,' Peggy flustered, her expression in direct denial of her words.

Cissy took them out of her hand and placed them on the floor by her mother's slippered feet. 'Go on, Mum, you know you want to.'

Peggy needed no further encouragement, and with a little gasp of delight, she kicked off the slippers and slid one foot into the sandal. 'Whoops,' she exclaimed, grabbing Cissy's arm to keep her balance while she put on the other sandal. 'Lawks, Cissy,' she breathed as she tried to stand without wobbling about. 'These are like stilts. How on earth can anyone be expected to walk in them?'

'It's all about balance, Mum,' said Cissy fondly. 'Hold onto my hands, keep your back straight and your knees firm. Walk confidently, heel first, and keep your hips in a straight line.'

Peggy tried, but her ankle went over and she ended up collapsing onto the bed in a fit of giggles. 'I'm clearly not meant to be a fashion model,' she managed.

Cissy had plans for her mother – exciting plans – and she wasn't about to let them fall at the first hurdle. She quickly removed the sandals and chose the midnight-blue silk slip-ons which had a glittering buckle across the toes and a much lower heel. 'You'll find these easier to walk in. Do give them a try, Mum.'

'But they're yours, darling. I don't go anywhere to warrant wearing such gorgeous things.'

'You never know what might be ahead,' replied Cissy mysteriously as she eased the shoes onto her mother's dainty feet. 'There, what do you think?'

Peggy stuck her legs out and wiggled her feet so the jewelled buckles sparkled in the weak sunlight that came through the window. 'They're very pretty,' she said, getting off the bed. 'And much more comfortable than those sandals.' She walked around the room and then sat on the dressing stool to take them off.

'No, Mum. Leave them on. I want you to get used to them.'

Peggy frowned. 'Whatever for, Cissy? I'm hardly likely to wear them again.'

Cissy was bubbling inside with excitement. She reached for her mother's hand. 'I'm hoping you'll wear them tonight, Mum. You see, I've organised a little surprise.'

Peggy's brown eyes widened. 'A surprise?'

Cissy nodded before unhooking the midnight-blue cocktail dress and carrying it over to her. 'What would you say to dressing up in this and going to a dinner and dance?'

'Oh, Cissy, I couldn't . . . it's too lovely . . . I'd look like mutton dressed as lamb, and besides . . .'

'You're far from over the hill, Mum, and you'll look stunning,' said Cissy firmly.

'Dinner and dance?' Peggy breathed, her eyes sparkling with hope.

Cissy nodded. 'It's being held at the County Hotel in Market Green, and I've booked a table for you and Dad, Grandpa and Rosie. I've ordered a taxi, so you can all enjoy the evening and not worry about driving.'

'Oh, Cissy,' Peggy said, tears welling. 'You shouldn't have, really. The County is very posh and four tickets must have cost you a fortune.'

'I wanted to do something special for the people I love most,' she replied, kissing her mother's cheek. 'And don't worry about the cost. I have money.'

'But that's for your future business,' Peggy snuffled into her handkerchief.

'It's mine to do with what I want,' Cissy said softly. 'And I want to treat you and Dad as well as Grandpa and Rosie. You've all been so wonderful, and this is my way of saying thank you.' She knelt before her, clasping her hands. 'Please let me do this, Mum,' she begged.

'Well, if you're really sure,' Peggy sniffed. 'Only it's a lot of money and . . .'

To stem her mother's tears and any further protest, Cissy stood and held the dress in front of her. 'It's a bit crumpled, but being silk, the creases will drop out before tonight.' She let the full skirt drift over her mother's hands. 'Why don't you just try it on?' she wheedled.

Peggy eyed the dress with the hunger of a woman starved of beautiful things for too long, and all resistance fled. She stripped off her jumper and skirt, eased off the lovely shoes, and with Cissy's help, stepped into the dress. The silk was cool against her skin, but she shivered in delight as Cissy fastened the silk-covered buttons at the back and adjusted the neckline.

Peggy was all for dashing to the mirror, but Cissy had other ideas. 'You can look in a minute,' she teased. 'Put the shoes on while I find the right accessories.'

Cissy took her time, and after a great deal of what an impatient Peggy thought of as fiddling about, was finally satisfied.

'Now shut your eyes until I tell you to look – and no cheating.' Cissy dumped the hanging clothes onto the bed and adjusted the wardrobe door to reveal the long mirror. 'You can look now,' she said excitedly.

Peggy slowly opened her eyes and stared at her reflection in disbelief. The pleated folds of blue-black shot silk rose from the tight bodice to drape elegantly off her shoulders. The skirt whispered sensually when she moved, flowing from her slim waist to just below the knee, the sunlight catching the rich, deep blue in a shimmer.

'Oh,' she breathed, turning this way and that to admire the elbow-length gloves, the sweet little evening bag, and the sparkling earrings and necklace that matched the buckles on her shoes. 'Oh, Cissy,' she managed again. 'I never imagined . . . I never thought . . .'

'You're beautiful, Mum,' Cissy sighed. 'No wonder Dad loves you so much.'

Peggy bit her lip, clearly overwhelmed by it all, but determined not to cry and spoil the effect. 'Do you really think so?'

Cissy nodded and put her arm about her mother's tiny waist. 'And tonight, he'll fall in love with you even more,' she murmured.

Peggy turned and gave her a fierce hug. 'Oh, my darling girl. How can I ever thank you?'

'You don't have to,' she replied, 'but I think we need to get this dress off before Daisy barges in and lets the cat out of the bag to Dad. I can hear her coming upstairs.'

Peggy waited for her to unbutton the dress, and then reluctantly stepped out of it to pull on her old jumper and skirt. 'I'd better see if I can get a hair appointment, and find some decent underwear for tonight,' she said, watching her daughter hang up the dress again. 'A gown like that calls for something special.'

Her thoughts went into overdrive and she snapped her fingers. 'As luck would have it, I've got just the thing at the back of my drawer that hasn't seen the light of day since your dad's first week home from Singapore.'

Cissy raised a brow. 'I'll leave that sort of thing to you, Mum,' she said wryly. 'But don't worry about your hair. I'll do it this afternoon.'

Peggy heard Daisy singing out of tune on the landing. 'Oh, no, I've just realised,' she gasped. 'Who will babysit Daisy while we're out? Charlie's off to the rugby club beano, and Grandma Cordy really can't be relied upon now.'

Cissy calmly carried on hanging up the clothes. 'No need to panic. Me and Sandra will babysit. It's all arranged.'

'But don't you want to go out tonight?'

Cissy shook her head. 'Neither of us is in the mood, and we've planned to make you all cocktails before the taxi comes, and then do some for ourselves while we play records for the evening. We'll listen to the wireless just before Big Ben strikes midnight and raise a glass to 1947 with Grandma Cordy and Bertie if they're both still awake.'

'Are you sure, Cissy? It's not like you to miss out on a party, and Ruby's promised to lay on a buffet and pianist at the Anchor.'

'I'm positive,' she said firmly. She hooked her arm through her mother's and gave it a squeeze. 'Come on, I'm gasping for a cup of tea, and I suspect Daisy will want some company. Have we got any of those lovely shortbread biscuits left?'

'We did the last time I looked, but if your father or Charlie has found the tin, there's no knowing.'

Daisy came running out of her bedroom with her rag doll to catch them up. 'Amelia would like a biscuit,' she declared. 'She's ever so hungry.' She grabbed her mother's hand as they continued down the stairs.

'Then we must see what we can find,' said Peggy, leading the way into the kitchen.

'Do cats like biscuits?' Daisy looked up at Peggy with large brown eyes.

Peggy regarded the few crumbs in the bottom of the tin. 'Not as much as the menfolk in this house,' she sighed. 'I'll have to find a better hiding place.'

Peggy had been very busy over the past couple of days, and now, with all the excitement for the coming night's festivities, she had to accept she could do no more to help raise awareness for the fundraising cause which had been splashed across the front page of the local paper this morning. She hurried back to the bedroom after Cissy had helped her into the glorious dress, which was now hidden beneath her thick dressing gown.

'I don't know why you went to all that trouble of printing flyers, Peg,' said Jim the moment she entered the room. 'The paper has really pulled out all the stops.'

'Solly agreed with me that it was a good idea,' she replied, making sure her dressing gown was buttoned to her neck. She didn't want Jim to see the dress until she was good and ready. 'It didn't take much to print off a few on the factory's Roneo copier and stick them up in shop windows. After all, not everyone reads that paper, and they'll act as a reminder for those that do.'

Jim gave a sigh as he sat down on the bed to pull on fresh socks. 'Then let's hope something comes of it, because we can't afford to pay for that funeral, and I doubt Florence can either.'

He laced up his highly polished shoes and reached for his tuxedo jacket. 'Are you sure Cissy can afford to pay for this treat? Buying those four tickets must have set her back more than a few quid – and it doesn't seem fair to leave her here looking after Daisy when she should be out having fun.'

'I had the same concern, but she was adamant she could afford it, Jim, and wouldn't take no for an answer. As for babysitting Daisy, she insisted.' She watched his reflection in the dressing-table mirror as he wrestled with his bow tie. 'And she won't be on her own, because Sandra's popping in, and both Cordelia and Bertie will be here.'

Peggy carefully applied lipstick, noting that she would soon have to buy a new one – in fact, most of her make-up needed renewing, which would rather dent her meagre savings. She'd be glad to get back to work and earning again.

Regarding the effect in the mirror, she patted her freshly styled hair, which Cissy had done that afternoon, clipped on the earrings, fastened the necklace, and reached for the bottle of scent Jim had brought all the way from Singapore. This would be their first proper night out since Jim had been demobbed, and despite all the worries and dramas of the past week, she was very excited about it and determined to make the most of Cissy's generous surprise.

'I'm worried about Cordelia,' confessed Jim, still fiddling with his bow tie. 'She's not eating properly and seems to be getting frailer by the day.'

Peggy was worried too, but as there seemed to be little she could do about it, she decided not to add to Jim's fears. 'Well, she is over eighty, so it's hardly surprising.'

She turned from the dressing table and slipped her stockinged feet into the blue high-heeled shoes. 'But I agree, she isn't her usual bright self.' She checked her stocking seams were straight, and silently prayed she wouldn't ladder them. 'There again, Jim,' she continued, 'you've got to remember she's been through a war, which is terrifying enough, only to be faced by the stark reality that life continues to be dangerous. I think hearing what happened to Cissy has really knocked her for six, and even Bertie's tender ministrations aren't enough to help her get over it.'

Jim was finally satisfied with his bow tie, and he crossed the room to pull her to her feet. Wary of smudging her lipstick, he softly kissed her powdered cheek. 'Maybe she's just feeling her age,' he said. 'And this cold weather isn't helping her arthritis.'

He grinned down at Peggy, his blue eyes bright with love and anticipation for the night ahead. 'Now, Mrs Reilly, are you going to take off that dressing gown and show me what you're hiding, or do I have to do it for you?'

She gave him a smouldering smile and very slowly began to unbutton the thick dressing gown. Sliding it from her shoulders, she let it puddle onto the floor. 'What do you think?'

Jim gave a long, low whistle as she gave him a twirl, the full skirt floating up to give him the merest glimpse of stocking top. 'You look smashing,' he breathed. 'Really quite stunning. I shall be the envy of every man there.'

He went to grab her in a hug, and she quickly stepped out of reach. 'Don't you dare, Jim Reilly. You'll crush Cissy's dress.'

He grinned and shot her a naughty wink. 'I'll wait until we get home, then, and help you take it off.'

She gave him a peck on the cheek and danced away

from his roving hands to pick up her evening shawl, bag and gloves. 'It's almost seven and we need to get downstairs. The others should be arriving any minute and Cissy has promised to make us cocktails to set us up for the evening.'

The shoes were comfortable, the heel just the right height, but Peggy was glad of the banisters and Jim's arm as she navigated the stairs. She'd got out of the habit of wearing heels, and it was taking a bit of time to get used to them again.

There was quite a jolly gathering in the kitchen, and the wireless was providing lively music to add to the party atmosphere. Cissy and Sandra had changed into pretty dresses for the evening; Bertie was wearing a rather flamboyant waistcoat under his suit jacket, and Cordelia had given a nod to the occasion by donning a black blouse and skirt that sparkled with sequins. Rosie looked like a Hollywood star in a shimmering silver sheath that showed off her curves to great advantage, while Ron was barely recognisable in a very smart tuxedo.

Ron's eyes widened as Peggy came into the room. 'To be sure, wee girl, you're a sight for sore old eyes and no mistake,' he gasped.

Peggy blushed. 'Thank you, Ron, and may I say you're looking dapper. Is that a new tuxedo?'

He looked quite bashful as he fiddled with the hem of the beautifully tailored jacket. 'Aye. My Rosie had it made for me for Christmas. Makes me feel a bit like a dog's dinner, but I suppose it doesn't hurt on the odd occasion.'

'Anything's an improvement on your usual attire, Ronan Reilly,' said Rosie without rancour, digging him in the ribs. 'But I do have to admit, you look very handsome when you make an effort.'

'Ach, now you're trying to sweet-talk me,' he retorted. 'And I'll not have me head turned, so I won't.'

'Well, I think you all look utterly splendid,' said Cissy. She picked up the tray laden with champagne coupes filled with something orange and bubbling and handed them out. 'Tropical champagne to get everyone off to a good start,' she announced.

Peggy eyed the concoction with mixed feelings. 'Goodness. That sounds a bit extravagant.'

Cissy giggled. 'I have to confess, I did cheat a bit. Ruby unearthed a cheap bottle of sparkling wine from her cellar, and I just added a drop of orange bitters to give it some colour, and vodka to add extra bite.' She raised her own coupe. 'Cheers, everyone. Here's to 1947.'

They all repeated the toast and Peggy took a tentative sip to discover that there was more than a drop of vodka in the mix. 'Whew,' she exclaimed. 'I'll be tiddly before I even leave the house if I drink all this.'

'Ooh, Cissy,' breathed Cordelia after taking rather more than a genteel sip. 'It's certainly got a good kick.'

'If you don't like it, I can make something else.'

'Oh, no, dear, this is just the ticket,' she chuckled. 'In fact, it's quite perked me up.'

'Well, I'd take it slowly,' warned Cissy. 'Too much and you'll be asleep before Big Ben strikes midnight.'

Cordelia waved away her caution. 'I'm sure I'll last you two young things out,' she said airily before taking another hefty swig. 'What's in it, by the way?'

As she clearly hadn't heard the last time, Cissy repeated the ingredients, and encouraged her to turn on her hearing aid.

Peggy exchanged a glance with Jim. The cocktail was strong, and she could see it wasn't really to his taste either, but as Cissy had made them as a treat, they'd drink them down, and hope the long drive to the hotel would give them a chance to clear their heads.

The rap of the knocker on the front door sent Cissy hurrying to answer it, and she returned to the kitchen moments later to announce the arrival of their taxi. There was an excited scramble for coats and scarves, and having kissed everyone goodbye, they hurried down the front steps to find not only a thick fog coming in from the sea, but a very smart chauffeur standing by the open door of a black limousine.

Once everyone was settled and assured that the fog would pose no problem, the chauffeur closed the doors and climbed behind the wheel. The others stood in the doorway of Beach View to wave them off, and the engine purred beneath the shining bonnet as they almost silently pulled away from the terrace to begin their journey to the outskirts of the county town some miles away.

Stanislav had finally managed to get an appointment to see his consultant at the hospital, but it seemed fate was against him, and he was burning with frustration. The short flight back from Scotland had been delayed because the delivery trucks had been late, and it had taken an inordinate amount of time to load the cargo of food, medicines and temporary shelters. Now, a freezing fog was threatening to blanket the south of England, and it was a race against time to land the C-47 before it closed in.

'Well done,' said Charlotte, his co-pilot, as the wheels finally hit the tarmac and he applied the brakes. 'Even my poor Freddy would have been proud of that landing in such awful conditions.'

At the mention of the long-dead Freddy Pargeter – air ace and all round jolly good drinking companion – Stanislav grinned. 'Coming from you, that is high praise indeed,' he replied, bringing the heavy plane to a standstill before executing a slow, careful turn.

He taxied the plane back along the runway to the hangar where the ground crew was waiting to unload, service and refuel it ready for the next day's flight. Switching off the engine, he quickly filled in the logbook, got Charlotte to counter-sign it and then heaved himself out of his seat. 'I am late for an appointment,' he explained. 'Will you give the logbook to Martin for me?'

'Of course,' she said, regarding him evenly. 'I hope all this rushing means you've finally decided to see someone about your leg.'

'For a check-up only,' he replied dismissively. 'It is routine.' He turned his back on her and moved awkwardly towards the door. Pulling back the lever, he swung it open and one of the ground crew quickly placed the set of steps in front of it.

He looked over his shoulder at Freddy's widow and smiled. 'Goodnight,' he said with all the cheer he could dredge up and then handed her his sticks. Grasping tightly to the rails, he made his tentative way down the steps, but the effort and pain this caused made him sweat, and he was glad the peak of his cap and the gathering gloom shadowed his face as he retrieved the sticks and headed for his car.

The short drive to the hospital for injured servicemen was hampered by the low-lying fog that swirled in the valleys of the winding country road, and cleared dramatically at the high points. Aware that he was now almost an hour late, the frustration ate into him, making him careless of his speed.

The tree loomed out of the fog from nowhere and, heart hammering, he slammed on the brake with such vehemence, he stalled the engine but narrowly missed crunching the car bonnet against the sturdy tree trunk.

Cursing from the pain this caused and furious at his own foolishness, he restarted the engine and manoeuvred the car out of harm's way until he was back on the road and then set off at a snail's pace.

It was a huge relief to finally see the large, illuminated white sign outside the hospital entrance. Making his way into the car park, he took a moment to steady his still racing pulse before climbing out and awkwardly lumbering through the main door to the consultant's waiting room.

Sir Julian Carmichael-Blackstock looked up from his copy of the *Lancet* and got to his feet with a welcoming smile. Tall and youthfully trim for a man in his early sixties, he was a handsome man who wore the tailored pinstriped suit with panache, the Oxford college tie precisely knotted. A discreet pin in his lapel proudly proclaimed his membership of an elite London gentlemen's club, and there was a gold signet ring with his family's crest gleaming on a finger of his well-manicured hands.

'It's good to see you, Stanislav,' he said in his rich bass tones as he shook hands. 'I didn't think you'd make it once the fog came down.'

'Neither did I. I'm sorry to have kept you waiting.'

Julian's sweeping gaze took in the beads of sweat on Stanislav's brow, and the slight trembling in his hands as he leaned all his weight on the sticks. 'Let's have a look at those legs and see what sort of damage you've done to them now,' he said with almost weary acceptance.

Stanislav knew from experience that Julian would stand no nonsense and see through any bluster, so didn't bother to contradict him as he meekly followed him into his consulting room.

Half an hour later, after being prodded, poked, X-rayed and asked endless searching questions, Stanislav braced himself for Julian's verdict. He could feel his pulse starting to race as the other man spent what felt like endless minutes meticulously writing his notes and studying the X-rays.

The consultant finally replaced the cap on his fountain pen, smoothed blotting paper over his notes and closed the thick file of medical records. He sat back in his leather chair, his elegant hands steepled under his chin as he regarded his patient with unnerving directness.

As the silence stretched, Stanislav could feel sweat bead his moustache and trickle from his hairline, but he didn't dare wipe it away under that all-encompassing gaze.

'I think you already know what I'm going to say, Stanislav,' Julian began. 'You need to lose weight, cut down on the drinking and give that leg some rest from the prosthesis. If you don't, you will end up in my theatre again.'

He raised a hand to stem any protest. 'You know as well as I do that your right stump has become infected, and if you continue to wear that prosthesis, it could become gangrenous – and then I shall have no option but to incise the dead flesh away to leave you with less than you already have left of that thigh. And if that is the case, a new prosthesis may not be practicable and you'll have to learn to live with one leg.'

Shocked, Stanislav gasped. 'It won't come to that, surely?'

'It will if you don't keep that prosthesis off and use your crutches,' the consultant retorted, his tone brooking no argument. 'Which is why I am going to confiscate this one until I see an improvement in that right stump.'

He sat forward, his forearms resting on the desk. 'I cannot express too urgently how important it is to do as I say, Stanislav. If you continue to ignore my advice, you could very well have to resort to using the wheelchair again.'

Stanislav's blood ran cold at the thought. He wanted to argue – to bluster his way out of this nightmare. But held by the other man's gaze for a long, silent moment, he slowly came to the realisation that it was time to be accountable for his gung-ho attitude and try to redeem the situation. He hated the crutches even more than the sticks, but the thought of having to be pushed around in a wheelchair again was even worse.

He looked down at the empty trouser leg which had been pinned up and swallowed his fear. 'I will do as you say,' he mumbled.

Julian heaved a sigh and got to his feet to perch on the corner of the desk. He looked back at Stanislav with great understanding. 'I know it's a dent in your pride, Stanislav,' he said quietly. 'It's the same for all my amputees when they have to revert to wheelchairs after having the freedom of their prostheses. But my advice really is worth following if you want to avoid such a thing.'

Stanislav couldn't meet his gaze. He knew that everything the man said made perfect sense, and he'd been a fool to think he could go on living as he had before losing his legs.

The consultant seemed to read his thoughts. 'You've come a long way since the initial amputation,' he continued. 'And I'd hate to see you back in that wheelchair.' He reached out and laid his hand on Stanislav's broad shoulder. 'Just please promise me you'll cut down on the drinking, try to lose some of that extra weight and take good care of *both* stumps. You really can't risk damaging the other one.'

Stanislav finally looked back at him, ashamed. 'I will, I promise.'

'And tell your wife what I've just said,' Julian

ordered. 'There's no shame in letting her help you. She is a nurse, after all, and can see you keep to a sensible diet, as well as maintaining the care of those stumps.' He reached for the leaflets on his desk and handed them over. 'This is a diet sheet – and this is a guide to sensible alcohol intake. I urge you to read them, Stanislav. You'll feel very much better if you follow their advice.'

Stanislav secretly thought there was a great deal of shame in being half a man in front of Danuta, but he kept silent. He shot a cursory glance at both leaflets and shoved them into his coat pocket. 'I'll do my best, Sir Julian, but how can I fly with only one prosthesis? There are two pedals on a C-47, and I can't afford not to work.'

A flash of humour lit the other man's grey eyes. 'Oh, I'm sure you'll find a way, Stanislav,' he said cheerfully. 'You're a man of many talents, with the capacity to think of ways and means to get around such minor problems.' He got to his feet to show that the consultation was over.

Stanislav reached for the hated crutches, struggled to stand on his one leg, and shook the man's cool, firm hand. 'I will wish you good health in 1947,' he said, sketching an awkward bow.

'And I to you. I will see you at the end of January. My secretary will write to inform you of the date and time.' Julian's grin was quite boyish, the formality melting away in a genuine show of friendship. 'Chin up, old chap. You'll come through with flying colours, I'm sure. Now go home to your wife and enjoy your evening.'

The limousine had slowed to almost walking pace as they'd travelled over the fog-bound hills, and then speeded up as they reached the clear green valley surrounding the county town. Entering the village of Market Green, the car turned in through an impressive gateway, and as the tyres crunched over the gravel of the turning circle in front of the hotel's grand entrance, there was a general sigh of relief that they'd made it – and in time.

Peggy refused to worry about whether they'd ever get home again. This was all far too exciting. She turned her attention to the marble columns of the impressive portico, the liveried staff waiting to help them from the car, and the rows of brightly lit windows set in the honey-coloured walls draped in bright red Virginia creeper.

The car door was opened and she slid from the leather seat, steadied by the young man's gloved hand as her heels dug into the gravel. In the moments it took for everyone to gather their things and prepare to make their entrance, her gaze swept over the ornamental bay trees set in terracotta pots on either side of the imposing front door. They had been strung with fairy lights, as had the surrounding birch trees, with the tiny white lights artfully wound around the slender white trunks to make it look like a fairyland.

'It's quite magical, isn't it?' whispered Rosie. 'And look at those chandeliers. I bet even Buckingham Palace don't have ones like that.'

Peggy could only stare in wonder at the glittering display she could see through the downstairs windows. 'It's ever so posh,' she hissed to Jim who'd come to escort her indoors. 'We'll have to mind our Ps and Qs, and no mistake.'

'It's no smarter than some of the hotels in Singapore,' he replied, 'and the way you look tonight, you'll be forgiven anything. Now stop fretting, and let's get inside before we freeze to death.'

The reception hall was full of the sound of clinking

glasses, laughter and chatter, under which was the siren music of a dance band. A liveried doorman directed them to the cloakrooms, and having left their coats, Peggy and Rosie admired the powder-pink carpet, plush chairs and fluffy towels in the pristine ladies' loo, before rejoining the men.

'It's a palace in there,' murmured Peggy.

'It's like a gentlemen's club in ours,' muttered Ron, looking round with a frown. 'To be sure I could do with a drink after that long drive in the fog.'

A waiter in tailcoat and starched shirt appeared as if by telepathy to offer them crystal coupes of champagne from a silver salver. Ron and Jim both dug in their pockets to pay, but the waiter shook his head. 'These are included in the price of the ticket, sir,' he said. He gave a discreet wink. 'As are the bottles of wine you'll find on the table.' He wished them a good evening and melted into the crowd.

'Gosh,' breathed Rosie. 'This must be setting your Cissy back a fair few bob.'

'Let's just enjoy it,' replied Peggy, her excited gaze trawling the crowd, the chandeliers, the fur stoles and flashing jewellery displayed by the other women. 'I'll find a way to pay her back.'

Rosie's gaze flitted about the room. 'That's the Lord Lieutenant of the county,' she informed Peggy, 'and look, there's our mayor and his wife talking to Lord Cliffe. We *are* in good company. I'm surprised your Doris isn't here. It's right up her street.'

Peggy prickled in horror at the idea. Doris was the last person she wanted to see on this perfect night. She did another swift trawl of the room just to check, but thankfully there was no sign of her. As a muffled gong announced it was time to go into the ballroom, she hooked her hand into the crook of Jim's elbow and joined the orderly queue from the reception hall. She was starting to feel rather light-headed with all the champagne and excitement, so was rather glad she'd soon get the chance to sit down.

The ballroom ran the entire breadth of the enormous building, with windows overlooking the back gardens, and vast chandeliers hanging in a line from an ornate ceiling. The dance band was set up on a stage by the large dance floor which was overshadowed by a cargo net filled with balloons that would no doubt be released at the stroke of midnight. The rest of the room was filled with round tables covered in pristine white linen that sat eight people. Silverware and crystal winked in the light from the chandeliers, and bowls of white hot-house roses formed perfect centrepieces.

Jim went to check the large table plan and returned with a frown. 'We're on number four,' he said quietly.

Peggy wondered why he was looking so glum, decided it must be because it was way past his usual teatime, and walked with him across the room to the table set up right by the dance floor. Waiters hurried to pull out the plush velvet chairs and drape stiff white napkins on their laps. She eyed the empty seats and idly pondered on who would be joining them as she picked up the embossed menu card and ran her gaze down the appetising food on offer. Rationing seemed to have bypassed this particular place, for there was roast beef, a salmon starter and several choices of pudding.

'Good heavens! Fancy seeing *you* here.'

Peggy went cold. She'd recognise her sister's voice anywhere.

6

It had been a long day for Danuta and, because she'd popped in to see Bobby at the end of her shift, it was now almost eight o'clock. She had seriously thought about not risking the drive and staying in Cliffehaven at Beach View where she knew she would always be welcome, but the draw of her own bed had won her over. Having battled the swirling fog on her way home, she felt wrung out, so she parked the car and sat for a moment to ease the tension in her neck and shoulders before wearily making her way down the slope to her beach-side home.

It was eerily dark, the frail beam of her torch barely penetrating the thick fog as she reached the beach and stumbled her way to her front door. All was silent and still but for the slap of the waves on the shingle and the muffled moan of the lightship's foghorn out at sea. There were no welcoming lights in any of the windows, and as she unlocked the door and stepped inside, she was greeted by an empty silence and deep chill which told her Stanislav was not yet home.

The thought that he was probably stranded in Scotland by the fog was swiftly followed by the dread that he might have flown anyway, and risked life and limb trying to land. She wouldn't put it past him, and could only hope that the sensible Charlotte would make sure he didn't do anything so hare-brained. She chose not to admit she'd been just as reckless by driving home. Heaving a sigh of weariness and frustration, she switched on the kitchen light and was faced with a cold and very dead stove.

'That's all I need,' she muttered crossly in Polish. 'And if that man of mine has dared to fly in this fog, I'll have his guts for garters.' She kept her coat, scarf and gloves on as she grimly set about relaying the fire. Once it was burning brightly, she slammed the door on it and made a cup of hot tea, thanking her lucky stars for her new electric kettle.

The chill of the day felt as if it had eaten into her bones, but the tea went some way towards thawing her out, so she braved the icy bedroom and quickly changed into a pair of old corduroy trousers and two thick sweaters. With her feet shoved into slippers, she returned to the kitchen which was warming up nicely, and hunted about for the makings of supper. They had planned to go to the Anchor tonight, but as Stan wasn't home – and was unlikely to be – and the fog made driving too hazardous, she'd have to put something together to eat.

There was very little in her small larder, but she found a large baking potato, so scored it with a knife and popped it onto the top shelf of the stove. Grating carrot and finely chopping an onion and some red cabbage, she made a rough coleslaw with the last of the mayonnaise. Eyeing the dry heel of Cheddar cheese, she decided it would be better to keep that to melt on toast tomorrow. But she really would have to knuckle down and do a proper shop. If Stanislav was right about the weather forecast, she'd need a well-stocked larder.

Her attention to food was broken by the sudden twin beams of blinding car lights piercing the curtainless window. Her jaw tightened as she watched the unmistakable figure of her husband clamber out to steady himself on crutches, a torch in his mouth to light the way. 'He dared to fly in this?' she exclaimed. 'I'll kill him.'

She snatched the door open before he had a chance to slot in his key. 'What do you mean by flying in this bloody fog?' she shouted in Polish. 'Did you actually risk your damned life – and Charlotte's – by landing at Cliffe, or did you by some miracle manage to get here on the hot wind of your bloody arrogance?'

Stanislav tucked in his neck and eyed her with trepidation as he withstood the barrage of Polish aimed at him. It was most unlike Danuta to shout – let alone swear – and he was amazed at how fluent she was at it. 'I can explain,' he said as she paused for breath.

'You'd better,' she stormed, standing aside to let him in before slamming the door.

Stanislav swung himself into the kitchen and sank into the nearest chair. The crutches clattered to the floor but he chose to ignore them, for Danuta had her arms folded and her expression told him he was in very deep trouble. With an inward sigh, he accepted that she wouldn't be any happier once he'd told her what the consultant had said, and just wished he hadn't finished that bottle of whisky last night.

'Well?' she snapped. 'I'm waiting.'

He smiled up at her more in hope than expectation of any relenting of her temper. 'You are very lovely when you are cross, Danuta,' he said softly in English. 'I am sorry I am late, but it couldn't be helped.' He waved his hand vaguely towards the window. 'The fog is not so bad now the wind has changed to come from the sea.'

'Don't give me that,' she snapped. 'I've only been home for about half an hour and it was what the English call "a pea-souper" out there.'

He was rather put out that she'd dared to drive home and yet was giving him earache because he'd done the same thing. 'It is true,' he admitted reluctantly. 'But it was far worse when . . .' He realised he'd said too much and clamped his lips together.

'Worse when you landed at Cliffe.' It was a statement, not a question.

'I wanted to get home to you, and because . . .'

'So you risked your life as well as Charlotte's by showing off. You're lucky you both weren't killed.' She took a breath, her arms tightening about her waist. 'And another thing. Why are you on crutches – and what's happened to your right leg?'

'Ah, well, that's the reason why I'm a bit late,' he said carefully.

She was not to be mollified. Plonking down on the chair next to him, her expression was stony. 'Then you'd better explain. Fully, and with no evasions or frills.'

Stanislav bit down on a smile, knowing it would only infuriate her further, but he was totally awed by this new aspect of Danuta. He'd always known she had spirit, but she was quite magnificent in her rage. 'Well, you see, my love, I had an appointment with Carmichael-Blackstock, and it was really important I didn't miss it.'

He could see Danuta's anger slowly melt away as he told her what the consultant had said, and when he took her hand and looked into her eyes, pleading silently for her to understand how vulnerable he suddenly felt, he saw he was forgiven. With a sigh of thankfulness, he welcomed her warm embrace.

'I'm sorry I was cross,' she said, mopping away her tears. 'So sorry I shouted at you like a fishwife, but I was frightened, Stan. I know the sort of risks you take, and I was terrified you might crash.'

'But I am home now, my love,' he crooned, stroking her hair. 'We are both safe. And you must promise me you will never again drive home in such fog.'

She lifted a tear-stained face and looked into his eyes. 'Only if you promise not to fly or drive in it either,' she said gruffly. 'Honestly, Stan, you take far too many risks, and you worry the life out of me.'

'You are sounding like Peggy,' he teased.

'Mama Peggy is a very sensible woman,' she retorted. 'She would agree that you are too eager to tempt the fates. It is why your leg is in a mess and you have to use those crutches.'

Since there was no answer to that, he watched her as she moved from the table to the stove to check what was in the oven, and hoped it was something tasty. He hadn't eaten very much since breakfast this morning, and his belly was grumbling.

'There is only a baked potato to share with coleslaw for supper as we were expecting to eat at the Anchor tonight.' She looked woebegone. 'I'm sorry, Stan. I didn't have time to go shopping.'

'Stop apologising,' he said, ignoring the squirm in his stomach as he drew her back to perch on the better of his two thighs. 'We will eat like kings compared to those poor devils across the Channel.'

Danuta sighed and kissed his cheek. 'We have a lot to be grateful for, Stan, and we must never forget it.' She wriggled off his lap, suddenly businesslike. 'While we're waiting for the potato to cook, I'll read those leaflets. If you're to watch what you eat, then I need to know what to buy tomorrow.'

'It won't be easy with rationing being so strict,' he said mournfully, digging the leaflets out of his coat pocket.

'Rationing might actually help,' she replied. 'It's basic, with very little fat and sugar, and few treats – and as long as you don't fry everything, you'll soon lose the pounds.' She scanned the leaflets. 'Not drinking will help,' she added. 'Help your weight and my housekeeping. Do you know how expensive vodka and whisky are?'

Stanislav had the feeling his lovely wife would be a hard task-master, and once again mourned the empty whisky bottle he'd consigned to the dustbin that morning.

Peggy looked up at her sister, well aware of how her unwanted presence had cast a cloud of gloom over the table.

'Hello, Doris,' she said, taking in the black velvet gown, the double string of pearls and rose corsage pinned above her bosom. *If nothing else,* she thought, *my sister is stylish*. 'What have you done with John?'

'He's over at our table with our other guests,' she replied. 'We made up a party from the Officers' Club.' Her gaze swept down her nose and round the table. 'I'd ask you to join us, but we are already eight.'

'We're quite happy where we are, thanks. Shouldn't you be getting back to your guests?'

Doris glanced across at the table which was at the far end of the room, and rather too close to the kitchen doors to be entirely comfortable. 'Yes, I suppose I should,' she said reluctantly.

She eyed Peggy from head to toe in that snooty way which made Peggy itch to poke her on the nose. 'I have to say, Margaret, you seem to have been given a very good table. As there are only four of you and we have some very important people in our party, I don't suppose you'd consider swapping over?'

'You suppose correctly, Mrs White.'

Doris turned sharply to find Lord Cliffe and his glamorous new wife standing behind her. 'Oh, I didn't realise this was your table,' she stammered.

'It is indeed,' he replied coolly. 'Now, if you would excuse us, we'd like to greet our guests.' Lord Cliffe regarded her steadily as he and his wife were joined by the Lord Lieutenant of the county and his wife, Lucinda Ambrose.

Doris had no option but to awkwardly shuffle to one side as the four dignitaries ignored her and moved towards the table with welcoming smiles. Ron and Jim shot to their feet to greet them and, turning her back on Doris, Peggy felt a deep satisfaction at having seen the shock and bewilderment on her sister's face before she'd scuttled off to her own table. It served her right for being horrid to Cissy.

Lord Cliffe gave Peggy a conspiratorial wink as he shook her hand, and she grinned back at him, still rather perplexed as to how she'd ended up in such illustrious company. However, he'd become a valued friend over the years and Peggy knew he'd never been able to disguise his dislike of Doris and her snobbery, and had been appalled when it had become clear she'd set her cap at him shortly after his first wife had died.

He'd been widowed for many years, so when he introduced his new, much younger wife, Edith, Peggy was fascinated to finally meet the woman who'd been the talk of the town ever since he'd brought her home to Cliffe House at the end of the war. She was pleasantly surprised to find that she was very jolly, easy to talk to, and not at all grand.

He greeted Rosie with a peck on the cheek – they'd known each other for years – and Ron as an old comrade and adversary, having accepted long ago that his poaching on his estate was all part and parcel of country life so long as he didn't get too greedy, or be caught by his gamekeeper. It had become almost a game over the years, and both men enjoyed it.

Jim had relaxed into the occasion very quickly, but Peggy had, at first, felt a little daunted by finding herself in such company, for although the two families knew each other well, they didn't move in the same circles. But she was soon put at ease, for Edith, the new Lady Cliffe, seemed to have a wide range of interests, and Lucinda Ambrose was adept at recounting some very funny anecdotes relating to her husband's tenure as Lord Lieutenant. As the first course was served, Peggy forgot all about Doris, and plunged wholeheartedly into making this a night to remember.

Danuta lay wide awake staring into the darkness as Stanislav snored beside her. They'd gone to bed early to save on firewood and coal, and to keep warm after their meagre supper. They were both exhausted, but as usual, Stanislav had fallen asleep almost immediately, while she lay here battling with a legion of worries.

She'd suspected for some time that he'd been overdoing things and putting too much pressure on his prosthetics, and now, having insisted upon dressing the right stump, she knew just why the consultant had forced him to use the crutches again. Perhaps the short, sharp shock of the doctor's warning would be enough to bring him to his senses and make him see how reckless he'd been – how close he'd come to losing more of that leg and being confined to the hated wheelchair. And it could still happen.

If the infection didn't heal and surgery became the only solution, then he would never fly again, and for a man like Stanislav, that would toll a death-knell, not only to his pride but to his very manhood. There were too many wounded returning servicemen already scrabbling to find work and shelter – any work that would keep a roof over their heads and food in the bellies of their children – and the thought of Stanislav joining those ranks was unbearable. They would be left struggling on pitiful welfare payments and her wages, doomed to live in this shack until it fell down around their ears, with absolutely no hope of adopting Bobby and Noel – or any other child.

Danuta turned onto her side and hugged the pillow as the thoughts and fears went round and round in her head. Stanislav had said he was happy for them to adopt, but was he really? Had he just said that to please her – to hide his true feelings, and the fact he was already battling with his health? Was this careless attitude to his well-being merely a cover-up for his fear that he could end up in a wheelchair, or a sign that he really didn't want the responsibility of taking on someone else's children?

He'd been reluctant to commit himself either way when she'd first told him about Gracie's wishes for the children, and even after their successful visit to see Bobby, he'd been quite taciturn, refusing to make plans for the future, and clearly upset. She suspected she knew why he'd reacted like that, and it cut her to the quick. Bobby had shown trust in Stan, and she knew her husband well enough to realise that his soft heart had been touched by the little boy.

However, his disability had been brought sharply into focus when he'd tried to carry Bobby to his bed and found that it was almost impossible. Stanislav was a proud man, and she had seen how it had shaken him to the core to realise he could never be what he saw as a proper father to Bobby and his brother – a father who carried his sons on his shoulders, a father to play football with, to take part in school sports days, and not be pointed out as the father with no proper legs.

Danuta gave a sigh as the first tear dampened the pillow. Why couldn't he see that he could be all those things if only he'd take better care of himself? Surely, a man in possession of such pride should harness it and use it to fight against further disability – not let it make him reckless to the point of destroying everything they treasured?

Florence was at her wits' end. Bobby had been restless ever since Danuta had left the house. He was too full of questions she couldn't answer, and wouldn't be cajoled into staying in his bed, even after she'd broken her own strict rule and treated him to hot cocoa and a digestive biscuit. She'd finally given in and allowed him to sit with her to listen to the wireless, but his constant chatter and demands for attention had ruined the comedy show as well as the concert that followed, and she'd found it hard to contain her impatience.

Now it was almost two in the morning and Bobby was finally asleep on the couch next to her, the fire merely a dull glow of dying embers. Not wanting to wake him, she eased herself off the couch to place a blanket over his shoulders, then put the guard in front of the fire, switched off the table lamp and went to her bedroom.

She'd had plans for tonight, but of course they'd had to be cancelled, and her friend, Beatrice, had made it clear she hadn't been too happy about going to the theatre and dinner without her. Not that she would be alone, thought Florence; there were four other women who regularly met up for such evenings, so she'd be amongst friends. However, the responsibility of taking on Bobby was beginning to take its toll, both on her social life and her pocket, and with little idea of how much longer this state of affairs might last, it was a worry.

Florence slowly got undressed and changed into her nightclothes, then, after a hurried trip to the icy bathroom, climbed into bed to savour the warmth of the hot-water bottle at her feet. She reached for her hairbrush and ran it through her long dark hair with the usual one hundred strokes before loosely winding it into a single plait. She was proud of her hair – it was her only redeeming feature – or at least that's what her mother had told her in her usual despairing tone. But Florence knew she was blessed with far more attributes than her mother deigned to admit. She might not have snared the wealthy husband her parents had wished for, nor been given the chance to go to university, but she held down a responsible job at Solly's factory, was smart and capable – someone to be relied upon to get the job done efficiently, and a loyal friend to those she trusted.

She set the brush aside and leaned back against the pillows. Her parents had not been rich, but they'd had aspirations for their only daughter which sadly had not borne fruit. There had been no money for the university engineering degree course she was interested in, even though she had passed the entrance exam, and it had soon become clear that she preferred the company of women to the men who'd come courting in her younger days. She knew she was a disappointment to her parents, but until now she'd been very content with her life and the circle of friends she'd made since coming to Cliffehaven. However, since taking on Bobby, she could see how that comfortable life she'd forged here could soon be disrupted.

Sliding down beneath the blankets, she stared up at the damp patch in the corner of the coving which the landlord had promised to sort out, but never had. The long Christmas holiday, the shock of losing Gracie so unexpectedly and in such a traumatic way had all taken its toll, and now she had the added worry over Bobby.

How long would she be expected to keep him, and would she finally break the habit of a lifetime to ask for financial help from the government? Would the authorities allow Danuta and her husband to adopt the children – and how on earth was she going to manage once she went back to work? It could take months for any adoption to go through, and if it didn't, how could she refuse to keep him and still hold up her head? The guilt would be too much to bear if they were both sent to some orphanage – perhaps even be split up if it was easier to find a home for them that way. But to take them both on would be impossible, and she'd forever be tormented by the knowledge that she'd let Gracie down.

She hadn't been in love with Gracie, not the way she loved Beatrice, but she had been very fond of her – almost motherly. She smiled at the thought, for she'd never hankered after motherhood, but Gracie had got under her skin with her vulnerability and cheeky ways, her determination to do her best for her children, but unfortunately inclined to be distracted by the first man who showed any sign of affection for her.

'Oh, Gracie,' she sighed. 'I so wish you'd trusted me enough to tell me about the baby. If only you had, you'd be here now with your children, and I wouldn't be worrying myself silly.'

Realising she was feeling sorry for herself, she impatiently reached out, turned off the bedside lamp and buried herself beneath the bedclothes. The school term would begin on Monday, and she'd be back at work. With money coming in and Bobby distracted from his mother's death by his classes and friends, things would get easier. Of course she could manage one small boy.

It was two in the morning and Peggy held tightly to Jim's arm as they joined the slow exodus from the ballroom. She felt happily tipsy from rather too many glasses of real champagne, her feet were killing her after being whirled round the floor for every dance, and the waistline of her beautiful dress was under strain from all the lovely food. But her head was still buzzing with the music, and she felt more alive than ever with the sheer joy of being with her Jim on the dance floor again.

Collecting their coats and scarves, they wrapped up to face the weather outside, only now giving a reluctant thought to the long journey home and what they would do if the fog had worsened and it proved impossible. Peggy could see that Jim was worried, for they couldn't afford to stay at the hotel like the others in their party, and she suspected they'd have to settle down in one of the lounges if they were allowed, which would certainly put a dampener on what had been a spectacular night.

They said their goodbyes to the Cliffes and Ambroses, the women making tentative plans to meet for coffee in the near future, and then headed for the doors. Emerging from the stuffy heat of the hotel, they found that the fog had lifted to leave an inky black sky studded with cold, bright stars and a crescent moon. The air was icy, their warm breath steaming as they laughed and chattered on the top step.

'It was a jolly good night, wasn't it?' said Doris, suddenly appearing from behind the potted bay tree.

Suspecting she'd been lying in wait to hear any gossip, Peggy wasn't about to tell her very much at all. 'It was lovely,' she replied. 'And so much fun. I can't remember how long it's been since I danced so much.'

Doris's expression was sour. 'Yes, I saw you making a fool of yourself with Lord Cliffe.'

Peggy giggled. 'Jealousy will get you nowhere, Doris.' She tugged on Jim's arm and they hurried to where the chauffeur was waiting to help them into the car.

'You are naughty, Peg,' murmured Jim as she

snuggled against him on the back seat. 'Poor old Doris was only on a fishing trip. She's clearly desperate to know how we ended up on that table.'

'Yes, she is, isn't she,' she replied happily. 'And I wouldn't tell her even if I knew.'

Jim sighed. 'Well, I'm blowed if I know what's going on, Peg. Was it just luck we ended up there, or did Cissy plan it somehow? And besides, I thought you and Doris were on friendly terms again.'

'It's a mystery, Jim,' she replied, becoming sleepy in the warmth of the car. 'I doubt we'll ever know for sure.'

The journey didn't take half as long on the way home, and as the car pulled up silently outside Beach View, she kissed Ron and Rosie goodbye and let the driver help her out onto the pavement. 'We'll catch up tomorrow, when you pick up your car, Rosie,' she called, waving goodbye as they were driven towards Havelock Road.

Jim steadied her as they negotiated the steps which were now white with thick frost, but as he was about to put his key in the lock, the front door opened.

'Did you have a wonderful time?' asked Cissy, her face alight with hope.

Peggy stepped inside and swamped her in a hug. 'We had the most marvellous time,' she replied, giving her a kiss. 'I haven't danced so much in an age, and the champagne has left me feeling quite light-headed.'

Jim flung his overcoat over the newel post and gave his daughter a kiss. 'We dined like kings and danced until our feet were sore.'

'And you'll never guess who was at our table,' breathed Peggy, shedding her coat and scarf.

Cissy looked her most innocent. 'Who was that, then?'

Peggy regarded her steadily, not fooled one bit. 'You

knew all the time, didn't you? But how did you fix it? And why on earth didn't you warn us?'

'That would have spoilt the surprise,' she replied. 'As for fixing anything, that wasn't really to do with me.'

'You can explain while I put the kettle on,' said Peggy, heading for the kitchen. 'I'm gasping for a cup of tea after all that rich food and wine.' She switched on the kettle and lit a cigarette. 'Are the others in bed?'

Cissy nodded. 'Sandra's only just gone up, but Cordelia went straight after Big Ben and Bertie drove home. I offered him a bed upstairs, but he seemed keen to get back.'

Peggy made the tea, plonked the pot on the table and sat down while Jim hunted out milk, sugar and cups. 'So, Cissy, how did you manage to sit us at that table with Lord Cliffe and the others?'

Cissy grinned. 'It was by pure chance, really,' she admitted. 'I'd gone to the County to see if I could book you in, and Lord Cliffe came in right behind me with his wife. She's rather fun, isn't she?'

'Don't go off the subject, Cissy,' warned Jim. 'Your mother will burst if you don't enlighten her.'

'Well, there weren't any tickets left, but Lord Cliffe was at the reception desk and must have overheard my conversation with the manager because he came to the rescue. It turned out that he'd booked a party of eight for the evening, but two of the couples had informed him that morning that they couldn't come. Stranded in far north Scotland by snow, I think he said.'

'Get on with it, Cissy,' growled Peggy.

'So instead of cancelling the tickets, he immediately added you all to his table, and gave strict instructions that it should be close to the dance floor and nowhere near the kitchens.' Her blue eyes sparkled as she shot them a cheeky grin. 'I think he was rather looking forward to catching up with Grandpa Ron – and of course he's always had a soft spot for Rosie.'

'Well I never,' said Jim. 'That really was a stroke of luck.'

'It certainly was,' said Peggy, giving a dry chuckle. 'Especially as it put Doris's nose right out of joint. You should have seen her face, Cissy. It was a real picture.'

'Good,' said Cissy. 'I'm glad it all went so well.'

'But how did you know Doris would be there?'

'I saw the tickets displayed on her mantelpiece, and they gave me the idea.'

'Clever girl,' murmured Peggy, squeezing her daughter's hand.

'I rather thought so,' Cissy replied before they both collapsed into giggles.

Jim eyed the pair of them with a frown. He had no idea what all that was about, and probably never would. Women really were a mystery.

7

On Wednesday 1st of January 1947, while most people were using the day to recover from their revelry of the night before, both Danuta and Stanislav were expected to be on duty. Danuta finished dressing his stumps, and then quickly made the breakfast of cheese on toast which was washed down with plenty of tea.

'I've made a list of everything I'll need to buy, but with most of the shops closed, I don't hold out much hope. I'm really sorry, Stan. I should have planned ahead.'

'I'll see if Martin will let me buy a couple of tins from the stores. They should do for tonight, and you can go shopping tomorrow.'

'I suppose so,' she sighed. 'But those stores are part of the airlift, and it doesn't feel right. Besides, how on earth are you going to fly with only one prosthesis? If Martin grounds you, we can hardly expect him to let us have supplies.'

Stanislav waved away her doubts. 'I will not be grounded,' he said airily. 'You worry too much, Danuta.' He heaved himself out of the kitchen chair onto his crutches and struggled into his coat. 'I can do it,' he snapped when she tried to help him. 'Stop fussing, woman.'

'If you're going to be like that, then I'm off to work,' she retorted mildly. 'I'll see you tonight.' She picked up her nursing bag and turned to kiss his cheek. 'And please be in a better mood. I do so hate it when you're grumpy.'

'I'm sorry,' he muttered, grabbing his hat. 'None of this is your fault.'

They left the little house together, and she measured her pace to match his as they went up the slope to the cars. The sky was a pale grey with thick cloud cover, and an easterly wind had them burying their chins into their scarves as they scraped the thick frost from the car windows. This achieved, they waved goodbye to each other before starting the engines and letting them run for a minute in the hope of warming the icy interiors.

Danuta followed him as far as the country lane where he turned right towards Cliffe airfield, and she went left towards Cliffehaven. The narrow, twisting lane was icy in patches where the trees from the Cliffe estate kept it in permanent shadow, but once she'd reached the main road, the way was clear. The gritting lorries had clearly been out, and thankfully there was no fog today because of the wind.

She reached Elms Avenue in plenty of time for the morning clinic, and parked the car outside the large Victorian villa where the aged Jacob Kaplin was struggling to manage on his own. It had once been an elegant house, but since losing his wife, and with no other family to help him, Jacob had let things slide. The paintwork was flaking on the door and windows; the front step was crumbling; the colourful tiles on the path were cracked or missing; some guttering was loose, and the garden had been sadly neglected behind the privet hedge that needed a severe pruning. It would take work and money to put it to rights, and although Rachel had promised to help them buy it once Jacob was found more suitable accommodation, the reality was she and Stan would never be able to afford it.

Danuta tried not to feel depressed, but with everything that had happened over the past two weeks, it was difficult not to see that fate was against her – especially now Stanislav was feeling so vulnerable, and his future as a pilot was in doubt. Refusing to dwell on this latest blow, she took her medical bag from the passenger seat, locked the car and walked across the road to the surgery.

Alistair was already in his consulting room and looking cheerful. 'Good morning, Sister Danuta. And a very happy New Year to you.'

Danuta couldn't remain glum in the beguiling light of Dr Darwin's winning smile. She grinned back. 'And the same to you. Did you manage to get to the Anchor last night?'

His brown eyes crinkled at the edges most attractively as he smiled. 'Indeed I did, but Ruby and I expected to see you and Stan there. What happened?'

'The fog happened, and once we'd both got home, we felt it was wiser to stay there.' Not wanting to dwell on the unpleasant row she'd had with Stan, she changed the subject. 'I don't suppose Gracie's autopsy report is through?'

'It came in late yesterday afternoon,' he replied. 'The findings went straight to the coroner, and he signed it off as death caused by septicaemia.' He leaned back in his chair. 'That was the main cause, not helped by the fact she was malnourished and had a previously undetected heart defect.' He gave a sigh. 'It's hardly surprising she was unable to fight the blood poisoning after giving birth alone in that filthy old caravan, but it's amazing that the baby has come through the ordeal seemingly unscathed.'

Reaching to pluck the buff-coloured folders from his desk, he riffled through them. 'I was concerned that Gracie's heart defect could be congenital so I checked Bobby's medical records. Thankfully, there's no sign of any problems. And that also applies to Noel. Dr Granger at the hospital gave him a thorough examination when he was first admitted and passed him fully fit.'

Danuta sank into a nearby chair. 'That is a relief,' she sighed, her thoughts immediately turning to all the things she had to do to get the adoption application in place now the coroner's report had finally been signed off.

Alistair Darwin seemed to read her mind. 'There's a very long way to go before you'll be able to take them both on, you know, Danuta. Both children are now under the watchful eye of the local authority, and if they are concerned about their future welfare, they could very well make them wards of court and put them into the care system.'

Danuta gasped in horror.

'But I doubt that will be the case here,' he said quickly. 'Both Miss Hillier and the Goldman couple are very reliable foster parents. However, I strongly advise you to get a solicitor, Danuta. Adoptions can be fraught with difficulties, and you'll need legal representation to help you through the minefield of paperwork and red tape.'

'Rachel Goldman said the same thing. She's recommended someone, but I have the feeling he's going to cost far more than we can afford.'

'Yes,' he replied thoughtfully. 'They aren't cheap. Would Mrs Goldman help with the fees, do you think?'

'I don't like to ask her. She's already been so supportive to me and Stanislav.'

'But surely she must know you can't afford a solicitor, and if she's willing to sponsor your application, then she must have taken the cost of a solicitor into account?'

Danuta's shoulders slumped. She felt helpless and rather foolish, but the last thing she wanted to do was to go cap in hand to Rachel again. 'I don't know, Alistair. We never got to discuss it.'

He patted her arm. 'Try not to worry about it now. None of the offices will be open until Monday, so you'll have time to discuss it with your Stan and Mrs Goldman. At least now we have the autopsy and coroner's report, the funeral arrangements can go ahead. I see the local paper has started fundraising.'

Danuta nodded, her thoughts still centred on the complexities which lay ahead. 'Anything they raise will be a help,' she said. 'Neither Peggy nor Florence can afford to pay for it – and we certainly can't.' She met Alistair's gaze. 'But if it means she'll be buried in a pauper's grave, I suspect Rachel will save the day again – although it doesn't seem fair.'

'I'm sure it won't come to that,' he soothed. He drew himself up and reached for the day's roster. 'We'd better get on, or the day will be lost with little achieved. There's no surgery this morning, but I'm on call should you need me. You have quite a long list to get through, so I've asked Sister York to come in this afternoon.'

'That's a bit unfair. She was on duty last night and will be for the rest of the week.'

'She was quite happy to do it,' he replied. 'It was a slow night, thankfully, and the only call-out she had was to Mrs Lester who lives in the centre of town, so she didn't have to go far and the delivery went very smoothly.' He looked up from the notes with a grin. 'It was a third boy and Mrs Lester decided there and then that she'd try again for a girl.'

Danuta grinned back. 'Let's hope she doesn't have to try too many times, or she'll end up with a football team.' She read down the list. Jacob Kaplin was at the top to have his leg ulcer cleaned and re-bandaged, and then the majority of the calls were to newly delivered mothers. With Sister York helping this afternoon – and barring any emergencies – she should get home at a reasonable time for once.

Folding the list and placing it in her coat pocket, she looked at him hopefully. 'I don't suppose you know if any of the shops are open?'

'That little place on the corner of Leaf Lane might be, but their stock is rather limited. Perhaps I can help?'

Danuta shook her head. 'That's kind, but I'm sure they'll have something to see us through until I can do a full shop tomorrow.' She got to her feet. 'I'll just sort out my medical bag and then be on my way.'

Stanislav leaned heavily on his crutches as Martin paced the floor of the office hut. 'Of course I can still fly the damned plane,' he blustered. 'It will be easy. I will use this crutch on the pedal instead of my false foot.'

Martin turned on his heel and glared at him. 'Don't be so bloody stupid,' he snapped. 'I will not put Charlotte's life at risk – or yours for that matter. This is a professional outfit, Stanislav, and there's no way on this earth I'll let you fly that plane with one leg and a bloody crutch.'

'I don't see why not,' he retorted. 'The crutch is just as good as my foot.'

'It damned well isn't and you know it!' shouted Martin.

'What on earth is going on? We can hear you down by the hangars.' Charlotte and Roger appeared in the doorway, swiftly followed by Roger's wife, Kitty.

'Stanislav is proposing to fly that C-47 with one foot and a crutch,' stormed Martin. 'And I will not have it. Do you hear?'

'I expect they can hear you in Cliffehaven,' said Kitty dryly. 'I really don't see what you're getting so het up about, Martin. Stan is experienced enough to know what he's doing, and he's right – a crutch is as good as a false foot if you really have a feel for the plane.' She tapped her own false leg. 'I'm sure that if I had to, I could use the pedals with a stick.'

'That's all very well,' snapped Martin. 'But none of it will wash with the insurance company. The premiums are already astronomic, and if they find out we're letting our pilots fly using crutches, they'll blacklist us.'

'I think he's right,' said Roger, his expression doleful. 'Sorry, Stan, old chum, but we really can't risk it.'

Stanislav's shoulders slumped as he regarded the four pilots, and realised there was no point in arguing. The insurance company had not been keen to take them on when they discovered that two of them were amputees, and despite the fact they'd both attained their full pilot's licences after the surgery, had insisted on rigorous medicals before agreeing to exorbitant premiums. He sank into a nearby chair, his spirits plummeting as Kitty began to argue with Roger.

'You and Martin are being very short-sighted,' Kitty stormed. 'Of course he has to fly and is quite capable of doing so, even if he does use a crutch.'

'It isn't safe, and I'm not letting you or Charlotte take that risk,' he snapped.

'We have two flights scheduled to go out today,' said Charlotte, cutting through the argument. 'Kitty is minding the children, and if Stan is grounded, it will leave us one short. The insurance company won't like that either, so I suggest Stan comes with me as navigator. Now, can we please get on?' she said in exasperation. 'We're running late as it is.'

'I don't like it,' muttered Martin.

'Neither do I,' said Roger on a sigh. 'But Charlotte's right; we can't legally fly those planes without two of us on the flight deck, and those supplies are urgently needed across the Channel.'

As the argument seemed to be settled, Kitty rounded up the three toddlers, tucked her new baby more snugly into his pram and set off for home.

Stanislav struggled to his feet and followed the others out of the office to where the huge cargo planes were waiting. He had won a victory, but he could tell there would be a long battle ahead if he was to keep flying.

'Thanks for supporting me, Charlotte,' he murmured, as they settled into the cockpit.

'It's what friends do,' she replied, busy at the controls, and waiting for instructions from the control tower to begin taxiing up the runway. 'But I don't think Martin and Roger will put up with it for too long. Did the doctor give you any idea of when you might get the leg back?'

Stanislav repeated the checks and studied the flight-plan. 'It won't be for long,' he assured her. 'The stump is just a bit sore, but it'll soon heal.'

Charlotte regarded him for a long, silent moment, clearly not convinced.

Peggy was still feeling the heady effects of the previous night, but a welcome cup of tea was dealing with that as she planned her day. Jim had driven off early to go to the local British Legion's head office and collect his daily schedule of visits before he went up to Parkwood House to check on his mate Ernie, who unfortunately had taken a turn for the worse over Christmas. The rest of the household were still in their beds as she sat at the kitchen table, and although she rather envied them, she was eager to feel useful again and had dressed and put on her make-up while it was still dark. The factory was closed until 2nd January, but there were things she had to do, and she really couldn't afford to sit here much longer.

The cleaners were due to arrive at the factory in an hour ahead of reopening, and as she was the keyholder, she would have to let them in. It was important they did a good job so that everything was ready for when the machinists and the warehouse staff started work tomorrow.

She had spoken to Solly before Christmas, and he'd agreed to Florence taking the weekend off so she could mind Bobby until he went back to school on Monday, so it was down to Peggy to pick up the reins over the weekend, sort out the post and any orders that might have come in over the holiday period, as well as do a quick stock-take to make sure Florence had kept the books properly. Which she was sure she had, for Florence was very efficient.

Peggy sipped her tea. She loved her home and her family, but the time off had seemed endless – particularly as she'd had an extra week at home to look after Daisy who'd had the measles. Now she was looking forward to going back to work and earning again. Christmas had been expensive as well as traumatic, and although Jim didn't know it, she'd given Florence a few quid to help her out with Bobby, which had left her a bit short. She could only hope that once everything was open again, Florence would get some sort of help for Bobby from the welfare. It wasn't fair to expect her to pay out when none of what had happened had been her fault.

Her thoughts stayed on Florence as she poured a fresh cup of tea and lit the first cigarette of the day. On her return to work, Florence would take up her old position as Peggy's deputy and shop-floor manager, her dip in wages reflecting the step down from the responsibilities she'd taken on during Peggy's absence.

Peggy made a mental note to look into any assistance Florence might be entitled to, because she suspected the other woman would be too proud to seek it out for herself.

Peggy had a long-held suspicion that Florence was one of those women who preferred the company of other women, and going by the odd bit of gossip she'd overheard on the factory floor, she wasn't alone in thinking that. There were several women in Cliffehaven who'd been living together as friends or companions for many years, but were in truth as devoted and tied to one another as any married couple. It didn't bother Peggy at all, for she'd always believed in letting people live their own lives as long as they didn't frighten the horses or hurt anyone. But it had to be a clandestine sort of life, built on secrecy and often leading to ridicule – but unlike their male counterparts, at least they weren't hounded by the law and thrown into prison.

Florence lived alone – or had done until she'd taken in Gracie and the boy as lodgers to protect them from a vengeful Phil Warner, whom Gracie had testified against in court following the robbery at the factory. She had never been linked romantically to anyone – man or woman – and she'd taken on a huge responsibility by caring for little Bobby after Gracie had died. Peggy wondered fleetingly if there had been anything between her and Gracie, but quickly dismissed the idea.

She finished her cigarette, drank down the last of the tea and got to her feet. Glancing up at the clock, she pulled on her coat, stuffed her feet into her boots, found the car keys and headed for the front door at a run. If she didn't get a move on, the cleaners would be left standing outside the factory door, and the day would not begin well.

The car was a bit reluctant to start after standing in the cold all night, but it eventually got going and, with a sigh of relief, Peggy drove down Camden Road, passing Solly's main clothing factory and crèche. That too was closed until tomorrow, and another army of cleaners would be going in to prepare it. She carried on up the empty High Street to turn off at the bridge by the station and up the hill to the large factory estate which had sprung up on the waste land beside the dairy during the war years.

Usually a hive of industry, the place was deserted, and she drove past Jack's motor workshop, the canteen and Red Cross warehouse. The large, prefabricated buildings had, during the war, housed aircraft manufacturers, rope makers, heavy machine shops and parachute packers. These huge edifices had now been transformed by the local council into smaller units which had been snapped up by entrepreneurs like Jack Smith to run their one-man businesses. The roofs were mostly corrugated iron, the floors concrete, the walls thin plasterboard, but there was running water and electricity, and the rents were low enough to be affordable.

Peggy drew the car to a halt outside the clothing factory, relieved that as it was closed, her sister would not be in the estate office. Her husband, Colonel White, was the overall manager of the whole factory site, responsible only to the local council who owned it. Doris was his secretary – which was how they'd met – and she seemed to have an uncanny knack of waylaying Peggy every time she came up here.

All was quiet as Peggy stepped out of the car and she breathed a sigh of relief as she pulled up the fur collar of her lovely new coat and headed for the main door unhindered. Turning the key in the heavy-duty padlock, she stepped inside the cavernous building, picked up the pile of post, switched on all the lights and made her way across the factory floor to the office cubicle on the far side, her footsteps echoing in the eerie silence.

Unlocking the office door, she found that everything was as she'd left it on that last awful day when Gracie had been rushed to the hospital, and she'd hurried up here to make sure everything was running smoothly in Florence's absence. It had been a minor blessing that it was the last day of work before closing for Christmas, and therefore easy to let everyone go home straight after Solly had doled out the Christmas bonuses.

Peggy put her handbag on the desk and shivered. It was freezing in here after being shut for so long, so she switched on the five-bar electric fire to warm up her office and then went back into the main body of the building to turn on the large heaters. It would take at least a day and a night to warm the place through, and as most of the machinists would be sitting down all day, it was hardly fair to make them keep their coats on.

She had just checked that there were no problems in the staff lavatories and the storeroom was securely locked to prevent pilfering, and was heading back to her office when the ten women from the cleaning company arrived. Loaded down with mops, buckets and brooms, they seemed to be eager for the day's hard work, and after giving them their instructions, she went back to her office to deal with the mail, make a couple of telephone calls and go through the books.

With repeated glances through the large window which looked over the factory floor, she kept an eye on their progress, and was glad to see they'd thought to bring their own flasks of tea and packets of sandwiches, for the canteen was shut until tomorrow, and cleaning was a thirsty business.

Solly's main factory in Camden Road had supplied

the forces uniforms, having won a contract from the war-time government. He'd had to take on extra machinists to fulfil the orders, but he'd kept them on after peace had been declared, for although the demand for uniforms had waned, he'd gone back into the business of making affordable women's clothing and men's suits.

The large factory now provided cheap versions of the suits, leisure wear and dresses to be found in the popular women's magazines. The orders had come in thick and fast, for the women of war-torn England were fed up with making do and mending, and having nothing but dull utility clothing to spend their clothing coupons on, and were hungering for colour, style, and to be feminine again.

This smaller factory produced baby and children's wear, with special orders for maternity dresses and christening gowns. Peggy admired Solly's business acumen, and his quick eye for seeing which way things were going, for once again, he'd got in on the ground floor of a new and growing market. There was a baby boom sweeping across the country now the men had returned from war, and their order books were full.

Peggy had dealt with the post and most of the order book when her office door opened to let in a cold draught that ruffled the paperwork on her desk. Looking up, she was surprised to see Florence standing there with Bobby. 'Hello, Florence. I didn't expect you to come in today.'

'We needed some fresh air and exercise after a rather disturbed night,' she replied. 'I hope you don't mind me bringing Bobby.'

'Of course I don't mind.' She smiled at Bobby. 'Why don't you sit down by the fire, Bobby? You must be cold after your walk.' As the child scrambled up onto the chair and held his hands out to the fire, Peggy regarded Florence and noted the dark shadows under her eyes.

'I'm sorry I can't offer you anything to eat or drink. I wasn't planning on staying very long.'

'We've had porridge and tea for breakfast, so we're fine, thanks.' Florence dug her hands into her coat pockets. 'I've actually come to tell you the latest news on you-know-who.' She pulled the other chair closer to the desk and sat down.

'The autopsy report?' asked Peggy, aware of the child sitting within earshot.

Florence nodded. 'Dr Darwin telephoned early this morning. The autopsy and coroner's report has been signed off, so I can finally arrange her funeral. I rang the undertaker, and it's all set for next Friday at eleven o'clock.'

'That's a relief,' said Peggy on a sigh. 'The waiting hasn't been easy for any of us. But how did you persuade them to arrange it when we don't know if we can pay?'

'It was very awkward, and I felt terrible about having to explain. But they're an old family firm who've been in Cliffehaven for at least three generations, and of course knew all about G . . . You know who.' She glanced across at Bobby who was clearly listening to every word and shot him a fleeting smile before turning back to Peggy.

'They've agreed to a small deposit of two pounds, which must be paid tomorrow, and then, if the fundraising doesn't come to enough, it will be monthly instalments until the debt is settled. I've said I'll go in tomorrow and sign their papers agreeing to the arrangement, but I really have no idea how I'll manage,' she sighed. 'Things are already very tight.'

'Hopefully, you won't have to, but if there is a shortfall, I'll make sure you're not lumbered with it.' Peggy reached across and squeezed Florence's arm. 'Please try not to worry, Florence. You aren't alone in this, and if push comes to shove, I'll ask Solly to stump up for any shortfall.'

'Well, if you're sure,' murmured Florence. 'It all feels so mean, somehow, and Gracie deserves better.'

Peggy agreed that it was penny-pinching, but as Gracie had died leaving barely a pound in her purse, there really wasn't much she could do about it.

A movement on the shop floor caught the corner of her eye and she glanced out of the window. The cleaners had downed tools and gone into a huddle where they seemed to be engrossed in animated conversation. 'I wonder what that's all about,' she murmured, hoping they weren't about to walk off site because of the cold.

She pulled her wandering attention back to Florence. 'Where is the service to be held?'

'St Cuthbert's. I've spoken to the priest – such a lovely man, and so understanding. He said that there was no rush to pay the fees – he was sure he could wangle some sort of deal with his bishop – and he would see to it that she was decently laid to rest beside her husband's memorial stone.'

'Oh, that is kind. But you're right; Father Finlay is a lovely, caring man, which I suppose comes from being an army padre during the war. Unlike his predecessor, he's had real experience of the darker side of life outside the church, and understands his parishioners. He even conducted Danuta and Stan's wedding in Polish, which I thought made it even more meaningful.'

Realising she was rambling on, she changed the subject. 'I forgot about Gracie's husband's memorial,' she murmured. 'It was so sad that his remains were never found after the Germans blew up that French oil refinery.'

Catching Florence's warning look and aware that Bobby was listening, Peggy changed tack. 'I just want to assure you that you will not be expected to pay for anything, Florence. With the newspaper on board with the fundraiser, and both the funeral directors and the priest willing to wait for their fees, I'm positive we'll manage somehow.'

'I hope so,' sighed Florence, 'because I simply don't have that sort of money to spare. Especially now,' she added with a meaningful sideways glance at Bobby.

Peggy was about to reply when there was a light rap on the half-glazed door. Looking up, she saw a deputation of cleaners standing there and her heart sank. *Please God they aren't here to moan or make impossible demands*, she silently prayed. She signalled for them to come in and braced herself for trouble.

The leader of this deputation was a sturdy middle-aged woman in overalls, headscarf and with a glint of determination in her eyes. She got straight to the point. 'We was having a talk, Mrs Reilly,' she said, meaty arms folded beneath a large bosom. 'We heard about what happened,' she went on, tilting her head towards Bobby who was staring at them in fascination. 'And it don't seem right.'

Peggy frowned. She'd been wrong-footed, but certainly didn't want a discussion about Gracie in front of Bobby – especially if prejudices and vicious gossip were to be aired. 'Please be careful what you say,' she warned.

The woman's chin went up, the pale eyes gimlet. 'I ain't saying nothing what can't be heard by little ears,' she retorted. 'I'm just saying it ain't right asking strangers for money to see things are done proper for her. She was one of us – a widow, with kids, and scarcely two brass farthings to rub together. It weren't her fault things happened like they did.'

'She certainly was one of us,' agreed Peggy. 'Unfortunately she left very little, so it was necessary to get the newspaper involved, if things are to be conducted properly. I'm sure the good people of Cliffehaven will dig deep when they realise how tragic her passing was.'

The shoulders slumped and the belligerent expression softened. 'Yeah, poor little cow didn't stand much chance, did she? But it's the kids we really feel sorry for.' The woman dug into her dungaree pocket, pulled out an envelope and placed it on the desk. 'We had a whip-round, Mrs Reilly. It ain't much, but at least it's something.'

'That is very generous of you Mrs . . . ?

'Ida Banks. No need for thanks; just see it goes where it's needed. We'll get back to work now. Sorry to have barged in.' She turned, shooed the other women out of the office and closed the door firmly behind her.

'Well, I never,' breathed Florence.

Peggy picked up the envelope which was heavy with coins. 'It's a good sign, Florence. It means people want to help regardless of how little they have.'

Danuta had finished giving Mr Kaplin his weekly bath and shave and had dressed his leg ulcer. Now they were back downstairs in the dark but warm old-fashioned kitchen, and she was waiting for the kettle to boil so she could make him a fresh pot of tea before she left. She stood by the fire and surreptitiously watched him as he struggled to read the newspaper in the weak beam of the overhead light, and felt sad for what he'd become since his wife of many years had died.

Jacob was in his eighties and had been such a proud man – always well dressed and neatly groomed – who'd forged a career as a successful goldsmith and jeweller and been a driving force on the boards of many charities. Now he was round-shouldered in his good quality but shabby clothes which hung off him, and was weighed down with almost crippling grief and loneliness. It was as if he'd given up on life, and no longer cared that his home was slowly crumbling around him.

Danuta bit her lip, eyeing the stuffed wallet he'd carelessly left on the sideboard. It wasn't as if he couldn't afford to do repairs or look after himself properly, for there had to be at least twenty pound notes in that wallet; there was plenty of coal in the shed, and the walk-in larder was well stocked with tins, eggs, milk, sugar, butter, cheese, biscuits and bread. A bag of potatoes sat on the floor of the larder alongside some carrots and onions in a basket, and there was a large tin of coffee on the side which was a real luxury. Someone was clearly shopping for him, and yet he was starving himself. She had to do something about it.

'Those carrots and onions are looking a bit sad, Mr Kaplin,' she ventured. 'Would you like me to cook you something before I go?'

'Too much bother, my dear,' he said, waving away her offer with a delicate, pale hand. 'I've not much of an appetite, and a tin of something will suffice.'

'What if I put together something now? It won't take long, and at least I'll know you haven't gone hungry today.'

'You have better things to do than look after me,' he replied, glaring at her over the glasses perched on the end of his nose. 'I don't need your charity. Go and leave me in peace with my paper.'

Danuta regarded him affectionately and carried on making the tea. He might be sour at times, and far too independent for his own good, but like her Stanislav, he needed help.

'Looking after you is not charity. It is part of my job,' she replied, heading for the larder again.

He muttered something unintelligible as she hunted through the larder and took out a tin of corned beef, an onion and two large potatoes – the carrots were so rotten they had to be thrown out, and some of the contents of the jars of preserves looked questionable – but she'd sort those another time.

Continuing to ignore his mild protests, she quickly peeled and chopped the potatoes into small pieces and put them on to boil while she hunted out a heavy frying pan, gave it a thorough scrub, and then sliced and fried the onion. In her hurry to feed him and get on with her long list of calls, she broke the key which opened the tin of corned beef and almost cut her finger. Biting back on her exasperation, she rooted about in one of the cluttered drawers of the old kitchen dresser and finally found a can opener. It was stiff from little use, but she eventually got it to work and managed to coax out the pressed meat with a knife. Chopping the meat into cubes, she tossed them in with the onions and let them simmer while she hunted in the larder for some Worcester sauce.

'I don't like you poking about in my cupboards,' he complained.

'I'm sorry, Mr Kaplin, but you have to eat, and I'm not leaving here until you do.'

She unearthed a half-empty dusty bottle of Worcester sauce from the back of the larder and gave the contents a wary sniff, as it looked as if it had been there for at least a decade. But it smelled all right, and after she'd tasted a drop on her finger, she sprinkled a generous amount onto the sizzling meat and onion, and added pinches of salt and pepper to give added flavour. The aroma was making her mouth water and her stomach rumble, but she ignored her own needs, determined that Mr Kaplin should have at least one decent meal today.

'What are you cooking?' he demanded. 'I cannot eat shellfish or pork or meat with dairy.'

'It's corned beef hash,' she replied. She turned from the stove to smile at him. 'I know you have a kosher diet, Mr Kaplin. Please don't be concerned.'

He glared at her for a moment and then dipped his chin and grunted. 'You young people think you know everything,' he muttered.

Danuta didn't bother to reply to this familiar grumble. The potatoes were now soft, so she drained off the water and added them to the mix in the heavy old frying pan. Pressing everything down to crisp up the bottom, she let it sizzle in the beef fat while she placed the fresh pot of tea on the table, and checked that the milk hadn't gone off. Once she'd gauged it had fried enough, she carefully turned the corned beef hash over to fry and crisp up on the other side.

'You are a good girl for a *shiksa*, Danuta,' he murmured as she finally put the plate of food in front of him and poured out the tea.

She patted him on the shoulder, knowing his use of the word *shiksa* hadn't been meant as an insult. 'I might be a gentile woman, but it doesn't mean I can't cook. You eat while I clean up the mess I've made, and if you're still hungry after that, I found a tin of rice pudding you might like. How's that?'

He nodded and tucked into the food so hungrily, she wondered how long it had been since he'd had a proper meal. She made a mental note to have a talk with Rachel to see who was doing his shopping and if they might agree to come in regularly to clean the place and look after him. His pride would be assuaged by the fact he would be paying her, and therefore it couldn't be seen as charity.

She began to clean the top of the stove which had splatters of long-forgotten meals caked all over it, and once that was done, turned her attention to the sink. One of the taps was dripping, and there was a stain on the porcelain which meant it had been leaking for a while, so would need a plumber to fix it. She scrubbed the sink clean, gathered up the peelings and put them in the overflowing waste-bin, which she carried outside and emptied into the big dustbin before giving it a good scrub clean.

Glancing at her watch, she realised she was now very late for the rest of her calls. She pulled on her coat, checking that the fire in the hearth would last out the day, and placing the guard in front of it. Mr Kaplin wasn't that steady on his feet, and the open fire was always a worry.

'It's good to see you've enjoyed that,' she said as he pushed aside his empty plate. 'There is a little more in the pan if you're still hungry, or would you like some rice pudding? I'm sorry I don't have time to heat it through, but I could open the tin for you.'

'You must go,' he ordered, waving her away. 'Shoo, shoo. I can manage.'

Danuta wasn't all that sure that he could, but she simply didn't have time to argue. She quickly opened the tin, wished him a good day and hurried to her car, praying that the small corner shop would still be open.

Ron had fixed up a permanent bed and dirt-box for the kittens in the dining room. They had finally learnt how to lap at their milk and water, and were now taking a little of the food he put down twice a day, which was why he hadn't worried about leaving them the previous night.

He'd wanted to shut the door on them so Monty wouldn't eat their food and they couldn't explore the house, but Harvey had plumped himself down beside the door and howled until he'd been let in to babysit. Monty showed no sign of being interested in the kittens, but it had soon become clear that he was jealous of all the attention they got, for he'd begun to pester Ron and Rosie every five minutes by demanding strokes and fuss.

'They can't stay in there permanently,' said Rosie, absent-mindedly stroking Monty's head as she leaned on the door jamb to watch Harvey lying on the floor while the kittens climbed all over him. 'It's all very well having that dirt-box, but they don't seem to be using it and the room's starting to pong.'

'I'm doing me best to teach them how to use it,' he replied. 'I'm sure they'll get the hang of it soon enough – and it won't be long before we can let them out into the garden.'

'Let's hope so, or that rug will be ruined.'

'I'll take it outside, give it a good scrub and let it air on the washing line.'

'That won't be enough, Ron. They'll mess on the floor and once it sinks into the boards we'll never get the smell out.' She gave an exasperated sigh. 'I wish you'd put them in the kitchen. At least it's easier to clean up after them with lino on the floor.'

'Your wish is my command,' he said cheerfully. 'Only be prepared for Monty snaffling their food.'

'I suspect Harvey will have something to say if he does,' she replied dryly. 'That dear old dog is a devoted nursery maid.'

As if Harvey understood what they were saying, he lifted his head and eyed them dolefully before giving a sigh and going back to sleep, unbothered by the kittens who were playfully using his tail to pounce on and chew.

'You grab the cats, I'll do the rest,' said Ron. 'And

once we're done, I'm off to Beach View to collect your car and check on Cordelia.'

Rosie nudged Monty to one side and caught the kittens to nestle them in her arms as Ron picked up the cardboard box he'd made into their bed, and Harvey lumbered to his feet, curious as to what was happening. 'Why do you need to check on Cordelia?'

'She's not right in herself,' he replied before returning to the dining room for the second cardboard box he'd adapted for use as a litter tray. He took it outside to clear out the sand and mess and as Monty shot off into the garden, quickly shovelled in more sand from the bucket by the back door and added fresh paper.

Rosie rounded up the kittens who'd decided that kitchen cupboards made excellent climbing frames. 'Cordelia's been frail for some time,' she said as Ron came back indoors. 'You've got to remember she is in her eighties now, and after all she's been through, it's hardly surprising that Cissy's bombshell has unsettled her.'

'Aye, that it has, and poor old Bertie Double-barrelled is very worried about her. Which is why I'm going over there to see if there's anything I can do to help him lift her mood.'

Monty's head appeared at the half-glazed back door, his paws scrabbling at the paintwork. Ron let him in and he made straight for the food in the cat bowls.

Harvey stiffened and growled deep in his throat. The kittens froze and Monty backed off to sit on the doormat, eyes rolling back and feigning innocence. Harvey nudged the kittens, giving each of them a reassuring lick to encourage them to finish their food.

'That seems to have settled things,' said Ron. 'I'll take Monty with me and give him a good run before I see Cordelia, so don't expect me back until lunchtime.'

Rosie ran her fingers through her tousled hair and

yawned. 'I'm going for a long, hot soak in the bath. All that champagne last night has left me feeling a bit under the weather.'

'But it was a good night, wasn't it?'

She smiled and nodded. 'We should go dancing more often. I love seeing you all dressed up and on your best behaviour. I think you made quite a hit with the new Lady Cliffe and Lucinda Ambrose.'

He gave her a wink and grinned. 'There's still life in this old dog yet, but you're the only woman for me, Rosie.' He put his arm about her waist. 'I could go to Beach View later if you'd be wanting help with scrubbing your back,' he murmured against her neck.

Rosie giggled and gently pushed him away. 'Go for your walk. I'll see you later.'

Ron watched her go up the stairs and then gave a sigh as he turned to Monty who was still sitting by the door and eyeing Harvey warily. 'Come on then, ye heathen beast,' he muttered. 'Let's get rid of some of that energy.' He grabbed his hat and poaching coat, patted Harvey's head and left the house with Monty at his heels.

The sky had darkened throughout the morning, turning from deep purple to inky black in the afternoon before the rain came down in a deluge. Danuta had finished her round later than she'd hoped, and finally handed over to Sister York mid-afternoon. The small corner shop had been on the point of closing when she'd eventually managed to get there, but the owner had noted her nurse's uniform and kindly let her in to buy a tin of corned beef, a large onion and two big potatoes as well as a rather stale loaf of bread which he'd let her have at half-price. The aroma of the meal she'd cooked for Mr Kaplin had stayed with her and that was what she and Stanislav would have tonight.

There hadn't been time to visit Florence and Bobby, but she would make up for that tomorrow. For now, she was on her way to Rachel's, and she hoped she'd get the chance to cuddle Noel while she discussed what to do about Jacob Kaplin, and broached the awkward subject of hiring a solicitor.

The wipers were struggling to clear the rain from the windscreen and, as she drove out of Cliffehaven and up into the hills, she could see that the water was already flowing in a fast river down both sides of the road. It was a filthy afternoon, the sky so dark it was almost like night, and the headlights were struggling to pierce through the gloomy downpour.

Having finally made it to the Goldman house, she parked and grabbed her umbrella. Scrambling out of the car, she struggled against the wind and rain to keep the umbrella from blowing inside out as she ran down the path to the welcome shelter of the deep porch.

'Danuta! What a lovely surprise,' welcomed Rachel. 'Come in, come in,' she added, holding the door open.

Danuta quickly shook out the umbrella and propped it against the side wall of the porch before she stepped inside and cleaned her shoes on the doormat. 'It's truly awful out there,' she said, unbuttoning her coat. 'The English say it rains cats and dogs, but it is more cows and elephants today,' she joked, mopping her damp face with her handkerchief.

Rachel laughed as she took Danuta's coat to hang it up. 'It certainly sounds like elephants trampling on my conservatory roof. Come through to the kitchen and we'll have some tea. Solly's at the factory in Camden Road overseeing the cleaners, so we won't be disturbed.'

'And Noel? How is he?'

Rachel smiled. 'He's in his pram in the kitchen, waiting for you to play with him.'

Danuta's heart leapt at the thought and within seconds, she was leaning over the pram cooing at the baby who laughed up at her, his arms and legs waving. 'He's changed so much in such a short time,' she said, smiling down at him and making him giggle as she tickled his tummy.

'They do change very quickly at this age,' Rachel replied. 'But he's a bonny baby, and he's starting to look more like Gracie – which can only be a blessing considering who his father probably was.'

'I didn't know the father, except from what I read in the newspapers. And although Noel has dark hair, he has his mother's clear blue eyes.' Danuta looked over her shoulder to find that Rachel was watching her with an indulgent smile. 'May I pick him up?'

'Of course. I'll make us some coffee. He's not due a feed for another hour, so we should be able to talk without too much interruption.'

Danuta carried Noel to one of the kitchen chairs and sat down with him on her lap. She made the silly noises that had him chuckling, and marvelled at how solid he felt. He was certainly thriving in Rachel's care.

Rachel placed a Victoria sponge cake on the table and went back for the two cups of coffee. 'I made the cake earlier. It's not one of my best but I felt the need for something sweet, and as I had the ingredients, I thought I'd treat myself.' She cut two generous slices and slid them onto small plates accompanied by pristine linen napkins and delicate bone-handled cake forks.

The heavenly smell of real coffee and the sight of the Victoria sponge had Danuta's mouth watering. She hadn't eaten since the slice of cheese on toast this morning and was ravenous. She tasted the cake. It was delicious, the sponge, jam and cream melting in her mouth in one glorious burst. Unable to stop herself, and keeping Noel's searching little hands away from the loaded cake fork, she tucked in until the last crumb had gone.

'Have you eaten today?' Rachel's expression was almost accusing.

Danuta felt the blush rise up her neck and into her face. 'I had breakfast, but there wasn't time for lunch. That cake was delicious, Rachel,' she added hastily to cover up her embarrassment. 'Better than anything from the bakery.'

'Would you like some more?' She didn't wait for an answer and cut another slice which she plopped onto Danuta's plate.

'You must think me very greedy,' she said, looking longingly at the cake.

'No, I think you're hungry. And that's not good enough, Danuta. You have a demanding job, and you must eat properly to keep yourself fit and able.'

'I do know that,' she protested mildly, unable to resist tucking into the second slice. 'But I forgot to do the shopping yesterday, and also forgot everything was shut today.' She smiled ruefully. 'Luckily that little corner shop was open, so we have supper tonight.'

'Yes, he's very useful, if somewhat lacking in choice. But if you ever need anything again, you are to come to me, Danuta. My cupboards are full, and I will not have you both going hungry.'

'That's very kind, Rachel, and I'm truly humbled by your generosity, but you have already done so much . . .'

'Tsk, tsk, tsk,' Rachel interrupted. 'Enough already with that sort of talk. We are friends. I do not wish you to be humbled or grateful – just sensible when planning your household needs.' She pushed aside her empty plate and leaned her forearms on the table, her hands cupping the mug of coffee. 'But you have come for a reason – and I don't think it's only because you want to cuddle Noel. What's troubling you?'

Noel was getting sleepy, so she moved him on her lap until he was cradled more comfortably in her arms. 'I'm worried about Jacob Kaplin.'

'Ah. Yes. He is a great concern to us too. But he's very stubborn and much too proud to ask for help. I have to find cunning ways to make sure he has groceries and enough coal.'

'I saw him this morning on my rounds. He's not eating despite the fact he has a full larder, and is neglecting himself. Do you do his shopping?'

Rachel shook her head. 'I pay the woman in the downstairs flat next door to him to do that. I've arranged for coal and wood to be delivered regularly and have asked the coalman to fill his coal scuttles when he's passing.'

'Do you think she would be willing to go in each day to cook and clean for him? His hygiene is poor, and he's become terribly thin and unsteady on his feet.'

'Oh dear, I was afraid of that. As to Mrs Hughes doing a daily stint, I'm not sure,' Rachel replied with a frown. 'She works a full shift for Solly in the Camden Road factory, and has a husband and two children to look after. She does his shopping once a week when she does her own, but I doubt she'd have time to do much more.'

'He really needs a closer eye kept on him,' said Danuta. 'I could write a report stating my concerns in the hope he'll get some assistance, but I don't really want to do that. The system is inclined to take over once an alert is put out, and I think he'll see any help from them as intrusive.'

'I agree. It's a great shame there are no vacancies in

the local retirement homes where he can be looked after properly, and he absolutely refuses to go further afield.' She sighed. 'I'll put out a few feelers, Danuta. It's not as if he can't afford to pay for someone to clean the place and do a bit of cooking, and there are plenty out there looking for work. It's just making sure it's the right person. Someone we can trust. He gets very careless at leaving money and bits of his wife's jewellery lying about.'

'Yes, I noticed that.' Danuta sipped the delicious coffee. 'Oh, and the kitchen tap is leaking. It only needs a new washer, I think, but it's probably best to get a plumber in so he can check the rest of the house.'

Rachel grabbed a notebook and pencil from the counter. 'I'll see about that in the morning.' She looked up from the pad, her eyes sad. 'I've rather neglected him, I'm afraid. Having Noel to look after as well as Solly is time-consuming.' She took a deep breath and let it out in a long sigh. 'And I doubt things will get any easier once we start doing battle with the authorities over Noel and Bobby.'

'That was the other thing I wanted to talk to you about,' Danuta said hesitantly. 'Do you think I really will need a solicitor?'

'I'm afraid so. It's very important you have someone on your side to help you understand what is going on when the authorities try to blindside you with jargon and barely understandable rulings with their numerous sub-sections. Believe me, Danuta. A solicitor is vital.'

'I see,' she murmured, her thoughts on Stanislav struggling to fly, their meagre savings, and her own very tightly stretched wages.

Rachel put her hand on her arm. 'Let me worry about paying the solicitor,' she said softly. 'I have a very good friend who happens to be a partner in

Golding, Golding and Meyer – and he owes me several favours.' She grinned cheekily. 'I learnt long ago that it's always useful to have lots of favours to call in when the occasion arises – and Marcus Golding is quite the most charming man. You'll get on with him like a house on fire.'

'I'll never be able to repay you.'

Rachel patted her arm. 'I don't expect you to, and Solly would never forgive me if you lost those children because you couldn't afford a solicitor. Now, no more of that. It's time you woke up Noel to give him his feed.'

8

There were now only two days to go before Gracie's funeral, and it hadn't stopped raining for the past week, which made everything even more depressing for those living in the beachside shacks at Tamarisk Bay, to the point where the family next door had moved back to Bolton to live with the mother-in-law. Frank had tried to shore up the damage and make the place more habitable, but the damp was seeping through the wooden walls, mildew was blossoming on their clothes, black mould stained every nook and cranny, and the roof was beginning to leak under the strain as the gutters struggled to cope.

'It's almost a biblical deluge,' said Stanislav as he stood by the window to watch the rain beating the tamarisk into soggy submission on the chalky bank. 'We'll soon have to build an ark.'

'Biblical or not, we've got to go out in it.' Danuta dodged the bucket catching the drips from the ceiling to pull on her raincoat, tie her headscarf under her chin and reach for the umbrella. 'Are you ready? Only we mustn't be late for our appointment.'

Stanislav reached for his heavy coat and struggled into it before grabbing his crutches. 'I'm not sure about letting Rachel pay for this Marcus Golding. It feels too much like charity.'

'We have no other choice, but we'll find a way to repay her somehow.' Her words sounded confident, but reason told her it would be almost impossible – and she suspected Stanislav knew it. She opened the door, thankful that the steep bank of chalk and sand gave some shelter from the rain which was sweeping across the headland like horizontal stair rods. Opening her umbrella, she waited for him to lock the door and steady himself for the uphill climb.

With their heads down, and chins buried in their scarves, Danuta battled to keep her umbrella from blowing inside out as they made their slow way up the steep slope to Stanislav's car. Especially adapted so it was entirely operated by hand, it was an absolute godsend, for it gave him a sense of independence and normality which he needed at this particular time when everything else was so uncertain.

Stanislav drove into Cliffehaven, turned off to the street behind the Town Hall and parked in the bay designated for the clients of Golding, Golding and Meyer. He looked at the neat brick building with its imposing front door, frosted window glass etched with gold lettering, and the three brass plaques on the wall. 'Expensive,' he sighed.

'I know, but we need him.' Danuta reached for his hand. 'Come on, Stan, if we're to have any chance of adopting those children, we have to do this.' She gripped his fingers. 'You do want us to adopt them, don't you?' she asked fearfully.

'Of course I do,' he replied. 'It just doesn't feel it's the right time, and it's all so rushed, I've barely taken it all in, and what with this . . .' He plucked at his empty trouser leg. 'And where we live . . . I can't bear the thought of you being hurt if it all falls apart, Danuta,' he finished softly.

'We have to at least try, my love. I made a promise to Gracie, and this is the first step. We can't falter now.'

He gave a great sigh, wrestled his crutches from the back seat and struggled to get out of the car. Danuta knew better than to try and help him, so she just sheltered them both with her umbrella and walked beside him to the solicitor's door.

They entered a pleasant, well-lit reception area furnished with comfortable chairs, a dark blue carpet and framed seascapes on the white walls. The smartly dressed young woman behind the desk greeted them warmly and escorted them straight to Marcus's office.

Marcus Golding looked to be in his late fifties. He was of medium height and build, with dark hair and brown eyes, and a face so striking he could have been a matinee idol. Dressed in a tailored pinstriped suit, crisp white shirt and silk tie, he had an air of capability and trustworthiness. His handshake was dry and firm, his smile putting them at ease.

He asked the receptionist to bring coffee, and once everyone was settled, he got straight down to business. 'Mrs Goldman has given me some details of the application you wish to make, but I will need to ask you some quite personal questions first. It's necessary, I'm afraid, if we are to get the groundwork of the case firmly embedded before we go to court.'

The coffee was delivered almost silently on a tray and in bone china cups, and the young woman closed the door behind her with a discreet click.

Marcus reached for a legal pad and a gold pen. 'I will need your full names, your ages, current address, a copy of your birth and marriage certificates, and of course your British citizenship papers.'

Danuta went cold and turned to Stanislav, seeing the same dread in his eyes. 'We have our marriage certificate and British citizenship papers. But we were both born in Poland, and all our family documents were destroyed during the war. Now the Russians have taken over, it would be impossible to search the Warsaw archives for them.'

'I think we can get around that. Let's begin with your full names, birth dates and address.'

As Danuta carefully spelled out their surname, she constantly glanced at Stanislav, who was looking very tense.

Marcus looked up from his neat writing and grinned. 'I won't attempt to pronounce your surname, so would it be all right if I used your first names?'

'It is what most English people do when they see so many consonants together,' said Stanislav, breaking the silence he'd maintained since entering the office. 'But if you break it up it is easy. Kuh vall check.'

Marcus grinned. 'I take your point. Thank you.'

Danuta handed over the large envelope which held their precious papers. 'Our British passports and a copy of Gracie Smith's will is in there too.'

Marcus took time to read everything and then set the papers to one side to make more notes on his pad. 'The will is legal as it was made on Mrs Smith's deathbed and has been witnessed by a doctor and a registrar. As she left nothing of value it will not have to go through probate, but it will have to be registered. Her wishes were made very clear.'

He looked up from his notes. 'I understand from Mrs Goldman that you were her nurse, Danuta.'

'I was called in to her lodgings as the district nurse when she collapsed. The hospital nurses tended her after her operation, but when it was clear she would not recover, I stayed with her until the end. I did not want her to be alone as she was a widow and had no one else but Florence, who was looking after Bobby.'

He nodded and then turned to Stanislav. 'And you are in full employment as a pilot for Phoenix Air Transport?'

At Stan's nod, he made another note and then regarded him evenly. 'I couldn't help but notice you have to use crutches. Is that a temporary thing, or will it affect your ability to continue flying?'

Stan's chin went up. 'It is temporary. I am flying as navigator until I am able to use my other prosthesis again.'

'May I ask how you lost your legs?'

'My plane was hit during a dogfight and crash-landed in Holland in the final months of the war. I came to and discovered that both legs were amputated just above the knee.' Stanislav regarded the other man almost defiantly. 'I regained my full pilot's licence after the surgery. The reason I'm using the crutches is because my stump became irritated. It only needs a rest and then I'll be perfectly fine again.'

'You are to be congratulated on your stoicism and bravery, Stanislav. Our country owes you a great deal.' Marcus turned his attention once more to his notes. 'I see by your address that you live at Tamarisk Bay.' He looked up with a frown. 'I know it well. Is this also temporary?'

'We are looking for a better place, but it's very difficult with so little available,' said Danuta, her voice unsteady through nerves.

'That, I fear, could be the stumbling block to the adoption,' Marcus replied solemnly. 'I know those shacks, and they really aren't suitable for raising small children.'

Danuta's hopes plummeted, and she reached for Stanislav's hand, gripping his fingers until her knuckles turned white. 'We realise that, and Rachel ... Mrs Goldman, has promised to try and help find us somewhere. We've been to every letting agency both in Cliffehaven and the surrounding areas. But of course our work means we cannot move too far away, and so far we have found nothing.'

Marcus nodded, made a note, and then sat back in

his chair. 'I have already obtained the birth certificates and medical records for both children, and also approached the authorities on your behalf. They are very willing to consider your application for adoption. It seems they are overwhelmed by the sheer number of children needing to be placed, which actually might help your cause – as will the fact you are Catholic, as Gracie was. As I've set the ball rolling, and both children are safely fostered, they will stay where they are and not be made wards of court, which would have complicated things considerably.'

'That's a huge relief.' Danuta dared to relax a little, but she still kept Stan's hand tightly clasped.

'It is certainly a step in the right direction.' He smiled the smile that must have had the female population of Cliffehaven swooning but which barely affected Danuta, who was so on edge, she hardly noticed.

'Now, we must go through your financial status. Your earnings, savings and so on. It's important we can show the authorities you can afford to take on two children even though it will probably mean there will only be one income coming in once you, Danuta, give up work to care for them.' He turned to Stanislav. 'Tell me, what happens if the planes are grounded and you cannot fly?'

'We have full pay while we're grounded as there is other work to do at the airfield. If we are sick and cannot work, then we are paid a nominal sum as a retainer, and must rely on our savings or apply for what you call "the dole".'

Danuta saw Marcus frown and handed over their bank statements, tamping down on the nerves so she could speak coherently and defuse his concern. 'As you can see, we have some savings, and I will be able to support us if that should happen,' she said quickly. 'I have discussed my work schedule with Dr Darwin and the others in the Elms Avenue practice, and they have agreed to me going part-time during the school terms, or when Stan is grounded and can look after the children. Mr Goldman has kindly promised to keep a free place in his factory crèche for Noel when I am working.'

'You seem to have thought of everything,' he said, his dark eyes full of understanding. He set aside the bank statements and leaned back in his chair. 'I think I should warn you that you'll both have to take a medical test to prove you are fit and able to look after a baby and a small boy.' He regarded Stanislav. 'Will that pose a problem?'

'I might have two half-legs, but the rest of me is very fit,' he replied confidently. 'My consultant, Sir Julian Carmichael-Blackstock, will confirm this.'

Danuta looked down at their linked fingers and wished her husband wouldn't make such statements when he knew full well that Sir Julian would do no such thing until his stump was much improved.

Marcus appeared to accept Stanislav's declaration and made a note. 'And you, Danuta?'

'I have regular health checks because of my work. I was passed fit at the beginning of December.'

'How well do you know these children? Did either of you meet Bobby before Mrs Smith died? Have you been in regular contact with them since?'

'Neither of us knew the family until I was called in to tend Gracie. Since then, I've got to know Bobby and now visit him almost every day. Stan comes with me if he's not flying, and they have struck up a good rapport. Baby Noel is with Rachel, as you know, and we try to spend time with him when work allows.'

Marcus nodded. 'It's certainly important you forge a relationship with them both, but please be aware that the process of adoption can be quite a long slog, and it will be up to the authorities to decide the outcome – which might not be in your favour.'

He let the warning hang in the air as he regarded them solemnly. 'I know it will be difficult for you, but I do advise you remain aware of this, and try not to let your hearts rule your heads.'

Danuta bit the inside of her cheek as tears welled. Her heart had already been given to those two small boys, and the thought of losing them was unbearable – and yet reason told her that he was offering good advice, and she must heed it. Bobby had already lost his beloved mother – it would be too cruel to let him get to love her and Stan, and then lose them too.

Marcus seemed to read her thoughts. 'It will be tough, Danuta, but this is about what is best for the children.'

'I know,' she managed, her throat tight with unshed tears.

He became businesslike. 'My role will be as an intermediary. You will be called to numerous meetings with the adoption services and the local authority in charge of child welfare to which I shall not be invited, although the reports on those meetings will be forwarded to me so that I can explain the process as we go along and answer any questions you might have. They will want to see where you live and how you interact with the children – and each other – and poke and pry into every corner of your lives.'

He sat forward to emphasise the seriousness of his next words. 'It's vital you're totally honest with them – for if they discover you have kept something back or not been wholly truthful, your application will be immediately dismissed with no hope of ever applying again.' His expression was earnest as he waited for that warning to sink in.

'It's clear to me that you are willing to go to great lengths to secure this adoption, and I will do my very best to make sure that it happens. Once the authorities are satisfied that you fit the criteria, you will go to court, and a judge will sign the official papers.' He smiled to reassure them. 'But we have a long way to go before then, so you must be patient. Are there any questions you want to ask me?'

Danuta and Stan looked at one another and knew there was a legion of doubts over their housing, their finances, the willingness of Phoenix Air Transport to let Stan keep flying, and Stan's health, but silently acknowledging it was better to keep them to themselves for now.

Danuta turned back to Marcus. 'I think you've covered everything.'

'Then I'll get things underway, and if you should have questions, please don't hesitate to ring the office and I'll get back to you. You should receive a letter from the authorities with the date of your first appointment within the next seven days. Please make sure you both keep the appointment, as it will count against you if you don't.'

'What if Stan is flying into Europe and can't make it – or I'm called out to a woman in labour?'

'They will accept a valid reason for not attending, but please don't do it too often. It's really important that both of you attend every meeting.'

He stood to signal the interview was over and they shook hands before making their way back through reception and into the teeming rain.

They slammed the car doors and sat there staring through the streaming windscreen at the blurred reflections of those brass plates. Danuta released the breath she hadn't realised she'd been holding and burst into tears.

'My love, my love, what's the matter?' Stanislav gathered her into his arms. 'It's all right. Everything is all right.'

'But it isn't, is it?' she sobbed. 'We live in a leaking shack; you're struggling with your leg; and we've had to rely on Rachel to pay for a solicitor. What if your leg doesn't get better? What if we never find a decent place to live? What if you can't fly again, and what if . . . ?'

He silenced her with a kiss. 'Enough of this talk,' he murmured. 'You are imagining that everything is against us, but it's not. It might not look like it now, but things will come right for us – and they will, Danuta. Really, they will. I promise you.'

'I don't see how,' she sniffed, mopping fresh tears from her face with a handkerchief. 'From where I'm sitting, it looks utterly hopeless.'

He grasped her by the shoulders and forced her to look at him. 'This is not the Danuta who faced the SS and survived. Not the Danuta who returned time and again to continue her vital work behind enemy lines. Not my Danuta who is so strong and fearless when she has a battle to fight.'

'I don't feel brave or strong, Stan. It was different in the war – we knew our enemy and had the ways and means to defeat him – but this battle is personal and I have no idea what we'll be up against.'

He pulled her close. 'We have Marcus. He knows how to cut his way through the bureaucracy and red tape. We are meant to have those children, Danuta – Gracie wished it so. Something will come up, you'll see.'

'I wish I shared your faith in this vague something,' she replied, shooting him a watery smile. 'But perhaps it wouldn't hurt to do the rounds of the letting agencies again, now we're in town.'

He gave her a hearty kiss before starting the car. 'We will find something today. I just know it,' he declared.

It was almost time to go home when Peggy put down the telephone receiver and smiled with delight. She was still grinning as she poured a cup of tea from her flask and turned to look out of her rain-streaked office window to the building site beyond the factory fencing.

The workmen had gone home and the machinery was lying idle, for the whole churned-up area between the station and the allotments was now a quagmire. The few lines of prefabs that had been erected looked miserable beneath the leaden sky, as did the solitary woman, laden down with shopping, who was trudging her way through the mud to her front door. It was not a day to be outside.

'You're looking cheerful, Peggy.' Florence closed the door behind her and handed over the worksheets.

'I have reason to be cheerful, Florence. Rosie just phoned to tell me the target for the fundraiser has been surpassed, with more money coming in every hour.'

'That is a relief. I was starting to worry I'd have to find the money to pay for it all as I'd signed the agreement with the funeral directors.'

'Well, you no longer have to. Rosie has rung the funeral parlour to give them the go-ahead, and the newspaper editor is sending them a cheque by hand today. There's enough for a decent send-off, with some left over which will be put into a fund for the children.'

Peggy beamed with relief and happiness. 'I knew the people of Cliffehaven would come up trumps.'

'You certainly had more faith in them than I did,' admitted Florence. 'But I'm glad she'll have a proper funeral.' She looked at her wristwatch. 'I'm going to have to pick up Bobby from school in ten minutes. Is there anything you want me to do before I leave?'

'Everything's in hand, thanks. How is Bobby now he's back at school?'

'I had a quiet word with the headmistress, asking her to keep an eye on him. With all the gossip surrounding Gracie, I was worried there could be some name-calling, or bullying – you know how spiteful children can be. But he seems to be less fretful and is sleeping better, so things are a bit easier. I couldn't have lasted much longer with all those sleepless nights.'

'Poor little boy. He's had a lot to contend with.'

'School has been a lifesaver, though. It's given him other things to think about, and all that dashing about with his friends during his break-times means he's tired when he gets home.'

'I hope you don't mind,' said Peggy tentatively, 'but I've had a discreet word with a friend of mine who works in the child welfare office, and she told me you are entitled to an allowance while you foster Bobby.'

Florence's smile quickly faded and her expression turned stony. 'I have no need for charity handouts,' she said stiffly.

'It's not charity, Florence. It's money the government pays to foster parents, and all you have to do is fill in a form.'

'Which will mean some busybody turning up to poke their nose into my business, in which case, I'd rather go without.'

'Florence,' soothed Peggy, 'we both know things are already tight without the extra food and bills incurred by taking the child on. And this money is not for you, but for Bobby, so he can eat well and have new clothes and shoes when he needs them.'

Florence's shoulders stiffened and her chin went up. 'Are you suggesting I'm not feeding him properly?'

Peggy hadn't meant that at all and hurried to smooth her ruffled feathers. 'I'm not saying that and you know it, Florence. Bobby's very lucky you were willing to take him on, and I know you're doing a sterling job. But he's a growing boy who will soon need new shoes and will start to eat you out of house and home.'

She smiled in the hope of coaxing Florence out of her huff. 'I know, because I've brought up my own two – and it's not easy. He's entitled to that money, and you really have no choice but to apply for it.'

Florence stiffened further. 'That's me told, then, isn't it? If there are no more instructions, I'll be off.'

Peggy hurried round the desk and caught her arm as she turned towards the door. 'Come on, Flo. There are times to hang onto your pride, and this isn't one of them. You know very well that I'm only trying to help.'

Florence's shoulders relaxed and she gave a sigh. 'Yes, I do know, Peggy. I just hate the thought of the welfare people getting a foot in the door. I've paid my way from the day I left school and never asked anyone for anything. It simply doesn't feel right.'

'I can understand that, Flo, and I'm sorry if you thought I was interfering.'

Florence met her gaze, her expression softening into a reluctant smile. 'Not interfering, Peggy – just being your usual caring self. But I just wish you'd discussed it with me before talking to anyone.'

'I'm sorry, but it was done with the very best of intentions.'

Florence nodded and then looked at her watch. 'I'm going to be late to pick up Bobby.'

'Of course; just promise me you'll give that allowance some consideration.'

'I'll certainly think about it,' Florence replied, before

leaving the office and closing the door rather too firmly behind her.

'That's torn it,' muttered Peggy, plumping down into her chair to reach for the cup of tea which was now lukewarm. Jim had warned her about meddling when she'd broached the subject of welfare payments with him the previous evening – and he'd been right. What was that old saying about the road to hell being paved with good intentions?

Tutting at her inability to mind her own business, she finished the tea and set about checking the worksheets. Cissy was picking up Daisy from school and giving her a snack to keep her going until teatime, so there was no rush to go out in the rain.

She was just making a note about one of the women who needed time off for medical reasons when she was disturbed by a tap on the door. Looking up, she was astonished to see Doris standing in the doorway.

'I hope you don't mind me intruding during your working hours,' she said, stepping into the room. 'But the weather is so abysmal, I didn't want to stand about outside waiting for you to finish.'

Peggy was still in shock as she got to her feet and took in the sight of her perfectly groomed sister who looked as if she'd just come straight from the beauty parlour. 'Come in and sit by the fire. I hope nothing's wrong. It's not like you to visit me here.'

Doris flapped a handkerchief over the chair and carefully sat down, drawing the hem of her expensive raincoat away from the floor, the leather handbag tightly clasped in both gloved hands on her lap as if she was afraid it might get snatched away. 'I wouldn't dream of it usually,' she said, 'but I felt I simply had to come and apologise.'

Apologise? Good grief, thought Peggy. *Whatever next?*

'I wasn't aware of any need for you to apologise, Doris,' she said carefully.

'Oh, but there is,' she replied. 'I'm afraid I must have given *quite* the wrong impression to you and your distinguished dinner companions on New Year's Eve. You see, I genuinely thought there had been a mix-up over the seating arrangements.'

'I don't understand why you thought that.' She saw Doris pull out her cigarette case and gold lighter and quickly put up a hand to stop her. 'Sorry, Doris, you can't smoke in here.'

Doris's severely plucked eyebrow shot up. 'Why ever not?'

'The place is full of combustible materials, which makes smoking a fire hazard and therefore breaches our insurance cover.'

'But I can see an ashtray over there,' she retorted.

'It's for Solly when he comes in with his cigar. At the end of the day, it's his responsibility to pay the insurance premiums and if he wants to take the risk – well, that's up to him.' She took a breath, intrigued to know why Doris felt the need to apologise. 'You were saying about the table arrangement,' she prompted.

Doris huffily put her cigarettes and lighter back in her handbag. 'It was all most unfortunate, really. You see, I booked that specific table months ago for the party from the Officers' Club, so you can imagine my horror when I discovered we'd been placed right by the kitchens and you were at the table I'd booked.'

Peggy firmly quelled the rising need to giggle. 'Oh dear, well, I'm afraid I had nothing to do with all that. Lord Cliffe booked the table and invited us to join him.'

'Well, of course he had every right to book any table he wanted – especially as he was entertaining the Lord Lieutenant of the County and his wife – but I do think the hotel was remiss in not giving us a better position in the dining room.'

'It sounds to me as if it should be the hotel apologising to you, rather than you to me,' said Peggy dryly.

'I will of course demand an apology and warn them we will never book a party from the Officers' Club again if they can't assure us of a decent table.' She gave a delicate sniff. 'But I do feel I must apologise to you for making things awkward in front of Lord Cliffe and the Ambroses.'

Peggy rather suspected that her sister really wanted to apologise to Lord Cliffe but didn't quite have the courage after they'd snubbed her. But she could be magnanimous in the light of this unusual occurrence. 'Apology accepted.'

'I doubt you'll see either Lord Cliffe or the others any time soon – after all, you hardly move in the same circles – and his invitation that night was most unusual. But should your paths cross, I do hope you'll pass on my sincere apologies.'

'Neither of us move in the same social circle as Lord Cliffe,' Peggy reminded her evenly. 'But I'll certainly pass on your message should I bump into him.'

She glanced at her watch, pushed back from the desk and plucked her coat from the hook on the wall. 'Apologies and table mix-ups aside, Doris, did you enjoy the evening?'

'It was extremely pleasant,' she replied. 'John and I don't often get the chance of dressing up to dance the night away, and I have to say the catering at the County is superb considering the times we're living in.' She got to her feet. 'I meant to ask, Mar . . . Peggy. How on earth did you manage to afford that Balmain gown?'

Peggy paused momentarily in buttoning up her coat. 'Cissy very generously lent it to me. She came home with a suitcase packed with the most gorgeous things. But how did you know it was Balmain?'

'Oh, I recognised it at once,' Doris said airily. 'I remember seeing it in a fashion magazine when Pierre Balmain was launching his first post-war collection two years ago. Still, even second-hand it would have been frightfully expensive. I wonder how Cissy got hold of it.'

Peggy belted her coat and reached for her umbrella. *Always the sharp-tongued cat*, she thought wearily. *She just can't help herself.* 'I really have no idea, Doris. But I have to see everyone off the premises and get home now. Jim will be wanting his tea.'

She tried to get past Doris so she could shut the door, but her sister stood squarely in the way, seemingly determined to continue the conversation and delay her.

'John was asking this morning if you and Cissy might like to come to afternoon tea on Saturday. He quite rightly pointed out that we see so very little of you now that you're working here.'

Peggy very much doubted John had suggested any such thing, or that her daughter would want to step foot in that house again. She had the nasty suspicion Doris was only inviting them because she wanted something – though what that could be, she had no idea.

'I'll have to see what arrangements the family has made for the weekend,' she hedged, nudging Doris out of the way so she could lock the office door.

But Doris was not to be shifted that easily. 'Do try and come, and bring Jim and Daisy too. I have a box of toys I keep for when my grandchildren stay, and I know John does enjoy Jim's company.' She hesitated for a beat. 'And perhaps Cissy could bring some of the clothes you mentioned?' she said casually. 'We could have so much fun trying them on.'

So, that's your game, Peggy thought crossly. 'I'll let you know about Saturday once the funeral is over and I have more idea of what the family are doing,' she said coolly.

Catching sight of one of the machinists trying to get her attention, she nodded in acknowledgement and then turned back to her sister. 'Sorry, but it looks as if Mrs Rayner needs to speak to me. I'll ring after the funeral.'

Doris regarded her sourly for a long moment and then turned on her heel and marched towards the door.

Peggy tamped down on her annoyance with her sister and headed towards Alice Rayner. 'What's the matter, Alice?'

'Sorry to bother you, Mrs Reilly, but the others have asked me to speak to you about Gracie's funeral.'

'I put all the details on the noticeboard, Alice. What's the problem?'

She dug her hands into her overalls pocket, looking decidedly awkward. 'Not a problem as such. We know the factory can't close for the morning, so we've had a bit of a meeting and five of us will be representing Gracie's workmates on the day. We had a whip-round for a wreath, but . . . Well, we were wondering if there would be a wake?' she finished in a rush.

'Mr Goldman, Miss Hillier and I talked about that, Alice, and came to the conclusion that with all the publicity – and the likelihood of a big turn-out of people who probably don't even know Gracie, and just turn up to pry – it would be best not to do one.'

'Oh, that's a shame,' she sighed. 'Gracie loved a good knees-up.'

'There's nothing to stop you and the others meeting to remember Gracie and raising a glass or two. But I would urge you to keep it quiet and respectful. There's been enough gossip already, and we have to think of the children.'

Alice nodded solemnly. 'Of course. I'll tell the others.'

Peggy watched her bustle off to relay this to her workmates, and then glanced up at the clock. The day's shift was over, and the women were already collecting their things to clock off and get home. It had been a long day, but it warmed her heart that these hard-working women had cared enough for Gracie to club together and buy a wreath, and to want to attend her funeral. It was a shame about the absence of a wake, but the publicity had added an uncertainty to the proceedings; catering would be costly, and there was the possibility of trouble should a drunken wake get out of hand.

Dispirited, Danuta and Stanislav hurried through the rain to the car. They'd found nothing suitable, and even the agent had gloomily admitted that the three places they had seen were the dregs of the barrel. The single squalid rooms in the overcrowded tenement houses had only a gas cooker and sink, no bathroom and an outside lav in back yards so littered with rubbish they were a prime breeding ground for vermin.

'Even our place is better than that,' said Danuta on a sigh. 'You'll have to speak to Frank and get him to do more repairs to the roof and guttering. At least then we won't have to have buckets all over the house catching the drips.' She grimaced. 'Even our clothes smell musty, and it's almost impossible to get the washing dry.'

'We'll just have to persevere,' he replied. 'At least we have a roof over our heads, even if it is leaking.' He turned the key in the ignition. 'Bobby will be out of school now, so let's go and see him. I found a good storybook he'd like in that second-hand shop and managed to get a small bag of jelly babies too.'

Stanislav's eagerness to get to know Bobby warmed her heart, and despite the disappointment in not finding better accommodation, and the continuous downpour, her spirits lightened. 'Perhaps after that we could drop into Rachel's on the way home? You've only seen Noel once, and it's important you get to know him too.'

He let the engine idle and looked out at the rain gathering in deep puddles. 'If you want. But he is too young to know or care who we are, and I think we'd unsettle him.'

'Nonsense,' she said rather sharply. 'He might be very young, but if we are regular visitors, he'll soon recognise us by our voices and how we handle him. Besides, he's Bobby's little brother, and if we are allowed to keep them, you'll need to get to know him.'

He raised his hands in defeat. 'Whatever you say, Danuta. But I have no idea how to handle babies, and I'm worried I'll drop him or do something wrong to make him cry. You're the expert, so it's probably for the best if I keep my distance.'

She regarded him for a moment and then giggled. 'Don't tell me you're frightened of the baby.'

'Of course not,' he blustered. 'It's just that Bobby is easier to understand. I was a boy once and can remember how I was at that age, so it is easy.'

'You were a baby too,' she reminded him gently. 'Though it's hard to believe it now,' she added, eyeing his huge frame. 'But Noel isn't made out of glass, Stan. In fact, he's now quite sturdy and beginning to take an interest in things. I think you'll find he's far easier to handle than he was at first.'

Stanislav grunted and drove out of the parking bay. 'What's for supper? I'm starving.'

'I'm doing rice with steamed chicken and vegetables, and there's jelly and custard for pudding.' She grinned at his dour expression. 'You're doing really well on your diet, Stan; another couple of pounds and you will have lost over half a stone.'

'At this rate I'll fade away to nothing,' he grumbled.

Weighing in at almost fourteen stone, she doubted that very much, but she made no comment. He might grumble at what he saw as starvation rations, but he was doing very well, and because he'd stopped drinking, the weight was coming off quite rapidly. His stump was improving too now it was free of the prosthesis, and she could only hope that his consultant wouldn't be persuaded to let him have it back too soon and undo all the good work.

Peggy parked outside Beach View and eyed the flatbed truck already there. It was unusual for Frank to call in now his father had his own house in Havelock Road, and she could only hope his visit didn't mean there was some kind of trouble awaiting her indoors.

Running through the rain to the front door, she quickly got into the house and shook out her raincoat and scarf, plopped the brolly into the stand at the bottom of the stairs and went into the kitchen.

Frank was sitting next to his brother Jim at the table, his large hands cupping a mug of tea as Daisy chattered to him about her day at school, and Cissy stirred something on the stove. There was no sign of Cordelia, but then she remembered Bertie was taking her out to the Lilac Tearooms for a treat.

Frank got to his feet. 'Hello, Peg. Sorry to drop in like this, but I needed a word with you and Jim.'

'Why, what's happened?'

He plumped down in the kitchen chair. 'It's my place out at Tamarisk Bay,' he said gloomily. 'The whole terrace is leaking. My roof is about to collapse under the weight of this rain, and there's mould growing everywhere. It's got so bad that one of my tenant families has already left.'

'But what do you expect me and Jim to do about it, Frank? Your dad warned you that a lick of paint and a bit of repair work wouldn't be enough to see them through a bad winter.'

'I didn't have time to knock it all down and start again,' Frank explained, 'because I needed the rents to boost my income when the council upped the cost of our licences to moor our boats on Cliffehaven beach and sell from our stall.'

He gave a deep sigh. 'Now, it seems, someone has made a complaint and really dropped me in it. I had a visit this afternoon from some pompous ass on the local housing committee, who poked and pried about and then had the audacity to declare that if I didn't do an immediate and full refurbishment, they would condemn the whole lot as uninhabitable.'

'You can't be surprised, Frank,' said Jim in reasonable tones. 'Those shacks have been falling down around your ears since we were boys. But I wonder who complained to the council? That was pretty low.'

'I'm sure it wasn't Danuta,' said Peggy, quickly defensive. 'She and Stanislav are glad to have a roof over their heads, and they certainly wouldn't want the place condemned as they're trying to adopt Gracie's children.'

'I suspect it was that know-all Barclay who was renting the end one and then did a flit last night with rent still owing.' Frank's expression was grim. 'He was forever moaning and telling me what to do – going on about his friends on the council. He forgot he and his family were homeless when I let them have that place. He was grateful enough then,' he finished bitterly.

Jim squeezed his older brother's shoulder in

sympathy. 'Whoever it was, it's too late to bother about it now. So what are you going to do, Frank?'

'What can I do, Jim? The man was right. The place is falling apart and I feel awful that Danuta and Stan are living in such conditions, but with all this rain coming down day after day, it's impossible to make any repairs – and yet the longer I leave it, the worse it gets.'

He took a deep breath. 'The only thing I can suggest is to get it condemned. At least then, the council will be forced to find Danuta and Stan alternative accommodation – and I have that straight from the pompous ass.'

'That's all very well,' said Peggy, 'but there isn't any alternative to be had. I know for a fact they've been trying to find somewhere, and all that's on offer is just as bad – if not worse – than what they already have.'

Frank shrugged his broad shoulders. 'It's out of my hands, Peg. Until this rain stops, I can't do repairs, and the rest of the month is going to be just as grim as they're forecasting high winds and heavy snow.'

'If the council can't find anywhere suitable for Stan and Danuta, then they must come here,' said Peggy. 'In fact, if the conditions really are as bad as you say, they should move in tomorrow. But what about you, Frank? Where will you go?'

'I've asked Dad and Rosie if I can move in with them until the weather improves and I can get on with pulling the whole place down and starting again. Dad's agreed and has even offered to help with the building work, but he's getting too old really for that sort of heavy labour. Just doing up that house in Havelock Road nearly poleaxed him.'

'I wouldn't let Dad hear you say that,' said Jim with a wry smile. 'He still thinks he's twenty and as fit as a butcher's dog.'

The two brothers grinned at one another. 'Aye,' said Frank. 'The auld fella's tough, but rebuilding those shacks would be a step too far.'

'Can you actually afford to rebuild the whole place, Frank?' asked Jim. 'It'll cost a pretty penny and the price of materials has gone through the roof.'

'The fishing has been good, the sales to the shops and on the beach are getting better by the month, and I have a fair bit put away. As long as I can keep fishing, and the powers that be grant me planning permission, the rebuild will be finished by the end of the summer.'

'I don't see how they can refuse you, Frank,' said Jim. 'Dad bought the freehold of that land and those buildings from the council when they decided they had no use for it. It's prime position too, and they're encouraging new building works at the moment – which is why half the town is covered in scaffolding.'

Peggy stepped in. 'Have you told Danuta about all this, Frank?'

He shook his head. 'They've been out all day, so I haven't had the chance. To be honest, I was quite glad they weren't there, because I'm dreading telling them.'

'It won't be so bad now you know me and Peg are happy to take them in,' said Jim comfortably. 'For Danuta, it will be like coming home after the years she lived here during the war.' He reached over and grasped Peggy's hand. 'Home to her Mama Peggy who will no doubt spoil her rotten,' he teased.

'She deserves to be spoilt – they both do,' she retorted. She turned to Frank. 'Stay and have tea with us, and then go and tell them they can move in as soon as they like.'

Frank's handsome face creased into a smile that made his blue eyes twinkle. 'Thanks, Peg. I knew you'd have an answer.'

9

Danuta was doing the washing-up after their meal when they heard the heavy knock on the door. She glanced at Stanislav with a frown, for they rarely had visitors and it was now almost nine o'clock – far too late for anyone to drive all the way down here.

'Stay there,' Stanislav ordered as he hauled himself out of the kitchen chair, grabbed his crutches and went to see who it was.

Danuta nervously edged away from the sink, very aware of how isolated they were, and how dark the night was.

'Frank! Come in, come in,' boomed Stanislav. 'I cannot offer you vodka, I'm afraid – my Danuta has forbidden it in the house – but there is tea or cocoa.'

Frank's deep voice replied and Danuta breathed a sigh of relief, whipping off her apron and drying her hands to welcome him.

Frank Reilly came into the room, his sheer size making her kitchen feel smaller than ever, but as the two men manoeuvred around the tight space to sit at the table, she sensed Frank's unease and had a nasty feeling this was no social call. 'Hello, Frank,' she managed. 'Is there something we can do for you?'

'It's more a case of what I can do for you two,' he replied, dragging off his sodden cap to reveal a mop of thick, silvery hair. 'I had a visit today from some know-all from the council – and it's not good news, I'm afraid.'

As Frank went on to tell them the outcome of that visit, they grew ever more concerned, and sat hand in hand getting tenser by the minute.

'I have it on good authority that the council will be forced to rehouse you if this place is condemned,' he said. 'But there is a long waiting list for housing, and you could be sent anywhere as a stopgap before you're offered anything half-decent. And that could take months with the way things are at the moment.'

He shot them a hopeful smile. 'However, it needn't come to that as Peggy and Jim have invited you to live with them. In fact, they insist upon it, and Peggy suggests you move in tomorrow.'

'Oh, darling Mama Peggy,' breathed Danuta. 'How can we ever thank her enough?'

'But if we move into Beach View, won't that stop the council from finding a permanent place for us?' asked Stanislav.

Frank slowly lifted his shoulders and lowered them with a deep sigh. 'I have no idea how councillors' minds work,' he replied. 'But you could have a point there, Stan.' He chewed his lip as he gave it some thought. 'Perhaps we should get Dad's Rosie onto it? She'll fight your corner.'

Stanislav nodded. 'Yes, she is on the council. She will know what is for the best, and perhaps help us to get somewhere of our own. Peggy and Jim are very generous and kind, but if we are to adopt the little ones, then we cannot risk losing our place on the housing list.'

'Whatever you decide to do, you'll have to be out of here within ten days,' said Frank. 'That's how long they've given me to do the most urgent repairs – and there is no way of achieving even that in this weather. Besides, heavy snow and gale-force winds are forecast, which will make living here even more difficult.'

'I see the Barclays next door have already left,' said Danuta. 'Did they know this would happen?'

'I think it was him who sent the councillor round to cause all this trouble – but there's not much I can do about it now, as he's long gone, and still owes me a month's rent.'

'Our rent is due next week,' murmured Danuta.

'I shan't ask you for it in the circumstances,' he replied. 'I'm just so very sorry I've dumped this on you both. You work so hard, and really don't deserve it. But then you shouldn't have to live like this.' His gaze drifted to the two buckets which were collecting the water that dripped from the roof. 'I've tried my best to keep this place habitable, but I'm at sea so much, there never seems to be enough time.'

Danuta left the table to pour some milk into a pan and stir in cocoa powder as it heated through. Her thoughts were in a whirl, her anxiety high. With only ten days to decide what to do, she and Stan were in an almost impossible position. To be evicted from here and be at the mercy of the council who might rehouse them in some hovel like the ones they'd seen today was her worst fear. But if they moved in with Peggy, they could very easily lose their place on the housing list – and their savings might not be enough to persuade a bank to give them a mortgage so they could buy somewhere. There seemed to be no easy solution.

'Dad and I will help to move your furniture,' said Frank into the uneasy silence which had fallen in the room. 'My truck is big enough for that large bed, and we can do several trips.'

Danuta put the steaming mugs of cocoa on the table. 'We don't have much; just the bedroom furniture, two easy chairs and this table and chairs, but if we move in with Peggy everything will have to be put into storage, and that will cost.'

'I'll ask Dad if you can use his garage. It's weather-proofed and dry and he rarely uses it for the car anyway.' He smiled warmly at her, clearly trying to ease her worries. 'I can keep an eye on it too, as I'll be living there until I can rebuild this place.'

'That's very kind of you, Frank. But what about all your stuff?'

'I've arranged to store it up at Jack Smith's place. That bungalow of his has a big double garage.'

'Are you sure Ron won't mind?'

'Of course he won't mind. He thinks the world of you, Danuta.'

She dipped her chin to hide her blushes and took a sip of the cocoa. Stanislav had said that something would happen today, but neither of them had expected this upheaval, and she feared for what the future might hold now they were about to become homeless.

'They're in an impossible situation,' said Rosie from the fireside chair as she gently stroked the kittens which were curled together on her lap. 'I'm not on the housing committee, so I really don't know what I can do to help.'

'But I'm right in thinking they won't get help from the council if they move in with our Peggy and Jim?' rumbled Ron who was enjoying a last pipe before bedtime.

Rosie bit her lip. 'I suspect that will be the case. There are too many families already in dire straits, and as they don't yet have children, they'll be a very low priority.'

'It's been quite a night all round,' sighed Ron. 'I know why Frank rushed into renting those places out, but it was never going to end well.' He puffed on his pipe, his gaze on some distant place far from the cosy sitting room. 'It'll seem strange to see Tamarisk Bay without those shacks,' he said wistfully. 'They're a part of our family history, and the memories of my younger years are woven into their very fabric.'

'You're getting maudlin,' she teased. 'Our memories are always rose-tinted, but unfortunately, today's reality is rather more sobering. The fabric is failing, the roof is coming down and soon they'll be no more than a pile of firewood. Tamarisk Bay will be vastly improved once Frank builds something sturdy and smart to withstand the weather.'

'Aye, I know you're right, Rosie, but those old walls were witness to our lives. My parents lived and died there; I learnt my lessons at the kitchen table and courted Mary who lived next door; my boys were born there, and the three of us left its shelter to fight a war.' He paused to stare into the fire. 'We were amongst the lucky ones who made it home, and after that, Frank settled there with Pauline to raise their boys. That house saw laughter and tears and deep mourning, but it was our mainstay.'

Rosie rolled her eyes. 'You really are laying it on rather thick, Ron. I seem to remember you saying how cold and damp it always was – and how isolated. Your sister certainly didn't stick it for very long, did she? I remember you telling me that the minute she felt she was old enough, she took off with that chap from the farm. What *was* his name?'

'Jack Chisolm,' he muttered with a grimace. 'And Roisin was barely fifteen; not old enough by half to get entangled with anyone, least of all that ne'er-do-well.'

'You were only a couple of years older when you married Mary,' she reminded him. 'And if things were as tough as you've always made out, you can't blame Roisin for running off in the hope of a better life.' She regarded him thoughtfully. 'Do you ever wonder where she is now and what happened to her?'

Ron knocked the dottle from his pipe into the fire and got to his feet. 'She was my younger sister, so of course I thought of her over the years. But she knew where I was if she needed me, so in the absence of any contact, I have to believe she's come to no harm. As to where she went, I have no idea. Now, I'm for me bed. It's going to be a long day tomorrow.'

'I'll be at Gracie's funeral in the morning and then have a council meeting in the afternoon. What are you up to?'

'Clearing out my garage to store all Danuta's stuff, so it will probably mean several trips to the tip.' He raised a brow. 'Why are you going to the funeral? I didn't realise you knew Gracie.'

'I didn't, but I thought I should be there to represent the local council as the mayor, and the majority of the other councillors have refused to be involved.' She gave a derisive sniff. 'They feel their reputations might be tainted if they're seen to be supporting a girl who abandoned her baby. Pompous asses.'

Ron grinned, gathered up the sleeping kittens and kissed her cheek. 'You're a good woman, Rosie Reilly, and don't let anyone say otherwise.'

'They wouldn't dare,' she giggled. 'Not with you as my knight in shining armour.'

There was no discernible horizon as the sea and sky melted into a gunmetal grey on the morning of Gracie's funeral. A damp mist enveloped the surrounding hills and trailed cold tendrils over the rooftops and smoking chimneys of the town. The atmosphere was made eerier still by the deep, regular moans of the lightship foghorn.

Peggy looked out of Beach View's sitting-room window and regarded the miserable day which seemed to echo her mood. She had rung Danuta earlier to urge her to move in as soon as possible, but although the girl had been very grateful, she was understandably worried that Peggy's act of kindness would hinder any help from the council. They had come to an agreement that Danuta and Stan would stay where they were for now, but use Beach View as a warm, dry refuge and somewhere to do her washing and have a proper bath.

Peggy gave a deep sigh. Such things were the basics of decent living, and to think the pair of them had struggled for so long without them made her feel not only guilty, but depressed. She should have done something sooner.

With a final glance out of the window to the drifting fog, she turned away and headed back to the kitchen where the usual morning chaos greeted her.

Jim was hunting about for his car keys; Daisy's piping voice continued unabated as she dripped jam from her toast onto her school jumper; Charlie was wrestling to pack his sports kit – still damp from the machine – into his already bulging school bag, and Cordelia had spread the newspaper over the table so she could read the obituaries, thereby knocking over her cup of tea.

Cissy looked across at her mother as she mopped up the spilt tea. 'Is it always like this?' she asked in exasperation.

'I'm afraid it is now everyone's back to work and school.' Peggy spotted Jim's keys on the mantel above the range and handed them over before reaching for a cloth to try and get the jam off Daisy's sweater without leaving a stain.

'I'll be off then,' said Jim, donning his coat and hat before planting a kiss on Peggy's cheek. 'I hope it goes well today.'

'So do I,' Peggy replied, turning her attention to the

jumper once he'd left the room. 'Daisy, you'll have to start wearing a bib again if you can't be more careful.'

Daisy glared at her. 'I'm not a baby,' she retorted. 'Don't want a bib.'

'I'm off too before Daisy throws a tantrum,' said Charlie, hoisting the heavy bag over his shoulder. 'There's rugby practice tonight, so I'll be late home.'

Peggy handed him the packet of sandwiches she'd made earlier. 'Make sure you eat them,' she ordered. 'And don't miss that last bus. Your father is not coming out to fetch you after a long day at work.'

'All right, all right,' he muttered. Charlie stuffed the packet in his coat pocket and slammed his way out of the kitchen to thud down the basement steps and crash through the back door. Peggy and Cissy rolled their eyes at one another before continuing to clean up.

Once the table had been cleared and the tea-stained tablecloth rinsed through and dumped into the washing machine, order was once more restored. Cordelia took her newspaper to the fireside chair and settled there for the morning with a blanket over her knees and a hot-water bottle to ease her arthritic hands.

'You'd better have my car for the day, Cissy, but you'll need to top up the petrol at Jack's – he's cheaper than the other one.' Peggy had finally sat down for a cup of tea and a well-earned fag. 'As Florence will be absent, I'm needed at the factory and won't be able to go to the funeral. I suggest you drop Daisy off at school and me at the factory before driving Sandra to the church. Danuta and Stan are taking Florence, and of course the Goldmans will make their own way.'

'Isn't Grandma Cordy going?'

Peggy shook her head. 'She didn't know Gracie, but Bertie has decided to represent them both, and will drive there.'

'Will Florence bring Bobby to the service, do you think?'

'I doubt it. He's far too young to understand what's happening today, and will be better off at school.'

Cissy nodded. 'I suppose it's for the best, but he'll surely realise something's going on. The parents at the school gates will be full of gossip, which he's bound to overhear.' She gave a sigh. 'I still haven't really taken in the fact that Gracie's gone, and I feel so guilty at not going to see her when I first came home.'

Peggy reached for her hand. 'You had a lot on your mind, darling; please don't feel guilty. I'm sure Gracie would have understood.'

'That's the trouble, though, isn't it? We'll never know.'

Florence held Bobby's hand as they walked the short distance to the school. She was still in two minds as to whether or not she should take him to the funeral. Her friend Beatrice had advised against it, but the child was already sensing that something was happening today, and was becoming difficult. There had been a wrangle over him finishing his breakfast, and he'd been reluctant to leave the house; now he was dragging on her arm and scuffing the toes of his shoes on the pavement.

She reached the school gates and warily regarded the huddle of women who were deep in conversation now their children had abandoned them to race into the playground. As one by one they stopped talking and turned to regard them both, she was relieved to see sympathy in the majority of those faces. Murmuring a good morning to them, she bent to straighten Bobby's cap and give him a hug.

'Poor little kid,' murmured one woman.

'Yeah, it's the kids what I'm sorry for,' said another. 'It ain't right what she done.'

'Good morning, ladies,' said Peggy, striding into the circle that was now surrounding Florence and Bobby. 'There's been enough chit-chat, don't you agree? And I really don't think this little one needs to hear it.' She smiled down at him and held out her hand. 'Daisy's waiting for you in the playground, Bobby. Let's go and find her, shall we?'

Florence gratefully nodded her agreement and encouraged the child on his way. She didn't linger once she saw he was happily playing with Daisy, for she was unwilling to be the centre of attention for the gossips, whatever their opinions on Gracie. She quickly walked towards home to prepare for what she suspected would be a difficult and very sad day.

Danuta was determined to keep her spirits up, despite the grim day ahead, and had packed the majority of their clothes into suitcases and stored them in the boot of the car. To her shame, most of it stank of damp and mould, so would have to be thoroughly washed and aired once they were at Beach View.

However, that was the least of her problems. Today would be hard enough to get through without the fog and the worry about where they would be sleeping in ten days' time, but Stanislav needed careful watching. His mood had plummeted after Frank's visit, and if there had been alcohol in the house, he would no doubt have drunk himself into a stupor. As it was, he was like a bear with a sore head, growling his way around the shack, cursing his inability to provide a proper home, getting impatient with everything – especially the buckets catching the drips which he kept knocking against.

'Are you almost ready? Only the fog's quite thick,

and it could take longer than usual to get to Florence's.'

'As ready as I'll ever be,' he grumbled. 'This shirt smells damp and I've cut myself shaving.'

She ignored the moaning and carefully adjusted her dark blue hat before pulling on the standard-issue grey gabardine mac over her plain navy dress. She did possess an overcoat which Stan had given her for Christmas, but it was dark red and not at all appropriate for a funeral. Reaching for her good leather gloves and black handbag, she shot him a smile of encouragement. 'The cut has stopped bleeding, so you can take that bit of tissue off now.'

He gingerly obeyed her, eyed his reflection in the fly-spotted mirror and grunted. 'Everything is so damp that even my moustache is drooping.' He glanced at Danuta, realised she was laughing at his vanity and grinned. 'We'd better go, my little one. I am sorry things are so bad, but I will make them better. I promise.'

Danuta smiled to encourage this attempt to bring a lighter mood to the proceedings, even though she doubted Stan could do very much to rescue them from this latest disaster. Locking the door behind them, they trudged slowly up the slope into the fog that silently and eerily drifted and cleared, drifted and cleared as a cold wind from the sea gathered strength, and the lightship's horn continued to moan.

The drive into Cliffehaven was easier than they expected, so they were in good time to pick up Florence and then wait at the kerb outside the undertakers, ready to follow the hearse. Florence was pale-faced and very quiet in the back seat, clearly reluctant to make small talk, so after a short discussion about Bobby, they sat in silence as the minutes ticked away.

The Goldmans' sleek car drew up behind them just

as the double gates opened and the long nose of the shining black hearse appeared. The polished oak coffin was almost buried in wreaths and bunches of flowers, which gladdened Danuta's heart. As they matched the hearse's dignified progress towards the ancient church of St Cuthbert's, she saw people standing at their gates or on the pavements to doff their hats or bow their heads in farewell. Moved by this show of unity from the people of Cliffehaven, Danuta determinedly held back her tears.

St Cuthbert's was perched on the side of a hill, protected from the wind on two sides by tall yew trees which were rumoured to have been planted over 900 years before. The ancient church had a Saxon tower and a Norman nave and chancel which had survived the Reformation. The peg-tiled roof sheltered the much-repaired flint walls and the precious surviving stained-glass windows. The undulating grounds of the cemetery surrounded the church and, on clearer days than this, offered a stunning view of the English Channel.

Danuta gasped as she saw the vast crowd gathered by the gate and spreading through the churchyard. There were even men with cameras, who she suspected must be from the press, and it seemed to her that there was an air of expectation, even excitement amongst them all as they leaned and stretched and jostled to peer into the hearse at the coffin, and then into the cars that were following.

The vigorous and handsome Father Finlay was waiting in the church doorway, the fringed edges of his purple stole fluttering, his long black robe and white vestment billowing in the wind to reveal a pair of well-worn army-issue boots polished to a shine.

The hearse came to a gentle halt, and those that had followed quickly parked their cars and made their way through the mass of people to the gate and then down the uneven brick path to the church.

Danuta watched Stanislav struggle to keep his balance on the pathway and tensed, ready to catch him should he stumble. Solly Goldman seemed to realise her concern, and quickly moved to his other side as Rachel, Rosie, Cissy, Sandra and Florence followed. Gloria and her sister Beryl joined them as they hurried into the packed church to sit in the reserved front pews and wait for the service to begin. They all noticed that the five girls from the factory who'd been closest to Gracie were already seated and respectfully sober in their Sunday best.

Quiet organ music played over the hushed voices, the fidgeting of feet and rustle of prayer book pages being turned. And then silence fell as the first solemn toll of the ancient bell announced Gracie's entrance. Everyone stood to watch the coffin being carefully carried down the stone-flagged aisle to be placed on the bier at the foot of the altar steps, the many floral tributes placed on and around it.

'The grace and peace of God our Father, who raised Jesus from the dead, be always with you.' Father Finley's rich baritone voice rang out to accompany the tolling bell as he sprinkled holy water over the coffin.

'And with you,' the congregation replied.

As the requiem mass continued in the customary Latin, Danuta gained comfort in Stanislav's close presence, for although she'd been raised a Catholic and had been married in this very church, her faith in a loving, all-seeing, forgiving God had been erased by what she'd witnessed and endured during the war. Now she felt like an intruder, uncomfortable with the once familiar words, the incense and holy water and especially the candles that flickered on the statue of a blue-robed Mary, and the tortured figure of Jesus on the gold cross above the altar.

And yet, she reminded herself, she was here for Gracie, to witness and fulfil her dearest wish to be buried here, and to listen to the moving eulogies from Florence and those who'd known her far better than she ever had. However, she and Gracie had forged a strong bond during those last awful days before she'd slipped away – and that bond had been strengthened by the love Danuta now felt for her precious children.

She must never lose sight of that, she thought, as the service came to an end and they began the slow procession out of the church to the shorter service of interment. No matter what lay ahead, she silently vowed, she would fight with every ounce of her being to keep her promise to Gracie, and be a mother to her little ones.

The fog had cleared, but the wind was now coming from the east, and it cut through the thickest of clothing as they gathered at the graveside. Father Finlay conducted the service with reverence and solemnity, his melodious voice holding them in thrall as he promised Gracie eternal rest with God.

When the last handful of earth had been sprinkled and the final muttered prayer was whipped away by the wind, the crowd began to slowly disperse until there were only a few left by the graveside to ponder on the inevitability of death, and the awful realisation that it didn't always come to those who'd lived long lives, but could strike at any time.

Danuta's thoughts turned to her stillborn baby who was lying beside her brother Aleksy in this very graveyard – and to her lover, Jean, who'd been betrayed to the Nazis and executed by a firing squad. She had no idea where he'd been buried and would probably never know, but she would always keep him in her heart – as she would the rest of her family – gone but never forgotten.

She looked up at Stan, and from his expression, she knew that he too was thinking of his lost family, and all the young men he'd known who'd been killed in serving this country. She reached for his hand, and together they silently acknowledged the departed.

'Are you all right, you lot?' Cissy asked, pushing between Danuta and Florence to link arms.

Drawing back from her dark thoughts, Danuta firmly sniffed back her tears and nudged both women into slowly following Stanislav who was moving awkwardly towards the path. 'I'm fine, really. It's just so sad to lose someone as young as Gracie. Don't you agree, Florence?'

The other woman nodded but was clearly still affected by the moving service and not in the mood to talk.

Cissy filled the silence. 'Sandra and I knew her from when we were both very young, and we still can't believe she's gone. But Father Finlay was just the right man to do the service – and the funeral directors did a smashing job considering they didn't know if they were going to get paid.'

'I think the whole thing went off really well,' said Rosie as she joined them. 'Though I did see the reporters with their cameras, so no doubt the local paper will be making the most of it. But I suppose you can't really blame the editor; he did after all manage to raise a very healthy sum for all this, and more besides. If it's invested wisely, those children will have a nice little nest egg when they come of age.'

Danuta kept her arm linked with Florence's and an eye on Stan's progress over the rough grass until they reached the even more treacherous path. They shook hands with the priest and exchanged short pleasantries before the cold wind defeated them all, and he went back inside while they headed for the cars.

Gloria was waiting by their car looking quite splendid in a black coat with a fake white fox fur collar, huge-brimmed black hat adorned with feathers and rather too much make-up. 'I thought you was never coming,' she grumbled, holding the collar up to her chin and trying not to set it alight with the cigarette stuck in her mouth. 'But now you are here, I want to tell you I'm splashing out on a bit of a wake back at the Crown for the factory girls and Gracie's mates. You're welcome to join us.'

Danuta couldn't think of anything she'd like less and noticed that Stan had slunk away to climb into the car. 'That is very kind,' she said politely, 'but we must get home.'

'Sandra's coming back to mine if that's all right, Gloria,' said Cissy firmly.

'I will be needed at work before I have to collect Bobby from school, but thank you for asking,' said an ashen-faced Florence rather stiffly.

'Fair enough. I just thought I'd mention it. Cheerio then.' She staggered off down the gravelled parking area in her very high heels, swiftly followed by her sister Beryl, and climbed into a waiting taxi.

Rosie chuckled. 'That could turn into a rowdy affair,' she murmured. 'But I hope none of you are really going home or to work, because I've given a few bob to Ruby to lay on a little something upstairs at the Anchor – very discreet, and for just a select few.'

'That sounds ideal,' said Cissy, looking round at the few people still milling around. 'Would it be all right if I invited Bertie to join us? Only he's looking a bit lost without Cordelia.'

'But of course,' Rosie exclaimed. 'You and Sandra

round him up, and if Cordelia is up to it, perhaps you could dig her out of Beach View for the afternoon.'

'Well, I'll try, but she's not been too keen on going anywhere just lately.'

'I really should go to work,' said Florence, who'd finally emerged from her grief and now looked torn between duty and the chance of pleasant company. 'Peggy's having to manage on her own and . . .'

'Peggy is quite capable of running that place single-handed,' said Rosie firmly. 'Please come and have at least one drink with us to Gracie's memory.'

'All right,' she replied. 'But just the one. I really do need to relieve Peggy at some point before I have to pick up Bobby.'

Rosie grinned in delight. 'That's more like it.'

Danuta looked over at Stanislav who was listening to their conversation from the car's open window. From his expression, she realised that he too was just as reluctant to go back to Tamarisk Bay to face the damp and cold – and it was far too early to descend on Beach View with their washing. 'We'd love to come, but first I want to say goodbye to Rachel and Solly.'

She left Florence with Stanislav and just caught the Goldmans as they were about to climb into their car. 'Gracie would really have appreciated you coming to the service,' she said, grasping Rachel's hand. 'I know you're of different faiths, but at times like these, it doesn't seem to matter, does it?'

'Our thinking exactly,' said Solly, removing the yarmulke he'd donned during the service as a sign of respect. 'And it was interesting to see how things are done in the Catholic Church.'

'I do like your Father Finlay,' said Rachel. 'He could read out the dictionary with that voice and keep me utterly bewitched. Such a great pity your church doesn't allow priests to marry – it seems a terrible waste of a very fine man.'

'Now, Rachel, my dear, you mustn't get carried away. He's a man of God, and you should show more respect.'

Rachel slapped him playfully on the arm. '*Oy vey*, Solomon Goldman, can you not let a girl get a little carried away by a handsome face and thrilling voice to brighten a sad day?'

Solly grinned. 'I've no doubt he's handsome and thrilling, my dove, but please remember you are in your sixties, and old enough to be his mother.'

'Gosh, you really know how to make a girl feel old, don't you?' she pouted, jabbing him playfully in his rather large stomach.

Danuta tried not to giggle at their antics, but gauged it was time to break up the fun. 'Rosie's arranged a discreet wake upstairs at the Anchor if you'd like to join us.'

'I'm dropping Solly off at the factory and picking up Noel from the creche,' said a rather more sober Rachel. 'Then I'm going home to feed him and sit *shiva* for Gracie for the rest of the day.' She gave an elegant shrug. '*Shiva* is usually sat for a week, with many rules and regulations to be observed. But as she is not of our faith, it will be just my way of thinking of her and thanking her for the beautiful children she has left in our care.'

Danuta dearly wanted to talk to Rachel about the trouble at Tamarisk Bay, but realised this was neither the time nor the place. 'We won't disturb you then by coming to see Noel later.'

'You come whenever you want,' Rachel insisted, 'but first, go to the wake and try to relax.' She patted Danuta's cheek. 'You are far too young and pretty to have such weighty cares on your shoulders.' She didn't wait for a reply, but instead turned and climbed behind the steering wheel. Within moments their car was out of sight.

Ron was thankful that the fog meant his son, Frank, wouldn't be out fishing so could give him a much-needed hand. They'd spent the entire morning clearing out the garage in Havelock Road, hindered by a less than helpful Monty who insisted upon getting under their feet. They'd loaded up Frank's flatbed truck and taken the rubbish to the tip, and returned to the house to check on Harvey and the kittens and eat a quick lunch of soup and the fresh bread they'd bought on the way back.

'We'll check on Jack's place, but he says there's nothing much in it, so we should be able to start shifting your stuff before it gets dark and the fog thickens again.'

Ron cleaned up the mess the kittens had made in the kitchen and closed the door to stop them getting into the rest of the house, as they'd discovered the joys of climbing curtains and using the furniture to sharpen their claws – which Rosie had not been happy about.

Harvey plumped down by the door, his nose pressed to the gap at the bottom, his ears flicking back and forth as the kittens scampered across the lino on the other side. It seemed that having the kittens in the house had given him second wind, and he was quite like his old self again. Monty slumped by the front door, watching every move Ron made, alert to the first sign they might be going out again.

Frank pulled his cap over his hair and dragged on his heavy coat. 'I feel badly about Danuta and Stan,' he said. 'They have enough on their plate without all this upheaval. But I did manage to get a couple of tarpaulins, so you can help me cover the roof in between the downpours.'

'Aye, I'll help you with that, but it's a bit like shutting the stable door after the horse has bolted,' said Ron. 'I've talked the problem of Danuta over with Rosie and she'll do what she can with the housing people, but she really doesn't have any influence in that direction. It seems the housing committee is a law unto itself.'

'I'm just relieved Peg and Jim have room to take them in, although they've said they'll stick it out at Tamarisk Bay until the last possible moment in the hope the council really will find them somewhere decent. I just wish I'd done a better job on the place before I rented them out.'

'It's all in the lap of the gods,' sighed Ron. 'Hindsight is a wonderful thing, Frank, but it helps no one. Come on, Monty, let's get to Mafeking Terrace and see what Jack's hiding in his garage – and then, if you behave, I'll give you a good run on the hills while Frank sorts out his belongings.'

'I don't know why you talk to that dog as if he understands you,' muttered Frank. 'He might look like a lurcher, but he's got the brains of his whippet mother.'

Ron placed a heavy hand on his eldest son's broad shoulder and gave it a squeeze. 'He isn't to blame for his unfortunate heritage, Frank, but he's brighter than you give him credit for.'

Frank's snort of derision was his only reply as they left the house to climb into the truck with Monty between them.

Ron knew his son had never had a high opinion of Monty – in fact, he'd never understood his passion for keeping a menagerie of pets in the first place. It was the only thing Frank and his sour-faced ex-wife, Pauline, had ever agreed upon.

They fetched the garage key from Jack at his workshop, and soon found that he hadn't exaggerated, for the only things in the garage were an old bicycle, a box of tools and a roll of stained carpet. Having permission to dispose of the bike and the carpet, they loaded them into the flatbed, and headed for Tamarisk Bay.

Ron released Monty to the freedom of the hills and went to sit on the back of the flatbed to keep an eye on him while Frank sorted through his things and decided what to keep and what to throw away. He regarded the shacks which had already taken on an aura of desolation, and saw that although it was no longer raining, there was water pooled on the flat roof and it dripped and splashed down the walls which were slowly turning green with moss and lichen. The gutters gurgled and spat out more water into puddles on the path, and the windows were rotting. If they were to get a tarpaulin over it, then all that water would have to be brushed off first – and that would be quite a tough job.

'Ach, to be sure, one puff of wind would have the whole lot down,' he sighed, reaching into his pocket for his pipe.

However, as derelict as it was, he could still remember how it had been when his family had arrived all those years ago. Coming from the poverty of Ireland and the despotic rule of their English landlord, this place had looked like heaven to the Reilly family. For these shacks were their own, the lease willed to them by his da's older brother, with two fishing boats and a viable business he'd run from the beach in the nearby bay.

He grimaced as he remembered himself in those days, for he'd been a raw youth of thirteen, on the cusp of manhood and already as tall as his father. He'd outgrown his clothes and boots; his arms were muscled and his hands roughened by the long hours he'd spent on his father's fishing boat now he no longer attended school.

And his sister Roisin had been there, a wee girl of twelve, with the long tangle of auburn curls she'd inherited from their mother, and eyes that turned almost violet when she was full of some emotion. She'd been their family treasure, and Ron had loved the very bones of her until she'd left with only a scribbled note to say she was off to a better life with Jack Chisolm.

Ron gave a deep sigh and tried to concentrate on filling his pipe while he kept an eye on Monty who was digging furiously beneath a gorse bush. He hadn't really thought about his sister for many years, not for more than a few moments, anyway, but the conversation with Rosie was stirring up the memories, and seeing this place falling into ruin seemed to bring them more sharply into focus.

He had tried to find out where she'd gone, and he'd even approached Dolly who seemed to have the sort of contacts who might know where she was. But it was as if she and Jack had vanished into thin air, and as time went on and his life had become occupied with Mary and his boys, he'd given up looking for her.

'Dad? Dad!' Frank shouted from the beach. 'I need a hand to shift this lot.'

The images in his head were shattered and Ron waved a hand to his son before clambering down from the truck. But he knew he would return to memories of Roisin again.

10

The women were clearly thinking of Gracie's funeral for the mood in the factory had been sombre all day, with none of the usual chatter and laughter ringing out over the whirr of the sewing machines. Peggy had been surprised to see Florence come in just after lunch, and although she seemed willing to tell her about the service and the small gathering at the Anchor, it was clear the whole day had upset her to the point where she was reluctant to feed the curiosity of the machinists.

Peggy had suggested she stay in the office to deal with the telephone and the order books while she went out and pacified the women with a second-hand retelling. They seemed satisfied with this edited version, so Peggy went for a slow walk around the factory to see if everyone was concentrating on their work, or needed help with something, and ended up in the sorting room where the day's output was quality-checked before it was packaged up and sent to the mail room. Half an hour later she was back in her office to find that Florence had already gone to pick up Bobby.

The day had seemed to drag, and Peggy was relieved when it was time to lock up after everyone and make her way home. She followed the staff out of the factory into the winter darkness of the late afternoon to be assaulted by the wind which tore through the estate to cut any exposed flesh like a knife. It was only then that she remembered she didn't have the car, and Cissy had clearly been so preoccupied, she'd forgotten to come and pick her up.

Cursing under her breath and with her head down to avoid the first needles of sleet that were bouncing off the concrete, she ran to Jack's repair shop, praying he was still there. The light emanating through the narrow gap in the large double doors of his workshop was a welcome beacon, and she dashed inside. 'Jack? Jack, are you there?'

He emerged from under the bonnet of an Austin, wiping his hands on an oily rag, his round face beaming a welcome smile as he switched off the wireless. 'Hello, Peg. Where's the fire?'

'Any fire would be doused in seconds. Have you seen it out there?'

He glanced over her shoulder and grimaced before tossing the rag aside. 'I've been under cars all day with the wireless on and didn't notice. How can I help, Peg?'

'Cissy's got my car, so I'm a bit stuck. Any chance of a lift home, Jack? Only I'll drown if I try to walk in that.'

'Give me five minutes to clean up properly, and I'll run you home.' He dug in his oil-stained overalls and pulled out a flimsy blue air-letter. 'Have a read of that while you're waiting, Peg.' He shot her a beaming smile before heading for the washroom at the back of the unit.

Peggy knew instantly it had to be from her evacuee chick, Rita, who'd married her Australian flier, Peter, and was now living in Queensland. She found a stool to perch on and quickly opened it, eager to see her news.

As she read Rita's usual scrawl she began to smile and suddenly the bleak world outside no longer existed, for the girl described the heat, sibilant with the sounds of insects, so vividly, and she could almost see the elegant wooden Queenslander home on stilts that they'd finally finished renovating. Rita and Peter's plot of land had been partially cleared to make a firebreak around the house and machine workshops, but the ghost gums, ironwoods, jacarandas, oleanders and golden wattle trees had been preserved for the myriad colourful budgies, magpies, parakeets and cockatoos who nested in them and filled the air with their songs. Their machine repair business was going from strength to strength as the owners of the vast, far-flung Outback properties began to rely on them to keep their farming machinery in tip-top order, and the locals brought their cars in for servicing.

But the very best news came right at the end of the letter, and Peggy gave a little whoop of pleasure.

'Good news, eh, Peg?' Jack was still beaming as he emerged from the back room, pulling on his coat.

Peggy grinned and gave him his letter back. 'Congratulations, Grandpa Jack. Will you be going over there to see your first grandchild when it's born?'

'I always said I'd consider it once the nippers started coming along, but I don't know, Peg. Australia's the other side of the world and it takes weeks to get there. Who would look after my business while I was away?'

'You could always sell up here and start again, Jack. You're still young enough, and it sounds as if the pair of them could do with an experienced mechanic now they're doing so well.'

Jack grinned as he opened a large umbrella to shelter them from the heavy downpour while he slid the big doors closed and applied the padlock to the bolt. 'Are you trying to get rid of me, Peggy Reilly?'

Peggy just smiled and climbed into his car. They were the same age and she'd known him all her life, and although he'd joined up and done his bit in the war, he wasn't the sort of man who liked change. He was actually a real homebody, perfectly content to stay in the town where he'd been born to follow in his late father's footsteps as a mechanic. It was one heck of a dilemma that he faced now, and she could only imagine how he must be torn between going and staying. But she had the feeling he wouldn't be able to resist the lure of a grandchild, for he'd raised Rita on his own after her mother had died, and Peggy knew how bereft he'd been once she'd left for Australia.

Jack climbed in behind the wheel and they set off, the sleet turning to hail, making the windscreen wipers work even harder. Peggy smeared away the mist on her window and saw that the High Street was deserted, and so was Camden Road but for a couple of hardy souls, bent against the windblown sleet and walking their dogs. She shivered, glad she no longer had a dog to walk in all weathers.

As Jack pulled up outside Beach View, she turned to him with a smile. 'Thanks, Jack, you're a lifesaver. Do you want to come in for a cuppa?'

He shook his head. 'I'm swimming in tea as it is, but thanks, Peg. I need to get home to my account books.'

She dug out her keys and small umbrella from her bag, and dashed through the hail with the key in her hand to get into the house quickly. Once inside, she turned and waved to Jack who was doing a three-point turn and heading back into the town. Slamming the door on the weather, she stuffed the brolly in the stand and whipped off her sodden headscarf.

'Hello,' she called. 'Anyone home?'

Danuta emerged from the kitchen. 'Hello, Mama Peggy. Cordelia and Bertie are still at the Anchor, and Cissy and Sandra have taken Daisy to the Lilac Tearooms for an after-school treat. I hope you don't mind me letting myself in, but I couldn't bear the thought of going back to Tamarisk Bay in this weather.'

'Darling, of course I don't mind.' She took off her coat and changed into her slippers. 'It's absolutely filthy out there, and getting colder by the minute. I do hope Charlie isn't playing rugby in it. He'll catch his death.'

'But how did you get home without your car?'

'Jack brought me home, thank goodness. And ...' She just managed to stop herself from telling Danuta about Rita's news, realising it probably wasn't what she wanted to hear at this moment. 'And I'm just glad to be home. It's been a long day.'

'How is Jack? Still dithering about going to visit Rita?'

Peggy grinned. 'He's thinking about it, so that's progress of a sort.' She headed for the kitchen. 'I could do with a cuppa and no mistake. Just those short dashes back and forth in the hail and sleet have chilled me to the bone.'

'I will make it,' insisted Danuta. 'You sit down and relax.'

'That would be lovely,' Peggy sighed, holding her cold hands towards the fire in the range. 'It's been a strange sort of day all round,' she added as she lit a cigarette. 'I heard from Florence that the service went well, the church was full and a huge number of people turned up to stand about outside.'

Danuta nodded and set the teapot on the table with two cups. 'The press were there, so no doubt it will be in the paper tomorrow. Florence gave a very good little speech about how Gracie had battled to bring up Bobby after her husband had been killed, and how she'd been such a loving and hard-working mother. I don't think many had dry eyes after that.'

Peggy poured the tea and took a welcome sip. 'Where's Stan, by the way?'

'He went back to the airfield after dropping me off at

the Anchor. He cannot drink because he must be on a diet, and he knew that although the planes had been grounded, there was much to do up there before the really bad weather sets in.'

'Yes, Frank mentioned snow, and it's certainly cold enough.' Peggy patted her hand. 'But at least you have a decent roof over your head now. I've made up the big bed in the room off the hall where Jim and I used to sleep. With the new bathroom in the basement, I thought it would be easier for Stan to avoid going up and down all those stairs.'

'That is very kind, Mama Peggy, and we are so grateful. And of course we will pay you rent while we are here, and not expect you to cook for us.'

'I won't hear of it,' retorted Peggy. 'You're one of the family, Danuta, and have been since you first walked into this house. You'll keep your money for more important things – like a mortgage and a home of your own.'

Danuta said nothing, but Peggy could tell by the light in her hazel eyes that she meant to pay rent regardless. *Well*, she thought, *I'll just put it aside and give it back when she finds somewhere permanent.*

'Mama Peggy, I have something I wish to talk to you about while we are alone.'

Startled, Peggy eyed her keenly. 'What's the matter?'

Danuta's shoulders slumped. 'I don't know what to do for the best,' she admitted. 'There will soon be a letter from the adoption people with a date for our first meeting. Marcus, the lawyer Rachel introduced us to, said we must be honest and tell these people everything. But if I tell them we are to be evicted, surely they will refuse to let us go any further in the adoption process? Do you think we should say nothing until the eviction order comes through in the hope the council will find us somewhere decent? Or do you think they will already know that the shacks in Tamarisk Bay have been condemned by the council?'

Peggy noted the stress in her voice as the tone rose and the words tumbled out. 'That's a very tricky set of questions, Danuta, and I have to admit I don't really know how to answer them. I've always found that honesty is the best policy. But you're right; if you tell the adoption people the truth in this case, the whole process could be put into jeopardy.'

She reached for Danuta's hand. 'I'm sorry, my love, this is something only you and Stanislav can decide. Perhaps you should trust Marcus with your dilemma, because that's what he's being paid for, and he will give you far better advice than I ever could. But I must warn you, Danuta, that you must not lie to the authorities. If you're caught out, then it will definitely be the end of you adopting those children.'

'That's what Marcus said, and what I'm afraid of,' she whispered, a tear clinging to her lashes. 'Stanislav says we shouldn't tell anyone anything – not even Marcus – until we know more and have an actual date for the appointment at the adoption services. He reasons that with every day that passes, the council is more likely to find somewhere suitable for us to have the children.'

'Why can't you just tell them you're moving in here? After all, there's plenty of room and this is a respectable home in a good neighbourhood.'

'Do you think they would agree to us having the children here until we can find somewhere permanent?' Danuta's hope filled her teary eyes and wrung at Peggy's heart.

'I don't know, but it will sound better than you being homeless, or forced to live in some slum tenement with four other families,' she replied rather more flatly than she'd intended, but it was important the girl saw the true picture.

Danuta nodded and dried her tears. 'You are right, of course. Stanislav says I worry too much.'

Peggy thought she had every reason to worry, but she did seem to be overthinking the whole terrible mess, and although she was more than willing to give a home to Danuta and her husband for as long as they needed, it would be a bit of a scrum if they were given custody of the children as the adoption process went on. But she said nothing and just enveloped her in a warm hug, hoping to imbue her with all the love and support she felt for her.

Florence had collected Bobby from school, noticing immediately that something was bothering him. As they'd walked home, he'd remained silent and thoughtful, so she'd decided to wait until he'd had something to eat and drink before gently finding out what it was – although she could guess it had to concern the events of the day.

It had begun to sleet as they hurried up the path and she'd quickly got him inside and slammed the door on it. Bobby had refused help with his cap and blazer, hanging them on the low peg she'd fixed beneath the others for just that purpose, and then plodding into the kitchen to sit morosely by the range fire.

Florence realised she would need help, for as practical as she was, she had absolutely no idea of how to tackle the questions that were, no doubt, going to be asked before the day was out. She picked up the telephone to ring the one person she knew who could come to the rescue.

Bobby's dark mood lingered through a silent cup of cocoa and a slice of bread and jam, and on during his playtime and his favourite radio programme. Florence kept glancing at the clock, aware of the time ticking away and wondering where Father Finlay had got to, for he'd promised to come before Bobby's bedtime.

It was now almost seven o'clock, and she'd fed and bathed Bobby, and was preparing him for bed. Bobby had been compliant but still silent, refusing to look at her or communicate in any way, which worried her. If only the priest would come; he would know how to get the child to talk about what was worrying him.

Dressed in his pyjamas and dressing gown, she sat him on a chair by the fire so she could towel-dry his hair, the soft music on the wireless breaking the silence which had fallen between them.

Bobby gave a deep sigh and stared into the fire. 'My mum's dead, ain't she?' he said baldly.

Startled, Florence's hands stilled, and the towel fell about his shoulders.

'My friend Alfie said she was taken to the church today. But you said she's gone to heaven.' He turned to look up at her, his big brown eyes regarding her accusingly. 'You told a big fat fib.'

Florence stared back at him, flustered and unsure of what to say. 'I didn't fib, Bobby,' she began. 'Not the way you think. You see when someone dies . . .'

The loud rap on the door made her jump, and praying it was the priest, she quickly went to answer it.

Father Finlay stood there looking flustered as he sheltered under an enormous umbrella. 'I'm so sorry I'm late, Miss Hillier, but I was called to another parishioner and it took longer than I expected. Is Bobby still up?'

'He is indeed,' she replied, stepping back so he could enter the hall and divest himself of his overcoat and umbrella to reveal a dark suit and dog collar.

'And how is he?' His voice was low and his expression concerned.

'Mostly uncommunicative until a moment ago when he accused me of lying to him.' She related the short conversation they'd had. 'This is way beyond me, Father. I have no idea what to say or do.'

He placed a hand on her arm and smiled. 'We all have difficulties at times like these, and for a small boy, the events of today must be confusing. You are doing a splendid job with him, Miss Hillier, so please try not to think you're failing him in any way.' He picked up his briefcase. 'Where is he?'

Florence opened the kitchen door, and as Father Finlay stepped inside, Bobby beamed with pleasure and ran to hug his legs. They were old friends.

'Hello, Bobby,' said the priest, bending to ruffle his hair. 'Do you think if we ask nicely that Auntie Flo will make us some cocoa and perhaps offer us a biscuit?'

Bobby glanced round him to Florence and shrugged. 'Dunno,' he muttered.

Florence put milk in a pan and hunted out the biscuits, surreptitiously watching as the priest gently disentangled himself from Bobby's clutches and sat down at the table. He patted the chair beside him to encourage the boy to sit, and then opened his briefcase to take out a large picture book. He then tugged Bobby's chair closer to the table so he could see the picture of the tearful little boy on the front, and she wondered how many times this good man had been called to soothe a child's troubled mind.

'This boy's name is John,' he said quietly. 'And his mummy has died too and he's feeling really sad.' He turned over the page to show the boy looking very cross. 'But sometimes he feels really angry too and doesn't understand why, but everything is so different without his mum, and that makes him feel a bit scared.'

Florence silently placed the mugs of cocoa and plate of biscuits on the table, noticing that the priest had Bobby transfixed, so signalled that she would leave him to it. She went into the sitting room and sank onto the couch with a blanket wrapped around her to ward off the chill. There was no fire in the hearth for she was waiting for a coal delivery and it was important to keep the range fire going so she could cook.

Hating to be idle, she picked up her box of darning and, as she sewed, she let her thoughts dwell on Bobby, and how he must be looking at the world now. Danuta had said that children had the same emotions as any adult, but they didn't know how to express them, or how to understand the difference it made to everything they'd known when a beloved parent had gone. How clever of Father Finlay to know exactly the right way to explain and soothe and sympathise – although it had surprised her that he hadn't spouted on about angels and heaven but had got straight to the practicalities of death and all it entailed for those left behind.

Florence wasn't a Catholic, and although her parents had been churchgoers, she'd always suspected that was only because it was the right thing to do on a Sunday. Her own faith was tenuous; she was too sceptical to believe most of what the holier-than-thou vicar had pontificated about from the pulpit, and once she'd left home, going to church had not been on her agenda. But a man like Father Finlay restored what little faith she had, for it was clear he truly was a man of God who served and cared for others, no matter what their faith. And if he could help little Bobby through the labyrinth of emotions and fears, then she might be tempted to attend one of his services.

She gave a wry smile and dumped the darning back into the basket. It was amazing how lack of sleep and too much worry made the mind play tricks. She'd almost believed she really would go back to St Cuthbert's.

Stanislav grimaced as the icy wind blew sleet in his face and made every step on the greasy concrete hazardous. He'd been helping to organise the storage of the aid boxes and crates in the empty hangar while the others carried them from the C-47 which sat on the runway. He felt useless and miserable, and try as he might, he simply couldn't force a smile or join in the usual banter with the ground staff or fellow pilots.

'For goodness' sake cheer up, old chap,' boomed Roger, heartily slapping him on the shoulder and almost making him lose his balance on the crutches. 'Even your fine moustache is drooping with depression.'

'So would you be if your wife fed you rabbit food and refused to let you have a drink,' he grumbled.

'I have to say, old boy, you do look better for it,' he shouted above the thunder of the hail on the tin roof. 'Chin up. You'll soon get that leg back and feel on top of the world again.'

Stanislav nodded before heading off to check on the last batch of large boxes filled with medical supplies and emergency tents. He'd told no one about the looming eviction, or their fruitless search for a permanent home, and although Peggy had probably told Martin's Anne that she'd given them shelter, he had not mentioned it – and neither had the others.

The trouble was he'd always been independent, proud to hold up his head in the knowledge that he could earn a good living despite being an amputee, and would one day provide a proper home for Danuta where they could raise the children they adopted. Now he felt as if the world – and the weather – was against him; beholden to Peggy and Jim, and at the mercy of the faceless bureaucrats who ran the council and adoption service.

'Stanislav. A word if you wouldn't mind.'

He turned to find Martin had followed him and was looking very serious. His heart stuttered. 'Is there something wrong?'

'Come with me. We need to talk.' Without waiting for a response, Martin headed for the large annexe at the back of the hangar where the ground crew usually met to rest and eat between flights. It was quieter in there, for the roof was tiled and insulated.

Stanislav followed him slowly, his mind whirling with the dark possibility that he was about to be laid off. As Martin closed the door behind him and indicated he should take one of the comfortable chairs, he shook his head and dredged up as much dignity as possible to remain standing and face his employer.

'You'll be more comfortable sitting,' said Martin quietly.

'I prefer to stand and take the bad news like a man,' he retorted.

Martin frowned, the scar on his cheek puckering. 'I'm not here to give you bad news, Stan. I merely wanted to discuss your situation at home, to see if I can help in any way.'

Stanislav's shoulders relaxed and his heart slowed to its regular rhythm. 'Unless you have a spare house to rent out, I don't see that you can help,' he sighed, sinking down onto a nearby chair.

'Peggy told my Anne about Frank's place, and I'm glad she and Jim are taking you in, but we both know it can't be permanent, Stan. Let's talk about alternatives and see if we can put our heads together to find a solution. And there will be one, I'm sure of it.'

Stanislav knew his expression showed his disbelief as his broad shoulders slumped in defeat. He couldn't share his friend's optimism.

Martin seemed to realise this and hurried on. 'There are a lot of people on your side, Stan, although it may not feel like it at the moment. And we all want to help.'

'So, everyone knows my shame,' Stanislav said softly.

'It's no shame, Stan; merely rotten bad luck and bloody awful timing. Now, are you willing to listen to what I have to say, or are you going to continue to wallow in misery?'

He sat up straighter, determined to show this man he hadn't quite given in. 'I am willing to listen to anything if it will give us a home of our own,' he confessed. 'My Danuta does not deserve this.'

'Good.' Martin plumped down in the chair beside him and offered him a cigar. Once they were both lit, he began to voice the idea he and Anne had come up with the night before.

Ron had cleaned out the ferrets and laid fresh straw in their wooden hutch before draping thick blankets over it to keep out the cold east wind. He'd fed the dogs and kittens, put the casserole in the oven, and was enjoying a quiet pipe by the fire as Monty snored at his feet and Harvey stretched out on the couch with the kittens curled against his belly. He was just starting to wonder where Rosie had got to when he heard the key turn in the front door, and Monty rushed to welcome her.

'Get down, Monty, you'll ladder my stockings.'

Ron looked across at Harvey, who hadn't moved, which was most unlike him. He stroked his head and then went to help Rosie fend off an over-excited Monty.

'It's chucking it down out there,' she said, dropping her umbrella in the stand by the door and kicking off her shoes. 'I got soaked through just running to and from the car. And I hope you've got the dinner on, because I'm starving.' She struggled out of her coat.

'Take a breath and slow down, Rosie. Dinner's heating through and the fire's blazing, so come into the sitting room and relax.'

'Sorry,' she murmured, giving him a kiss on the cheek. 'It's been one of those days, and I'm still absolutely seething over those bloody people on the housing committee.'

He didn't like the sound of that, but decided it could wait until Rosie had caught her breath and had her dinner. He left her to find her slippers and make repairs to her hair, and went to dish up the casserole into bowls, which he carried into the sitting room on two trays.

'There,' he said, carefully placing her tray on a side table. 'Eat that and get warm while I tell you about the disaster Frank and I had over at Tamarisk Bay.'

She looked at him in horror. 'Not another disaster, Ron. I can't bear it.'

'Neither did the roof on the Barclays' shack,' he replied dryly. 'We were up there trying to get a heavy tarpaulin over it when Frank's foot went straight through it, plasterboard ceiling and all, nearly cutting him in half. I had one hell of a job to get him out of there, because he was stuck as tight as a cork in a bottle, the roof was threatening to cave in under us, and the tarpaulin was flapping about so hard in the wind it was almost knocking me over.'

'Was he hurt?'

Ron shook his head. 'Frank's made of strong stuff and even managed to laugh about it in the end. But actually, it wasn't funny. He could really have done himself some damage, and he's probably bruised from his feet to his groin.'

'It's a good thing the Barclays had already moved out, or he'd have been in all kinds of trouble.'

'Aye, that's true enough.' He finished the rest of his meal and set the bowl aside. 'We finally managed to get the tarpaulin over his and Danuta's place, so they're a bit more weatherproof, but most of the damage had already been done. Both places are still damp and mouldy inside.'

'I don't like the thought of you climbing all over those roofs,' she said, pushing her empty bowl away. 'I do wish you wouldn't risk your life like that. It could so easily have been you stuck up there.'

'I don't weigh as much as Frank and am lighter on me feet,' he replied, airily ignoring the fact it had been dangerous up there, and he'd been quite scared of following Frank through one of the rotten roofs. 'Besides, it was a job that needed doing, and he couldn't have done it on his own.'

He crossed the room to the cabinet and poured two large brandies. 'To keep out the cold while you tell me why the housing people have made you seethe,' he said, giving her a kiss on the brow.

'They're talking about sending Danuta and Stan fifteen miles away to a one-bed council flat on one of the more notorious slum estates,' she said flatly. 'According to them, they don't qualify for one of the prefabs as they don't have children. They've disregarded the fact they're trying to adopt because they reason it might not come to anything; in which case, they'd have to be moved again to somewhere smaller.'

'That won't do,' protested Ron. 'Fifteen miles is too far from their work, and will cost a small fortune in petrol if they both have to drive in every day.'

'I know,' she sighed. 'I did vigorously argue the

point. The only other place they could offer is a single room in one of those villas behind the Crown, and I'm afraid that if they turn down both places, they'll be struck off the housing list and left to their own devices.'

'Then they'll have to stay with Peggy and Jim.'

'I popped in to see Danuta before I came home, which is why I was so late back,' she said quietly. 'I've advised them to take the single room in Cliffehaven and make it look as if they're living there, but actually use Beach View as their base. The only redeeming factor of that room is that it's on the ground floor, so at least Stanislav won't have the bother of tackling stairs.'

'But no adoption will go through if they're living there,' said Ron.

'It's the only way they can stay on the housing list, Ron. If the adoption does go ahead, then the housing people have promised to look into their case again, and do their best to find somewhere more suitable.' She gave a deep sigh. 'But promises are easily given – and just as easily broken.'

As Stanislav came through the front door, Danuta could see instantly that his mood had lifted. She embraced him once he'd struggled out of his coat. 'You look much more cheerful, and I have a lot to tell you,' she said. 'But first, you must eat. Peggy has made a vegetable stew which is keeping warm for us in the slow oven.'

'Where is everyone?' he asked as he entered the cosy but deserted kitchen.

'Peggy and Jim have gone to the Anchor for a drink with Cordelia and Bertie. Cissy is listening to records in the sitting room, Daisy is in bed, and Charlie is upstairs doing his homework.'

He gave a sigh of pleasure as he sank into a chair and held his hands out to the fire. 'This is more like home: warm, welcoming and clean, with my lovely wife smiling at me.'

Danuta dished out the stew and sat down. 'I agree, it is lovely, and we're very lucky, but we must not get too used to it,' she said after she'd eaten a couple of mouthfuls. 'Rosie came earlier, and we've been offered a ground-floor room in Eshton Road. It's a big house, but there are already many people living there, and if we don't take it, the council will remove us from the housing list.'

She looked back at Stan to see how he was reacting to her news, but couldn't read his expression, so carried on. 'But it is better than the flat they wanted us to take fifteen miles away. Rosie advised we take the local one, but use Beach View as our base until we can find somewhere better,' she finished in a rush.

'If the plans I discussed with Martin today come to something, then we won't have to take anything from the council,' he said, his eyes shining.

She eyed him suspiciously, feeling rather put out that he'd been discussing their problems with Martin behind her back. 'What plans?'

'Martin has made me a partner in Phoenix Air Transport, and as such, I will get dividends on top of my usual salary. It will mean that as long as the company is making a profit – which it is at the moment – I will have an income, even if we are grounded.'

He paused as Danuta stared at him in disbelief. 'And that means we will be able to go to the bank to ask for a mortgage.'

'It will be enough on top of our savings?' she queried.

'Martin has done the sums and worked out how much we can borrow without getting into difficulties. We both earn good money, Danuta, and even if you have to go half-time to look after the children, the bonus of those dividends means we can invest in a home of our own.'

'Oh, Stan,' she breathed, hardly daring to believe such a thing was within their grasp. 'Are you sure? Are you really certain we can do this thing?'

He reached for her hand across the kitchen table. 'Martin has written a letter of recommendation which has been signed by the other partners in the business. This I must show to the bank manager, and he will not be able to refuse me when he sees what they have written.'

He kissed her hands and held them to his cheek. 'We're on our way, my darling. On our way to a new home where we can raise our little family.'

Danuta smiled as the tears of happiness rolled down her face, for at last she could dare to believe that her dreams were about to come true.

Peggy snuggled against Jim as the hail rattled against the windows and the sea thundered to shore. It was a wild night out there, which only made the luxury of being in her warm bed with Jim even more satisfying. 'Thank goodness those two aren't sleeping in that shack tonight. If the tide gets any higher, the whole lot will get washed away.'

'Probably the best thing that could happen to them,' Jim murmured, his concentration fixed on the paperwork he'd brought from work.

'I'd have thought you'd be sad to see them go, considering it was your boyhood home.'

'Mmm. Not really. Sorry, Peg, but I really need to read through this lot before tomorrow. There's a meeting, and I have to keep up with some of these new regulations and guidelines.'

Peggy sighed, for although they'd made love earlier, she'd hoped they could cuddle for a while and forget about the outside world. But Jim took his job with the British Legion very seriously, and with so many injured servicemen under his care, it was right he should want to be up to date with everything. Thinking of Parkwood House where some of the most severely injured men now lived reminded her of Jim's friend.

'How's Ernie? You said he hadn't done too well over Christmas.'

'He's rallied, the old devil,' he replied on a chuckle. 'Everyone thought that chest infection would see him off, but he's back to his usual miserable, foul-mouthed self. I really don't know how he does it.' He immersed himself in the papers again and then remarked almost casually, 'By the way, I spoke to the psychiatrist up there, and he'll be glad to see Cissy whenever she's ready to talk to him.'

Peggy gave a little sigh of relief, for although Cissy seemed to be her usual self, there was still a brittleness about her in the way she laughed too loudly and couldn't seem to sit still for very long. It would be a relief to know that she would soon return to the counselling she'd started in London, for it was certainly doing Jim a lot of good.

Jim finally put the papers on the bedside chest, turned off the light and took Peggy in his arms. 'Perhaps you should come up and visit Ernie, Peg? It perked him up no end, last time.'

'Of course I will, once I have a minute to myself. But there's so much going on at the moment, and with only the weekends free, there just don't seem to be enough hours in the day to fit everything in.'

'Well, you know my feelings, love. Give up work and enjoy being a housewife and mother again. Florence sounds as if she's perfectly capable of taking over from you, and you deserve to put your feet up.'

Peggy inwardly groaned. Jim seemed to think that

being a housewife and mother was easier than going to work. Typical man. 'I'm not ready to hand in my notice, Jim. I enjoy having my own money to spend, and going to work keeps me in touch with what's happening outside these four walls.'

'You've always known the current gossip, so that's no excuse,' he chided softly. 'I'm earning good money, Peg. There's no need for you to go to work.'

'I know that, but it's what I want, so please don't keep on. We've had a lovely evening out, and it sounds as if Danuta and Stan are finally seeing the light at the end of the tunnel, so let's just agree to disagree, and get a good night's sleep.'

He pulled her closer and nuzzled her neck and shoulder. 'Are you sure you want to go to sleep?'

Peggy giggled. 'Jim Reilly, you are naughty.'

'I know – and if you're willing, I'll show you just how very bad I can be.'

'Oh, Jim,' she sighed. 'Yes, please.'

11

Stanislav had already contacted Martin to make sure nothing had cropped up over the weekend which would make it difficult for him to miss a morning's work. Satisfied that he wouldn't be needed until the afternoon for a short flight to Leeds, he settled down to a leisurely breakfast. He'd promised Danuta that he'd telephone the bank when it opened at nine, to make an appointment to see the manager.

Danuta was on night duty this week but had eaten a hurried breakfast and gone out early to drive over to Tamarisk Bay to see if there was any post, and to collect the last few small things she'd left behind. As she drove, she felt newly born, refreshed and full of optimism. It was almost spring-like, for the sun was shining, the awful wind had dropped, and she'd had the best night's sleep in ages. With her spirits high, she refused to contemplate the possibility that the bank manager might turn them down – for surely, on a day like this, nothing bad could happen.

Danuta drove past the Goldmans' house – resisting the urge to nip in and see Noel – and then along the lane before turning up the steep track to Tamarisk Bay. Coming to a halt in her usual parking space, she stared at the buildings with some dismay. A tarpaulin had been lashed over two of the shacks, but the one the Barclays had rented was open to the elements and, from her high viewpoint on the bank, she could see there was a huge hole in the roof.

She climbed out of the car, fetched the packing boxes Peggy had lent her from the boot, and then walked down the slope. Frank's boat was gone along with the generator and piles of ropes, buoys, creels, lobster pots, anchors and general fisherman's clutter which had always been stacked in an untidy heap by his door. Peering through the salt-stained window, she saw that most of his furniture was gone too. It looked as if he'd already abandoned the place.

She went to her own front door and stepped inside. It also felt abandoned, and she was assaulted by the stench of damp and mould which seemed to have strengthened in their short absence. She tried to switch on the light, and then checked the telephone. It appeared that Frank had disconnected both, which was understandable. The fire had long gone out, of course, but there was a bag of coal and a pile of logs she would need help with if she was to take them to Beach View, but they would have to wait. For now, she would gather up her cooking utensils, crockery, bed linen, light bulbs and spare blankets, load them into the car and come back for her cleaning materials, and any packets or tins she still had in the cupboard.

Once most of the boxes were loaded up, she hauled them to the car, dumped them in the boot and returned to what had been their home for the last of it. Wandering from kitchen to bedroom and tiny sitting room which looked over the beach, she remembered the happy times they'd had here.

Stanislav had carried her over the threshold on their first night of marriage; they'd made love in the big bed Rachel had given them as a wedding present, and in the summer they'd eaten picnics on the beach, and she'd paddled in the icy water of the English Channel while Stanislav lay shirtless like a beached whale on the shingle to improve his tan.

It hadn't all been bad, she thought with a smile. At first they'd managed to laugh off the cold and damp, snuggling down in that big bed to shut off the outside world, or sitting cosily by the temperamental stove with large mugs of tea or cocoa. But this cold, wet and stormy winter had proved to be too much, and she felt a little sad that these frail old buildings would soon be gone along with their history.

She heard a noise outside and went to investigate, hoping it might be Frank. But it was the young postman, Billy Frazer, standing in her kitchen.

'Just the two for you today, Sister Danuta,' he said cheerfully, his gaze trawling the cold, denuded room. 'Looks like this old place has about had it. On the move, are you?'

She glanced at the letters, saw the government franking next to the stamps and was desperate to open them – but with gossipy Billy there, it wouldn't be wise, so she shoved them into her pocket.

'Yes. We will be at Beach View from now on, Billy. And Frank is going to live with his father in Havelock Road, so if you could tell them at the Post Office not to deliver here any more.'

He pulled a notebook from his pocket, licked the end of a stubby pencil and carefully noted their new addresses. 'I'll make sure they know before the end of the day,' he said, putting the notebook back in his pocket. 'But you will still be coming to look after me gran, won't you, Sister?' he asked with a frown.

'Of course I will, Billy. In fact, she should be on my list for this evening.' She could see he wanted to stop and chat, but she really didn't have the time, and desperately needed to know what was in those letters. They felt as if they were burning a hole in her pocket, and she placed the large kitchen clock on top of the last of the boxes, picked it up off the table and inched towards the door, hoping he'd take the hint.

'Thanks for bringing the mail all this way every day, Billy. I bet you'll be glad to have this place off your round.'

'It'll certainly make it shorter,' he replied. 'Cheerio, then. Best of luck.' He doffed his cap and strode away up the slope to the bright red delivery van.

Danuta didn't bother to lock the door. Frank and Ron would soon be coming for the furniture, and there was nothing else left to steal. She tramped up the slope, shoved the box of cleaning materials and assorted bits and pieces into the boot, and carefully placed the clock on the back seat with her curtains.

Climbing in behind the wheel, she took the letters out of her pocket. Now she could open them, she was almost afraid to see what was inside, and her hands were shaking as she held them both up, trying to decide which to open first. She took a deep breath, chose the one in her right hand and then ran her finger under the seal to open it.

The single sheet of paper had the address of the adoption agency at the top. It was covered in neat typing, and had an illegible signature scrawled at the bottom.

Dear Mr and Mrs Kowalcyzk,

We have made an appointment for you on Wednesday 15th January at two o'clock in our offices at the above address. It is important that you both attend this appointment, for failing to do so might affect your application to adopt Robert and Noel Smith. Should you be unable to attend through illness or work commitments, then another date will be suggested on the production of proof of a valid reason for absence. Please be aware that this office is extremely busy and appointments cannot be changed at the last minute, or too often. It is important the process of your adoption application is carried out smoothly by all parties, and keeping appointments is paramount to maintaining this. A copy of this letter has been sent to your solicitor, Marcus Golding.

The typed name beneath the signature was Mrs Aurelia Johnston-Black.

Danuta thought she sounded rather grand, and just hoped she wasn't one of those daunting women with huge bosoms, cut-glass accents, and the bossy attitude of an English headmistress. She'd met a few, both at Bletchley Park and during her rounds, and on the whole, she hadn't liked them.

Danuta tucked the letter safely away in her bag and reached for the second. It was from the local housing department. She read through it quickly, and realised everything was as Rosie had said, and she had less than three days to confirm they would be taking on the room in Eshton Road, and if they missed the deadline, it would go to someone else and they would be struck off the housing list.

She folded the letter and placed it in her bag. They had no choice but to accept the room, for even if they did get a mortgage, it could be months before they found something, and then the process of buying it would take several weeks – and they really couldn't expect Peggy and Jim to put them up for that length of time. She instantly dismissed the thought they might not get a mortgage at all and would be stuck in that room for the foreseeable future.

She took a last, lingering look at the tumbledown home she'd shared with Stanislav, then drove back to

Cliffehaven. She had written a long letter to Marcus Golding explaining the dilemma of what to do about where they were living, and planned to drop it off before she went to Beach View to see how Stanislav had got on with the bank, but of course now she'd had the notification from the council, it was a bit out of date. But this was not a day to be pessimistic, for by tonight, if their luck held, they would have some idea of what their future could look like.

During breakfast, Peggy had noted how tightly strung Stanislav had been under the veneer of jovial confidence, and could only pray that the manager at the bank was the sort of man who wouldn't just look at the crutches and missing leg, and would be understanding and helpful. Unfortunately, she didn't know this particular one, for he was newly arrived from Chichester and she'd yet to hear anything about him. But new brooms were inclined to make sweeping changes, and she just hoped Stanislav wouldn't over-egg the pudding in trying to persuade him to give them what they needed.

As Charlie left for the grammar school and Daisy went upstairs to fetch her blazer, Peggy wondered if it might be better for Danuta to do the talking as she was straightforward and could lay out her reasoning clearly. But suggesting that to Stanislav probably wouldn't be wise, for he was like Jim when it came to such important matters, and he'd insist upon being the spokesman.

'Now Sandra's back in London, I'm at a bit of a loose end, so I'm going up to Parkwood House to meet Dad and his shrink later this morning, Mum,' said Cissy. 'Is it all right if I borrow your car again?'

Peggy forced her wandering thoughts into order. 'Not really, dear. I have to get Daisy to school and then go to work – and I need to do some food shopping during the lunch hour. I suppose you could run me and Daisy to school and the factory, but the shopping will be a problem without a car.'

'I will take you,' said Stanislav. 'And if you wish to do shopping, give me the list and Danuta and I will do it after we have seen the bank manager.'

'That would be a terrific help, but are you sure, Stan? Don't you have to be at the airfield this afternoon?'

He waved away her questions. 'Not until much later, Peggy. As long as the manager can see us this morning, there will be plenty of time for shopping.'

As Cissy thanked him with a smile and hurried upstairs, Danuta came bustling into the kitchen and made straight for Stanislav.

'We've got a date for the adoption people,' she said breathlessly. 'And the council have offered us that room in Eshton Road, just as Rosie said they would. But we must tell them if we want it before the end of the week.' She passed the letters over so he could read them.

'What date did the adoption people give you?' asked Peggy.

'The fifteenth. It's only two days away, Mama Peggy, and I'm already feeling on edge about it.'

'There'll be no need for nerves, Danuta,' she soothed. 'It's as clear as daylight how much you want to adopt those little ones, and how good you'll both be for them. Now, sit down and have a cup of tea. It sounds as if you've got a busy day ahead.'

Danuta sat down to pour the tea, but it was clear to Peggy that she was unable to settle. 'Eshton Road isn't too bad, despite the fact it's a bit close to the noisy Crown. The houses are large and mostly well maintained with spacious rooms and a decent-sized garden. It will depend on what the other tenants are like, of course, but then you won't have to have much to do with them if you're using here as your base.'

'I thought we'd go to see it once we've been to the bank,' Danuta replied, darting anxious looks at Stanislav who was frowning over both letters. 'What's the matter, Stan?'

'This woman who writes to us from the agency doesn't sound very helpful,' he muttered. 'She is all rules and regulations.'

'That's just the way things are. Marcus warned us that there would be if the adoption is to be done properly.' She looked at her watch and gave a sigh. 'The morning feels as if it has flown, but it is still not quite half past eight.'

'Oh, my goodness,' gasped Peggy, 'I have to get Daisy to school and go to work.' She shouted for Daisy to come downstairs and dashed about the kitchen collecting her coat, hat and bag and changing out of her slippers. 'Is your offer of a lift still on, Stan?'

'Of course, of course. I will get the car started.' Stanislav tossed the letters onto the table and grabbed his crutches, hauled himself out of the kitchen chair and swung his way out into the hall.

Danuta retrieved the letters and popped them back into her bag before helping Daisy into her blazer, gloves and hat. 'I will come too,' she said, hunting out Daisy's school bag from under the fireside chair. 'And then Stan and I will go straight to the bank and ask to see the manager. It will be better than using the telephone.'

'I'm off, Cissy,' Peggy shouted up the stairs. 'The car keys are on the kitchen table.'

Once Daisy and Peggy had been dropped off, Stan drove back into the High Street and parked outside the bank. It was not yet nine, but there was already a small queue outside the large, intimidating closed doors.

Danuta and Stanislav sat for a moment in silence, the tension of the moment like electricity between them. And then he kissed her. 'We can do this, my love,' he murmured. 'Trust me.'

Danuta had always trusted him, but could she trust the bank manager to see things their way? She pecked him on the cheek, then clambered out and waited for him to join her in the queue.

Once the door had been opened, they moved into another queue at one of the counters, and after explaining why they'd come, had to wait for several anxious moments before the teller came back and asked them to go and sit by Major Collingwood's office door.

They waited, the tension rising as the customers came and went, and the door to the manager's office remained firmly shut. Danuta gripped Stan's fingers, her pulse racing both with trepidation and excitement until she felt quite giddy from it all.

'Good morning. I understand you wish to see me about taking out a mortgage.'

They looked up to see a man who was probably in his early fifties and of average height, with the bearing of a military man, but wearing a smart suit and regimental tie. His thinning hair was carefully combed over a bald patch, but to counteract this loss, his moustache and eyebrows were startlingly bushy, which made him look rather like Groucho Marx.

As this comical image sprang to mind, Danuta had to swallow a rising fit of nervous giggles as she shot to her feet and Stanislav struggled to get out of the low leather chair. 'Thank you for seeing us today, Major Collingwood,' she managed.

His handshake was firm, his smile pleasant as he greeted them before ushering them into his well-appointed office. The room was warm and oak-panelled, with a large desk, a Turkish carpet and a line of filing cabinets beneath a wall of shelves holding hefty tomes related to banking. As they sat in the leather chairs facing his desk, Danuta caught sight of a photograph on the wall which she suspected was a keepsake of Major Collingwood's war.

He must have seen her interest, for he smiled. 'I was with the Eighth Army in Africa,' he murmured. 'A Desert Rat. It was all a far cry from where I am now. But I was one of the lucky ones and got home in one piece.' He turned to Stanislav, his expression sympathetic. 'I see you didn't fare as well, Mr Kowalcyzk.'

Stan blinked in surprise at the other man's perfect pronunciation of their name. 'You must be the only person in England to get our name right first time.'

'My grandmother was Polish,' he replied with a smile. 'I'm a little rusty, but I remember enough to hold a fairly decent conversation. Where did you see your service?'

'With the RAF, Polish Wing – though towards the end we were a mix of Irish, Australian, Kiwis, Hungarians and Brits. It didn't seem to matter where we'd come from as we were fighting the same enemy.' He patted both thighs. 'Lost the other end of these over Holland.'

Collingwood nodded and then became businesslike. He explained what a mortgage deed would entail and answered their questions, assuring Danuta that should she wish it, her name would also be on the agreement. He then reached for pen and paper to begin asking a long list of searching questions.

Once he was satisfied that they were both fully employed and had savings in his bank, he read the letter of reference signed by the partners of Phoenix Air Transport, and the one from Dr Darwin. He then asked about Stan's health and suggested that a letter from his consultant might help smooth their mortgage application along.

Having spent some moments jotting down numbers, he then leaned back in his chair. 'Have you seen a property you wish to buy?'

Stanislav shook his head. 'There isn't much about, and we didn't want to do anything until we had a secure mortgage agreement.'

'Very wise,' he murmured. 'These are difficult times. But I must warn you both that property prices are going up daily. With so much war damage, there is little stock to be had that is empty and in good repair, and new-builds are being held up by the lack of materials. The average price of a house in a reasonable area is over a thousand pounds now, whereas it would have been about five hundred pounds before the war.'

He paused to let this sink in, and Danuta gripped Stan's hand, willing Collingwood to tell them what he'd decided.

He seemed to read her mind. 'I know you'd like an answer today, but I'm afraid that's not possible,' he said. 'I'll have to consult with Head Office before anything can be decided – but I promise I'll get back to you as soon as possible.' He pushed away from the desk to show the interview was over.

Stanislav remained seated. 'But what is your opinion? Will you look on us with favour?'

'I cannot commit to anything until I've spoken to Head Office. I'm sorry, Stanislav, but I will certainly do my best for you.'

Danuta realised they could do no more, and after shaking his hand, they both left the bank feeling a little disheartened, but still holding tightly to the hope that Collingwood would come through for them.

It was still unseasonably warm and bright as they

drove up the steep High Street to the turn-off which would take them into the labyrinth of streets behind the Crown. Stan slowly drove along Eshton Road and parked outside number 26.

'It looks quite a nice area,' said Danuta hopefully, eyeing the neatly trimmed hedges at the front of the line of double-fronted Victorian villas, and the few slender trees that lined the narrow pavements on either side. There were no other cars in the street, and none of the houses had a garage, but there was a small, well-tended garden at the front of number 26, the front door looked as if it had been freshly painted, and the net curtains at every window but one were snowy white.

She eyed the ground-floor bay window with its tatty curtains and grey nets and wondered what it was like inside. 'Let's go to the council offices and fill in their forms so we can get the key.'

'All right,' he said on a sigh. 'But I can't see the point if we're staying at Beach View.'

'We don't have that mortgage yet,' she reminded him firmly. 'And we have to hedge our bets and take this on even if we do stay with Mama Peggy. But there will come a point where we'll outstay our welcome, and we must think of that, Stan, and not take advantage of her kindness.'

The short trip to the council offices didn't take as long as it did to actually see someone, fill in endless forms and take possession of the keys. The rent was a little more than they'd been paying Frank, but it was still manageable.

Returning to Eshton Road, they parked the car, noticing how quiet it was despite the fact it was quite close to the High Street, and went through the low wrought-iron gate and up the red-tiled path to the dark blue front door set between the two bay windows.

They entered a narrow, dark hallway which had doors on both sides and led to the back of the house. There was a coin-in-the-slot telephone to the side of the front door, and an uncarpeted staircase leading to the two top floors. Now they were inside, they could smell the lingering reminders of many meals, and hear a wireless blaring. There was also a baby crying, and a furious amount of shouting going on somewhere upstairs.

Stan grimaced and shared a look with Danuta before unlocking the door to their right. It swung open to reveal a room bare of furniture with scuffed and stained floorboards, a single light bulb hanging from a nicotine-stained ceiling, and a small range which looked as if it hadn't been cleaned since Queen Victoria had first sat on the throne.

Upon further inspection, Danuta found a dirty sink with a single leaking tap behind a filthy plastic curtain, several dusty shelves stained by rings from rusty tins, and a gas fire with a meter. 'It needs a good scrubbing,' she said, looking round. 'And those curtains and nets are fit only for the dustbin.'

She gingerly pulled the nets to one side to discover that the windows in the bay were far from clean. 'No wonder it's so gloomy in here,' she sighed.

'The house is facing the wrong way,' said Stan. 'The sun won't come in here until very late in the day – if at all in winter.' His expression was grim as the argument upstairs reached an even more furious pitch, and the baby continued to cry. 'Thank God we have Beach View,' he said with great feeling.

Danuta nodded in agreement. 'Yes, we are very lucky, but we can make this look nice with a lot of hard work and elbow grease, Stan. It's dry and sturdy for all the filth, and much better than Tamarisk Bay in that respect, so if we do have to live here, we won't be in constant danger of being washed away during a high tide.' She looked around and nodded. 'I'll make a start on cleaning it this afternoon.'

'But Frank and Ron will be bringing the furniture over soon.'

'Then I'll just have to work around it,' she said firmly. 'Come on, Stan, we have to get Peggy's shopping done before you go to work.'

'Aren't we going to have lunch?' he asked mournfully.

Danuta grinned and shooed him out of the room. Trust Stan to be thinking only of his stomach when their life was in turmoil and there was so much to be done.

12

The young woman was standing on her doorstep with a clipboard as Florence returned home, having collected Bobby from school. Florence took in the earnest expression in that youthful face; the untidy fair hair escaping the bun; the sturdy shoes and drooping pleated skirt which fell almost to her ankles; the briefcase and clipboard – and bristled. She knew immediately who she represented and what she'd come for.

'My name is Sarah Watts, and I'm from the children's fostering services,' she said, holding out a pale, slim hand and smiling brightly.

'Florence Hillier,' she replied coolly, ignoring the hand and thinking that this chit of a girl could barely have left school, let alone be experienced enough in childcare to come snooping where she wasn't wanted.

Sarah withdrew her hand, her smile faltering as her wide blue eyes darted from Florence to the boy fidgeting at her side. In an effort to break the awkward silence, she bent down to speak to Bobby. 'And you must be Robert,' she crooned. 'Aren't you a handsome boy?'

'My name's Bobby,' he retorted, edging away from her to escape having his hair ruffled. He looked up at Florence and tugged her hand. 'Can we go in now? I want me tea.'

Florence slotted the key in the door and he ran inside. 'You'd better come in, then,' she said ungraciously. 'But you'll have to wait until Bobby's had something to eat before you start with your questions.'

'Of course,' she replied, clearly on the back foot. 'Would it be all right if I just looked around the flat while you feed him? Only I need to fill in a report.'

'No, it wouldn't. You can sit in the kitchen with us until I'm ready to show you around.'

'Oh, I see. Well . . .' She looked at Florence beseechingly. 'Sorry, but I'm new to all this, and simply want to do the job I've been trained for,' she explained in a rush.

Florence nodded, deciding she was being rather harsh with the poor thing. 'Yes, I thought you might be.' She tidied away the shoes, cap and blazer Bobby had dumped on the hall floor. 'Come and sit in the warm. I'll make some tea.'

Bobby ate his bread and jam in silence, his brown eyes regarding their visitor with undisguised suspicion as he slurped tea from the mug.

Sarah Watts sat on the very edge of the kitchen chair and seemed determined to fill the awkward silence with chatter. 'This is very cosy, Miss Hillier,' she twittered. 'I do so love these old-fashioned ranges, and I see you have some copper pots too. I've always adored copper pots, haven't you?'

Florence rolled her eyes. She couldn't take much more of this. 'We'll leave Bobby to his snack and I'll show you round. It won't take long as there are only another three rooms and a bathroom.'

'So convenient to have an indoor bath and lavatory,' gushed Sarah, giving the icy room a quick inspection before ticking it off on her clipboard and writing a note.

Florence was relieved she'd tidied up before leaving for work this morning, but tightly held in her impatience as she showed Sarah the rest of the flat before returning to the kitchen. Bobby had left a mess on the table and was now in the hall with his toy cars.

Florence quickly cleared away his crockery and wiped down the oilcloth. 'I suppose you have to ask me endless questions, so you'd better get on with them before I have to start preparing our supper.'

Sarah seemed relieved to be able to set aside her clipboard and pull some paperwork out of the highly polished briefcase which looked very new.

Florence began to feel a bit sorry for her, and wondered why on earth they'd sent this girl out to her when she clearly didn't know what she was doing.

'You are not on our council records as having ever claimed any kind of benefit, so I'm afraid I will have to ask you some rather personal questions,' Sarah began nervously. Her eyes didn't quite meet Florence's over the table. 'Why haven't you applied for a foster carer's allowance?'

'I earn enough money to keep me and Bobby in food, clothes and anything else he might need. I'm not in the habit of asking for hand-outs.'

Sarah bit her lip and made a note. 'May I ask your age?'

'I'm thirty-nine. Not married – and never have been.'

'I see, thank you.' She carefully wrote this down on the form. 'And I believe you work at Mr Goldman's clothing factory up on the estate as a shop-floor manager?'

Florence frowned. 'I don't know how you know that, but yes. I've worked for Mr Goldman since the end of the war. Before that I held the rank of Sergeant in the ATS.'

Sarah's pale face flushed as if in guilt. 'Mrs Goldman told me when I saw her earlier.' She hurried on to ask the rest of the questions on her form, and then put down her pen.

'And how are you managing with Robert?' Her expression was earnest, her tone cloying as if she was addressing someone in their dotage. 'It must be difficult for you being on your own and without any experience of looking after children.'

Florence coolly held her gaze. 'Bobby doesn't need "managing", as you put it. He isn't a difficult child; but should I need help or advice, I have only to call on Sister Danuta, Peggy Reilly or Father Finlay. Bobby and I have worked out a good routine which suits us both. We're doing just fine, thank you.'

'But having him live with you must be restricting as far as your work and social life are concerned? You must be finding that difficult?' Sarah probed.

Florence folded her arms. She didn't like the sound of this at all. 'What are you getting at exactly?'

Sarah took a breath and began to fiddle with her pen, ducking her head and not quite daring to meet Florence's stony gaze. 'My superiors in the office are concerned that as a single woman with no experience of children, it might be better if Bobby went to live with Mr and Mrs Goldman,' she said in a rush.

'Grace Smith entrusted Bobby's care to me until Danuta and Stanislav adopt him. He's staying here.' Florence glared at the top of the girl's bowed head.

'I'm sure you're doing your best, Miss Hillier,' Sarah stammered, finally giving her a nervous glance. 'And I'm sure Mrs Smith had every faith in your ability to look after Robert, but you see . . . You see, it is thought that it really would be better if he was to go to live with the Goldmans and be with his little brother.'

'That's what your committee has decided, is it?' Florence was coldly furious. 'And have they considered the fact the Goldmans are in their sixties, and taking on a five-year-old as well as a baby will be far too much?'

'That was a consideration, yes,' she admitted solemnly. 'But Mrs Goldman seemed quite amenable to the idea. Of course we would need to speak to Mr Goldman before we could go any further.'

'You'll have your work cut out there,' retorted Florence. 'Solly has made it quite clear that one baby in the house is more than enough to deal with at his age. Besides, Bobby is settled here, close to his school and friends. He knows me and this flat, and feels comfortable, surrounded by memories of his mother. He's never met the Goldmans, is unaware of baby Noel's existence – and certainly doesn't need any more upheaval in his life.'

Sarah's gaze was steady, her tone of voice making it plain she would have no further argument on the matter. 'I do take your point, Miss Hillier, but I'm afraid it is not up to you – or me – to decide these things. If Mr Goldman agrees, then the committee will almost certainly send Robert to live with them and his brother until the adoption process runs its course. Depending on the outcome of that, of course, other arrangements might have to be made.'

Florence inwardly shivered as she saw the steely look in the girl's eyes, and knew that despite her milksop looks and nervous disposition, Sarah had the weight of authority behind her and meant to use it. Florence had underestimated her and was furious at being driven into a corner.

Cissy had been at the school gates to pick up Daisy and, having driven her home and given her a snack, she played dressing-up dolls with her for a while and then left her with Cordelia to go and fetch Peggy.

'Danuta and Stan have got the keys to the room in Eshton Road,' she said the minute her mother had climbed into the car. 'Danuta's over there now trying to clean it up before she has to go on night duty. It's a bit of a dump by all accounts, with noisy tenants.'

'Oh, poor girl,' Peggy sighed. 'It all seems so unfair. I'll pop in and see if I can help.'

'You've already done a day's work, Mum, and she'll be going on night shift in about an hour's time. Grandpa Ron and Uncle Frank are planning to take their furniture over there tomorrow, so I'd leave it for now.'

'It won't hurt to look in for a minute or two. It's on the way home,' she said purposefully. 'Turn left once we're over the bridge and then right after the greengrocer's.'

'Curiosity killed the cat,' teased Cissy.

'That cat has been dead a long time,' Peggy replied dryly. 'By the way, how did you get on up at Parkwood House?'

'It's quite a place, isn't it? I got there a bit early so managed to look into that sweet little chapel and take a turn around the grounds. I was expecting it to be terribly gloomy, but the men were all so much fun, and welcomed me like a long-lost daughter when Dad introduced me.'

Peggy laughed. 'I expect they were delighted to see a pretty face. Turn left here.'

Tutting, Cissy turned left and drove slowly down Eshton Road looking for the right number. 'It doesn't look too bad on the outside,' she murmured, drawing up behind Danuta's little car. 'And, look, there's Danuta cleaning the windows as if her life depended upon it.'

'We'll talk about how you got on with the counsellor when we get home.' Peggy got out of the car, wishing she had a bunch of flowers or something to give Danuta as a housewarming present – but on reaching the door, remembered this accommodation was merely a means to an end, so it would have been pointless.

Danuta opened the door clad in a pair of filthy dungarees and an old sweater, sturdy shoes, rubber gloves and a headscarf. There was a streak of dirt on her flushed cheek. 'Mama Peggy. I wasn't expecting to see you,' she shouted over the blaring music that was coming from upstairs. 'Come in, come in.'

Peggy could smell years of old dinners and hear the tramp of feet upstairs along with raised voices trying to compete with the music. She and Cissy followed Danuta into the room and she stared about her in dismay. 'You can't stay here,' she breathed.

'I'm not planning to, but it's a great deal drier than the place we had at Frank's. But I do need to get it clean before my furniture arrives.' Danuta made a helpless gesture with her hands. 'I'm sorry, but I can't even offer you both tea – my kettle's packed away in Ron's garage, and I didn't think to bring a flask.'

Peggy slipped off her coat and hung it on the peg behind the door. 'We didn't come for tea. Give me a cloth and some Vim and I'll make a start on that sink. Cissy, take those filthy curtains and nets and put them in the bin. There must be one around here somewhere.'

'You don't have to do this,' protested Danuta.

'Of course, I do,' retorted Peggy. 'You can't possibly have things like a mattress and bedlinen in this mucky place. Goodness only knows what sort of animal life there is lurking under those floorboards.'

She shuddered and began to give the porcelain sink and tiled splash-back a jolly good scrub with the Vim before trying to raise a shine on the tap. 'Jim will have to put a new washer in this,' she muttered. 'And I'll get Frank to sand down the floor and give it a coat of fresh varnish before he makes you some new, clean shelves – it's the least he can do.'

'It's really not necessary,' said Danuta in frustration.

'We have rugs to cover the floor, and these shelves only need a scrub and a lick of paint.'

Peggy ignored her and carried on cleaning to the sound of children squabbling in the hall and racing up and down the uncarpeted stairs. The range was disgusting, coated in so much congealed fat and burnt-on grime that it would need one of Jim's electric sanders to get it even partially clean. How people could live like this, she had no idea. Poverty didn't mean you had to be slovenly, and that stove was truly disgusting.

Cissy came back and picked up the dustpan and brush to sweep away the accumulated dust and cobwebs in the corners, under the sink and along the skirting boards. 'The bins are round the back next to the lav, and so full I had to squash those curtains and nets in. From what I could see, there's a decent-sized garden out there that someone has been looking after. There's even a vegetable patch.'

Peggy wrung out the cloth and waved her hands about to dry them as there was no towel. Without her faithful old rubber gloves to protect her hands, the Vim had taken off most of her nail polish, and she'd snagged her thumbnail. But it was all in a good cause.

Danuta stepped back from the window. 'That's a lot better. I can see out of it now, and Stan says the sun should come in during the summer afternoons, which will make the place feel a bit more cheerful.'

'You talk as if you're planning on moving in,' said Peggy fretfully.

Danuta pulled a face. 'We might have to one day. The bank manager will not give us a decision on the mortgage immediately, and even if he does agree to it, we still have to find a house to buy and that could take ages.' She grasped Peggy's damp hands. 'We don't want to impose on you any longer than we really have to, Mama Peggy.'

Peggy looked at her askance. 'Impose? You would never impose, Danuta. Beach View is your home and always will be. I'll never let you live in a place like this so long as I still draw breath.'

Danuta kissed her cheek. 'I must now go home to wash and change. I am on duty at six.'

'What about your tea? You can't go to work on an empty stomach,' Peggy protested.

'I put together a thick potato and leek soup for me and Stan.' She picked up her coat and headed for the door.

Peggy tutted at the thought as she waited for Danuta to turn the key and lead the way back outside to the cars. 'I'll get one of the men to put a proper Yale lock on that door,' she muttered, 'and make some corned beef sandwiches for her to eat later on. Soup, indeed. Whatever next?'

Florence hadn't slept well that night, so wasn't feeling quite the ticket on Tuesday morning. The girl's visit had upset her far more than she could ever have imagined, for now she was in danger of losing Bobby, she'd come to realise just how much she cared for him.

She wasn't at all hungry, so she sipped her morning tea and fondly watched him devour his cereal and toast. He was certainly more cheerful since Father Finlay's visit, and she'd noticed that the book he'd been given now took pride of place on his bedside table. The upsetting incident on Friday night had clearly been forgotten, as he chattered about his friend Alfie and the games lesson he was looking forward to that day.

Florence washed his face with a warm, damp flannel, and made sure that he cleaned his teeth properly before helping him on with his blazer, scarf, gloves and cap. 'There we are,' she said, giving him a brief enough hug for him not to complain. 'All ready for school.'

She checked that his gym shoes and shorts were in his satchel, then took his hand and shut the door behind them to be greeted by another bright but very chilly day.

Bobby chattered away as they headed for the school gates in Camden Road, and although she was tempted to give him another hug, she let him run off happily to join his friends in the playground. She watched him for a moment, surprised at the depth of her feelings, and fretting over the fact she might lose him.

'Would you like a lift to work, Florence?'

Turning, she saw Peggy waving off her Daisy. 'Thanks, that would save me the long trek up that hill.'

Peggy regarded her thoughtfully. 'You look tired. More trouble with little Bobby?'

Florence shook her head. 'He's been as good as gold since Father Finlay came round to talk to him. But I had a visit from the children's fostering service yesterday, Peggy, and it's rather shaken me.'

Peggy's brown eyes widened. 'Lawks, what did they want?'

Florence realised they could be overheard by the other women. 'I'll tell you once I've got the day's work underway and we can talk privately in your office.'

Peggy was deeply concerned over Flo's news and, as she drove up the hill to the factory estate, she silently prayed that the bad start to the day wouldn't be exacerbated by Doris spotting her from the estate office window. With all the other problems she'd had to deal with over the weekend, she'd forgotten about the invitation to tea and hadn't phoned Doris as she'd promised she would, and knew she was in for an earwigging next time their paths crossed.

She waved to Colonel White, Doris's husband and emergency key holder for the factory, and quickly parked. 'Let's get in before my sister catches me,' she said, hurrying from the car to join the flood of chattering women who were pouring in through the doorway to clock on.

Not waiting to see if Florence was following her, she went straight to her office to turn on the fire and switch on the kettle. She'd brought a fresh packet of tea, some milk and biscuits with her today, and as she'd had a hurried breakfast, she was in need of a decent cuppa before she was faced with Florence's problems.

Florence came into the office half an hour later, having checked that the machinists had their sewing for the day, grudges and grumbles had been soothed, and everyone was getting on with their work without too much tittle-tattle. 'I'm sorry to dump this on you, Peggy, but I don't know who else to talk to.'

Peggy had refreshed the pot of tea, so she poured Florence a cup, placed a biscuit on the saucer and pushed it towards her across the desk. 'A visit from the fostering people can't have been a pleasant experience. I'm not surprised you feel shaken.' She sat back and gave her an encouraging smile. 'Tell me what happened, Flo. You know it won't go any further.'

Florence took a sip of tea and then described the whole unpleasant interview, almost word for word. 'So you see, Peggy,' she finished. 'If Solly agrees to take him on with his baby brother, he'll find himself living with strangers – completely uprooted from all he knows, and too far from his little friends to be able to stay in touch outside school hours.'

'I can fully understand why you're upset,' said Peggy. 'The whole plan is utterly ridiculous. Don't those people have any common sense?'

'It's a committee, and you know what they're like,' replied Florence bitterly. 'To be honest, Peggy, I feel I'm in limbo, with no say in what happens next. It was hard enough to get Bobby through the initial bewilderment and shock of losing his mother, so I dread what this proposed move will do to him.'

Peggy smiled. 'It sounds as if, despite your initial doubts, you've become very attached to Bobby.'

'To my surprise, I discover that I have,' she admitted. 'He's a dear little boy, and the thought of him being shunted from pillar to post makes my blood boil. Gracie must be turning in her grave,' she added gruffly.

Peggy could see Florence was getting quite emotional, which was most unusual. 'We can only hope Solly refuses to take him on,' she soothed, wishing she could have a cigarette right now, for it always seemed to help her to think. 'But I am surprised Rachel hasn't spoken to Danuta about this,' she murmured.

'I've only met Rachel at work parties, and fleetingly even then. But you know her very well. Could you telephone her to see how the land lies at that end? I can't go through another night worrying myself silly.'

'I'll phone her later, once I've had the chance to speak to Danuta who'll be asleep right now after being on duty all night.' Peggy leaned forward, her arms resting on the desk. 'I know you feel let down by all this after the care you've given Bobby, but Florence, you have to look at the situation from the fostering people's point of view.'

'Why should I when all they do is poke and pry and meddle in things without any real care for that little boy?' She drew herself up, backbone rigid. 'I might be a single woman of a certain age living in a flat, but love counts for a great deal more than fancy houses and too many toys. And how on *earth* will he react when he discovers he's not only moving in with pensioners, but has got a brother as well?'

Peggy noted that her voice had risen in pitch as her emotions had taken over, and as Florence burst into tears, she moved from behind the desk to awkwardly embrace her. 'Oh, Florence, I'm so sorry this has happened to you. I'll speak to Rachel and Danuta, I promise, and between us, we'll sort out a solution that will suit everyone.'

Florence lifted a tear-streaked face. 'You really think you can? Only I can't bear the thought of Bobby being shunted about like a parcel until the adoption goes through.'

'We'll do our very best, Flo.' She glanced out of the large window and realised they were being watched by half the shop floor.

She moved away from Florence and resumed her seat. 'Why don't you sit and calm yourself for a while before going back out there?' she advised. 'And then I suggest you go to the canteen and have an early lunch, because I suspect you didn't have a proper breakfast, did you?'

Florence battled to control her tears and shook her head. 'I'm sorry to cause such a fuss,' she managed. 'This is most unlike me.'

'Children have a way of touching our hearts like none other,' said Peggy softly. 'It can be a blessing and a curse, for when they are hurt, so are we; but when they smile, it's like the warmth of the sun coming out on a cloudy day. Don't ever apologise for loving him, Flo. It means you're experiencing what all mothers feel at one time or another.'

Stanislav had left Beach View minutes after Danuta had returned from her night duty and crawled into the still-warm bed. He didn't need to be at the airfield for another two hours, but he had something important to do that couldn't wait any longer.

He drove out of Cliffehaven, pleased to see the sun again after the weeks of rain. It felt hopeful, somehow, and it lifted his mood. He approached the hospital and slowed to turn into the car park. It was doubtful the consultant would be in at this early hour, but he was prepared to wait.

The hospital corridors were bustling with porters pushing trolleys of breakfast dishes and nurses carrying bedpans and linen. He made his slow progress towards the consultant's waiting room, the rubber tips of his crutches squeaking on the highly polished linoleum. Pushing his way through the swing door, he saw Julian's terrifyingly efficient secretary sitting behind her desk.

She looked up and over the tortoiseshell-rimmed glasses that were perched on the end of her sharp nose. 'Mr Kowalcyzk,' she said with a frown. 'Do you have an appointment?'

He gave her his most disarming smile even though experience had taught him it didn't work on this particular harridan. 'I do not. But I need to see Julian rather urgently today.'

'*Sir* Julian is very busy today,' she replied. 'What is so urgent, may I ask?'

'That is between me and Julian,' he replied. 'But it is urgent that I see him today, and within the next two hours. I'm flying a cargo of medical equipment to Brussels at ten.'

She raised an eyebrow, smothering a sigh of impatience, and ran her finger down the page of the appointment book. 'Sir Julian is in theatre at ten, and then for most of the day. *If* he arrives early, he *might* be able to fit you in.' She looked up at him again, her expression severe. 'It would really have been better to make an appointment instead of just turning up.'

'I will wait.' He swung over to the line of comfortable chairs and sank down, his crutches propped against the arm, his prosthetic leg stretched out to ease the pressure on his stump. He didn't appreciate being talked to like a naughty schoolboy but would put up with it today because it was vital he spoke to Julian. He folded his arms and watched the door.

'Stanislav, you wanted to see me urgently?'

He woke with a start to find the consultant standing in front of him. 'Yes. It is very important.'

Sir Julian Carmichael-Blackstock grinned. 'You'd better come into my office then.'

Stanislav struggled to get up and followed him, noting that he'd been waiting for over an hour – and had dozed off into the bargain. As Julian closed the door and he took a seat, he felt the nerves kick in. 'I need you to examine my stump,' he said abruptly.

'Why, is it worse?'

'No, it is much better, and I have lost a stone in weight,' he replied proudly.

'That's good, but why the sudden urgency? You have another appointment at the end of the month, which is quite soon enough.'

Stanislav quickly explained why he needed him to write letters to the bank manager and to his solicitor passing him as fit – and if possible, to give back the other prosthesis.

Julian regarded him solemnly and then sighed. 'Let me have a look, then – and be warned, Stan, there'll be no letters if I don't think you're ready for that prosthesis.'

Twenty minutes later and after a lot of prodding, poking and frowning, Julian returned to his desk. 'The infection has cleared up very well over the past two weeks, so you can have the prosthesis back – but I want you to promise that you'll take it off as much as possible to give that stump a rest. It's healing nicely, but still very tender, and will be easily damaged again.'

'I will do as you say,' he replied quickly. 'And the letters? You will write the letters?'

'I will dictate them to my secretary after I've finished in theatre today. Keep up with the diet, Stanislav. The less weight you put on those stumps the better. Now, I really must prepare for theatre.'

Stanislav felt as if a great weight had been lifted from his shoulders, and then glanced at the wall clock and gasped. 'And I must fly to Brussels.'

He delightedly shook the other man's hand and began to fix the prosthesis onto his stump even before Julian had left the room. It was a joyous feeling to be able to ditch the crutches and use the sticks again, and to know that those letters would soon be winging their way to Marcus and the bank manager.

When he finally reached the front steps of the hospital, he lifted his face to the tenuous warmth of the winter's sun. Everything was going to be all right.

13

Danuta climbed out of bed at midday and went searching for breakfast. The night before had been quiet, so after she'd completed her house calls, including Billy's gran, she'd chatted with the other midwife between dozing on and off by the telephone in the clinic, leaving only to assist one of her regular patients who gave birth to a fourth girl without very much fuss at all.

Before returning home, she'd crossed the road to check on Mr Kaplin, and found him contentedly sitting by his fire, eating a fried egg sandwich – most of which had dripped down his pyjamas and dressing gown. She'd left him to the illicit treat his late wife would have frowned upon and headed for her bed at Beach View.

'Good morning, dear,' said Cordelia brightly from her usual fireside chair. 'Sleep well?'

'I did, thank you, Grandma Cordy. Would you like a cup of tea? I'm about to make my breakfast before I go back to Eshton Road.'

'Tea would be lovely, but I don't like the thought of you being there.' She sniffed. 'Peggy told me it was dirty and very noisy.'

'That's why I have to go this morning to finish cleaning before Frank and Ron bring the furniture.'

Cordelia folded her hands over the blanket which covered a hot-water bottle. 'Stan left very early and in a terrible hurry. Did he have an early flight?'

'I'm not sure,' she replied truthfully, concentrating

on making tea and toast. 'We didn't have much time to talk this morning and I was asleep almost before he left the room.'

'I don't know,' Cordelia sighed. 'You young things work long hours and yet you still seem to be full of energy. I'm exhausted just getting dressed in the morning.'

'I can always help you. I do it for a lot of my patients.'

'I'll carry on all the while I can, dear. I've learnt you soon lose the ability to do anything once you give up on it.'

Danuta had just poured the tea and rescued the toast when the telephone rang. 'Is Cissy in?' she asked, hoping she'd answer it.

'No, dear, she went out this morning on some mysterious errand. I have no idea when she'll be back.'

Danuta left her breakfast to cool and reluctantly went into the hall.

'I hope I didn't wake you, dear,' said Peggy. 'Only there's something I need to tell you.'

Danuta listened in growing horror as Peggy related the news about Bobby. 'That seems terribly unfair on Florence, and very unkind to poor Bobby who's had quite enough upset already. Have you managed to speak to Rachel yet?'

'I've tried ringing her, but I haven't got hold of her yet,' said Peggy. 'I'll try her again in a while. What are your plans for the day, Danuta? Are you going back to Eshton Road? Only I didn't make a note of the number there.'

'Neither did I,' admitted Danuta. 'I'm going over after breakfast to finish the cleaning and wait for Ron and Frank. I'll be home in time for supper.'

'Good, you must never go to work without eating first,' said Peggy. 'We'll talk further when I get home.'

Danuta returned to the kitchen, and seeing Cordelia's

look of enquiry, told her what Peggy had said. She didn't want the dear old lady to feel left out of things again.

Cordelia tutted. 'Trust the authorities to go rushing in like headless chickens when they're not needed,' she said crossly. She patted Danuta's hand. 'Never you mind, ducky. With Peggy and Rachel on the case, they'll soon see those busybodies off.'

Danuta sat at the table and sipped the lukewarm tea before scraping a sliver of butter onto the cold toast. Rachel and Peggy together would be an indomitable force, but she doubted that even they could defeat the over-riding power of the local authority.

Once she'd finished her unsatisfactory breakfast, she washed the dishes, made a flask of tea, and then went down into the basement to fetch Peggy's mop, scrubbing brush and bucket. She would stop off on the way to buy a large bottle of bleach, and then give that floor a good scrub before she put her rugs down.

'I'll see you at teatime,' she told Cordelia, kissing her soft cheek. 'Are you expecting Bertie to keep you company later?'

'Yes, dear; he's changing my library books today and promised to come and have a cup of tea with me after lunch.'

Relieved that she wouldn't be entirely alone all day, Danuta left Beach View, loaded up her car and set off for the hardware store in Camden Road to buy the bleach before heading for Eshton Road.

Pulling up at the kerb, she saw a robust elderly man in a flat cap, waistcoat, shirt and tweed trousers, vigorously pruning the hedge, and realised this must be the mystery gardener. She unloaded the boot and, laden with her bedroom curtains and cleaning apparatus, she headed for the gate, aware that he was watching her every move with all the inquisitiveness of a bright-eyed robin.

He pulled off his cap to reveal a mop of silver hair and held out a tanned and gnarled hand. 'Good morning,' he said. 'Hugh Wilton's the name and gardening's my game. You must be the new lass.'

She balanced the box on one arm, the mop wedged under her elbow, to shake his hand. 'My name is Danuta,' she said, aware her surname would probably confuse the issue. 'I am pleased to meet you.' She glanced at the hedge and the neatly tended flower beds where snowdrops were already pushing up their heads. 'You have made this look very nice.'

He tugged his cloth cap back on and straightened his shoulders, the brown eyes in the tanned face gleaming with pride. 'Ah, but you should see the back garden. I look after the vegetable plot too. Everyone chips in with seeds and whatnot, and we share what we grow.'

'A private allotment, what a very good idea,' she replied.

He stood in front of the gate, barring her way, and pulled a pouch of tobacco from his waistcoat pocket to begin rolling a cigarette. 'So, you're foreign then,' he said almost casually, his gaze sharply inquisitive.

'Yes, I am from Poland,' she replied. 'And so is my husband.'

'Right,' he drawled, his gaze still suspicious. 'So what work do you both do?'

Foreign accents were always viewed with suspicion nowadays. Danuta was feeling the weight of the box in her arms but didn't want to seem rude as he clearly suspected they might be German. She'd come across this before, and knew it had to be quashed very quickly to avoid future nastiness. 'I am the local district nurse and midwife,' she said. 'My husband was in the RAF and is now a pilot up at Cliffe airfield.'

His eyes lit up – all prejudice gone. 'Is he indeed? I shall enjoy having a chat with him, then. I've always liked planes and would have loved to learn to fly. But there wasn't much chance of that in the first shout, and I was too old for this last one.'

He cupped his hand around a match and lit his cigarette. 'So, you're moving into old mother Johnson's room,' he rasped through a fit of coughing as the smoke hit his throat. 'It will certainly need a good clean, and no mistake. The poor old girl wasn't up to doing much before they carted her off to the old folks' home.'

'I'm surprised she wasn't one of my patients,' said Danuta, her arms now cramping under the weight of the box.

He shook his head and grimaced. 'She refused any sort of help, and that daughter of hers was worse than useless when it came to looking after her. She's better off in the home if you ask me.'

'Well, I'd better get on,' she said quickly before he could get going again. 'My furniture will be here soon.' She edged round him and headed for the front door.

'If you want a cuppa, just give me a knock,' he called after her. 'My door's across the hall from you.'

She turned on the threshold to smile at him. 'Thank you, I will remember that.'

He waved the shears at her and resumed his clipping, and she hurried to unlock her door so she could put down the heavy box.

'Whew,' she breathed, easing her aching arms and flexing her fingers. 'I thought my arms would drop off. Still, at least I've now met one of my neighbours.' Wondering what the rest of them were like, she set to scrubbing and mopping the floor with a mixture of bleach and water.

The sharp tang of the bleach eventually became too much, and she went to open the window, aware that

Hugh was watching her from the other side of the hedge. She tugged and strained, but the latch at the top was sealed tight and wouldn't budge, so she propped open her door with the bucket in the hope the fumes would dissipate.

As she finished mopping, she arched her aching spine and used the back of her wrist to wipe the sweat from her face. The hard work was helping her to stop thinking about her worries, but as she paused to perch on the broad bay window's sill and drink tea from her flask, they all came flooding back.

'Hello, Sister Danuta. What you doing 'ere?'

Startled, Danuta looked up to see the brassy but cheerful Irene Smith standing in her doorway with her baby in her arms and a toddler peeking from behind her bare legs and short, tight skirt. She quickly got to her feet. 'Hello, Irene. I might ask the same thing of you.'

'The council moved me 'ere when me fella did a runner and I got behind on me rent. What about you?'

'We were evicted from our place out at Tamarisk Bay, and this was all they could give us,' she replied, taking in the bright red hair which clashed with an even brighter lipstick, the skimpy blouse which left little to the imagination, and the painted toenails peeking from the high-heeled sandals. She suspected she knew how Irene was managing, but she asked anyway. 'How are you coping, Irene? It can't be easy with the baby as well as Katy.'

Irene tossed back her hair, her eyes knowing. 'Oh, a bit of this and that, like before.'

'Well, I hope you're being careful,' she murmured.

Irene hitched the baby onto her narrow hip. 'Yeah, I know the drill, Sister, but the rent's gotta be paid, ain't it? And it's wot I know.' She shot her a beaming smile. 'Ta-ta for now then,' she said before clattering up the stairs.

Danuta shifted the bucket away from the door and closed it against any further intrusion. She felt saddened that Irene had gone back on the streets, but then she'd probably had very little choice in the matter once her man had left her with two small children to care for.

She finished the cup of tea and then picked up the broom to sweep the cobwebs from the nicotine-stained ceiling. The range was more than she could tackle; it would have to wait.

The knock on the door startled her, and hoping it wasn't Irene or Hugh, she hesitated before going to open it.

'Rachel? What on earth are you doing here?'

'I had to come, Danuta, I'm sorry to disturb you. Can you help me with the pram, please? It doesn't seem to fit through any of the doors, and I really don't want to leave it outside in case it gets stolen.'

'If Hugh is out there still, I'm sure he'll keep an eye on it. I'll come out with you and ask him.'

Hugh was indeed there, keeping a beady eye on proceedings and all too willing to look after the pram once he'd been introduced to the glamorous Rachel.

Danuta lifted Noel out and carried him inside. 'You'd better close the door, Rachel. They're a nosy bunch in this house.'

Rachel closed the door and stood there like an exotic creature from another world in her sleek mink coat, the diamonds glittering in her ears and on her fingers as she took in the room. 'What is this place? Why are you here?'

Danuta suddenly remembered she hadn't told Rachel anything about the events of the past week, and quickly brought her up to speed, assuring her it was a stopgap and that she'd actually be living at Beach View.

She cuddled the sleeping Noel against her heart, delighted to have this unexpected chance to hold him. 'We went to the bank yesterday to ask for a mortgage,' she said finally. 'Now we must wait to see what they have decided.'

'But the council expects you to live in one room until then?' Rachel gasped. 'Where is the bathroom – the lavatory, kitchen and laundry room?'

Danuta giggled. 'That's the bathroom,' she spluttered, pointing to the basin and single cold tap. 'The kitchen is that health hazard of a range. The lav is outside, and although I'm lucky and can use Peggy's machine, the other tenants have to take their washing to the public laundry in town, and use the council baths for a decent wash.'

Rachel shook her head and sank down on the windowsill next to Danuta. 'I must do something about this, Danuta. You nearly died in service to this country. It's shameful. And you cannot stay with Peggy for ever, my dear. With so few houses to buy at the moment, you could be stuck here for months.'

'There's no need for you to do anything, Rachel, really,' she insisted. 'Peggy and I have a plan. Now, why have you come to see me? Is it about Bobby?'

Rachel pulled out her gold cigarette case and lighter from her coat pocket, looked round for an ashtray, and finding none, put them back again. 'Is there any other subject to concern us both at the moment?' She didn't wait for an answer but carried on. 'I've spoken with Solly – in fact it got quite heated at times – you know what he's like when he feels he's being pushed into a corner.'

Danuta smiled nervously and nodded to encourage Rachel to get on with it.

'He calmed down eventually, as he always does, and we managed to discuss the problem sensibly. We both came to the conclusion that the authorities are being very high-handed with Florence, and that moving Bobby now would undo all the sterling progress she's made with him since Gracie died.'

Danuta was on tenterhooks. 'So, what decision did you come to?'

'Solly is adamant that Noel is quite enough to deal with, without having a five-year-old running about the place. And although I wouldn't have minded taking him on, I agreed that he was in the best place for now.'

'Rachel, please tell me what you've decided.'

'I telephoned the council as soon as I finished speaking with Peggy and demanded to speak to the department head. I've known her for years and am familiar with her circumstances – which are a little odd considering her position,' she added mysteriously.

Danuta raised an eyebrow.

'But never mind all that,' she said, waving her hand. 'The upshot is, Bobby will stay with Florence and his home will be with her until you adopt them both.'

'Oh, Rachel, that's perfect,' Danuta breathed, clasping her hand. 'You really know how to work miracles, don't you? Florence will be so relieved.'

Rachel giggled and tapped the side of her nose. 'It's knowing people's secrets that gets things done in this town, and I've lived here long enough to have quite a store of them; believe you me.' She got to her feet. 'I'd better go and let you get on.'

Danuta followed Rachel out onto the front step and allowed Hugh to coo over the baby for a moment until Rachel took him from her arms and gently placed him in the luxurious pram. 'Don't worry about telling Florence the news. Peggy said she'll let her know.'

Danuta bent over the pram and resisted touching the baby's cheek with her dirty finger. 'I'll be up to visit again when I'm off nights and have this place straight.

Thanks for coming to tell me, Rachel. It's eased my mind no end.'

Rachel gave her a hug and kissed her cheek. 'It was my very great pleasure, my dear, and now I'm off to work some more miracles. Bye, bye.'

Danuta stood at the gate and watched her stroll along in her high heels pushing the pram. She must have left her car at the Camden Road factory, she surmised, for there was absolutely no way she could walk the ten miles home in those shoes.

'You got some posh friends, and no mistake,' muttered Hugh, scratching his head beneath his cap as he openly admired Rachel's retreating figure.

Danuta laughed. 'She's not at all posh, just the kindest, sweetest, most cleverest woman you're likely to meet.'

Hugh looked at her askance and then shook his head. 'Now I've heard it all,' he muttered before returning to his gardening.

Peggy returned home that evening to find that Danuta was already dressed for her night duty, and that she and Cissy had made a large vegetable pie for supper, with mashed potato as a topping instead of pastry. She slipped off her coat and kicked off her shoes to sit down in her slippers by the fire while Cordelia read Daisy a story.

'It's been quite an emotional day all round,' she said after telling Cordelia and Cissy about the to-do with the fostering people. 'Florence was over the moon when she heard how Rachel had turned things round for Bobby.' She gave a wry smile. 'And here was me thinking she was finding the responsibility too much.'

She turned to Danuta. 'How do you feel about the new arrangements?'

'Delighted,' she replied. 'It's the best thing for Bobby, and that's all that really matters, isn't it?'

Peggy nodded. 'So, how did you get on at Eshton Road?'

'Very well, considering it was in such a state. I met two of my neighbours and got the place a bit cleaner than it was, although getting that range anywhere close to hygienic is beyond me. Ron and Frank brought my furniture, though it was a bit of a struggle to get our huge bed inside. They had to take it apart and then put it back together again.'

She grinned. 'There was a lot of muttering and sweating, but they managed it in the end – but it didn't leave room for much more. I've kept two armchairs for the bay window, and a small chest of drawers, but the rest will have to go in Ron's garage. They also promised to drop off the coal and logs we still have for you tomorrow.'

'They'll certainly be welcome. Did they put a proper lock on the door, and fix that dripping tap?'

Danuta nodded. 'They got the locksmith in and I now have a good Yale lock and two keys. They also fixed the rail, hung my curtains, and checked the gas fire worked properly. It's looking quite cosy now.'

She pursed her lips. 'The only really disappointing thing was the state of my lovely rugs. The damp from Tamarisk Bay has really got into them, so I've brought them home, given them a good beating and scrub, and then hung them out on your washing line. Which reminds me, I'd better get them in before the night air gets to them.'

As Danuta hurried outside, Peggy turned to Cissy. 'And what about you, darling? How was your day?'

'It was fine, although not very exciting. I had a potter around the shops, ate lunch upstairs at Plummer's, and then walked along the promenade. It was such a lovely crisp day it seemed to be a waste to stay indoors. Then I came back and had a cup of tea with Grandma Cordy and Bertie before picking up Daisy.'

Peggy regarded her evenly, suspecting she'd been up to far more than she'd admitted to, but she didn't question her. No doubt she'd tell her when she was ready.

The front door slammed and they all turned towards the kitchen door. Stanislav came in with his usual rolling gait, supported by his two sturdy sticks. 'Good evening,' he boomed cheerfully.

'Stanislav, you've got rid of your crutches,' Danuta cried out, hastily dumping the rugs on a nearby chair to rush and give him a hug.

'Steady on, darling, you will have me off my feet,' he softly protested, giving her a kiss. 'Yes, and Julian is writing letters to the bank and Marcus to tell them I am fit and well, and capable of anything. Martin and the others are delighted too, and I must admit, it is good to be back in the pilot's seat again.'

'Oh, that is such good news,' breathed Peggy. 'I'm so glad for you.'

Stanislav sat at the table and shot them all another beaming smile. 'Danuta and I must now prepare for tomorrow, but with everything going so well, I have no fear of it.'

'It's a big day,' said Danuta, carefully picking up the rugs again so they didn't leave a damp patch on her uniform dress. 'And although you might not be too worried about it, I'm a bag of nerves.' She gave the rugs a sniff. 'They smell a bit better. Would it be all right if I hung them up downstairs, Mama Peggy?'

'Of course.' Peggy got out of the chair to inspect the pie. 'The food's ready, so everyone sit down and eat.'

Once Danuta had returned to the kitchen, she tucked into the pie and told Stan all about the tussle with the foster people and how it had been resolved. 'Things finally look as if they're working out,' she said once she'd finished her meal. 'We'll just have to keep our fingers crossed that we get the mortgage and tomorrow goes smoothly. You have told Martin you'll need the afternoon off, haven't you?'

'Of course I did.' He ran a gentle finger down her cheek. 'Don't worry, little one, all is organised.'

Danuta had finally got into her bed at nine o'clock the following morning, and fallen instantly asleep. When Stanislav had woken her at one, she'd hurriedly washed and dressed, so she could eat something before they had to be at the adoption office at two-thirty.

'I had hoped for an easy night of it,' she said, stifling a yawn as they sat at the kitchen table to share a hurried lunch and watch the sleet dance past the window. 'Unfortunately, it was anything but. Mrs Brown had a seizure in the middle of her evening bath and I had to wait with her for over half an hour for an ambulance, which meant I was running late for the rest of my home visits – which didn't go down well with some of my grumpier old patients. They hate having their routine upset.'

She sipped her tea. 'Then two women living at opposite ends of the town went into labour at the same time – one of them with complications – so I had to quickly run to a phone box and call out Sister O'Neill to help. I'd only just got back to the clinic when Mr Kaplin's neighbour telephoned in a panic. She'd found him crumpled at the bottom of the stairs, out cold.'

'That doesn't sound too good,' gasped Stanislav. 'He wasn't dead, was he?'

'Thankfully, no, and he'd come round by the time the ambulance arrived. The hospital confirmed he'd broken his arm, and they're keeping him in just to be sure he doesn't suffer any ill effects after that nasty knock on the head.'

'He'll find it difficult to cope with one arm in plaster.'

Danuta nodded. 'He'll need someone calling in every day until it's mended, and although the woman next door said she'd try and pop in, I don't fully trust her, so I telephoned Rachel to let her know what had happened in the hope she knows someone more reliable. Actually, he was very lucky he didn't break his hip. At his age, that would almost certainly have finished him off.'

She pushed back from the table and glanced at the clock, her stomach clenching with nerves. 'It's time we went, Stan. We mustn't be late.'

He helped her on with her coat, and she spent a moment adjusting her hat over her freshly brushed brown hair, before applying a dash of lipstick to boost her courage. She turned to see Stanislav watching her with some amusement. 'First impressions are very important, Stan. And we have to let this Mrs whatever-her-name-is know we mean business,' she said firmly.

'Aurelia Johnston-Black,' he recited from the letter before returning it to the inside pocket of his overcoat. He twirled his moustache. 'How can she fail to be impressed when the baron and his baroness are honouring her with our presence?'

She giggled and poked him in the chest. 'Don't be daft, Stan. Foreign titles like ours don't open doors here as they did back in Poland. You have to be at least a lord, or a belted earl.' She kissed his cheek to take the sting out of her words, and then headed for the front door.

The drive to the council offices didn't take long, and it was a relief to note that although the sky was grey and ominous, the sleet had yet to turn to snow, but when they climbed out of the car to make their way into the building they were assailed by a bitter wind that almost took their breath away.

Danuta pressed the button for the lift, and they rode up to the third floor. She tried to calm her racing pulse by taking deep breaths. It was ridiculous to be so nervous when she'd faced far worse during her undercover work in enemy territory. But this interview mattered so much, and those two little ones relied on her to keep her promise to their mother, so the thought of failing simply had to be banished.

The lift door opened and they followed the signs until they came to the end of a long corridor where a closed door bore a plaque proclaiming 'Adoption Services Office'. She shared a look with Stanislav and squeezed his hand, then took a deep breath and opened the door – to discover a deserted room.

There were chairs lining two walls, with a low table in the middle, and a desk beneath the window that overlooked the roofs of the buildings in the High Street. They hesitated in the doorway before Danuta noticed the little silver hand-bell on the desk. 'Should I ring it, do you think?' she whispered into the silence.

He shrugged, and she was about to pick up the bell when a side door opened and a middle-aged woman of generous proportions in a twinset, pearls and pleated skirt stepped into the room with a welcoming smile.

'How very nice to meet you both,' she said in plummy tones, advancing on them. She stuck out a soft white hand with neat, unvarnished nails and only a gold wedding band as adornment. 'We're very informal here,' she continued once they'd shaken hands. 'Please, call me Aurelia, and you must be Danuta and Stanislav.'

Danuta felt marginally more relaxed now she

realised Aurelia perhaps wasn't quite the officious, bullying monster she'd expected, and fleetingly wondered if the reason for first names had anything to do with the fact the woman couldn't pronounce their surname. 'We are pleased to meet you too,' she said.

Aurelia dipped her chin in acknowledgement and indicated they should follow her into the inner office, which was far less formal. Another desk under another window with the same view was adorned with a blue folder, a rack of pens and a small vase containing what looked suspiciously like plastic daffodils. Three comfortable chairs had been placed around a low table bearing a tray of tea things, and there were numerous photographs of smiling babies and children covering one entire wall.

Aurelia noticed Danuta's interest. 'They are just a very few of our successes,' she said proudly. 'Do please sit down.' She picked up the folder from the desk, and then settled down to pour the tea and hand out the cups.

Danuta noted with dismay that her hand was shaking to the point where she was in danger of slopping the tea into the saucer, so she quickly put her cup down on the table.

'My dear Danuta, there really is no need to be nervous,' soothed Aurelia. 'This first meeting is really for us to get to know one another, and to answer any questions you might have as to the way your application will progress.'

Danuta knotted her hands in her lap, determined to quell the nerves and concentrate.

Aurelia opened the blue folder. 'I have received letters from your solicitor as well as from your consultant and employer, Stanislav. I have to say, they have given you glowing references, and I'm delighted to see that your health has greatly improved.'

'I am very fit,' said Stanislav, sitting bolt upright in the chair, and only just managing not to twirl his moustache. 'I will be an excellent father – and Danuta she will be the best mother.'

Aurelia smiled. 'I have no doubt of it,' she replied. 'Now, why don't you tell me about yourselves – what you do – where you're from – and how these two little ones will fit into your lives.'

Stanislav told her of his life in Poland before the war, his action during the Spanish Civil War and his career in the RAF which came to an end when he lost his legs – but how his flying had been resurrected when he'd become part of the team at Phoenix Air Transport. He went on to say how he and Bobby had become friends, and he was planning to take him to the park and the beach once the weather was more clement.

When it was Danuta's turn, she had to be careful not to reveal the part she'd played in the war for the SOE, so she simply told Aurelia that she'd managed to get out of Poland in the early days of the war to come to England to find her brother who'd also flown for the RAF before being killed during the Battle of Britain. She kept to the story made up for her at Bletchley Park that she'd gone to London to nurse during the war, bypassing the fact she'd become one of the most wanted saboteurs by the Nazis – had been captured and tortured by the SS – and could no longer have children as a result of what they did to her. The truth was easy when she went on to explain how her work could be continued around the children, but that they would always be the main priority.

'Do either of you have family still in Poland?' Aurelia asked.

They both shook their heads. 'All dead,' muttered Stanislav. 'I lost my ancestral estate too – now the Russians live in my fine house,' he added with a grimace.

'It must have been very difficult for you to learn another language and settle into a new country in the midst of a war.'

'We both speak the English we learnt in school in Poland,' said Stanislav. 'My Danuta, she already speaks English, French and German before she comes here.'

Aurelia looked suitably impressed by this, before she returned to her paperwork. 'I see you are living in Tamarisk Bay.' She looked up with a frown. 'But aren't those buildings due for demolition?'

'We've moved out already,' said Stanislav. 'The council have given us a room in Eshton Road, but we will be staying with the Reilly family at Beach View for a while until we have to move in there.'

Aurelia frowned. 'Yes, I have had a letter from Marcus Golding explaining this. I understand you are hoping to buy somewhere very soon? Will that be in Cliffehaven?'

'Cliffehaven has become our home,' said Danuta as Stanislav hesitated. 'We have work and friends here, so we very much hope to find somewhere local.'

Aurelia spent time writing in her folder and then closed it. 'I must warn you that you will be considered homeless until you find something more permanent.'

They stared at her in horror, and all of Danuta's hopes died.

Aurelia held up her hand. 'Please, let me explain,' she said quickly. 'The Eshton Road house is already overcrowded, and one room isn't remotely adequate for two adults and two small children – even less so if you take into account Stanislav's disability.'

She must have seen him take umbrage at being called disabled and hurried on. 'And although Beach View is of a higher standard and the Reillys are very well-respected people, it is still classed on the council register as a boarding house – making you lodgers, and therefore at risk of being evicted. The sooner you can find a home of your own, the better.'

Danuta swallowed the lump in her throat. 'Peggy and Jim would never evict us,' she protested.

Aurelia pursed her lips. 'You say that now, Danuta, but the legal rights of a lodger are a very grey area and, unfortunately, none of us can be certain of what the future might hold.' She leaned forward, her expression earnest. 'What if their daughter had to move in with her husband and three children? What if Jim lost his job and Peggy had to give up her work at the factory and start running it as a boarding house again?'

She gave a little sigh and fluttered her hands. 'I'm not saying these things will happen, but I have to play devil's advocate here and paint the worst scenario.'

Danuta digested this and glanced at Stan, who was looking shell-shocked. 'We do understand, Aurelia, and I agree it is wise to think of these things. But we aren't just relying on the Reillys or the council. We have been to the bank, and now have to wait for the manager to give us an answer to our mortgage application,' she finished in a rush.

'Jolly good. Please make sure you let me know immediately if your circumstances change, for a mortgage and home of your own will boost your adoption application no end.'

Aurelia set the folder aside and rested her hands on her lap. 'Please don't lose heart,' she said quietly. 'Both children are safe and being well looked after, and your application will just remain on hold for a while until your accommodation is fixed and more appropriate.'

'You won't refuse us?' Danuta pleaded.

She smiled. 'Not today – and not out of hand either. You're clearly doing the best you can in difficult circumstances. My advice would be to concentrate on finding a home while maintaining close contact with the children. Meanwhile, I will arrange for home visits to both children with you in attendance to see how you are all getting on, and also a home visit to you both to see if there are more questions to be answered once we're further down the line.'

She got to her feet, waited for Stanislav to struggle up and balance on his sticks, then shook their hands. 'It's been a pleasure to meet you both, and I hope to see you again very soon.'

The door closed behind them and, arm in arm, they slowly walked back to the bank of lifts, their thoughts and emotions in too much of a turmoil to be able to voice them.

Peggy's mind had wandered from her work responsibilities all afternoon, repeatedly returning to Danuta and Stan, making her wish she could have been a fly on the wall during that interview.

Thoughts of that office above the Town Hall naturally brought back memories of young April, who'd come to live at Beach View after she'd been turfed out of the Wrens and disowned by her mother for getting pregnant. The American GI responsible had denied even knowing her and had been whisked away by his commanding officer to another encampment, leaving the poor girl at her wits' end.

Peggy had gone with her to that office to see about having the baby adopted – but brown-skinned babies were hard to place, especially as the war had seen hundreds of girls in the same situation, and prejudice against them had been rife. Rescue had come from April's uncle who used to be Cliffehaven's stationmaster, and he'd taken her and her baby under his wing.

Peggy smiled at the memory, for once April had the love and support of her uncle, she'd come to the brave decision to keep baby Paula and hold her own against the opposition she would meet in a small town like Cliffehaven. April was still living in the old stationmaster's cottage with her uncle, but was now in charge of the local telephone exchange, and courting a nice young man who doted on Paula, who was thriving.

Dragging her thoughts back to the present, Peggy finished sorting through the dockets which had come through from the loading bay. They would need to be checked against the stock before she went home tonight, for she couldn't risk anything going missing after the debacle of Phil Warner's robbery.

She left the office and bustled through the main body of the factory to the back where the stock was stowed on racks, well away from the cold concrete floor. The latest delivery was stored close to the door which led to the loading bay, so she slowly ticked off each bolt of cloth on her inventory, and once she was satisfied that everything was as it should be, checked both doors were secure and returned to her office and the welcome warmth of her electric fire.

She held her hands out to the fire and watched the sleet driving across the deserted building site. The sky looked grey, the clouds swollen with the promise of snow. She could only hope they wouldn't wake up tomorrow to find themselves several feet deep in snowdrifts, as they had down the east coast during the previous night.

With that thought, she picked up the receiver and dialled Anne's number. It was answered on the third ring. 'Hello, darling. I know I'll see you when you pick the girls up from school, but I wondered if Martin had given you any idea of how much snow we can expect.'

'The forecast reckons we'll get quite a lot of it, Mum, and it's likely to stick around for a while too. But don't worry. I've done a huge food shop and laid in lots of cans and dried stuff. The coalman has been and Martin chopped a load of logs for me over the weekend, so we're all set up, ready for whatever the weather throws at us.'

'That's a relief. But you know you can all come to me if it gets too bad.'

'I know, Mum, but if it gets really bad we'll be stuck out here. They certainly won't clear these country lanes. But please don't worry about us. We'll be fine, really we will.'

'I'll ring Bob tonight and see how he's faring in Somerset, and then try to get through to your Auntie Doreen in Wales, although she ought to be used to heavy snow – they get enough of it there.'

'Are you well prepared, Mum? Do you want me to get in any tins for you?'

'I've got tins, and Ron delivered Danuta's left-over coal and logs early this morning. The coalman was due to call today as well, so we should be fine.'

'I'm glad to hear it. By the way, have you heard from Aunt Doris?'

Peggy stiffened. 'Why?'

'I bumped into her today when I was shopping, and she's definitely got a bone to pick with you.' Anne giggled. 'Whatever have you done to upset her now, Mum?'

Peggy told her about the invitation she hadn't replied to. 'I'm ashamed to say that I'm entirely at fault, and the truth is, I've been avoiding her. There's too much going on at the moment with Danuta and Stan and the children, and I really can't cope with trying to soothe her hurt feelings.'

'I don't suppose you know how Stan and Danuta got on today? Martin and the others at the airfield were asking after them.'

'I haven't heard anything yet, but it's a bit too soon, really. No doubt they'll tell us this evening.' She glanced up at the clock and then caught sight of Doris marching through the factory with a very determined look on her face. 'I'd better go. Doris has turned up and is clearly on the warpath.'

Doris didn't knock but walked straight in and closed the door behind her. 'I know you've been avoiding me, Margaret, and I'm appalled at your lack of manners.'

Peggy decided that only the truth would do. 'I'm sorry, Doris. Really I am. But there was so much going on at home, I completely forgot about your invitation to tea. By the time I'd remembered it was too late to do anything about it – and yes, I took the coward's way out and have been avoiding you.'

The wind of self-righteous anger was taken from Doris's sails and she was left standing there without a retort.

'Why don't you sit down and have a cup of tea with me? I've got some digestive biscuits,' Peggy coaxed.

Doris looked at the slim watch on her wrist. 'I don't really have time. John is waiting to drive me home as the weather's closing in.'

'Of course. Another day, then,' replied Peggy, shooting her a warm smile in the hope it might defrost her.

Doris's smile barely touched her lips. 'Perhaps,' she replied and reached for the door handle. 'When you do find time in your busy life, try and remember that I am family, and deserve just as much attention as all those other waifs and strays you have a habit of collecting.'

Peggy blinked at the barb as Doris exited the office and slammed the door behind her. 'Oh, Doris,' she sighed. 'When will I ever get it right with you?'

Stanislav drew the car to a halt outside Eshton Road and stared at the driving sleet. 'What do we do about this room, Danuta? If Aurelia thinks it will not be right for us to have the children, shouldn't we give it back to the council so someone else can have it?'

Danuta shook her head. 'We have to keep it until we know for sure we can get a mortgage and buy our own place. Besides, if the weather is going to be as bad as you say, Anne and the others might very well want to move into Beach View.'

'There is plenty of room at Beach View. They could have the big room upstairs next to Charlie.'

'It will be very noisy with those two girls, Daisy and baby Oscar,' she warned. 'We might be glad to have the room to escape to.'

He grimaced at the thought and then reached for the door handle. 'Come, show me what you have done with it.'

They tucked their chins into their collars to avoid the windblown sleet and she opened the door to their room with the new key.

Stanislav leaned on his sticks and looked round. The large bed took up most of the space, with the small chest of drawers beside it. The two easy chairs had been placed in the bay, and their curtains and pristine nets hung at the window. He noticed the lampshade from their bedroom now covered the central bulb, and the large kitchen clock took pride of place above the range.

He moved across the room and eyed the range, his lip curling. 'Anything cooked on that would poison us,' he muttered.

'Frank said he'd borrow Jim's electric sander to try to get it clean, but I doubt it's been used for years, which is why the gas fire was installed. I'd be very loath to light it in case the pipe is blocked – or there are bird nests in the chimney.'

He perched on the side of the bed and gloomily stared out of the window at the gathering darkness. 'I am sorry, Danuta. I never wanted this for you.'

She rushed to him and put her arm about his broad shoulder. 'It's not your fault, Stan,' she whispered in Polish. 'As long as we're together, then I am happy to live anywhere.'

He hung his head. 'But Aurelia called us homeless – and we are, my love. We're dependent on others to decide our future, just as we were when the Germans marched into Poland, and that is not what I wished for us. You would have been better off not marrying me.'

She took his face in her hands and looked into his eyes with all the love she felt for him. 'I never want to hear you say things like that again, Stanislav. I love you, and my place is at your side until my last breath. We will find a way to get through this – together.' She softly kissed his lips. 'Come on, let's get home to Beach View and have something to eat before I have to be on duty again.'

'But you can't drive about in that,' he gasped, indicating the sleet that was visibly turning to snow and coming down more determinedly.

She stood and put her hands on her hips. 'Stan, I have driven through the blizzards of a Warsaw winter and survived. A few Cliffehaven snowflakes aren't going to bother me.'

He laughed uproariously and pulled her onto his lap. 'I'm so glad I married you,' he said, nuzzling her neck. 'Please don't ever change.'

14

Bobby was jumping up and down in a fever of excitement as Florence struggled to wrap him in layers of jumpers beneath his coat and ram a woolly hat over his ears, a scarf around his neck and insist he pulled on his gloves. The east wind was bitter, but he'd been kept indoors at school all day, and was impatient to join his friends who were already playing in the snow, even though it had yet to settle.

She pulled on her thick overcoat, scarf, woolly hat and sturdiest shoes in the hope they'd keep her warm. They finally set off and she chuckled in delight as he turned his face up to the swirling flurries, trying to catch them on his tongue. And then he raced away from her to join the other little boys who were running about with their arms extended, pretending to be fighter planes avoiding the flak of the snow that was blowing across the playing field.

Digging her gloved hands into her coat pockets, and her nose and chin in her woollen scarf, she saw she was the only adult to brave the cold and keep an eye on the boys, but that suited her just fine. She didn't want or need company after being stuck indoors with all those gossiping women at the factory, and was just glad to be outside even though the air was freezing.

She stamped her feet in an attempt to bring some feeling back into her toes, and then decided a brisk walk around the perimeter of the field might be better than just standing on the sidelines. She was about to set off when she heard a familiar voice call her name.

Turning, she saw the tall, slender figure of her darling Beatrice approaching, similarly wrapped against the cold but somehow still managing to look elegant and glamorous in her camel-hair coat, fur hat and long leather boots. She felt the usual inner glow at the sight and hurried towards her, resisting the yearning to kiss her lovely cheek.

'Hello, Bea. What on earth are you doing here?'

'I might ask you the same thing.' Large blue eyes regarded her quizzically between fur hat and woollen scarf. 'This is hardly walking weather.'

'I'm keeping an eye on Bobby. What about you?'

'I saw you walk past my flat, and as you haven't been in touch since we were supposed to go out on New Year's Eve, I thought I'd brave the cold and find out how things are going.'

'Let's walk and talk. It's too cold to stand about.' Florence hooked her hand into the crook of Beatrice's arm and they set off on a slow circuit of the playing field as the boys ran and shouted and kicked a football back and forth.

She told Beatrice about the run-in with the council officials and the surprising outcome engineered by Rachel. 'I was so relieved to be able to keep him with me. He's a dear little boy and coping very much better now. I have Father Finlay to thank for that,' she finished with a warm smile.

'I heard on the grapevine that the fostering people wanted to hand him over to Rachel Goldman. Which, in my opinion, would have been the best thing all round, so I'm astounded to learn you're actually glad to keep him.'

Florence came to a standstill and regarded the woman she loved with some misgivings. 'I've grown to care for him, Bea,' she said simply. 'We've become used to each other, and I enjoy his company.'

The blue eyes widened. 'Good heavens, Florence, you really have changed your tune. You've always sworn you detested the idea of children.'

Florence smiled. 'That was before I got to know Bobby.'

'You're not thinking of adopting him, are you?' Beatrice asked sharply.

Shocked by Bea's tone, Florence shivered. 'What if I was? Would that be such a terrible thing?'

'It would be a ridiculous thing to do,' snapped Beatrice. 'You're a single, independent woman and your whole life would be turned upside down. You'd have no chance of a social life and lose all your friends into the bargain; you'd have to be constantly paying out for babysitters to look after him in the school holidays, and any dream you might have had of taking that correspondence engineering degree would be forever on the back burner.'

She grasped Florence's hand with surprising strength. 'For goodness' sake, Florence, think very carefully before you do something you'll regret.'

Florence looked into her blue eyes, hoping to see warmth and understanding, but they were as cold as the swirling snowflakes. 'It's a good thing I have no intention of adopting him and his brother then, isn't it?' she said flatly. 'But I tell you this, Beatrice, whether you approve or not, I shall remain a part of Bobby and Noel's life even after they are adopted.'

'More fool you then,' muttered Beatrice, her eyes narrowing as she watched the boys playing. 'He's not yours, and never was – and if all this sentimental tosh you're spouting is because you feel you owe something to Gracie, then you're deluded. You owe that girl nothing after what she did.'

Florence dug her hands into her pockets and calmly looked Beatrice in the eye, seeing for the first time how self-serving and bullying she was. 'Thank you for your candid appraisal, Beatrice. I'll be sure to ignore it – and anything else you have to say from now on. Goodbye.'

She felt strangely liberated as she turned her back on the other woman and headed towards Bobby, who was now quite red in the face with cold. 'Come on, love, let's get home for some cocoa before Uncle Stan comes to read you your bedtime story.'

Florence didn't look back to see what Beatrice was doing. Their relationship was at an end, and she felt few regrets.

Stanislav had driven straight from the airfield to Florence's flat so he could read Bobby his nightly story before he went to bed at six. Florence had already bathed and fed him, and so they sat close together on the couch while Stan read from the Enid Blyton book. Bobby had been full of questions as usual and, having asked Florence's permission, Stanislav had allowed him to look at the two false legs while he explained how they worked.

As the child's eyes began to flutter with sleep, Stanislav gathered him into his arms and very carefully carried him to his bedroom. Pulling the covers over his narrow shoulders, he softly ruffled his hair. 'Goodnight and sweet dreams,' he murmured.

Bobby muttered something, but Stanislav could see he was already well on his way to a deep sleep, so he lit the night-light and left the door ajar before going into the kitchen to see Florence.

'The snow is coming down faster now,' he said, taking the cup of tea she'd offered. 'It's settling too. I wouldn't be surprised if we woke tomorrow to find the world is white like Polish winters.'

'Will it be very bad, do you think?'

'The latest forecast says we could be in for the worst winter in living memory. There is an anticyclone sitting over Scandinavia – this is a high-pressure area blocking the movement of the depressions coming across the Atlantic Ocean and forcing them to the south. It will bring strong, easterly winds carrying snow, which the forecasters think will eventually cover the entire country. We must be prepared for such heavy snow that the town is cut off for some time.'

Florence frowned. 'I heard on the news that they'd already had a lot of snow on the East Anglian coast last night, but I was hoping the weather would go north and we'd miss it.'

'I very much doubt that will be the case, Florence. The forecasts we get at the airfield are extremely detailed and accurate.' He glanced across at the range fire. 'Do you have enough coal and logs to see you through a few weeks?'

'I should have enough for a week or two, but I do have a couple of electric fires, so I'm sure we'll be fine.'

'It might be an idea to call the coal merchant first thing tomorrow and get some extra stocks in – just in case.'

'You really think it will be that bad?' At his nod, she rubbed her brow. 'But what about you and the others at the airfield? Surely you won't be able to fly if the weather closes in?'

He tugged on his moustache. 'We already have the planes in the hangars, and everything we couldn't fly out today is now stored under cover. There will be no more flying until the weather changes.'

He drank the last of the tea and struggled to his feet.

'Thank you, Florence, but I must check on Danuta. She is on duty tonight, and I don't like the thought of her driving if the snow is thickening.' He smiled down at her. 'I will see you tomorrow evening. Thank you for letting me read to Bobby each night.'

She smiled back at him. 'It's the highlight of his day – although if the snow settles overnight, I suspect it will be snowmen and snowball fights that will be uppermost in his mind tomorrow.'

Stanislav waved to her before she closed the door behind him, and he stood by the car, noticing the silence that always came at times like this as he watched the snow fall softly all around. The air was bitterly cold, the black sky studded with diamond-bright stars, but this narrow street seemed to be sheltered from the wind.

He lifted his face and felt the feathery touch of the snowflakes settle on his nose, cheeks and eyelashes, reminding him of the Polish winters of his boyhood. The memories flashed through his mind, and he smiled. Tomorrow he would buy a toboggan and take Bobby to the hills so he could learn how much fun it was to be a boy racing downhill in the snow.

He climbed into the car, still smiling, and headed towards Elms Avenue and the surgery. He wouldn't tell Danuta of his plan because she'd only try and stop him, but he and Bobby would be able to share their first secret adventure – and adventures were very important to boys, for they moulded, educated and defined the character of the men they would become.

Danuta's schedule of home visits had taken longer than usual, so she hadn't managed to see to Mr Kaplin until after nine. She could see he was getting very frustrated at trying to do things with one arm in plaster, but once she'd managed to wash him and persuade him into fresh pyjamas, he'd calmed down enough to tell her that Rachel had visited earlier to inform him that for the time being, he would have to rely on the woman next door and the district nurses; but that she had arranged for two meals to be delivered each day from the Lilac Tearooms. Danuta had left him having a late supper of what looked like a very tasty pie and mash.

Relieved that he seemed quite happy, she'd gone back to the surgery across the road to find that the other midwife, Sister Patricia O'Neill, had left a note saying she'd been called out to a woman expecting twins. Danuta settled down to write up her notes, expecting Sister O'Neill to be back any minute as twin births were usually transferred to the hospital.

And then the telephone rang. It was a farmer whose wife had gone into a swiftly progressing labour. She listened as the man's panicked voice rattled down the receiver to the accompaniment of his wife's yells for help, and realised she didn't know the woman as she hadn't attended any of the antenatal clinics.

'It's snowing hard here and my lorry's got a flat tyre. Shall I bring her in on my tractor?' the man shouted down the phone.

Horrified at the suggestion, Danuta gripped the receiver. 'Good grief, Mr Green. On no account are you to even attempt that. Keep her warm in bed and I will get to you as soon as I can.'

She took down the address, listened to a garbled set of directions interspersed with Mrs Green's screeching, and eventually put down the receiver. She eyed the snow drifting past the surgery window and, with a sigh of impatience, looked up their farm on the detailed local area map she always kept handy – it was certainly easier to understand than Mr Green's broad countryman's brogue.

She bit her lip, for the farm was isolated, hidden deep within the hills some eight miles north of Cliffehaven, and the snow was now coming down quite fast.

Having written a note for Sister O'Neill to tell her where she'd gone, she gathered up her bag and extra blankets from the stores before checking the battery on her torch, filling a flask with hot tea, and then taking everything out to her car.

Knowing the roads would soon be treacherous, and she was about to encounter narrow country lanes which could already be icy and covered in snow, she quickly checked she had the foot-pump in the boot and then let some air out of her tyres. Soft tyres gripped better onto the road and were less likely to slip and slide than plump ones – but if the snow worsened over the next few days, she would have to dig out the chains from her boxes in Ron's garage.

The snowflakes seemed to be coming straight at her as she drove along Elms Avenue, her headlights shining on the tyre tracks someone had left in the thin white layer that was already making it difficult to gauge where the road ended and the pavement began. Aware that time was slipping away and the farmer's wife needed her urgently, she set caution aside and picked up the pace a little as she headed up the High Street and out onto the hills.

The snow was coming down harder and faster on the wind now she'd left the valley, and the wipers were struggling to clear it from the windscreen which was quickly steaming up. The blizzard of white coming out of the black night was hypnotising as it was driven towards her and Danuta was reminded of a kaleidoscope she'd once had as a child, for the darting flakes seemed to be drawing her into the very heart of the storm.

She blinked and forced herself to watch the road,

and not the snow, and to try and ascertain how far out of town she was and where the turn-off must be.

She almost missed the white wooden sign which was partially hidden by trees, but as she was going very slowly now, she managed to turn off without touching the brakes. With her pulse thudding, her hands gripping the steering wheel and her neck craned to see the road ahead, she was relieved to find that the surrounding trees had given the narrow lane a modicum of shelter, and the way was fairly clear.

Daring to speed up to twenty-five miles an hour, she kept to the middle of the rutted lane to avoid driving into the deep ditches on either side. She had no real idea of how far she would have to go before she saw the farm entrance, and although Mr Green had promised to put a lantern on the gatepost, there was no guarantee she would see it in this white whirlwind.

Coming out of the trees and climbing to higher ground, the snow and wind were buffeting the side of the car and she could see the snow was now slowly filling the potholes and ditches, and dusting the hedgerows. She slowed again to a crawl as she navigated her way along the twisting lane into the next dip. Then she saw a flicker of light in the distance, giving her a tiny beacon of hope that the farm was nearby.

Rounding another bend, the light was stronger and became twin headlight beams, and she realised the farmer had driven his tractor to the gate and was waiting for her. Breathing a sigh of relief, she turned in and followed him down the rutted track past the sprawl of farm buildings to the farmhouse itself. It was a welcome sight, with smoke coming from the chimney and lights at every window.

'Thanks for coming out, Sister.' The farmer opened her car door, holding it against the wind and snow until she'd climbed out and fetched her bag. 'I'm sorry you've had a wasted journey though. The missus couldn't wait, so I had to help her birth our boy.'

'Congratulations,' she said, ducking her head against the onslaught. 'But I will still need to make sure everything is all right with them both.'

'It'll be right enough,' he replied nonchalantly. 'I've birthed more sheep and cattle than you've had hot dinners.' He led the way into the warmth and light of the farmhouse kitchen where two dogs lazily watched her from in front of the roaring fire, and a tabby cat came to insinuate itself around her legs.

Danuta shed her coat, gloves and scarf, and followed him upstairs to the bedroom where his plump, fair-haired wife was looking very pleased with herself as she lay propped up by pillows holding her new baby to her breast.

'I'm ever so sorry, Sister, but this one was in too much of a hurry,' she said with a beaming smile. 'Luckily my Alf was in from milking so he could lend a hand.'

Alf muttered something about leaving them to it and stomped back downstairs, still in his mud-caked rubber boots.

Danuta asked her the usual questions and made notes for her files and then examined her and the baby. He was a big boy, weighing nearly eight pounds, and Alf had certainly dealt with the cord appropriately. She found nothing amiss, and as the afterbirth looked intact and Mrs Green's temperature and pulse were normal, she washed her hands in the bowl of tepid water by the bed and prepared to leave.

'You've done remarkably well for a first baby, Mrs Green, but perhaps next time you could call me a bit sooner?'

The woman laughed. 'I would have, Sister, but it all happened too quickly. I got a few twinges, then my waters broke, and before I knew it this one was on the way. But I'll remember what you said for next time.'

'May I use your telephone to ring the surgery? I need to tell the other midwife that I'll be back as soon as I can.'

'Of course, dearie. But you aren't really going back out in that, are you? We've got plenty of room if you'd prefer to stay.'

'That's very kind, Mrs Green, but I can't risk getting stuck here. There are only two of us on duty tonight, and there could be more call-outs.'

Mrs Green chuckled contentedly and stroked her baby's head. 'Babies are no respecters of the weather or the time, are they?'

Danuta glanced at the bedside clock to discover it was almost midnight. 'They certainly aren't,' she replied. 'If you have any problems at all, please ring the surgery; otherwise, we will see you at the clinic in ten days' time.'

She made the call from the telephone on the landing and then went back down to the kitchen to find Mr Green waiting for her with an offer of hot soup which she regretfully had to decline as she needed to get back before she was snowed in.

'I'll guide you down our track to the gate, then,' he said, frowning. 'Though, if you were my lass, I wouldn't want you out on a night like this.'

She just smiled and nodded, knowing Stanislav wouldn't like it either – and in fact, if she had the choice, she'd have much preferred to sit here by the fire to doze away the rest of the night and drink soup. But duty called.

She pulled on her coat, gloves and scarf, grabbed her bag and followed him out of the door to discover the snow was now covering everything in a thick blanket – including her car. She quickly cleared the windscreen and turned on the heater before following the tractor down the track to the lane. Sounding her horn to thank him, she headed back to Cliffehaven.

The drive was torturous, the snow splattering in great gobbets on the windscreen, making it almost impossible for the wipers to clear it. She was so tense her shoulders and spine were aching as she crouched over the steering wheel and peered into the swirling mass, looking for the road sign which would take her back onto the main road.

But as she carried on down the lane and came to a large farmhouse she definitely hadn't passed before, she realised she must have missed it, so then had the tricky job of doing a three-point turn in a gateway before heading back the way she'd come.

Driving at walking pace now, she peered through the window, watching the headlights pick their way through the maelstrom, and holding onto the hope she'd eventually find the signpost, and not end up in a ditch.

The headlights finally caught the white gleam in the darkness of the surrounding trees, and she breathed a great sigh of relief. But in turning onto the main road she was hit by the ferocity of the wind as it tore across the hills and buffeted her little car so hard, she had to fight to keep it on the road.

Gripping the steering wheel and trying to find her way across the hills, she was aware that she could easily lose the road and end up on the edge of the cliffs. Fear was copper in her mouth as she kept to what she thought was the middle of the road and prayed there was nothing coming the other way.

She had no idea where she was or how far it was from home when something large suddenly loomed out of the storm, headlights glaring and making straight for her at speed.

She swerved to avoid it, feathering the brake pedal in the hope of avoiding a skid. But her front left tyre bounced against the steep grassy bank at the side of the road and she was sent into a spin, coming to rest against the opposite bank with a crunch that cut off the engine and killed her headlights.

Shocked, she fought to catch her breath and to make sense of what had just happened. She looked into the rear-view mirror and saw no sign of the other vehicle, not even their red tail-lights. Whoever it was hadn't stopped – and perhaps hadn't even seen her or realised what they'd done.

She sat for a moment to calm her racing pulse, and then turned the key in the ignition. The engine coughed and spluttered and then died. She tried again, knowing she was risking flooding the engine but also knowing if she didn't get it started she could be stuck here without the remotest chance of anyone finding her.

The engine coughed again and again, but wouldn't ignite. Danuta sat in the car and stared at the snow as the wind continued to forcefully throw it at her car. Now the heater wasn't working she could feel the chill creeping in, and knew that if she stayed here she'd die of hypothermia, even though she had blankets and a flask of tea. It was not an option.

Grabbing her torch from the passenger seat, she climbed out and was almost knocked off her feet by the wind. Pelted by the snow and battered by the wind, she clung to the car and shone her torch on the crumpled wing and dented bonnet. The damage was minor and the wheels seemed to be undamaged and clear of the bank. There was no obvious reason why the engine wouldn't start, but as the car was facing the right way down the hill, there was a chance she could get it started again.

Danuta was chilled to the bone and soaked through as she climbed back in and dried her face with her handkerchief. What she was proposing to do was dangerous, but it was the only way she could think of that would get her off these hills.

She yanked the steering wheel round just enough so she was again facing the middle of the road, turned the key halfway in the ignition, selected second gear and took a breath before releasing the handbrake. The car started rolling down the hill, and as soon as she gauged it was going fast enough, she very quickly turned the key, lifted her foot off the clutch and stamped on the accelerator.

The car jerked and juddered as it hurtled downwards into the swirling white, but the engine fired at last, and the lights came back on. She touched the brake to slow down and the car fishtailed. Turning the wheels into the skid, she got it in a straight line again and, with nerves jangling, the sweat cold on her spine, focused on the road ahead.

It was after one in the morning and Stanislav couldn't settle to anything until he knew his Danuta was safe. He'd telephoned the surgery twice already and Sister O'Neill was beginning to lose patience with him.

'I've already told you, Stan,' she said briskly. 'Danuta telephoned me before she left the Greens' farm. She is on her way.'

'But that was over an hour ago. How do you know she has not had an accident? Have you seen the snowstorm?'

'To be sure, I am very aware of the weather conditions, Stan. I've been out there myself. Now, please stop ringing me. This telephone is for medical emergencies and call-outs only.'

Stanislav glared at the buzz of a disconnected line

and slammed the receiver back into its cradle. He thumped his sticks on the hall tiles as he made his way back to the kitchen where Peggy and Jim were waiting up with him for news.

'She tells me her telephone is for emergencies only,' he complained loudly, dropping his sticks to the floor with a clatter. 'But this is an emergency. My Danuta is out there and she could be hurt, or lost or ...' He plumped down into the kitchen chair. 'I fear for her, Peggy,' he managed through welling tears.

'I know, Stan, but there's really nothing any of us can do about it, and winding yourself up like this isn't going to help her.' She laid a reassuring hand on his arm. 'I'm sure that if Pat O'Neill was at all worried, she'd have called out the fire brigade or the police to go and look for her.'

'But I have seen on the map where she had to go tonight. It is far into the country with deep ditches and narrow roads, but should not take more than an hour for her to get home.'

'Stan,' soothed Jim, his hand on the other man's shoulder. 'She'll be driving very slowly, so of course it will take longer. Give her some credit, old son. She's tougher than you realise, and won't let something like a drop of snow defeat her.'

'I think it is best if I go and look for her,' he replied, bending to retrieve his sticks.

'Oh, no you don't, said Jim, grabbing his arm. 'You'll do her no good by rushing out there and possibly getting into trouble yourself. Just sit down, Stan, and have a drink to calm your nerves.'

Stanislav didn't want a drink. Didn't want to sit idly about waiting for Danuta to walk in the door – and certainly didn't want to give vent to his true feelings on the matter in front of these good people who'd refused to go to bed until they knew Danuta was all right. He got to his feet. 'I have a better idea,' he muttered, and went into the bedroom off the hall.

Slumping onto the bed, he gazed at the photograph of their wedding day that Danuta had placed on the side table. He had great faith in her ability to tackle most things, for she was brave and stoic and rarely got into a panic. But that didn't stop him worrying. Accidents could happen in the blink of an eye in such weather, and that road leading into Cliffehaven was very exposed at the best of times – and tonight the wind and snow would be driven across the hills from the North Sea to create hazardous conditions.

Refusing to dwell on all the scenarios that flashed through his mind, he reached into the drawer for his cigar case. He didn't smoke very often, but liked an occasional cigar when he felt the need for a bit of comfort. He carried the cigar case back into the kitchen and offered it to Jim.

Jim saw the name on the band as he rolled the cigar between his fingers and took an appreciative sniff of the rich Havana tobacco. 'Are you sure, Stan? These are some of the most expensive cigars to be had.'

'They were a gift from a grateful customer,' he replied. 'He owns a gentlemen's club in London and we supply him with cigars and brandy when we can.'

He snipped the end and passed the cutters to Jim before carefully lighting the Montecristo. The heavy scent of the finest Cuban tobacco filled the room, and as both men shared a grin of pleasure, Peggy coughed and went to open the door to the basement so she could breathe.

Danuta's pulse rate had returned to normal once she had the car's speed under control, and she could finally see some familiar landmarks. She was almost home.

She slowly drove down the High Street, the snow

still flying about her and settling thickly on the roofs and in gutters. Elms Avenue proved to be similarly carpeted, with no trace of any traffic, which must mean that Sister O'Neill hadn't been called out once the snow had started to settle.

She saw the welcoming light glowing from behind the curtains of the nurses' duty room and parked next to the other car in the driveway. Gathering her belongings, she scrambled out and hurried to get indoors.

'Thank goodness,' said Sister O'Neill, jumping to her feet to welcome her in a crushing hug that almost buried Danuta in her generous bosom. 'To be sure, Danuta, I was about to call the fire brigade and send out a search party.'

'Whatever for?' Danuta gently disentangled herself, genuinely puzzled and rather disturbed that her journey home should have caused such concern.

'It's after three in the morning, Danuta,' Pat O'Neill replied, hands on generous hips, her plump face wreathed in exasperation. 'I've not heard a word from you since you telephoned from the farm at midnight. Of course I was worried. And poor Stan – he's frantic, calling me every half-hour, and threatening to go out looking for you.'

'Oh, lawks,' Danuta sighed. 'I didn't realise it had taken that long. I am sorry, Pat.'

'There's no need to apologise,' she said briskly. 'I'm just thankful you're safe. Get your coat off and warm up by the fire. I'll be making you some hot cocoa.'

'That would be lovely, but I'll ring Stan first.' Danuta reached for the phone and then hesitated momentarily, unsure whether a call at this time of the morning wouldn't wake the whole household. Deciding he was probably sitting by the phone, she risked it, and her call was answered on the first ring.

'It's me, Stan,' she said quickly. 'I'm at the surgery,

safe and sound, so please, go to bed and I'll be home by six unless there's another call-out.'

'I do not want you going out again, Danuta,' he said forcefully. 'You have done enough for one night and I want you home.'

'I'm on duty until six, Stan,' she replied calmly. 'I'll be home then, and not before.'

'But why did it take so long for you to get back to Cliffehaven?' he persisted in rapid Polish. 'It's been over three hours since you left the farm, and I was imagining all sorts of things – unbearable things, my darling. Please, please come home so I can see for myself that you have come to no harm.'

The pain in his voice made her heart twist, but she couldn't allow it to side-track her from her duty. 'I can't leave Pat here on her own again, Stan. It's not fair. But I promise you that I'm perfectly fine, and I'll be home as soon as I can.' She cut the call before he could protest further, and went to sit by the electric fire, disconcerted that the delayed shock was making her hands tremble.

'He's not at all happy about me staying on until six,' she said, clasping her hands together in front of the fire in the hope Pat didn't notice how unsteady they were. 'I wouldn't be at all surprised if he turns up here just to make sure I'm all right,' she joked.

Pat O'Neill grinned and placed the cup of cocoa on the table next to her. 'By all the saints, Danuta, your man loves the very bones of you. I wish mine was half as passionate.' She plumped down in the chair beside her and took a sip. 'Harold's not one to show his emotions,' she continued. 'His upper lip is far too stiff, so it is.'

'That's what comes of marrying an Englishman, Pat,' she teased. 'Poles are almost too passionate, and it can be hard going at times.'

The sound of a car pulling up outside was swiftly followed by the slam of a door and the familiar heavy tread of a man using walking sticks. 'Told you so,' said Danuta, shooting her friend a grin before getting to her feet to let him in.

'I had to come to make sure you're all right,' he said, his face almost white with anxiety. 'I saw the damage to your car. You *are* hurt – aren't you?'

'Not a bit,' she reassured him firmly. 'I just got confused in the snow and bumped into something, that's all. It's nothing Jack Smith won't be able to fix.'

He threw an arm round her, holding her so tightly against him that she was finding it hard to breathe. 'Thank God,' he sighed before holding her at arm's length and scrutinising her face for the merest sign she was fibbing to him. 'You are very pale,' he murmured.

'It was cold out there, Stanislav, and I haven't had the chance to warm up yet.' She giggled and brushed the droplets of melted snow from his flaring moustache. 'I love you, Stan, but really, all this fuss is too much. Give me a kiss and then go home.'

He complied and hugged her again. 'I will wait for you in our bed,' he whispered, aware that Pat O'Neill was watching them. 'Do not be late.' With that, he headed outside to his car.

'I'm thinking your man is not meaning for you to be sleeping when you get home,' teased Pat, her brown eyes bright with innuendo.

Danuta felt the blush rising up her neck and into her face and concentrated on drinking the cocoa.

15

Ron pulled back the bedroom curtains and stared at the view from his window at the top of the house, marvelling at its stark beauty and simultaneously cursing it for the inconvenience it had caused. It was now late January, and it had been snowing solidly for two weeks; Cliffehaven was almost at a standstill, and by the look of the thick grey clouds that blotted out the sun, there was more to come.

He drew on his dressing gown and tied the belt, his gaze slowly traversing the bare branches of the trees of Havelock Gardens which were bowing beneath the weight of the snow, and then across the pristine white of the playing fields to Elms Avenue and beyond to the lines of bungalows and houses huddled along the hillside beneath their blanket of white. The world was in monochrome, the almost blinding white relieved only by the occasional dark chimney pot, cleared street or freshly shovelled footpath.

Rosie came to stand beside him, linking her arm through his as they looked out over the town. 'You and Frank had better clear our driveway, Ron,' she murmured. 'I'll need the car later this morning to get to the emergency council meeting.'

'There's not much point in trying to clear it when Havelock Road is still two feet deep in it,' he replied. 'There's thick ice under that drift which neither of us will be able to shift. And, anyway, the snow will cover it again before you can blink.'

He kissed her brow and gently stroked back a stray platinum curl. 'You'll just have to forgo your high heels, put on sensible boots and walk like everyone else,' he teased.

She gave a deep sigh. 'I don't have much choice, do I? At least it's not far to the Town Hall. But what about the dogs, Ron? You can't take Harvey out in this with his arthritis.'

'I'll be letting him out in the garden to cock his leg as usual, but Monty can go out on the playing field and get rid of some of that energy. He's being a blasted nuisance by constantly annoying those kittens.'

'I'm worried he'll do them harm,' she confessed. 'He's horribly jealous of all the attention they get.'

'Harvey's on watch – and so am I. But not to worry, Rosie. Tom Kitten's claws are very sharp, and his sister is a fast learner. Monty's nose has become their favourite target. He's slowly learning not to mess with either of them.' He lightly slapped her bottom and headed for the bathroom just as the telephone rang. 'I'll get it,' he called, thudding down the stairs to the hall.

Rosie couldn't make out who Ron was talking to, so went into the bathroom to prepare for another day of tramping through the snow in the freezing cold wind that was playing havoc with her fair and delicate complexion, and making her hair crackle with electricity every time she ran a brush through it.

It was important she attended the meeting today for it concerned the very worrying news that if this heavy snowfall continued for much longer, there would be a serious shortage of coal for fuelling the local electric power stations. There had even been talk at government level of restricting the electricity supply for both domestic and industrial use, which had caused a furious debate in Parliament, and strident headlines in the press. However, Emanuel Shinwell, the Minister for

Fuel and Power, seemed confident that the national stock of coal would be enough to see them through, so she just had to hope he was right.

Rosie grimaced at her reflection in the mirror and dabbed a bit more powder on her nose. It would be a disaster for the Labour government if they did run out of fuel and had to ration the electricity. Everyone was already sick to death of the food restrictions and it really would be a step too far.

'That was Chalky,' said Ron, returning to the bedroom. 'He's all but marooned down in that valley and has had to bring his goats and chickens into the barns. He's left the ducks to their own devices with their duck-house for shelter, but he doubts his vegetables and fruit crops will survive – which will mean no more damsons for his lethal slivovitz.'

He whipped off the dressing gown and quickly dressed in his thick old corduroy trousers, warm shirt and two sweaters. 'But he's really concerned about those sheep up on Arkwright's top fields. The man clearly doesn't know what he's doing and hasn't begun to move them to better shelter closer to the farmhouse – or even taken them winter feed now they can't get to the grass. Chalky reckons he'll lose the lot if he continues to ignore them and this freeze carries on. His barometer showed minus six last night, and it had to be even colder up on those exposed hills where the sheep are.'

'Why doesn't he go and see the man and warn him?'

Ron grunted. 'Chalky doesn't like him and the feeling is mutual. He's tried talking to him and all he got for his pains was being faced with a shotgun and told to get off his land before he filled him with pellets for trespassing.'

'Then he deserves to lose his flock. Those poor ewes,

though,' she sighed. 'They must be coming into lambing season too.'

Ron's expression was grim as he nodded. 'Aye, but there's nothing any of us can do about it now Arkwright's place is snowed in and unreachable.'

Danuta had taken to racing to the door the minute the postman delivered the mail, in the hope there would be news from the bank. But two weeks had passed since their interview, and still there was nothing.

Stanislav looked up hopefully at her from the breakfast table as she returned to Peggy's kitchen, saw the disappointment in her expression and gave a sigh. 'This snow is hampering everything. How long does it take for a group of men to decide to give us a mortgage?'

Danuta sat down and finished her cup of tea. She was determined not to give even a moment's thought to the possibility that they'd turned their application down and that was the real reason they'd heard nothing. 'Maybe there will be something in the second post,' she said cheerfully.

'I'm amazed we're getting any post at all,' said Cordelia. 'That poor boy can't use his bicycle in the snow and has to lug that huge bag through drifts that come up to his knees. At least the milkman can still use his shires and dray to get around the town.'

'It's all right for some,' muttered Charlie through a mouthful of toast. 'Me and the other grammar school lads have to rely on a tractor and trailer to get us from the last bus stop to the school. It's more than two feet deep up on the hills, you know. More like eight or even ten in the drifts, and where they've cleared the road, it's like passing through a great white tunnel.'

'They should close the school,' said Peggy. 'It's

utterly ridiculous you boys having to do that journey every day.'

Charlie grinned and grabbed his cap and scarf. 'But it's fun, Mum. We toboggan down the hills during break and have snowball fights.' Dragging on his coat, he picked up his heavy school bag. 'See you tonight unless we get stuck in a snowdrift,' he said, shooting his mother a teasing grin before thudding down the cellar steps and out of the back door.

'That boy will be the death of me,' sighed Peggy.

'He is young,' said Stanislav, 'and all young boys like an adventure.'

'Adventure or not, Stan, if this weather keeps on, we'll all be sitting at home doing nothing, and earning no wages. Rosie said there's talk of rationing the electricity, and if that happens, Solly will have to shut the factories and we'll all be on the dole. And the amount they pay out certainly won't cover anything but the bare essentials – even if we can get them. The shops are getting low on stock, especially fresh vegetables, and poor Alf is having the devil's own job to get fresh meat for his butcher shop. If it wasn't for men like Frank and his crew going out each day, we wouldn't have fish either.'

'And here's us thinking we had it tough during the war,' said Cordelia. 'I wouldn't mind betting we'll end up queuing again for whatever scraps we can find.'

'Let's hope it doesn't come to that, Grandma Cordy,' soothed Danuta. 'It's 1947, and the army is doing its level best to make sure the supply trucks get through.'

She pushed back from the table and put on her coat, scarf and boots. 'I must go to work.' She kissed Stan's cheek, wrapped the scarf round her neck and, waving goodbye to Peggy and Cordelia, went out to her car.

She was relieved to get it back, for although Jack had fixed the dents and touched up the scratches on the paintwork, as well as giving it a thorough service, she'd had to be without transport for three days. She now had the snow chains in the boot in case of emergencies, but luckily, there had been no further call-outs into the farmland beyond Cliffehaven.

As she carefully drove to Elms Avenue along the cleared and gritted roads, she mulled over the conversation in Peggy's kitchen. Perhaps Cordelia was right when she said they'd face long queues again, for the news of snowbound warehouses and marooned delivery trucks were in the papers every day now. There was further concern that the railways were rapidly becoming unusable, and rumours of a coal shortage were rife.

She parked outside the surgery and went in to find the waiting room full of people with hacking coughs and sniffles. Hurrying into the nurses' room to prepare for her morning rounds, she found Sister Lucy York busy cleaning her medical bag, her sterilised instruments already laid out neatly on a clean towel.

Lucy pushed back her fair hair and gave Danuta a tired smile, and then swallowed a yawn. 'Good morning,' she said. 'I hope today's quiet. I didn't get much sleep in that chair last night.'

'Why did you sleep here? You weren't on night duty.'

'I couldn't get home. My place is out on the country road near the Greens' farm, and by all accounts the snow is up to the roof in places. I telephoned my parents so they wouldn't worry, but if this weather doesn't change, I'm going to have to find somewhere to stay here.'

'I'm sure someone will gladly offer you a spare bed,' Danuta said.

Lucy frowned. 'My father is most particular about things like that, and he's already given me a sermon on the sorts of places I mustn't go. But I won't cope with work if I have to sleep here every night.'

Danuta's first thought was to offer her a bed at Beach View, but that would be taking Peggy for granted and stretching her hospitality too far. There was the empty room in Eshton Road, of course, but although Lucy was a fully qualified midwife, she was young, very naive and still living with her parents, who sounded very strict. Bumping into Irene each day would be a bit of an eye-opener, and that was without the noise and the arguments, and Irene's dubious customers.

And then she was struck by the perfect solution. 'I'll just make a telephone call,' she said. 'I think I might have an answer to your sleeping arrangements.'

'Hello, Ruby 'ere,' said the bright voice at the end of the line.

'Hello, Ruby, it's Danuta. How are things with you?'

'Hello, Danuta, love. All right, I suppose, but getting me beer delivered is proving a right carry-on. Lucky I 'ad some brought in before the snow come down, or me customers would be baying for me blood. What about you? Can't be easy getting about in all this bloody snow.'

Danuta smiled at the familiar Cockney voice of the young woman she'd briefly shared a home with under Peggy's roof. 'I was wondering if you'd take in a lodger,' she said. 'One of our nurses is stranded and can't get home.' She looked over her shoulder at Lucy and grinned. 'She's well house-trained.'

'Well, I never thought about 'avin' a lodger, but what with the weather being like it is, I suppose it's the right thing to do. How old is she? What's her background? Only I got to be careful who I takes in, yer see, because of me licence.'

'Lucy is twenty-one and from a respectable local

farming family. You won't have to worry about your licence.'

'All right, then. You'd better bring 'er round so I can meet her. But make it in between opening hours, love. It's been chaos in 'ere since so many have been laid off work.'

'Thanks, Ruby. It will save her from having to bed down in the nurses' room every night on an uncomfortable chair. I'll pop in later and introduce you.'

She disconnected the call and turned back to Lucy. 'Ruby and I were both evacuees at Beach View during the war. She married a Canadian and went out there with him but was widowed a few months later and returned here last year. She's now the landlady of the Anchor in Camden Road, and despite her no-nonsense manner she has a heart of gold. You'll like her, I'm sure, and you'll be quite safe there.'

Danuta paused, seeing the girl frown. 'Oh, and she's being courted by our Dr Darwin, so be prepared to bump into him as he visits the Anchor most nights now when he's not on call.'

Lucy twisted her hands in her lap, looking even more uncomfortable. 'The Anchor? But that's a pub. And even if Dr Darwin is courting this Ruby, I doubt very much if my father will allow me to stay there. He's a lay preacher and a leading member of the local Temperance Society, you see, and ever so strict.'

Danuta bit back on a flash of impatience. 'I don't really think he has the choice of voicing any opinions in the circumstances, do you, Lucy? You're stranded, and there's a perfectly nice bed at the Anchor, ready and waiting for you.'

'I don't know,' she muttered. 'It's really kind of you, Danuta, but perhaps I'd better telephone home and see how my parents feel about it.'

'You do that, Lucy, and I'll get on with my morning

rounds. Let me know your decision when I get back.' She picked up her bag and left the surgery before her patience snapped at the girl's dithering.

'You look as if something's ruffled your feathers this morning.'

Danuta whirled round to find Dr Darwin grinning at her from the front porch. 'It's nothing, really,' she blustered. 'Just Lucy trying my patience.'

'Oh dear. What's she done now apart from sleeping in the nurses' room overnight? I'm assuming she was unable to get home.'

Danuta told him about Ruby's offer to take her in, and Lucy's reluctance to step inside a pub because of her father's zealous adherence to the Temperance Society.

'Is she telephoning home now?' he asked. At Danuta's nod, he grinned. 'Leave it with me, Danuta.'

She watched him hurry back into the building and wondered if his charm really would work on a man who clearly ruled his household like a despot.

Her normal district nurse round took longer than usual because she'd been hampered by the fact that a lot of the smaller roads in Cliffehaven had not been cleared. This meant she'd had to park the car as near to her patient as possible and then tramp through the deep snow to get to them. Consequently, she didn't return to Elms Avenue until almost one o'clock.

She glanced across the street to Mr Kaplin's house and decided that although he wasn't due for a visit today, she'd just drop in to make sure he was all right.

'Hello, Danuta,' he said, eyeing her over his spectacles. 'What are you doing here?'

'I'm just checking to see you're keeping warm and that the Lilac Tearooms have delivered your midday meal.'

'I need more coal,' he muttered gloomily. 'And lunch was not very exciting. Just mince and mash with a few peas.'

'At least it was something,' she replied mildly, picking up the scuttle. 'I'll just fill this and then get your fire going properly.'

She went outside to the coal shed and returned with the heavy scuttle to poke at the fire and feed it with a few more lumps of coal. Once she was satisfied it would keep him warm for the rest of the afternoon, she washed her hands, made him a cup of tea and left him to his newspaper. The situation with Mr Kaplin was far from ideal, but it was the best anyone could do in the circumstances as Rachel had yet to find someone she could trust to call in every day.

Danuta returned to the clinic to find Pat O'Neill preparing to go out on a call. 'Stanislav telephoned at least three times while you were out,' she said. 'He said it was urgent, and to ring him the minute you got in. But he wouldn't say what it was about.'

Danuta rolled her eyes. Everything was urgent as far as her husband was concerned. 'Where are you off to – and where's Lucy?'

'Lorna Fairfax has finally gone into labour. Lucy's with another patient who fell in the snow and has a suspected broken leg, so they're waiting for an ambulance. Dr Darwin had no luck with her father, by the way, so I said she could stay in our spare room.' She picked up her nursing bag, grabbed a couple of blankets and with a wave goodbye, ran out of the clinic.

Danuta was relieved to hear Lucy would be all right. She held her hands out to the five-bar electric fire, knowing she was probably risking getting chilblains, but too cold to care. Once she'd warmed up a little, she rang Ruby to let her know that Lucy wouldn't be taking up her kind offer, and then she rang Beach View, bracing herself for Stanislav's emergency.

Her call was answered almost immediately, which told her he'd been sitting beside the telephone, probably in a lather of impatience. 'Danuta? Danuta, it is a disaster.'

She was determined to remain calm. 'What's a disaster?'

'They have given us a mortgage, but it is not the amount we asked for.'

Danuta gripped the receiver and sank into a chair. This was indeed a huge blow. No wonder he was in such a state. 'How much have they said we can have?'

'One thousand pounds only,' he barked. 'Added to our savings it will not be enough to buy anything.' His voice rose as his stress mounted. 'We have seen what is on the market, Danuta, and there is nothing that cheap except for a one-bedroom bungalow out in the sticks. And that is on a lease, so it would never truly be our own.'

Danuta's spirits plummeted. 'I wonder why he didn't give us what we asked for.' She took a tremulous breath. 'He must know that sum would never be enough, even with every penny we can scrape together to add to our savings.'

'I telephoned the bank, but he isn't there. He's been snowed in, and is not expected to return until the thaw. His assistant was not at all helpful, telling me we could take it or leave it as the board's decision was final.'

He fell silent and Danuta could almost feel his despair coming down the line. Her own spirits were so low, she couldn't think of any words that might comfort him.

'There is no point in accepting his offer, Danuta,' he said finally, his voice breaking. 'We will be paying the interest on money we cannot use. The whole thing is hopeless.'

'Don't do anything rash, Stan,' she urged, fearing that in this mood, he might telephone the bank and tell them in no uncertain language where to put their offer. 'Just stay calm and we'll discuss everything when I get home. If we think about this with clear heads, there still might be some way we can manage to scrape enough together to make that thousand pounds work for us.'

'We both know it will not buy a home fit for a family, Danuta. I see no point in even talking about it.'

'Stan,' she said sharply. 'Stan, you mustn't think like that. We'll sort something out, really we will.'

'But there is another thing,' he continued in the same gloomy tone.

She tensed. 'What?'

'The adoption people have arranged to visit Florence tonight at five-thirty, and we must be there too, so they can see if we are good with Bobby.'

Danuta relaxed. 'That's not a problem, Stan, although I'll have to meet you there as my shift doesn't finish until six.' She closed her eyes and sighed. 'Honestly, Stan, the way you were going on I thought there'd been some sort of accident.'

'There is no accident,' he said on a deep sigh. 'We are doomed.' He cut the connection.

Danuta replaced the receiver and stared into the electric fire as she replayed the conversation. She wasn't surprised that Stanislav was depressed, for they did indeed seem ill-fated, and this last crushing disappointment was almost too much to bear.

She took a deep breath and got to her feet. But bear it they would, she decided fiercely, for she still possessed the fighting spirit that had seen her through far worse than this. They would find a way to beat those who stood in their path.

The first day of February was ushered in with yet more snow as well as high, bitter winds. Peggy had spent the past month worrying about Jim out on the roads in this awful weather, but as he'd promised he wouldn't be going too far, she'd had to accept he'd be sensible and not take any unnecessary risks. The trouble was, his injured servicemen were scattered far and wide and well beyond the boundaries of Cliffehaven, and visiting Parkwood House was definitely out of the question as it was completely snowed in now. The same applied to the hamlet where Anne and Martin lived with their children, although they seemed to be managing very well.

And then there was Charlie, making his way to the grammar school each day on those treacherous, icy roads in an old school bus that must be really struggling to make it across the hills. The snow was reported to be very deep up there, even though the army had been called out to clear it with bulldozers every day. But having visited the school once, she knew the valley in which it was set could only be reached by a long, steep track, and the thought of those boys being taken down there by tractor and trailer made her fret even more.

Unable to settle her mind to anything sensible, she'd left the factory to come home that Friday lunchtime to check that Cordelia was keeping warm, and not suffering too badly from her arthritis now it was so bitterly cold – and to see if there had been any messages from Jim and Charlie, for she fully expected them to call to tell her they'd been stranded somewhere and were unable to get home.

She'd said none of this to Cordelia when she'd found

the old lady huddled by the range fire with a thick blanket over her knees, and a cooling hot-water bottle on the floor beside her. Having refilled the hot-water bottle and tucked it into the blanket to keep Cordy's hands warm, she'd stoked the fire in the range, and was now stirring a hearty vegetable soup on the hob for their lunch, her ears pricked to the one-sided and rather emotional conversation Stan was having on the telephone to Danuta.

It really wasn't fair of the bank to offer them less than they needed, and she couldn't understand why they had done so. It didn't make sense when house prices were soaring because there were so few to be had, and although Stan's circumstances had changed because of the snow, surely the bank's board must have made their decision long before the weather had closed in?

She continued to stir the soup she'd put together earlier this morning and shot Stan a smile of sympathy as he came back into the kitchen to slump despondently in a chair. 'I couldn't help overhearing, Stan, and I'm sorry. But I'm sure you'll find a way around this latest knock-back,' she soothed.

He looked up at her, his brown eyes soulful. 'I wish I shared your faith, Peggy. But with this snow laying us all off, I have no chance of adding to our savings – and they are not enough to buy a home for my Danuta.'

'Hot soup will go a little way to make you feel a bit more cheerful,' she said resolutely, her thoughts suddenly distracted by a rather startling idea. 'Danuta doesn't want to come home to that miserable face after fighting her way through the snow all day.'

He straightened his shoulders and sat more upright, seemingly determined to show her that despite everything, he would find a way to resolve things.

But Peggy could see in his eyes that he had little

hope of succeeding, and that made her yearn to do something about it.

She returned to the factory after lunch to find Florence waiting for her in her office, and clearly on edge. 'Whatever's the matter, Flo? You look as if you're walking on hot coals.'

'The adoption people are coming to my home tonight,' she said in a rush. 'They've asked Stanislav and Danuta too so they can see how we all are with Bobby.'

Peggy frowned. 'I don't see why you're in such a lather about it, Flo. They're not there to poke and pry into your life – and certainly not about to take him away from you.'

'I just don't like the thought of them in my home,' she muttered. 'I don't see why we couldn't all have met at your place, or Rachel's for that matter.'

'Beach View isn't Bobby's home, and it's getting increasingly difficult to get anywhere outside of town. Solly telephoned this morning to say he'd had to turn back on his way in as the top road is now completely covered by very deep drifts which the army has yet to clear.'

'Oh.' Florence looked deflated. 'Oh well, I suppose I'll just have to put up with it, then. I hope it doesn't upset Bobby. He's been such a happy little boy since Stan made him that sled.'

Peggy eyed her quizzically. 'I didn't realise he'd done that – but now you mention it, he has been spending time doing something mysterious in Ron's shed.'

Florence's smile was faint. 'They go off as soon as Bobby's had his snack after school and take the sled onto the hill above the playing ground. My heart's in my mouth every time they come hurtling down.' She shrugged. 'But boys will be boys, I suppose.'

Peggy chuckled. 'They certainly will, and Stan's the

biggest kid of all. But I'm a bit surprised that Danuta hasn't put a stop to it. After all, it can't be wise for a man with two prostheses to go hurtling down hills on a few bits of wood nailed together.'

'Oh, it's quite a work of art,' said Florence more cheerfully. 'Very sturdy and painted bright red, with Bobby's name picked out in yellow on the front.' She looked at her watch. 'I'd better get on with checking the stock again. We seem to be running low on that white broderie anglaise for the baby dresses. It's proving a popular line.'

'Let me know if I need to reorder, but with this weather, we might not get anything for a while. Transport is almost at a standstill all over the country, and that cotton comes from the Midlands.' Peggy gave Florence a warm smile in the hope of cheering her up. 'Thanks, Florence, and don't worry about tonight. I'm sure everything will be just fine.'

As Florence left the office, Peggy sat back, deep in thought. Now she had a chance to concentrate, the glimmer of the idea she'd had earlier was growing brighter and taking better shape by the minute. But how would it be received should she dare to share it?

She turned her chair to face the window, but her focus was not on the wintry scene on the other side of the glass as her mind went over all the points of her scheme, trying to find the reasons why it wouldn't work. Realising the pluses far outweighed the minuses, she reached for the telephone. It was time to test her theory.

Danuta had been thinking deeply about the dilemma which faced her and Stanislav, and had almost found the glimmer of a solution when the call came from one of the bungalows close to Mafeking Terrace. Emily Smithson had gone into premature labour, and as her train driver husband was stranded in the county town, she was alone with her three children.

She drove as quickly as she dared through town, the newly attached chains clanking and rattling on the wheels as the little car struggled up the steep hill towards the factory estate. The side roads up here had not been cleared, and the drifts reached almost to the roofs in some places as the snow had been blown by the wind from the east. Seeing that the estate was relatively clear, she drove in and parked outside Jack's repair shop.

Gathering up all she needed from the boot, she popped her head round the door. 'I've parked outside,' she shouted to Jack who was banging away at something metal with a hammer.

He simply waved the hammer to acknowledge he'd heard and carried on banging.

Danuta slid and slithered along the icy patches left on the estate concrete and then tramped through the thick snow to the Smithsons' house. The door was opened by Danny, a wide-eyed and ashen-faced boy of about ten. 'Mum's in the back bedroom,' he managed.

Danuta smiled at him and his two little sisters who'd crowded in behind him to stare at her. 'I am here now,' she soothed. 'There's no need to be afraid, Danny. Why don't you take your sisters into the sitting room, while I go and see how your mum is doing?'

'She's making a fair old racket,' he replied, biting his lip against the tears blooming in his hazel eyes. 'She will be all right, won't she?'

'She'll be just fine.' Danuta steered all three children into the sitting room and switched on the gas fire. She noted how clean and tidy it was and saw a box of books and toys in the corner. 'Why don't you read them a story, Danny?' she coaxed. 'They would like that.'

Once they were settled on the couch with the book

between them, Danuta hurried along the hall to the bedroom.

Emily was writhing in pain on a tangle of sheets and blankets, her hair damp with sweat. 'How long since the pains started, Emily?' Danuta asked, taking her pulse.

'About an hour ago, but they're getting stronger and with less time in between,' she gasped as another contraction took hold. 'It's too soon, Sister Danuta. Much too soon. I'm not going to lose it, am I?'

Danuta quickly listened to the baby's heartbeat and then examined her. 'Your baby's heartbeat is steady and strong, and you're almost fully dilated,' she said calmly. 'Early or not, your baby is on its way.'

As Emily groaned and dealt with the pain of another contraction, Danuta folded away the blankets and sheets, surprised to see that Emily had already placed the rubber sheet from her home delivery kit over the mattress.

'It's a new bed,' Emily rasped. 'Didn't want to ruin it.'

'Well done,' Danuta murmured, turning the damp pillows over to plump them up and make Emily more comfortable. 'I will just get a bowl of hot water.'

'Too late,' gasped Emily, now straining to push.

Danuta swiftly checked on the baby's progress and to her shock, saw the head slowly emerging from the birth canal. She cradled it in her hands and within seconds Emily gave a huge push and her baby was born, squalling, red-faced and furious.

'You have another beautiful little girl,' she told Emily as she rapidly dealt with the umbilical cord and checked over the baby to make sure her rapid birth hadn't damaged her in any way. 'She's small, but perfect,' she murmured, swaddling the tiny scrap in a blanket and placing her gently into her mother's arms.

Emily burst into tears and held the squalling baby

close as Danuta dealt with the afterbirth and cleaned her up.

'Let's make you tidy so your other children can see their new sister,' she said. She placed the baby in the nearby cot and helped Emily into a clean nightgown before remaking the bed and returning the baby to her arms. 'Leave the rubber sheet on for a few days,' she advised before opening the door to discover all three children standing outside.

'You have a baby sister,' she said, giving them a beaming smile.

Danny grimaced. 'Not another one,' he moaned before following the two excited little girls into the room to take a look at the new arrival.

Danuta washed her hands in the bathroom and then went back to the bedroom to find Emily surrounded by her children as the baby continued to bellow. 'It might be a good idea to put her to the breast, Emily,' she advised. 'Being so small, it's really the very best thing to nurture her. In other circumstances I would have you taken to the hospital for you both to be checked over, but as your husband isn't here . . . Well, I'll just have to try and call in regularly to keep an eye on you both. But if there is a problem, any problem at all, ring the clinic.'

'That's ever so good of you, Sister. I'm sure we'll be fine.'

Danuta left the bungalow and traipsed through the snow as she was pelted with the stuff being blown at her from the sea. For a premature labour, it had gone extremely well, and Danuta was relieved there hadn't been any of the usual complications, but Emily and her baby would need a close eye kept on them over the week ahead.

Returning to her car, she could hear Jack's hammering, so she popped her head round the door to let him know she was back, and then slowly drove down the hill to the High Street and on to Elms Avenue.

The surgery spaces were full, signifying that all the doctors and the other district nurses were indoors, so she parked at the kerb and sat for a moment deep in thought, her gaze drifting along the line of villas.

The idea that had come to her before she'd been called out now seemed to be pushing itself forward, and the more she thought about it, the more sensible it seemed – and it was so obvious she wondered why on earth she hadn't thought of it before. A flutter of hopeful excitement swept through her but she swiftly tamped down on it. Stan would have to be consulted, of course, and he might have strong objections to such a plan, but he surely couldn't fail to see that it was as close to the perfect solution as they could ever hope for?

16

Jim had spent the majority of his war in Burma and India and, despite having returned from the tropics over five months ago, he still felt the cold – even on a warm English day. Today it felt as if the winter weather was gnawing into his bones as he finished his visit to one of his veterans and slowly drove towards home.

The car suddenly skidded on a patch of black ice and, although he turned the wheels into the skid, he ended up with the car bonnet buried in one of the massive walls of snow that lined the road. These white monoliths had been thrown up by the army bulldozers that were working day and night to keep the road open, and as he hit it, the top of the unstable pile toppled over to fall with a thud onto the car roof.

Shaken and shivering, Jim managed to fight his way out to inspect the damage, and was relieved to see that the rear end of the car was sticking out far enough to be seen should anyone happen to pass. But he could also see that any attempt to clear the snow from the roof and bonnet, or reverse out of the steep, unstable bank, would bring the entire lot crashing down to bury the car and him along with it.

Returning to the driver's seat, he wrapped his arms around himself in an effort to retain what little body heat he had while he waited to be rescued. Despite being dressed in two sweaters, heavyweight trousers, two pairs of socks, his old army greatcoat and a woolly hat, gloves and scarf, he was freezing, and he knew without a doubt that if rescue didn't come soon he would die out here.

Jim lit a cigarette and opened the quarter-light window the tiniest notch to let out the smoke. He didn't really have many options open to him. There was no telling when – or even if – the army or the council workmen would turn up, and as the day became even darker, and the snow continued to fall, he doubted anyone would see him. There was only one way out of here, and that was to walk.

He smoked his cigarette, putting off the moment when he'd have to get out of the car again and brave the windblown snow. And then he thought of Peggy and his children – of home and the warmth and love in his Peggy's kitchen – and knew he could delay no longer.

Grabbing his briefcase and large torch from the passenger seat, he carefully pushed open the door to find that the snow mountain had slipped further and was now pressing against it. He breathed in and squeezed through the narrow gap, aware that one false move could bring the whole lot down on top of him. Now pressed between the wall of snow and the side of his car, he clicked the door shut and carefully inched his way out into the road.

He could just make out the distant haze of lights in the ever-darkening sky as he stood trembling in his sodden coat, and the sight gave him the impetus he needed to get moving. He strode out, confident that now he could see Cliffehaven, it was within reach, and therefore he would make it home.

However, he hadn't counted on the strength of the bitter wind, or the machine-gun pellets of snow that bit into any exposed flesh and stung as sharply as bullets. He ducked his chin, pulled the woolly hat right down over his ears and his scarf up to cover his mouth and nose. He could barely see the road ahead as his torch struggled to pierce the onslaught, and his feet slid and slithered in the icy patches hidden beneath the fresh dusting of snow on the tarmac.

The sound of the wind filled his head as its force seemed determined to bring him to his knees. It made him stumble and momentarily lose sight of the road. He bent at the waist, hands on his knees, to try and catch his breath and deaden the awful noise of that wind. But it continued to howl like a banshee and he felt as if he was being assaulted on all sides, as the wind snatched his hat to send it flying into the darkness.

Pulling the scarf over his head and holding his coat collar tightly to his chin, he staggered on, the siren call of home the only thing that kept him going.

Peggy had been home for three hours, and as each minute passed, she became more anxious. There was no sign of Charlie or Jim, and it was now long past their usual home-time. She'd telephoned the school to be told that all the boys had left, and the tractor and trailer driver had reported back to say they'd caught the bus. The headmaster assured her that the journey was taking a bit longer than usual because of the conditions up on the top road.

Peggy wasn't at all reassured by this, and told the headmaster that Charlie would not be coming back to school until the weather had improved. She'd banged down the receiver in a fit of pique, and promptly picked it up again. There was no answer from Jim's head office, despite the fact she let it ring for a good five minutes. Admitting defeat, she hung up and went back into the kitchen.

'Try not to worry, Mum,' said Cissy. 'I know they're both late, but I'm sure they're on their way. No one can keep to a timetable in this weather.'

Peggy tried very hard to believe her husband and son were all right, but she couldn't blank out the visions of them stranded on the hills, battling to get home but losing their way as they became disorientated, and left wandering until they died of the cold.

At this thought, she burst into tears, and Cissy rushed to take her into her arms to comfort her. 'Please don't cry, Mum. You're imagining the worst, and I'm sure they're fine. Really I am.'

Peggy lifted her chin and regarded Cissy through her tears and saw her own fear mirrored in her daughter's eyes. Pulling her emotions firmly under control, she kissed Cissy's cheek. 'I'm sure you're right, darling. Take no notice of me. It's been a long day and my imagination's run away with me.'

Peggy pushed back from the table, suddenly full of purpose. 'Will you keep an ear out for Daisy?'

Alarmed, Cissy shot to her feet. 'Why? Where are you going?'

Peggy pulled her thickest coat from the hook behind the door and stuffed her feet into her boots. 'I'm driving to the bus stop to wait for Charlie.'

'But you mustn't, Mum,' Cissy protested. 'The snow's coming down even harder and that stop is on the other side of town and at the top of a steep hill.'

'He'll be frozen to the bone after being hauled out of the school grounds behind that stupid tractor – and that old bus isn't much better. I don't want him to have to walk home after all that.'

She ignored Cissy's protests and hurried outside to be met by a gale-force wind driving the snow into her face. Whimpering with fear for her loved ones, she carefully negotiated the steps and then quickly got into her car. With the windscreen wipers working at full tilt, she left the cul-de-sac and headed down Camden Road, taking a right turn at the bottom and following the road past Elms Avenue which climbed up towards the northerly hills and the bus stop.

The stop was situated on one of the most remote and exposed places, as the route was the main one linking the county town and smaller seaside resorts on the other side of the hills – and then on to the isolated villages which dotted the countryside beyond.

She peered through the windscreen as the snow pelted down and the wind buffeted the car. The streets she passed were deserted, but as she approached the crest of the hill where the bus stop was, her headlights picked out a group of huddled figures slowly stumbling towards her.

'Charlie,' she breathed, as she saw his face lift towards her lights. 'Oh, thank the Lord.' She pulled to a halt. 'Get in, all of you,' she shouted above the wind and snow. 'It'll be a squash, but better than out there.'

The five bedraggled and shivering boys crammed in, slamming the doors behind them before Peggy turned the car around in someone's gateway and headed back into town. One by one she dropped the boys off into the welcoming arms of their frantic families and then drove home.

'Go and have a hot bath straight away,' she told Charlie as they entered the house. 'I'll make you cocoa when you come back down, and heat up your dinner.'

'It was all good fun to start with,' he said, shivering as he divested himself of his sodden clothes. He eased off his shoes to reveal wet socks which he pulled off to reveal bright red toes. 'But the bus broke down halfway back and we had to walk the rest of the way.'

'Well, you won't be doing that again,' she said. 'And I suspect the others won't either. I've already told the headmaster you'll not be returning until the weather improves.'

Charlie looked a bit sheepish beneath his damp mop

of dark hair. 'Thanks for coming to collect us, Mum. We honestly didn't think we'd make that last mile home.'

Peggy shooed him up to the bathroom and went into the kitchen to find Jim sitting by the fire as if it was just a normal evening. 'Jim!' she cried, running to hug him. 'When did you get back? Are you all right? Why were you so late?'

'Well, now, that's a fine welcome, so it is,' he replied, pulling her onto his knee to kiss her. 'And believe me, darlin', glad it is that I'm home on such a foul night.'

Cissy rolled her eyes. 'I'll leave you two lovebirds alone and go up to see if Grandma Cordy needs anything.'

Peggy giggled as Jim gave her an extra squeeze. 'So, Jim Reilly, what made you so late tonight?'

He told her about sliding into the bank of snow and getting stuck, and how he'd started to walk home. 'And then, the luck of the Irish came into play, Peg. The army lads turned up in their massive bulldozer and drove me back to the car. They pulled it out, and once I'd got it started again, I drove home none the worse for wear but for a frost-bitten nose and dead feet.'

She looked down at his bare feet splayed close to the fire. 'You'll get chilblains,' she warned.

'I don't care,' he replied. His expression became serious. 'Now, I'd like you to explain what the heck you were doing out on a night like this.'

She told him about Charlie's adventure as she went to make fresh tea and heat up the dinner. 'Those boys were lucky to survive that walk home,' she said eventually. 'Thank God I was there to meet them, for they were all exhausted and soaked to the skin.'

'Well, it looks as if we'll all be stuck at home for a fair while, Peg. Headquarters is closed for the foreseeable future, and we've been instructed to visit only those veterans within walking distance – of which there aren't many. I pity those poor souls stuck in the outlying villages. They must be completely cut off by now.'

He wiggled his toes by the fire. 'So, apart from going to the rescue of a bunch of schoolboys, what else have you been up to today?'

'Well,' she said, bringing the fresh pot of tea to the table, knowing he could tell from her face that she had something exciting to tell him, 'I've had an interesting day, actually, Jim, and I think you'll be thrilled with what I have to tell you.'

She sat down on the other fireside chair and grinned at him like a Cheshire cat. 'But it's a secret, Jim, and you mustn't breathe a word to anyone until we have absolutely everything in place.'

Jim chuckled. 'You'd better get on and tell me then before you burst your stays,'

She pouted and swiped him with the tea towel. 'I do *not* wear stays.' She giggled. 'Now shut up and let me tell you what I've done.'

Danuta had struggled to stay silent about the plan she'd worked out earlier, but she could tell that Stanislav was aware that she was keeping something to herself, and during the two hours with Bobby, Florence and the woman from the adoption agency, he'd kept glancing across at her with curiosity.

Now, finally, they were leaving the terraced villa and heading for their cars. 'Are you going to tell me what is going on, Danuta?' he asked, his head dipped into his collar against the onslaught of snow that was now being driven between the terraces as if they were in a wind tunnel.

'Not until we are back at Beach View and on our own,' she replied, unable to resist grinning.

Stanislav heaved a deep sigh and opened his car door. 'I'll see you there, then.'

Danuta drove carefully home to Beach View, bubbling with excitement and hope which she tried very hard to contain. For it was important to keep a level head. Although her plan was perfect as far as she could see, Stan might see some flaw and be against it, and then they'd be back to square one.

She climbed out of the car as Stan pulled up behind her and hurried up the steps to the front door. Checking that he was managing the short climb, she opened the door and they entered the hall together.

'Will you tell me now?' he asked gruffly.

'After we've eaten.' She pecked him on his cold cheek and helped him take off his heavy coat. 'It will be all the better for having to wait,' she promised him.

Stanislav rolled his eyes and headed for the kitchen.

Danuta followed to find Jim and Charlie eating their dinner while Peggy sat with them, clearly bursting with some secret she was finding hard to keep to herself. Danuta smiled at her and went to collect their dinner plates from the slow oven. 'You look like the cat that swallowed the canary,' she teased Peggy. 'What have you been up to?'

'Oh, nothing much, dear,' she said airily. 'Do sit down and eat. You both must be starving.'

Danuta caught the swift look that passed between Peggy and Jim and wondered what was going on – but as they seemed determined to say nothing, she'd just have to be patient. But it was very hard to stay calm when her own emotions were in turmoil. She started to eat as Charlie and Jim recounted their night's adventures in such a dramatic and lively manner that the tales could have come from one of Charlie's *Boy's Own* comics.

'And what sort of day have you had, Danuta? It

must have been a terrible blow to discover the mortgage loan was below your expectation.' Peggy's bright brown eyes were twinkling, although she was maintaining a solemn expression.

'It's what the English call a stumbling block,' Danuta replied, keeping her own expression bland. 'But we will find a way round it, I'm sure.' She pushed her empty plate to one side and sipped from her cup of tea. 'The meeting at Florence's went well, I think. Bobby seemed quite happy to answer the woman's questions, and of course Stan read him his usual bedtime story before we left.'

'That's good,' said Peggy. 'Have they given you another date to see them again?'

Danuta quelled the sudden fear that everything could go horribly wrong if her plan was flawed. 'They have put our application on hold as they say we are homeless. We must have a permanent and suitable home before we can go any further.'

'Oh, darling.' Peggy reached for her hand. 'I know you must feel as if the world is against you at the moment, but things will come right for you both. I'm certain of it.'

'This is my hope too, Mama Peggy,' she replied quietly before pushing back her chair. 'If you will excuse us, Stan and I have much to discuss, and as I have an early start in the morning, I will wish you all goodnight.'

Heading for the ground-floor room, once she'd prepared for bed in the upstairs bathroom, she waited impatiently for Stan to join her. When they were cosy between the covers, she turned within his arms and looked into his eyes. 'Stan, my love, I think I have found a way to get us a proper home,' she said.

17

It was only just light the next morning and, despite the fact she'd had to struggle through deep snowdrifts from her home in Mafeking Terrace to the Town Hall, Doris was in her element. She was once again in charge of the Women's Voluntary Service in Cliffehaven, and had made it her mission to prove to the town that she was capable of superb organisation in a crisis.

There had been no opposition to her taking control of the WVS, as the present chairwoman was snowbound out in the countryside, and the rest of the women had been too daunted by her commanding presence at the hurriedly convened meeting to oppose her. And so here she was, fulfilling her duty at the Town Hall where she'd arranged for beds, hot food and the most basic of washing and toilet facilities to cope with the number of people who'd become stranded in the town since the overnight snowfall had made the roads impassable.

The noise was terrific, with children running about yelling as their mothers bellowed at them; babies were crying and men were shouting to be heard above the noise as they argued the finer points of football. Some families had been trapped on their weekly shopping trip; men had been forced to abandon their delivery trucks, cars and vans in the snowdrifts; children had been stranded, unable to get home from school, and nurses found there was no accommodation left at the hospital. It was organised chaos, and Doris loved being at the centre of it.

It's quite like wartime, she thought gleefully, as she paraded along the lines of beds to make sure everyone was behaving, and not filching extra blankets and pillows. One had to watch these people, for if it wasn't nailed down, it disappeared.

A small boy stuck his tongue out at her and she lifted her chin and stalked across the huge hall to the long trestle tables loaded with used clothing that had been donated by the locals. The people of Cliffehaven had answered her rallying cry and come up trumps again with their generous donations – although some were fit only for the bin, she realised, as she plucked a woollen jumper from the pile, got a powerful whiff of body odour and quickly tossed it back again.

'Hello, my dear,' said John. 'All's very quiet on the factory estate, as so many have been unable to get in today. How are you doing?'

She smiled up at him and brushed the snow from his shoulders. 'I would cope better if I had some decent help, like I did in the war years,' she replied, her gaze trawling the room to check that her fellow WVS members weren't standing idly about. 'I had hoped Peggy would drop in to lend a hand, but it seems she's too busy.'

'She has a large household to care for as well as a full-time job, Doris. You can't expect her to do more.'

'I suppose not,' she muttered, her expression saying otherwise. 'But there's no reason why Jim couldn't come; he can mend things and help with the heavy lifting.' She sniffed. 'And of course there's also Ron and Frank, lounging about doing nothing. It's at times like this that families should pull together.'

John was clearly about to argue, but wisely kept his thoughts on the matter to himself. 'What can I do to help now I'm here?'

'You could find the other camp beds in the stores. We're almost at capacity, but I'm sure I could squeeze in a few more.' She looked at her watch. 'I'm going into the office to start my telephone calls. We'll soon be overwhelmed, and I have to source all the spare rooms available in the town.' *Starting with Peggy*, she thought as she strode off.

'You two look very pleased with yourselves,' said Peggy, looking up from the pot of porridge she was stirring. 'What's going on?'

'We have something we wish to discuss, Mama Peggy, and we'd appreciate your advice.'

Peggy pulled the pot off the hob and eagerly sat down next to Jim. 'I knew there was something you've been keeping from me, Danuta. Come on then, out with it.'

Danuta looked to Stanislav for support and at his nod, she took a breath. 'I think I have a solution to our housing problem,' she began. 'Stan and I talked it over last night, and although it isn't perfect, it's about as near as we can get.' She paused and bit her lip. 'But to make my idea work, it will depend on outside help, Peggy, and that is why we are turning to you.'

Peggy's eyes gleamed, and she couldn't quite disguise her excitement. 'By outside help, do you mean Rachel?'

Danuta sensed Peggy was bursting with her own secret, and fleetingly wondered if she and Rachel were in cahoots over some plan of their own. 'Well, yes,' she began cautiously. 'But not just Rachel. It would also involve the cooperation of Jacob Kaplin, and Marcus Golding as well,' she finished in a rush.

'Well, I'll be blowed, Peg; it sounds like you've had the same idea,' said Jim from the fireside chair. 'How's that for coincidence?'

Danuta frowned as she looked from Jim to Peggy. 'You know my plan? But how? I have said nothing to anyone but Stanislav.'

Peggy grinned and leaned her arms on the table. 'It's not so mysterious, Danuta – not if you think about it logically – and I was certain you'd eventually come to the same conclusion. You see, I was mulling over the situation all day yesterday, and having discussed it with Rachel, we agreed it was the best answer to your problem.'

Peggy paused, glanced across at Jim, and continued. 'Rachel suggested long ago that you should buy Jacob's house once she'd found a decent care home for him. But why wait until then when he's all alone and in great need of help and support during this awful weather? Why not make arrangements to buy the house with him as a sitting tenant – and then move in and take care of him?'

'That is exactly what I was thinking!' gasped Danuta. 'And Stan agrees with me, don't you, Stan? It is the best solution all round.'

'Apart from the cost of buying such a house, my main worry is not being able to manage all those stairs,' said Stanislav. 'Although I have never been inside, it is a big house, and looks as if it will need a lot of work doing to it, which I'm prepared to see to, but I have little experience in such things.'

'The stairs are a problem,' Danuta conceded, 'but there is a back room overlooking the garden, which we could turn into our bedroom. As to the price; it is run-down, so I'm hoping it will not be out of our reach, but I'm sure that with Rachel's help we can work out a way to pay for it – even if it is in instalments. My real worry is getting Jacob to agree to us buying it and moving in with him.'

Peggy giggled. 'You have no need to worry about

Jacob,' she said. 'Rachel telephoned him yesterday, and I popped in to see him before coming home last night. He grumbled a bit at first, but it was clear he realised it would solve a great many problems, and make his life a whole lot easier to have someone living in.'

'So, you and Rachel have already got things underway?' Danuta breathed. 'Why didn't you tell us this before?'

'I'm sorry, dear, I suppose I should have, but Rachel wanted to be sure she had Marcus Golding onside and willing to prepare the deeds of sale and negotiate a fair price. I didn't want to give you false hope, you see.' She grinned in delight. 'But she telephoned me earlier to say that luckily, Marcus lives in the flat above the office, so is on hand and very willing to help out with the legal side of things.'

Danuta was so nervous, she could barely speak. 'So what price does he think the house is worth?'

'In better condition, the estate agent reckons it would be worth about two and a half thousand pounds or more. However,' she added quickly to reassure them, 'as it does need quite a lot of repairs, Marcus is aiming to negotiate a lower price and repayment plan with Jacob today. He's hoping he'll agree to you paying one thousand, two hundred pounds up front for the title deeds, and act as housekeeper and handyman for no wages until the weather changes for the better. Then you will pay a sum into his account each month – like rent, really – until the five-hundred-pound balance is cleared, or he dies.'

Stunned, Danuta looked from Peggy to Stanislav. 'It is a very good scheme,' she breathed. 'It will mean Jacob can stay in his own home, and we can restart the adoption process again.'

'Do you think Jacob will agree to those terms?' asked Stanislav.

'Rachel says Marcus is very persuasive, and to be frank, Stan, he won't get a better offer.'

Stanislav frowned. 'But I am worried that if we are to pay a sum each month like rent on top of the interest on our loan, it will prove too much.'

'Marcus has done the sums, Stan. He knows your financial limit and won't see you overstretched,' soothed Peggy.

Danuta had a sudden awful thought. 'But what if Jacob doesn't want the mess and noise of a small boy and a baby in his house?'

Peggy laughed in delight. 'You need have no fear of that, my dear. Jacob surprised me and Rachel by being quite excited by the idea once he got used to it. You see, he and his wife never had children, but they'd always longed for them. I think he's hoping the presence of you and the little ones will give him and that old house a new lease of life.'

'Oh, bless him,' said Danuta, the tears welling. 'He must have been so very lonely after his wife died if he's willing to take us all on.' She pushed back from the table. 'I will go and see him before I start my day's duties.'

'Not yet,' said Peggy quickly. 'Let Marcus do the negotiating and get things underway first. The minute I hear from Rachel that everything is in hand, I will let you know.'

Danuta sat back down again, suddenly very much on edge. The knowledge that their future was now in the hands of an old man and a sharp lawyer troubled her. There were so many things that could go wrong, even though Rachel seemed to be holding the reins, and she had every faith in her. But Stanislav had been right to worry about paying Jacob as well as the bank, for they'd have very little left out of their wages each month – and the repairs could cost a fortune if they had to get tradesmen in. And although they wouldn't be paying Jacob his money until Stanislav was back to work, they'd still have to find the money out of her wages for the interest on the mortgage.

'I can see you're worrying about being able to afford everything on just your wages at the moment, Danuta,' said Stanislav. 'Please don't. Martin paid me my wages for the last month when we shut the airfield down. With the added bonus of the dividend, it will be enough to cover the first few mortgage payments.'

'Are you sure?' At his nod, she gave a sigh of relief.

'And don't worry about those repairs,' said Jim. 'Me, Da and Frank will pop round there once everything's agreed, and see what's to be done. Dad has a shed full of building materials, and we're all experienced enough to repair most things.' He grinned at them both. 'It'll be something to keep us occupied until we can go back to work, and won't cost you a penny.'

Danuta rushed to hug him. 'You are so kind. Thank you,' she said tearfully.

Jim awkwardly patted her shoulder. 'No need for that, wee girl. It's what families are for.' He got to his feet. 'Now, Peg, are we going to get that porridge or not? All this excitement is making me hungry.'

Peggy had just finished her porridge and was about to get ready for work when the telephone rang. Thinking it might be Rachel, she hurried into the hall.

'Goodness me, you're difficult to get hold of this morning,' said Doris crossly at the other end of the line.

'What's the matter, Doris? Only I have to get to work.'

'I doubt you'll be needed. John told me that most of the workforce hasn't turned up this morning. But that's neither here nor there,' she rushed on. 'I'm now in charge of the WVS and need you to house a family in that attic bedroom. It's a mother and two children – aged five and seven. They seem quite respectable, but got stranded last night when she came to collect them from school.'

'I'm really not sure,' Peggy replied, having been caught on the hop. 'Charlie's home from school and will want to study for his summer exams. Having two more young children in the house might prove too noisy.'

'It's your civic duty, Peggy,' Doris said firmly. 'Ruby has taken in one of the nurses, as has Brenda, and even the ghastly Gloria has opened up her rooms to take in several lorry drivers and a couple of travelling salesmen. In times like these, one has to put aside the inconveniences and work as a community.'

'How many are you taking in then, Doris?' she asked suspiciously.

'One of the junior doctors from the hospital is moving into our spare double, and a young midwife is moving into the room I keep aside for when my grandchildren stay.'

Peggy realised she couldn't really refuse in the circumstances. 'All right, but I need to go to the factory first to see what's happening. I'll drop into the Town Hall later to meet this woman, but I really would have preferred to have had a couple of girls up there instead of small children. Daisy is quite enough on her own – especially if they close the school and I have them running about the house all day.'

'I'd have thought you were used to having children running about,' said Doris sniffily.

'I am, but Jim finds the noise difficult to cope with. He still hasn't got over his experiences in Burma.'

'If you say so, but it sounds like an excuse to me. I'll see what I can do.'

Peggy blinked as the call was abruptly cut off. She replaced the receiver and hurried back into the kitchen to chivvy Daisy into her school blazer and coat. But as she was about to leave the house the telephone rang again. It was the headmistress of the junior school. They were closing down as most of the teachers couldn't get through; fewer pupils were managing to get in and they were getting very low on fuel to heat the classrooms.

Peggy gave a deep sigh and told Daisy, who whooped with joy and rushed upstairs to tell Cissy and Cordelia who had yet to get out of bed.

She turned to Jim and shrugged. 'It looks like you were right about things shutting down. And on top of that we'll be taking in a couple of lodgers until the roads are cleared.' She told him about Doris's demands. 'I made it clear to her I didn't want children,' she said. 'The disruption would be too much for you and Cissy, and poor Charlie would never get his schoolwork revision done.'

'Will the factories shut too?'

'That's what I'm going to find out,' she replied, pulling on her coat. 'Whew, it's been quite a morning, Jim, and it's barely half past eight.'

He pulled her to him and gave her a kiss. 'Don't pretend you aren't enjoying every minute of it, Peggy Reilly,' he teased. 'You know very well that if you weren't surrounded by chaos, you'd get horribly bored.'

'Chance would be a fine thing,' she retorted as she left the house smiling.

Danuta had arrived at the surgery to discover there was an emergency meeting of all the staff going on in the large back room that overlooked the snow-covered garden. She beamed at everyone and took a seat, hugging her excitement to herself as she tried to concentrate on what Dr Darwin was saying.

'All roads out of Cliffehaven are now closed, and there are some parts of the town which are difficult to access, so please be careful. There was a traffic accident last night on the top road, and although one of the ambulances did get through to help the injured, they had difficulty getting back to the hospital, and unfortunately, one of their patients died on the way.'

He paused to let this sink in before continuing. 'Both the fire and ambulance services are limited in what they can do because the army and the council workers are unable to clear the snow, even with their bulldozers. The outlying hospitals are now out of action and the local one isn't working at full capacity as a lot of the staff can't get in.'

His audience stirred uneasily in their seats.

'There are bound to be emergency situations which we simply won't be able to attend to, and I cannot stress enough the need for every one of you to take great care out there. The other doctors and I will run the surgery as usual and be on call day and night should you need us. And although it is asking a lot of you, I'd like all the nursing staff to remain on duty – or at least on call – for the duration.'

His gaze found Danuta. 'I note that Sister Danuta has put chains on her tyres, and I suggest you all do the same, as they will give you a better grip on the road. I spoke to Jack Smith earlier and he has a good supply, which he'll fit at no charge for medical staff.'

He paused and looked round the room. 'Are there any questions?'

Pat O'Neill put up her hand. 'What are we to do if we're called out to a birth and have to bring the patient into the hospital for an emergency C-section?'

'Call an ambulance as usual if the access is clear;

otherwise, you'll have to call one of us, and we'll do our best to get to you.' He paused. 'And if we can't, then I'm afraid you'll have to perform the C-section yourself. The same will apply to any other emergency, so make sure you're fully prepared for all eventualities before you set out.'

He turned back to face his solemn audience. 'We're asking a lot from our district nurses and midwives, but we have great faith in your skills and in your common sense. If we all work together, and keep clear heads, we'll get through. Good luck.'

Danuta exchanged a glance with Pat O'Neill as everyone got to their feet and they headed for the nurses' clinic. 'It sounds as if we're in for some fun,' she said dryly. She looked round to make sure they weren't overheard. 'I don't know about you, Pat,' she murmured, 'but I'm not sure young Lucy would handle a C-section on her own – she's not long qualified and still inclined to panic when faced with a difficult situation.'

'It's probably best if we give her the nursing mother check-ups and general district nurse duties until the snow clears; you, Sister O'Neill and I can handle the emergency call-outs.'

Danuta nodded and looked at her list of calls, which were nothing out of the ordinary. 'How are you and Lucy getting on now she's moved in?'

Pat grunted. 'Her father didn't approve of her living with an Irish Catholic,' she said crossly. 'So she's gone to stay with Doris and John Williams – and good riddance.'

Danuta giggled. 'Good luck to her then. Doris isn't the easiest person to get on with, and Lucy will have to be on her best behaviour.'

'It's not our problem, thank goodness,' sighed Pat. 'Right, I'm off to see my usual old dears and make sure they're keeping warm. It's worrying to hear that our fuel stocks in the town are running low. With so many elderly relying on coal for heating and cooking, we could have some serious cases of hypothermia on our hands if this arctic weather goes on for much longer.'

Peggy had made it to the factory in her car but noted that all the streets leading off the main road and winding along the side of the hill were several feet deep in snow. She parked outside Solly's factory and went inside to find Florence there with Bobby, and only a handful of staff still in their overcoats.

'Goodness me,' said Peggy. 'Where is everyone?'

'It's pointless to stay open, Peggy,' Florence replied. 'None of the warehouse staff or delivery drivers are in, and only five machinists have turned up this morning. I've already had Solly on the telephone and it seems the situation isn't quite as bad in Camden Road, as most of the staff there live very locally. He's keeping that open for as long as he can but told me to shut this place down today to conserve heating expenses.'

'A wise decision. But I'm afraid it will mean we'll all be on the dole until it opens again. And it's all very well keeping the other place open, but how will he get the orders out if the transport system has ground to a halt?'

Florence shrugged. 'I don't know, but he is concerned about that, and he's burning with frustration that he's stuck all the way out there and can't be hands-on.'

'Well, the local trains aren't running, and it said on the news last night that nothing much is going in or out of London – and that's his marketplace. He has every reason to worry.' Peggy dredged up a smile for little Bobby, but she couldn't help thinking that if this weather continued for much longer, Solly could be facing a complete shut-down.

The telephone call had come from Marcus late that afternoon, and as Danuta listened to Peggy relay his message, the weight of worry began to lift from her shoulders. Asking Dr Darwin for permission to use the surgery telephone, she rang him back and, after a long, reassuring conversation, put down the receiver and shot him a radiant smile. 'It looks as if we are about to own our first home,' she breathed. 'Our solicitor has done all the paperwork and Jacob has signed the agreement. It will not be fully finalised until it has been stamped by the Land Registry Office and the bank has paid the money into Jacob's account. But that agreement means we can move in whenever we're ready, and our adoption application can be restarted.' She took a breath. 'Marcus is writing to them today.'

'I'm delighted for you, Danuta,' he said, beaming. 'And you'll be so handy for work too. I hope Mr Kaplin has a telephone.'

She nodded. 'I've put his number on my contact details already. May I go and see him? I have done my rounds and the other three nurses are not occupied at the moment.'

'Off you go,' he replied cheerfully. 'I'll get someone to call you if you're needed.'

Danuta didn't waste another minute. She grabbed her coat and scarf and hurried outside to cross the road and let herself into the side door that led straight into Jacob's kitchen.

'Ah, there you are,' he said, looking up from his plate of food. 'I hope you're not looking for supper. This is all they sent me this afternoon, and it's not very appetising.'

Danuta looked at the mess of mince and potato and

agreed. 'Thank you, but I will eat with Stanislav at Beach View.' She sat down next to him at the table. 'I have come to thank you for agreeing to sell us your home, Mr Kaplin. You have no idea how much it means to us.'

He regarded her through smeared spectacles, his brown eyes doleful. 'Oh, I think I do, my dear,' he replied softly. 'You're a good girl, Sister Danuta, and I count myself lucky that you'll look after me and this home I shared with my beloved Naomi. We wanted children, you know, but it was not to be,' he ended on a trembling sigh before wiping his eyes with his handkerchief.

'We promise we will take great care of you and your home, Mr Kaplin,' she said, 'and make sure that it is a happy place again. We will be your family from now on, so please just call me Danuta.'

He nodded but didn't ask her to call him Jacob. 'It will feel strange having people around again,' he murmured, easing his plastered arm to a more comfortable position in the sling. 'You won't make too many changes, will you?' he asked fretfully.

'We won't be moving in straight away and of course we will discuss the repairs that need doing before we touch anything – we will always ask you first before we make any changes. But there is one thing I would ask you to consider now.'

His eyes were suspicious. 'Oh, yes?'

'I have been worried about you having to use those stairs. Would you consider moving your bedroom down to the dining room? There's a fire in there, and the small bathroom is only down the hall.'

'I can't start moving furniture about,' he protested. 'It's all solid oak and antique. Besides, a lot of my memories are up in that room. Memories of my wife and all the years we spent together.'

'I know someone who can help move the furniture down, and we can make the dining room just as full of memories. But it will be much easier for you than negotiating those stairs twice a day.'

'Hmm. Rachel said the same thing. Bossy woman.' He eyed her sharply. 'I hope you're not bossy, Danuta.'

'Not at all,' she replied, preferring to get her way with a smile and gentle coaxing. 'So, what do you say? Shall I ask my friends to come in to move everything down?'

'I'm not sure,' he muttered. 'I agreed to all this nonsense because I thought you were going to look after me, not start moving all my furniture about and forcing me to sleep in the dining room.'

Danuta realised there was no point in going any further. 'It's all right, Mr Kaplin, we won't move anything. But if you should change your mind, you only have to say.'

'Will you be doing the cooking?' he asked sharply.

'I will do it when I'm not on duty, and Stan will cook when I am.'

'Just remember I keep a kosher kitchen. Meat, cheese and dairy are to be kept separate – and the same goes for the cooking utensils used for each – and no pork or shellfish are to be brought into the house.'

'Stanislav and I are familiar with your customs and will respect them, Mr Kaplin,' she said patiently. 'I promise.'

He grunted. 'So when am I going to meet this husband of yours? Peggy Reilly told me he lost both lower limbs during the war. How's *he* going to manage the stairs?'

'I will bring him to see you tomorrow morning, and if you agree, I thought we could turn one of the back reception rooms into our bedroom so he doesn't have to cope with them.'

'What about Naomi's antique furniture and the china, glassware and figurines she spent a lifetime collecting? They're valuable and very precious.'

'We will ask your advice on what to do with them before we touch a thing,' she promised. 'Now, would you like me to help you up to bed?'

'It's too early. I'll go up when I'm ready,' he replied grumpily. He eyed her over his glasses, his expression softening. 'Will you bring the children to visit soon?'

'Baby Noel is with Rachel and she's been snowed in, but Bobby doesn't live far away. Would you like to meet him tomorrow?'

His face lit up. 'What time? We must make tea and sandwiches, and I've got a cake somewhere. Boys like cake.'

Danuta giggled and resisted hugging him. 'They certainly do. I'll talk to Florence who's looking after him at the moment, but I should think about eleven would be right.'

'Eleven it is. Now, shoo. I want to listen to my wireless programme.'

Danuta left him to his wireless and hurried back across the road to the surgery. Life wouldn't be easy with Mr Kaplin, but she suspected a lot of his grumpiness was for show, and that really, he had a heart of gold.

18

It was almost six o'clock and Doris was keeping a beady eye on proceedings as the hot food was served from the kitchen to the lines of crowded trestle tables. The women had done splendidly considering they had so little to work with – they'd managed to make a thick, nourishing stew from donated vegetables and a few scraps of meat added to by lots of mashed potato. The bakery had donated the bread and rolls they hadn't sold that day, and there were two huge urns bubbling away to provide enough cups of tea to satisfy an army.

The main trouble was that if the weather didn't improve – and soon – it would be impossible to feed so many people without money coming in. Neither could she expect those kind souls who'd taken in her waifs and strays to do so without recompense. Money was tight with so many people being laid off work; food shortages were already becoming apparent; and if the appalling weather continued, there would soon be no coal to feed the local electricity station – which in turn meant the Town Hall would soon be freezing. That was the trouble with a Labour government, she thought sourly. They simply couldn't govern.

'What kept you?' she asked as Peggy hurried in, laden down with shopping bags.

'Work, family, other people's problems and food shopping,' panted Peggy. 'I'm here now. So who have you got for me?'

Doris pursed her lips as she eyed her sister from

head to foot, wishing she'd smarten herself up instead of dashing about in that old overcoat and woolly hat. She wasn't even wearing make-up. She turned her attention back to the matter in hand. 'Those two girls on the end of that table,' she said, pointing. 'They work on the beauty counter in Plummer's, so will have good references should you wish to ask their manager.'

'They look very young,' murmured Peggy, musing that Charlie would think all his Christmases had come at once if those two moved in.

'They're both eighteen; old enough to be responsible house guests,' said Doris. 'You'll find them no bother as they'll be at work during the day and they'll eat their meals in the Plummer's staff canteen.'

'I'm not sure it's wise to take them on with Charlie in the house,' Peggy murmured, noting the sophisticated make-up and clothes each girl wore, and the way they were flirting with a group of workmen on the other side of the table.

'Then you will need to keep a rein on your son, Peggy.' Doris's expression was stern.

'It's not my son's behaviour I'm worried about,' she retorted. 'Those two would eat Charlie for breakfast.' She picked up her shopping bags. 'I'm sorry, Doris, but I'm not taking them. If you've got a couple of middle-aged women, then I'll think about it, but no more young girls – and no children,' she added firmly as three toddlers dashed past screaming their heads off.

'It's a good thing not everyone is as picky,' said Doris crossly.

'I have a right to be picky when it comes to people living in my home. Now, I must be off.'

Doris glared at her sister's back as she left the hall and had to admit defeat. Three families had turned down those girls for the same reason, but she had thought that, with all her experience of the young girls she'd taken in during the war, her sister would have coped very easily.

And then she thought of Jack Smith, living alone in that big bungalow. He'd brought up his daughter, Rita, single-handedly, and would be a perfect host. With a smug smile, she hurried to the office telephone.

Danuta had slept much better now that the stress of everything had been lifted, and she climbed out of bed feeling ready and able for whatever the coming day held. She left Stanislav snoring and dashed down to the basement bathroom, surprised to see a deserted kitchen and no sign or sound of Peggy.

As she prepared for the day, her mind was busy with everything that had to be done. She'd come to realise they wouldn't be able to move their furniture into Elms Avenue until Jacob's back room had been cleared. Once Naomi's precious collection was carefully stored somewhere else, she'd have to ask Ron, Jim and Frank to move her bed and bits of furniture from Eshton Road and bring over the rest of their belongings from Ron's garage. Perhaps, given the current situation with the weather, she should ask around and see if there was anyone who'd like to move into the room until things improved.

As she made a mental note to ask Doris if she knew of anyone, she realised that the Reilly men would also need to be introduced to Jacob, to make sure he had no objection to them going in and out of his home. They'd need to take the opportunity to look around for any repairs and discuss how they'd go about them with him.

She didn't want Jacob inconvenienced in any way and was determined to plan this move so it went as smoothly and swiftly as possible without disruption or upset. Jacob was used to being on his own, and although he'd said he was looking forward to having company, the reality of lots of strangers tramping about and shifting things might prove upsetting.

Now the school and the factory were closed, she had arranged for Florence to bring Bobby to Jacob's for morning tea at eleven. Stanislav was coming too so he could get to know Jacob and take his first look inside the house they'd just bought. It was a lopsided way of doing things, but these were extraordinary circumstances, and they had to grab this opportunity with both hands.

She finished brushing her hair and pinned it back into a loose bun at her nape, before checking that her white collar was pristine and there were no creases in her uniform dress. It was important she kept tidy as everyone at the surgery was on permanent duty until the weather changed for the better, and a call-out could happen at any minute.

Returning to the hall-floor bedroom, she left a hastily scribbled note to remind Stan he was due at Elms Avenue at eleven. She grabbed her coat, nursing apron and bag, and hurried outside into the wind-driven snow.

All four cars were thickly covered, and it took a while to brush the snow off the windscreen and bonnet so she could see where she was going. It was also reluctant to start after being out all night, but she eventually got it going and headed for the surgery. The bulldozers could no longer even attempt to clear the roads beyond the hills, but the ones in the town were relatively easy to navigate, although the mountains of snow on the sides seemed to be growing daily, and walking on the icy pavements was hazardous.

She parked the car in her usual spot close to the front door and headed into the clinic to find all three midwives sitting there drinking cocoa. 'I'll be across the road at number forty-eight for the most part,' she told them in delight, 'and plan to spend as much time as I can there preparing for the big moving-in day. If you need me, this is the telephone number.'

She handed the slip of paper to Pat O'Neill with whom she'd shared her news the previous day, answered the many questions the others fired at her and then left them cosily huddled by the gas fire.

She entered the side door as usual and was surprised to find a deserted, cold kitchen and no sign of Jacob. With a dart of alarm, she hurried into the hall to find him sitting trembling in his nightclothes on the bottom stair, clinging onto the newel post as if his life depended upon it. It was what she'd feared the most.

'What's happened? Did you fall again?' She rushed to squat beside him and saw how pale and shaken he was.

'I missed a step,' he gasped. 'Managed to grab the banister in time, but then lost my footing and missed the next step. It's shaken me up a bit,' he confessed, his breathing ragged. 'I thought I was going to fall again.'

'Just sit there until you've got your breath back,' she soothed. 'Did you hurt your arm or your leg?'

He shook his head, his eyes bright with unshed tears. 'But I think I pulled something in my chest when I grabbed the banister.' He blinked rapidly and tried a brave smile.

'All right,' she crooned. 'You stay there and I'll make you a cup of tea.'

'I'd prefer a brandy,' he panted, his eyes now twinkling with mischief. 'For the shock.'

She grinned. 'I think I can manage that. Do you feel strong enough to stand? It's draughty here in the hall, and I don't want you getting a chill.'

His legs were so weak it was a struggle to get to his feet, so she let him use her arm to hoist himself upright, and then carefully steered him into the kitchen. 'I'll get you that brandy and then relight the fire. I don't suppose you've had breakfast yet?'

He shook his head. 'Slept in late for once, and it was so cold, I was loath to leave my warm bed.' He plucked anxiously at his dressing gown. 'Sorry for my lack of suitable clothing, but with this arm it's impossible to do anything.'

She handed him the glass of brandy and saw how his hand trembled as he held it to his mouth and tried to drink. But he'd forgotten to put his teeth in, and his hand was shaking so badly, most of it dribbled down his chin and onto his dressing gown. She decided she wouldn't hurt his pride by saying anything, but went quickly upstairs to find his teeth, hairbrush and fresh clothes.

The room was a shrine to his dead wife, with her clothes in the wardrobe and draped over the low chair by the window. There were pictures of her everywhere, and her jewellery was scattered amongst the pots and jars on the dressing table. Pulling back the heavy velvet curtains, she had a clear view of the street and the surgery across the road, and right up to the crest of the hill lined with bungalows. Everything was white and so bright it hurt the eyes.

For a moment the world seemed to stop turning and she was back in the family home in Poland, for this room and the snow outside were redolent with memories of a time never to be seen again. These memories were to be found in the dark red velvet of the dusty curtains; the faded Turkish rugs on the floor; the padded stool at the dressing table and the gilded pictures of faded beauties on the wall, and even in the faint, lingering scent of a flowery perfume. All that was missing were the sounds of music floating through the house; of her mother's voice and the deep bass of her father's as he answered her.

Feeling almost overwhelmed by memories, she quickly gathered up what she needed, and went back downstairs to see to Mr Kaplin and get the fire going again.

For only the second time in his life, Stanislav was nervous. He'd showered and shaved, and brushed his moustache into its usual twirled and waxed ends and then very carefully combed his thick, dark hair, setting it in place with a drop of pomade. Having dressed carefully in his best suit, white shirt and RAF tie, he checked his nails were clean and neatly cut, and then pulled on his airforce-blue overcoat and scarf. He wanted to make a good impression on Mr Kaplin, not only for Danuta's sake but for his own, and yet, like his wedding day, the importance of the occasion made butterflies flit in his stomach.

'My goodness, you look the business,' gasped Peggy admiringly as he came into the kitchen.

'Do you think Mr Kaplin will approve?' he asked, unusually subdued.

'Oh, Stan, don't be silly. Of course he'll approve – although there's no reason why he should have to. You and Danuta are doing him an enormous service by buying that place and promising to look after him.'

She reached up and gave the silk tie the merest tweak. 'There, perfect,' she sighed. 'Now, don't let him intimidate you, Stan. He can be brusque and rather rude at times, but that's only because he detests losing his independence – and I'm sure you know how that feels,' she added quietly, looking into his eyes.

He did indeed, but his confidence remained low. 'It will be interesting to see this house I have bought without going inside, but if my Danuta says it's a good thing to do, then I trust her.'

Peggy smiled. 'I only saw the inside for the first time

yesterday, and it is in a bit of a state. But it will be a fine home once the repairs and renovations are done. A lick of paint, some wallpaper and judicious scrubbing will soon bring it back to life.'

He nodded and reached for his hat. 'I am sure you are right,' he murmured before grasping his sticks. 'Thank you, Peggy.'

The car started first time as he'd already given it a bit of a run to make sure it would. He drove down Camden Road, looking longingly at the Anchor and repressing the urge to pop in for a morale-boosting drink. He would not give a good impression if he had whisky on his breath, and the Anchor didn't sell vodka.

He parked outside number 48 Elms Avenue, thinking it was a good round number for a house, and sat for a moment to take a long, hard look at it. The front door was central, with bay windows on either side, the roof forming an M-shape over the two top windows. Two chimney stacks rose above it all, both emitting smoke.

Stanislav could see that although the roof looked all right, the guttering needed mending in places, the weatherboards beneath the eaves needed replacing, and that some of the red and blue Victorian tiles on the path would also need to be fixed. The paint on the front door and window frames was flaking and the garden was overgrown with weeds. But the crowning glory was a fine magnolia tree which was trying to bud behind the untidy hedge, and he could imagine how beautiful it would be once the snow had gone and spring brought the waxy white candle-like flowers into bloom.

Stanislav gave a sigh at the thought of all the work it would entail to get the house right, but he could see why Peggy had said it had all the promise of being a good, solid home, and a sound investment. Which was a good thing, because it was too late to back out now.

The sight of Florence approaching with Bobby stirred him into action and he pushed open the door to struggle out and meet them. 'Bobby, my boy,' he called, waving one of his walking sticks to catch his attention.

Bobby let go of Florence's hand and ran to him, almost knocking him over as he grasped what was left of his knees. He looked up, his brown eyes alight with excitement. 'Auntie Ditta said we're going to have cake,' he announced, jumping up and down. 'Will it have icing and chocolate, do you think?'

'I don't know about that, young man,' replied Stan, suddenly feeling more confident about the meeting now the boy was with him. 'You'll have to wait and see.' He straightened the boy's school cap and fastened the top button of his coat, wrapping the scarf more firmly about his neck. 'There, very smart and ready to meet Mr Kaplin. Has Auntie Ditta or Auntie Flo told you about him?'

'He's the man who is going to live with us when you and me and Auntie Ditta move into the house.' He looked up at Stanislav with a frown. 'Why is he going to live with us, Uncle Stan?'

'He is an old man – like a sort of grandfather – and your auntie and I are going to look after him. So you must be very polite to him, Bobby, and be on your best behaviour.'

Bobby scuffed his shoe and scowled. 'I always have to be on my best behaviour,' he moaned. 'And it's boring.'

'It won't be for long, and then we'll go and have some fun in the snow, yes?'

'All right,' he said cheerfully, grasping the cuff of Stan's coat sleeve.

'I'll leave you to it,' said Florence. 'There's no need for me to be here, and while I have the time, I want to go to the library.'

'We'll bring him home later,' said Stanislav.

'No rush,' replied Florence, who clearly didn't want to hang about.

Stan and Bobby went up the short garden path. They were about to rap the brass knocker when the door was flung open.

'Hello, darling,' Danuta said, giving Bobby a hug. 'Come in quick before we let the heat out.' She began to take Bobby's cap, coat and scarf off to hang them on a nearby coat stand.

Bobby stood wide-eyed while she did this, staring all round him at the generously sized hall with doors leading off on both sides, its tiled floor; the high, ornate ceiling with its glittering crystal chandelier, and the impressive oak staircase. 'Is this going to be our flat?' he asked in a whisper.

'It's not a flat, Bobby,' Danuta quickly explained. 'We are going to live in the whole house – upstairs and downstairs.'

'Cor,' he breathed in awe. 'I never lived in a whole house before. Can I go and explore?'

'Later, perhaps. Come into the kitchen and meet Mr Kaplin first.'

She shot Stanislav a quick smile of encouragement and took Bobby's hand to lead the way past the staircase and into a large, warm kitchen, which Stanislav suspected hadn't been changed one iota since the house had been built over a century ago.

He gave it a quick glance before turning his full attention on the old man who was sitting in a chair by the roaring fire, in what he guessed was his best suit. He whipped off his hat, balanced on one stick and held out his hand. 'I'm so pleased to meet you at last, Mr Kaplin. I am Stan, and this is young Bobby.'

The old man shook Stan's hand and regarded him sternly over his glasses. 'I've heard a lot about you,' he muttered ominously. Then he broke into a smile. 'All good, though. All good. Sit down, young man. We don't stand on ceremony here, do we, Danuta?'

Stanislav finally relaxed and, with Bobby still clinging to his coat cuff, sat down at the table which had been laid for tea, intrigued by the old man's expression as he gazed at Bobby.

Mr Kaplin shook his head as if in wonder. 'My, my, what a fine boy you are, Bobby. I have heard so much already about you from your auntie Ditta. She tells me you are doing well at school and that you like to play football.'

Bobby was struck unusually dumb and Stan had to give him a little nudge to encourage him to reply. 'What you done to your arm?' he blurted out.

Mr Kaplin laughed. 'That's what I like in a boy,' he chuckled, slapping his knee. 'Straight to the point and no fiddle-faddle.' He grinned in delight and moved his arm so Bobby could see it more clearly. 'I broke it falling on the stairs.'

Bobby advanced a step to examine the plaster cast. 'Does it hurt?'

'Can't feel a thing,' he replied almost proudly. 'Now sit down and tell me all about your adventures.' Mr Kaplin leaned towards him, his eyes twinkling behind the smudged lenses of his spectacles. 'You do have adventures, I hope?'

'Oh, yes, loads.' Bobby forgot his shyness, and settled into the opposite fireside chair, his legs dangling several inches from the floor. 'Me and Uncle Stan have got a sled, and we go racing down the hill in the snow. It's ever so much fun,' he rattled on, 'cos it's got no brakes and we have to use our feet to stop it. Only Uncle Stan's feet aren't very good at that, and sometimes we end up in one of the big drifts, and he has to dig us out.'

As the old man and the boy laughed uproariously, Stanislav heard Danuta's gasp and avoided her gaze which he could feel boring into him. He struggled out of his coat and slung it over the back of his chair as Bobby carried on about how Stan had built the sled in secret, so it was kept at Florence's flat.

'Well, that all sounds terrific fun,' said Jacob, his eyes merry as his gaze went from Stan to Danuta. 'I wish I was a boy again to have such adventures.' He leaned towards the boy. 'But I think the secret's out now, Bobby,' he said in a stage whisper.

'Oh.' Bobby looked from the frosty-faced Danuta to the sheepish Stan. 'Sorry, Uncle Stan. It just slipped out.'

Mr Kaplin broke the awkward silence. 'Why don't you tell me about the football, Bobby? Which team do you support?'

'Preston North End,' Bobby replied proudly

'Good heavens,' exclaimed Jacob. 'But that's up in the wilds of Lancashire – why not a southern team like Gillingham, Guildford or Dartford?'

'Tom Finney plays for them and he's the best footballer in the whole world,' replied Bobby, stoutly defending his favourite. 'Can we have cake now? Only I'm starving.'

'Give the boy cake, Danuta. And lots of it,' commanded Jacob, his face alight and almost youthful with the joy of Bobby's company.

'Preston North End indeed,' he chuckled as he moved from his fireside chair to the table. 'There is some serious educating to be done here, Stan,' he said with a wink. 'We can't have a local boy supporting Preston North End.'

19

After that initial meeting it became part of the daily routine for Stanislav to collect Bobby from Florence's flat so he could spend time with Jacob and they could both get used to being part of a family again. It also gave Florence much needed respite and the time to return to her engineering studies, as she still hoped to get into university as a mature student.

However, as the snow blizzards continued throughout the rest of February, there had been no word from the adoption people, and this lack of communication cast a dark cloud over what should have been a happy and exciting time. Danuta tried telephoning the office but there had been no reply, and they could only surmise that the staff had been unable to get into the town which was now completely cut off from the outside world.

The room in Eshton Road was now a temporary home to a lorry driver, and Peggy had taken in two middle-aged women who were stalwarts of the local library and determined to keep it open. Danuta and Stanislav were still sleeping at Beach View, but spent as much time as possible with Jacob as the Reilly men started work in the house. With no word from the adoption people, and baby Noel still snow-bound with Rachel and Solly, Danuta was beginning to fear that their dreams would never be realised.

It was almost the end of February when a letter arrived from the adoption agency to say that everything was in hand, and that although the weather had caused disruption of services, it was hoped the adoption of both children would be brought to a satisfactory conclusion. But it was ultimately up to a judge to sign off the papers, and that wouldn't happen until the local courts were back in session. In the meantime, it was agreed that Bobby could visit Elms Avenue whenever he wanted to, but not to stay overnight until his adoption was fully processed.

'Oh, Stan,' Danuta murmured. 'What if the judge says no?'

Stan put his arms around his wife and held her to his heart. 'He won't – not now the adoption people have given us their blessing. I told you not to worry, my darling. It's this weather making everything impossible. We just have to be patient.'

Danuta snuggled into his embrace, feeling the burden of worry lift slightly now there was a real glimmer of hope that things were going in the right direction. She smiled against his chest, remembering how horrified she'd been to learn of the secret sled and the escapades her husband and the boy had been up to in the snow, but she could forgive Stanislav in the light of how warmly the relationship was growing between him, Jacob and Bobby, who'd quite naturally started to call Jacob Grandpa.

The only person missing from her life was Noel, who she hadn't seen since the beginning of January, and although she telephoned Rachel each day for news of him, her arms felt empty and she missed him terribly. It was all very well for Stan to advise patience, but it was hard not to yearn for the sight and feel of him when they were so close to fulfilling the promise she'd made to Gracie.

'We'll have to tell Bobby about Noel,' she said, drawing back from the embrace. 'We've left it too long already.'

'I have thought of this and don't know where to start,' Stan replied, reaching for his coat. 'He's got used to us, but having a little brother suddenly foisted on him might come as a shock.'

Danuta lifted her nursing bag from the bed and gave a sigh. 'We should have said something right at the start; but it never seemed to be the right time.' She looked up at Stan. 'I think we should do it round at Flo's. It's much quieter there, and he won't be distracted by everything that's going on at Elms Avenue.'

'I agree. But it won't be easy, Danuta.'

She nodded and led the way out of Beach View to the car. There were so many things to worry about and her head was spinning. On the brighter side, and much to her relief, Jacob seemed to have discovered a new lease of life, for although his home was slowly being renovated – his quiet routine disturbed, and his furniture moved – he'd established new friendships with Jim, Ron, Frank and especially young Charlie who enlivened him with wonderful tales of grammar school high jinks and daring exploits on the rugby pitch. Charlie had also soon become little Bobby's hero, and he'd begun to follow him everywhere – except when Daisy was around, and he avoided her like the plague.

They pulled up outside number 48 and went in to make a start on Jacob's breakfast before Danuta had to check in at the surgery. Jacob's bedroom was now downstairs in its entirety, in what had been the dining room off the hall. Although he'd grumbled a bit at first, he'd quickly settled in, for there was a fireplace to keep him warm during the bitter nights, and a large window to sit by and watch the goings-on outside.

Danuta had soon realised that far from being disturbed by all the comings and goings, Jacob was thoroughly enjoying himself, taking huge interest in everything that Ron, Jim and Charlie were doing to the house, while Frank continued to go to sea, risking life and limb to bring in the much-needed daily catch.

These new friendships had enlivened Jacob, and he looked forward to sitting over endless cups of tea, discussing football, rugby and cricket with them, while admiring the kitchen cupboards they'd restored. He also thoroughly enjoyed listening to Peggy's endless fund of local gossip, for she reminded him of his beloved Naomi. But it was little Daisy who most enchanted him, with her big brown eyes and dark curls, and her endless chatter, and Danuta suspected Bobby was a little jealous of this burgeoning mutual admiration, which was why he avoided her.

Having made sure Jacob was bathed, dressed and happily tucking into breakfast, Danuta checked the daily roster at the surgery and headed for Flo's flat. Stan had agreed it would be best if she handled the tricky meeting with Bobby, as it really called for a woman's touch.

'It's a bit early,' said Florence rather grumpily. 'We're still eating breakfast.'

Danuta apologised and explained why she'd come. 'I was rather hoping you'd help me explain about Noel,' she said, following her into the kitchen.

'Who's Noel?' piped up Bobby, his cereal spoon dripping milk onto the cloth.

'He's a very important little person who is going to come and live with us when we move in with Grandpa Jacob,' Danuta began.

Bobby eyed her quizzically. 'Why?'

'Because he is one of us. He's part of our family,' said Danuta, not at all sure she was doing this the right way.

'I never met him.' Bobby abandoned his cereal and held Danuta's gaze. 'Where is he, then?'

'He's living somewhere else at the moment,' Danuta

floundered. 'And because of the snow, he can't come and see us.'

'Noel is just a baby,' said Florence. 'And he has to stay where he is for now. But once the snow clears, he'll come and live with you.'

Bobby grimaced, shrugged and returned to eating his breakfast. 'Babies are no fun – worse than girls.'

'But this baby is special, Bobby.' Danuta retrieved the spoon and halted his eating. 'I need you to listen to me. There is something important that I have to tell you.'

Bobby eyed her and folded his arms. 'He's my brother, ain't he?' he said flatly.

'How did you know?' gasped Danuta.

'My friend Alfie told me, and I bashed him in for telling fibs,' he said crossly.

'Oh dear,' sighed Florence. 'I knew the gossip would get to him sooner or later. It's a shame we didn't say something earlier.'

'What's done is done, Flo,' said Danuta. 'Bobby, your friend wasn't telling you fibs. You really do have a little brother. His name is Noel, and he's nearly three months old now.'

Bobby screwed up his mouth as he contemplated this piece of news. 'Can he play football?'

Danuta smiled. 'He's a bit too young, but you could teach him when he's bigger.'

Bobby gave a sigh. 'I suppose so, but babies are boring. Does he have to live with us?'

'He's your little brother, Bobby. Of course he does. But just think, you'll be his big brother and he'll look up to you like you look up to Charlie.'

Bobby chewed his lip and then fiddled with his spoon as he thought deeply about this. 'Will you and Uncle Stan still love me when he comes to live with us?' he asked quietly.

Danuta swiftly gathered him into her arms. 'Oh, my darling, of course we'll always love you. You're our precious boy, and nothing will change that.'

He remained in her arms for a moment and then rubbed his eyes before returning to his breakfast. 'That's all right then,' he muttered.

'It will be OK, Bobby. I promise. And we'll love you always.' She glanced across at Florence, who mouthed, 'Well done.'

But she wasn't convinced she had done that well, and she could only pray that Bobby wouldn't have his nose put out when Noel did move in with them. Bobby was clearly still uncertain about things, and it could be some time before he fully accepted the situation and stopped worrying. She kissed his hot cheek. 'Uncle Stan will come and fetch you soon. We love you, Bobby – very much. Never forget that.'

While the weeks passed and the snow blizzards continued to form huge drifts which cut Cliffehaven asunder from the outside world, Naomi's precious china and glass collection was carefully moved to cabinets in the other large room at the back, which had now become a cosy sitting room instead of a repository for years of junk. The downstairs cloakroom had been brought into the twentieth century with a new bath, basin and lavatory that had somehow been left spare from the building site behind the station – although no one could explain why. The fresh lino and white tiles had also mysteriously appeared with Frank one morning, and he'd been very vague as to where he'd got them.

The second largest room at the back of the house had been papered and painted, the floor sanded and varnished in preparation for the big day when the large bed could finally be brought from Eshton Road, and they would move in permanently. But that day still seemed far off as the weather conditions worsened and dragged on into March, which proved to be the wettest month in three hundred years of records. The shortage of coal meant people turned to electric fires for heating. This put added strain on supplies, and power stations across the country had to be shut down – and in turn, forced the government to bring in a restriction of nineteen hours' usage a day for each household, and eventually to cut all industrial supplies completely.

With over four million people now forced out of work and claiming unemployment benefit, there was a fear of public disturbance – but morale was so low, it was a case of hunkering down and surviving as best one could. There was little joy to be had, for radio broadcasts were limited, telephone lines were broken, television services were suspended, some magazines were ordered to stop publishing, and newspapers were once again reduced to four pages.

Blackouts became the norm, hundreds of villages were cut off, and thousands of sheep, cattle and chickens died. In the end, the Royal Navy launched Operation Blackcurrant, which used diesel generators aboard submarines to provide supplementary power to coastal towns and dockyards. Food rationing was further tightened, and for the first time, potatoes were rationed too.

By the beginning of April it had finally stopped snowing, although the snow still lay in huge drifts all round the town, and the top road was closed because of fallen trees, flooding and downed power lines. Despite not being able to get to see Noel, or hearing anything more from the adoption people, Danuta was buzzing with excitement as she returned from her nursing duties to number 48 – for this was the day they would finally move in. She dashed into the hall and greeted Jacob and Stan with a beaming smile. 'Where is everyone?' she enquired as she shook off her coat.

'They've gone home,' said Jacob. 'The work's finished.' He grinned at Danuta. 'But Stan has something to tell you, haven't you, Stan?'

Stanislav was beaming as he held up a letter. 'This came, Danuta. It is from the adoption agency.'

'What does it say?' she asked, hardly able to breathe.

'The adoption has been passed. The children are ours,' he managed through his tears before taking her into his arms.

Danuta's legs could barely hold her up as she all but collapsed into his embrace. 'Really? It is true? Really true?'

'Look, read it for yourself, my love.' He shoved the letter at her, and unable to keep still in his excitement began to move about the kitchen.

Danuta read the typed words that looked so bland and matter-of-fact but which warmed her heart and brought tears of joy. 'Oh, Stan,' she breathed. 'They're ours. They're really ours.' She folded the precious letter back into the envelope and blinked away her tears. 'When will we have them?'

'Bobby can come today, and Noel will come the minute Rachel can get into town. And everything is ready, Danuta. You must come and see.'

Danuta took his hand and let him lead her to the back room where she found that the bed was made, and her dressing table and stool were placed perfectly beneath the large window that overlooked the back garden. There was even a vase of flowers on the bedside table next to their wedding photograph, and her precious rugs covered the floor.

'We are home at last,' she sighed with pleasure, as they sat on the bed to look out at the snow-covered garden and the recreation ground behind the neatly trimmed hedge. 'I can hardly believe it, Stan.'

'We have come a long way in what has felt like a lifetime, my love.' He cupped Danuta's chin in his large hand and looked deep into her eyes. 'I know you miss baby Noel, but with Rachel still marooned up there in the hills, it could be quite a time before we see him again.'

Danuta nodded. 'We'll find he's changed a lot the next time we do see him,' she said wistfully. 'Babies do a lot of growing in these first few months, and we will have missed most of that because of the damned snow.'

'It will all come right,' he soothed with a hug. 'Come and see what we've done upstairs.'

'I thought upstairs was out of bounds to me until the work was finished?'

'Not today,' he replied with a wink.

She followed him as he very slowly wrestled his way up the grand staircase to the broad landing from which several doors led to the four bedrooms. He opened the door to the double room at the front with a flourish. 'What do you think?'

'Oh, my goodness,' she gasped, taking in the fresh white paint and the hand-drawn mural on the wall of Tom Finney in full flow, kicking a ball. 'Who did that? It's a terrific likeness, and Bobby will absolutely love it.'

Stan grinned. 'Frank is a secret artist, I think. When he could no longer go fishing because of the icebergs in the Channel, he let his imagination run riot. Come and see what he's done in Noel's room.'

Danuta glanced at the neat single bed that had already been made up for Bobby's first night in his new home; the box of toys, miniature blackboard and easel, and the small desk and chair placed beneath the window. It was utterly perfect.

She eventually turned away, her heart full, and followed Stan to the smallest bedroom, to burst into tears of happiness when she saw the pretty blue and white wallpaper, the painted chest of drawers, the white cot, blue check curtains and soft rag rugs on the floor. But it was Frank's depiction of Mother Goose and her goslings on the wall that really made her sob. 'It's beautiful,' she managed.

'Frank copied it from the Beatrix Potter book Ron's been reading to Daisy. Peggy made the rugs and curtains, and I painted the cupboard. The rest was down to Ron and Jim.'

He put his arms around her and held her close. 'Noel will come soon and then we will be a real little family,' he murmured into her hair. 'Please don't cry, my Danuta.'

'They are happy tears, Stan. Such happy tears. I feel so very blessed.'

But much to their disappointment, the break in the weather proved to be only fleeting, and the snow came again, thicker and heavier than before, trapping Rachel and baby Noel in their hilltop home for several more days. When the snowfall finally stopped, the country was hit by heavy rain and gale-force winds. Rivers breached their banks and the melting snow caused heavy flooding, which made travelling hazardous. Rachel refused to risk driving over the windswept hills with a baby in the car, and because of fallen trees and other hazards on that road, Stan refused to let Danuta go and fetch him. Danuta burnt with frustration, but there was nothing she could do. She simply had to knuckle down to work and keep the home fires burning for Stan, Jacob and little Bobby.

As the weather continued to worsen through March into April, and the country emerged from months of snow with flash flooding making matters worse still, it became clear that Cliffehaven had come out of the devastation comparatively lightly, although the outlying farms had fared badly.

The chalk hills and the underground springs had absorbed much of the snowfall run-off, leaving only a few of the houses on the hills or in the deep valleys with some minor damp problems. The town was back to its usual bustling self, with the shops, offices and factories once again in full swing as the new cinema and Woolworths buildings came close to completion and the estate of prefabs was finally finished.

Danuta and Stan were in a lather of excitement as they woke that beautiful spring morning, for today was the day they would finally bring Noel home. Now it would be only a matter of hours before Rachel arrived to hand him over, and Danuta leapt out of bed to go upstairs and wake Bobby who'd been given special permission to have the day off school.

Bobby still wasn't totally convinced that having a baby brother was a good thing, and although they'd shown him the photographs of Noel that Rachel had sent by post, he didn't show much interest.

'Bobby, darling, it's time to wake up,' Danuta murmured, giving his warm cheek a kiss. 'Your little brother will be here soon, and Grandpa Jacob has bought a special cake for elevenses.'

At the mention of cake, his eyes opened and he sat up. 'Are Uncle Frank and Charlie coming too?' he asked. He adored Frank, because he'd painted his football idol on his bedroom wall, and Charlie was his absolute hero now he'd started to teach him the rudiments of rugby.

'Not today, love. Frank's had to go out on his fishing boat, and Charlie's back at school. But I expect they'll drop in this evening with Ron and the rest of the family to see you and Noel.'

Bobby grinned. 'I like Grandpa Ron. He's funny.'

'He certainly is,' she giggled. 'And you're a very lucky boy to have so many grandpas and uncles. Now, come on, get washed and dressed. I have to see to Grandpa Jacob while Uncle Stan gets the breakfast on.'

He leapt out of bed and dashed along the landing to the bathroom as Danuta went back downstairs to help Jacob get washed and dressed. Jacob's spirits had been lifted now the house was alive again, but he was getting very frail, and had come to rely on Danuta for most things. But to her relief, he'd asked her some time ago to drop the formalities and call him Uncle Jacob.

Once everyone was in the refurbished kitchen – a bonus due to the many weeks of horrendous weather which had given the men plenty of time to do the work – Danuta dished up the breakfast. But she was too excited to eat, and to the amusement of the others, kept getting up to check that everything in the house was perfect for their new arrival.

With breakfast cleared away and the kitchen tidied, Danuta went to make Jacob's bed, and then went upstairs to Noel's room. The cupboard drawers were full of the sweetest baby clothes and nappies, and all the accoutrements needed by one tiny person were neatly stowed on the changing table.

With a sigh of pleasure, she tweaked the curtains and flicked a non-existent mote of dust from the windowsill, then returned downstairs. She was so on edge with anticipation and excitement she couldn't keep still, so she fussed about, moving a flower vase an inch on the hall table and unnecessarily dusting the newel post and brass stair rods.

'You'll wear that post down if you rub any harder,' teased Stanislav, coming out of the kitchen with Jacob and Bobby in tow.

She was about to reply when the rap on the door

knocker made her heart skip a beat, and she dashed to answer it, Stan, Bobby and Jacob crowding in behind her.

A smiling Rachel stood there, having somehow dispensed with the woman from the adoption office who was supposed to witness the handover. Noel was tucked beneath the blankets of the luxurious Silver Cross pram.

'Special delivery service,' she said brightly, wheeling the pram into the hall. 'I bring you one very important little person.'

Danuta's heart swelled with love as she looked down at Noel who was beaming toothlessly back at her, his chubby arms waving as his legs kicked off the blankets.

'Oh, my darling,' she whispered through her tears as she reached to pick him up and cradle him to her heart. 'Welcome home, little one,' she murmured tearfully against his dark curls as an emotional Stanislav drew Bobby and Jacob closer to encircle them in his arms. She closed her eyes, and thought she could feel Gracie looking down on them with a smile. 'I kept my promise, Gracie. They're safe now,' she whispered.

'We are truly a family,' Stanislav managed through his tears, 'and I will love and cherish you all to my last breath.'

WELCOME TO
Cliffehaven
ELLIE DEAN

A Map of Cliffehaven

1 Café
2 Beach View Boarding House
3 Vet
4 Doctor's Surgery
5 Cliffehaven General
6 Lilac Tearooms
7 The Anchor and Ruby's home
8 Ethel's House
9 Station
10 Pier
11 Home and Colonial Stores
12 Plummer's Department Store
13 Town Hall
14 Fire Station
15 Uniform Factory
16 Bombed School
17 Bombed Odeon Cinema
18 Bombed Church

MEET THE CLIFFEHAVEN FAMILY

PEGGY REILLY is in her late forties, and married to her childhood sweetheart, Jim. She is small and slender, with dark, curly hair and lively brown eyes. As if running a busy household and caring for her youngest daughter, Daisy, wasn't enough, Peggy is now the manager of a local clothing factory, yet still finds time to offer tea, sympathy and a shoulder to cry on when they're needed. She and Jim took over the running of Beach View Boarding House when Peggy's parents retired. During the war years when her family were scattered and Jim was fighting in Burma and India, Peggy took in numerous evacuees who remain to this day an intrinsic part of her life.

Peggy and Jim have three daughters, two sons and three grandchildren, and their permanent lodger, Cordelia Finch, has become a surrogate grandmother to them all. Peggy can be feisty and certainly doesn't suffer fools, and yet she is also a romantic at heart and can't help trying to match-make.

JIM REILLY is in his late forties and was a projectionist at the local cinema until it was bombed, and he was called up to fight for king and country in India and Burma. He had previously seen action in the last few months of the First World War with his older brother, Frank, and father Ron, and the experiences he'd gone through in both wars are now affecting him to the point where he needs help. Returning from the Far East, he is now employed by the British Legion and finds great solace in the fact he's doing useful work.

Jim is handsome, with flashing blue eyes and dark hair, and the gift of the Irish blarney he'd inherited from his Irish father, which usually gets him out of trouble. He likes to flirt with women and although he would never be unfaithful to Peggy, he enjoys the chase. Now he's returned home, Jim is finding it hard to settle even though it was all he'd dreamt about while away – but there have been too many changes and Peggy has become far too independent for his liking.

RONAN REILLY (Ron) is a sturdy man in his late sixties who led a very private life away from Beach View during the hostilities as a member of the highly secretive sabotage and defence arm of the Home Guard. Widowed several decades ago, he's recently married Rosie Braithwaite who used to own the Anchor pub. They now live in the posh end of Cliffehaven in a detached house in Havelock Road.

Ron is a wily countryman; a poacher and retired fisherman with great roguish charm who tramps over the fields with his dogs, Harvey and Monty, and his two ferrets. He doesn't care much about his appearance, much to Rosie's dismay, but beneath that ramshackle old hat and moth-eaten clothing, beats the heart of a strong, loving man who will fiercely protect those he loves.

ROSIE BRAITHWAITE is in her late fifties and is extremely happy to be finally married to Ron, even if he does drive her to distraction with his shenanigans. Having sold the Anchor to Ruby Clarke, she is now a local town councillor with a passion for improving the lot of those who have been left homeless after the war. Rosie has platinum hair, big blue eyes and an hour-glass figure – she also has a good sense of humour and enjoys sparring with Ron when he's got himself into yet another tangle. And yet her glamourous appearance and winning smile hides the heartache of not having been blessed with a longed-for baby, and now it's too late. Peggy is her best friend, and the people living in Beach View have taken the place of the family she'd never had.

HARVEY is a scruffy, but highly intelligent brindle lurcher, with a mind of his own and a mischievous nature – much like his owner, Ron. His pup, Monty, is the product of an illicit courtship with a pedigree whippet, and the pair of them like nothing more than being out on the hills with Ron. Harvey adores everyone but Peggy's elder sister, Doris.

DORIS WHITE was once married to the long-suffering Ted who'd secretly been having an affair for years. They used to live in a large house in Havelock Road until it took a direct hit from a doodlebug and she was forced to move in with her sister Peggy. She has always looked down on Peggy and despite having recently married the gentle and loving retired colonel, John White, is a terrible social climber and snob.

Doris is a leading light – or would like to be – in Cliffehaven society and enjoys being married to John who is captain of the golf club and on the committee of the Officer's Club. They have converted their two bungalows into one grand house in Mafeking Terrace. Doris insists upon calling Peggy, Margaret, because she knows it winds her up like a clock and loathes Ron because he calls a spade a shovel and refuses to change his nefarious ways. Yet, despite her snooty attitude and her refusal to unbend, Doris has realised that her marriage to John is in danger if she doesn't change.

ANTHONY WILLIAMS is Doris's much beloved only son. He was a teacher in a private school before the war and worked for the Ministry of Defence during it. He still works for the government and is now married to Suzy, who was a lodger at Beach View Boarding House during the war and was a theatre nurse at Cliffehaven General. They have now moved to Oxford and are the proud parents of baby Angela and little Teddy.

DOREEN GREY is the youngest Dawson sister and although she loves Peggy, cannot stand Doris. Doreen has long been divorced from her ne'er-do-well husband, Eddie, and after the tragic death of her lover, Archie Blake, is raising their baby boy along with her two young girls. She works as a school secretary in Swansea.

FRANK REILLY is in his early fifties and has served his time in the army during both wars, but at heart, he's a fisherman. He was married to the very difficult Pauline, who left him for a job in London, and now he lives alone in Tamarisk Bay in the fisherman's cottage where he was born. Free of Pauline who has demanded a divorce, Frank is now courting Brenda – a childless and very attractive widow who works at the Anchor pub with Ruby Clarke.

CORDELIA FINCH is a widow and has been boarding at Beach View for many years. She is in her eighties and is rather frail due to her arthritis, but that doesn't stop her from bantering with Ron and enjoying life to the full. She adores Peggy and looks on her as a daughter, for her own sons emigrated to Canada many years before and she rarely hears from them. Everyone who lives at Beach View, including Peggy's youngest, Daisy, regard her as their grandmother. Cordelia's close friendship with Bertie Double-Barrelled has come too late in their lives for romantic potential, but they're content in each other's company.

BERTRUM GRANTLEY-ADAMS (Bertie Double-Barrelled) is a retired army officer in his eighties. Raised in an orphanage and numerous foster homes, he found his family in the army. Old habits die hard and he's a stickler for time-keeping and efficiency, and his daily routine is unvarying. He lives in a bungalow which overlooks the golf course and acts as church warden. He adores Cordelia, but knows friendship is really all he can offer her now they are so elderly.

RITA SMITH came to live at Beach View after her home in Cliffehaven was flattened by an air raid. She worked for the local fire service as a mechanic during the war where she met an Australian flier, Peter, who shares her love of motorbikes. Once the war was over, she married Peter and went with him back to Australia to set up home in Northern Queensland.

FRAN is from Ireland and is a talented violinist who worked as a theatre nurse at Cliffehaven General. She was one of Peggy's evacuees until she married Robert – a Ministry of Defence colleague of Anthony Williams. They now live in London with their baby.

SARAH FULLER and her younger sister, **JANE**, came to England and Beach View after the fall of Singapore. They are the great-nieces of Cordelia Finch who welcomed them with open arms. Having worked in the Timber Corps and for the government's secret service, both girls returned to Singapore to search for their father and Sarah's fiancé, Philip, and to reunite with their mother and much younger brother. The tragic news that neither man had survived was tempered by the fact they had their mother and Jim Reilly to help them through. A double wedding in Singapore saw both girls finally settled with the men they'd met during the war years. They now live in America.

IVY is from the East End of London and was billeted for a time with Doris where she was expected to skivvy. Now married to Fire Officer Andy Stevens, they have moved to Walthamstow, and have a baby boy and another on the way. Ivy and Rita are best friends and are still in touch despite living on opposite sides of the world.

DANUTA is in her early thirties. Originally from Poland, she managed to escape Europe and come to England in search of her brother, who was a pilot. She arrived at Beach View to learn that he was killed during the Battle of Britain and, after losing the baby she so desperately wanted, tries to make the best of things by using her nursing skills at Cliffehaven General. But she is soon recruited to the Secret Service where she meets Dolly Cardew who becomes her mentor and guide during the dangerous missions into war-torn Europe. Following her capture by the SS and a miraculous escape, she meets the Polish flier and amputee, Stanislav, who she eventually marries. She is now the local district nurse and midwife in Cliffehaven.

RUBY CLARKE is in her late twenties and has taken over the Anchor pub from Rosie Braithwaite. She met and married a Canadian soldier in Cliffehaven and went to live in the wilds of Canada but never settled. When her husband was killed in a logging accident, and she lost her baby during a brutal winter, she returned to Cliffehaven and the only family she ever really knew at the Beach View Boarding House. The memories of what happened in Canada still haunt her, and although she is being very sweetly courted by Dr Darwin, the local GP, she is not yet ready to make a commitment.

DOLLY CARDEW is in her sixties, married to retired American General Felix Addington, and living in California. She is mother to Pauline – from whom she's estranged, and Carol, who lives in Devon. Dolly is a live-wire and spent the First World War working with the resistance in France – and the Second World War training girls like Danuta in unarmed combat and sabotage. She spent her lonely childhood holidays roaming the hills surrounding Cliffehaven and her first love was Ronan Reilly – a man she will always think of as the one who got away. But she is very happy with Felix – Carol's father – and thoroughly enjoying the liberating life in the warmth of the Californian sunshine.

PEGGY'S CHILDREN

ANNE is married to Station Commander Martin Black, a retired RAF pilot. Together they have two girls, Rose Margaret and Emily Jane, as well as newly born Oscar. Martin is now a partner in Phoenix Air Transport and Anne is a full-time mother since giving up teaching at the local primary school.

CICELY (Cissy) was a driver for the WAAF and stationed at Cliffe aerodrome. She once had ambitions to go on stage but found great satisfaction in doing her bit. She invested her life savings into a private hire chauffeur company with three other young women she met during the war years and for a time was enjoying the bright lights of London. But when things turn sour, she returns home to Beach View and her loving family.

BOB and **CHARLIE** are Peggy's sons of eighteen and sixteen who spent most of their childhood in Somerset because of the war. Bob is serious and dedicated to running the farm, while Charlie is still mischievous and, when not causing trouble or playing rugby, can usually be found under the bonnet of some vehicle, tinkering with the engine. Charlie has plans to join the RAF, and is proving to be quite a scholar, while Bob is making his life in Somerset on the farm which he will inherit.

DAISY is Peggy's youngest child, born the day Singapore fell. She found it difficult to relate to Jim on his return home as he was a stranger, but is now a real daddy's girl, and can wind him round her little finger. She has just started school and is in the same class as Anne's Rose Margaret.

Lose yourself in the world of Cliffehaven

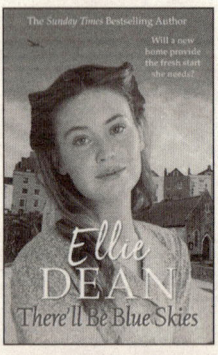

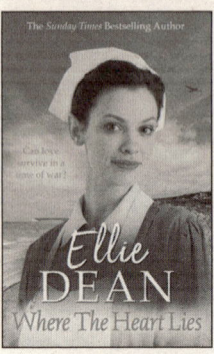

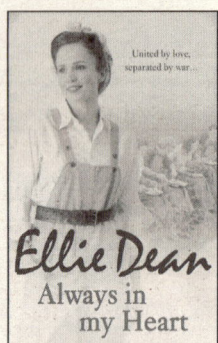

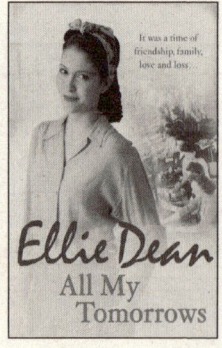

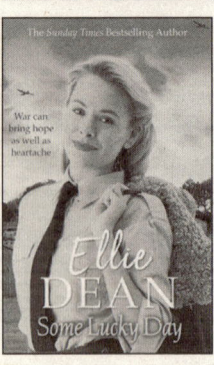

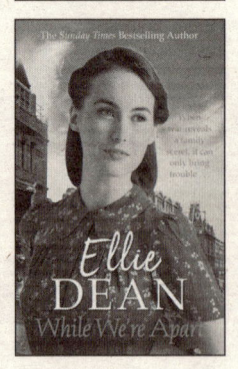

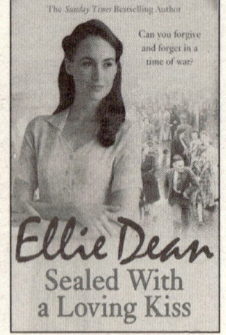

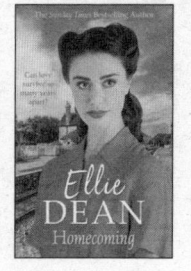

All available in paperback and eBook now

SIGN UP TO OUR SAGA NEWSLETTER

Penny Street

The home of heart-warming reads

Welcome to **Penny Street**, your **number one stop for emotional and heartfelt historical reads**. Meet casts of characters you'll never forget, memories you'll treasure as your own, and places that will forever stay with you long after the last page.

Join our online **community** bringing you the latest book deals, competitions and new saga series releases.

You can also find extra content, talk to your favourite authors and share your discoveries with other saga fans on Facebook.

Join today by visiting
www.penguin.co.uk/pennystreet

Follow us on Facebook
www.facebook.com/welcometopennystreet